"Why have you and your sister joined this wagon train?"

Thatcher's eyes were hidden below his hat's wide brim, but Emma was sure he was scowling. She gripped the lantern with both hands. "And how is that your concern, Mr. Thatcher?"

"I am responsible for getting this wagon train to Oregon before winter, Miss Allen. *Everything* that can endanger that mission is my concern."

He called her an endangerment! Emma gave him her haughtiest look. "And how does our presence imperil your mission?"

"If you want me to name all the ways, you'd best let me light that lantern. We will be a while." He held out his hand.

"I think it would be best for you if I continue to hold the lantern, Mr. Thatcher. At this moment, you would not want my hands to be free."

Laughter burst from him, deep and full. Surprising. She had thought him quite without humor.

"Seems you might not need quite as much protecting as I figured you would." He chuckled.

Dorothy Clark
and
Pamela Nissen

Prairie Courtship
&
Rocky Mountain Match

LOVE INSPIRED
INSPIRATIONAL ROMANCE

LOVE INSPIRED®
INSPIRATIONAL ROMANCE

ISBN-13: 978-1-335-45473-7

Prairie Courtship & Rocky Mountain Match

Copyright © 2020 by Harlequin Books S.A.

Prairie Courtship
First published in 2010. This edition published in 2020.
Copyright © 2010 by Dorothy Clark

Rocky Mountain Match
First published in 2010. This edition published in 2020.
Copyright © 2010 by Pamela Nissen

This edition published by arrangement with Harlequin Books S.A.

For questions and comments about the quality of this book, please contact us at CustomerService@Harlequin.com.

Love Inspired
22 Adelaide St. West, 40th Floor
Toronto, Ontario M5H 4E3, Canada
www.Harlequin.com

Printed in U.S.A.

CONTENTS

Award-winning author **Dorothy Clark** lives in rural New York. Dorothy enjoys traveling with her husband throughout the United States, doing research and gaining inspiration for future books. Dorothy believes in God, love, family and happy endings, which explains why she feels so at home writing stories for Love Inspired Books. Dorothy enjoys hearing from her readers and may be contacted at dorothyjclark@hotmail.com.

Visit the Author Profile page
at Harlequin.com for more titles.

PRAIRIE COURTSHIP

Dorothy Clark

Delight thyself also in the Lord; and he shall give thee the desires of thine heart. Commit thy way unto him; trust also in him; and he shall bring it to pass.
—*Psalm 37:4–5*

This book is dedicated to my sisters, Jo and Marj. My thanks to you both for being so understanding of my time constraints, and for praying me through these last two months. I wouldn't have made it without your help. I love you both.

And to my critique partner, Sam. You stand tall, cowboy. Thank you again for your encouragement and prayers. And for sticking with me through the crunch. I will return the favor when your deadline hovers! And, yes, you may have Comanche— after the next book is written. Blessings.

Chapter One

Independence, Missouri
April, 1841

"Break camp!"

That was not Josiah Blake's voice. Emma Allen turned in the direction of the barked order, stiffened at the sight of an imposing figure atop a roan with distinctive spots on its hindquarters. So the autocratic Mr. Thatcher had returned to take command. She had hoped his absence since their arrival at Independence had meant he would not be leading the wagon train after all.

Brass buttons on the front of the once dark blue tunic that stretched across the ex-soldier's shoulders gleamed dully in the early morning light. Pants of lighter blue fabric skimmed over his long legs and disappeared into the knee-high, black boots jammed into his stirrups. He rode forward, began to wend his way through the wagons scattered over the field.

Emma frowned and stepped out of sight at the back of the wagon. Mr. Thatcher did not need to wear the faded blue cavalry uniform to remind people he had been a military officer. It was in his bearing. And in the penetrating gaze of the bright blue eyes that peered out from beneath his broad-brimmed hat. Eyes that looked straight at a person, noticed everything about her— including a lace-trimmed silk gown that was inappropriate garb for an emigrant. Eyes that had unfairly impaled her on their spike of disapproval at that first meeting in St. Louis when he had simply *assumed* she was William's wife and would be accompanying him on the journey to Oregon country—and judged her accordingly. Had the man bothered to ask, she would have informed him William was her *brother* and that she was not traveling with the train.

Not then.

But that was before everything in their lives had turned upside down. Emma sighed and stroked Traveler's arched neck. How she had hated telling William that the severe nausea Caroline had developed was not normal for a woman with child. That his wife and the baby she carried were in peril, and would, of a certainty, not survive the journey to Oregon country. Her face tightened. Another prayer unanswered. Another hope shattered. William had to give up his dream of teaching at his friend Mitchel Banning's mission in Oregon country.

Emma glanced at the two wagons sitting side by side, lifted her hand and combed through Traveler's mane with her fingers. How many hours had she sat watching William plan and design the two wagons' interiors— one to hold their personal necessities and provide for Caroline's comfort, the other to carry needed provisions, the teaching materials and provide shelter for Caroline's mother? He had had such faith that things would turn out all right. *Misplaced* faith. William was, at this moment, aboard one of their uncle Justin's luxury river steamboats taking his wife home to Philadelphia. And she and Annie—who should not be traveling at all in her injured condition—were—

Traveler tossed his head, snorted. The thud of a horse's hoofs drew near. Stopped. *Mr. Thatcher*. Emma stood immobile, aware of a sudden tenseness in her breathing, a quickening of her pulse.

"Good morning, Mrs. Allen."

Emma turned, looked up at Zachary Thatcher sitting so tall and handsome in his saddle and gave him a cool nod of greeting. He was a lean man, muscular and broad of shoulder. But it was not his size, rather the intensity, the firm, purposeful expression on his weather-darkened face, the aura of strength and authority that emanated from him that produced an antipathy in her. Autocratic men like Zachary Thatcher were the bane of her life, had caused the demise of her dream. She refused to feed this one's vanity by exhibiting the slightest interest in him or what he had to say.

A frown tightened his face, drew his brows together into a V-shaped line. "I see your lead team is not hitched yet. Tell your husband from now on every wagon is to be ready to roll out by first light."

Emma stared up into those judgmental, sky-blue eyes. Clearly Mr. Thatcher expected an acknowledgment. "I will relay your order." Her conscience pricked. She quelled the unease. It was the truth as far as it went. As for the rest, let the pompous Mr. Thatcher who formed his own conclusions believe what he chose.

He glanced toward the second wagon. "I understand your husband hired the oldest Lundquist sons to help him out—drive his wagons, herd the stock and such. Is that right?"

"They have been hired, yes." There was that prick of conscience again. She clenched her hands and yielded to its prompting. "But I must explain that William is not—"

"I have no time for explanations or excuses, Mrs. Allen. Only make sure your husband passes my message on to his drivers. Tomorrow we start traveling at the break of dawn. Any slackers will be left behind to turn back or catch up as best they can." He touched his fingers to his hat's brim and rode off.

Tyrant! It was a wonder he did not make the members of the train salute and call him "sir"! Emma glared at Zachary Thatcher's strong, straight back and shoved her conscience firmly aside. She had tried to tell him the truth about William. It was not her fault if he would not take the time to listen.

"Whoa, now, whoa!" Oxen hoofs thumped against the ground—stopped. Chains rattled at the front of the wagon.

Emma hurried forward. "Mr. Lundquist, Mr. Thatcher has returned. He ordered that from now on all wagons are to be hitched up and ready to leave by first light, else they will be left behind. Please inform your brother."

Her hired driver's head dipped. "I'll see to it." He

leaned a beefy shoulder against an ox and shoved. "Give over, now!"

Emma left him to his work, glanced around the field. Everywhere she looked men were making last-minute checks of equipment, climbing to wagon seats or taking up their places beside oxen teams. Women and girls were dousing cooking fires, stowing away breakfast paraphernalia and gathering small children into the wagons. All was as she had watched their company practice over the past few days under Josiah Blake's guidance—and yet completely different.

"Form up!"

The words cracked through the cool morning air, sharp as a gunshot. Zachary Thatcher's order was picked up and echoed around the camp. Emma caught her breath and tugged her riding gloves snug. This was it. There was no more time. A tremble rippled through her, shook her hands as she loosed the reins tethering Traveler and led him to the side of the wagon to use the spoke of a wheel as a mounting aid. The light wool fabric of the long, divided skirt of her riding outfit whispered softly as she stepped into the stirrup and settled herself into the strange saddle with the horn on the front. William's saddle. William's horse.

Tears flooded her eyes. Her brother, her staunch protector, the only one of her family who shared her blood, would soon be out of her life—forced by his wife's illness to remain at home, while she, who wanted only to return to Philadelphia, traveled with this wagon train bound for Oregon country. Oh, if only William had sold the wagons! But he had kept hoping. And then Annie had declared she would go to Mitchel Banning's mission and teach in William's place!

Emma's shoulder's slumped. When Annie would not be dissuaded, *her* fate had been decided. What choice had she but to come along to care for her injured sister? The sick, hollow feeling she had been fighting for days swelled in her stomach. Would she ever see William again? Or Mother and Papa Doc, who had taken them into their hearts and adopted them so many years ago she could remember no other parents?

Emma blinked to clear her vision, brushed the moisture from her cheeks and focused her attention on the last-minute rush of activity to block out the dear, loved faces that floated on her memory. Her heart pounded. Men's mouths opened wide in shouts she could not hear over the throbbing of her pulse in her ears. Whips snaked through the air over the backs of the teams. Here and there a wagon lurched, began to move. She tensed, counted. William's wagon—no, *her* wagon—was to be fourth in line...to what? A primitive, unknown land inhabited by heathen. It was insanity!

"Haw, Baldy! Haw, Bright!"

The command penetrated her anxiety, the roaring in her ears. Emma drew her gaze from the camp, watched the oxen her brother had purchased lean into their yokes and move forward at Garth Lundquist's bidding. The wagon shuddered and creaked, rolled over the trampled grass. She swallowed hard against a sudden surge of nausea, made certain only the toes of her riding boots showed from beneath the fullness of her long skirts and rode forward beside the wagon. All through the eight-day steamboat journey from St. Louis up the muddy

Missouri River to Independence she had managed to hold her apprehension at bay. Even when the steamer had run aground on one of the many sandbars, or when it had been raked by hidden snags, she had maintained her calm. But now…

Now there was no more time.

Emma closed her eyes, took a deep breath to steady her nerves. Still, who could blame her for her fearfulness? She opened her eyes and stared at the western horizon. This was not merely another drill to ensure everyone could drive their wagons and herd their stock on the trail. This was *it.* She was leaving behind family, friends and all of civilization and heading into untold danger. And for what? Someone else's dream. If Mitchel Banning had not started that mission in Oregon country none of this—

"Haw, Big Boy. Steady on, Scar."

Emma glanced over her shoulder, watched Garth Lundquist's brother, Ernst, bring William's second wagon into line behind hers. Anne's wagon now. She and her adopted sister were on their own. A tremor snaked through her. Traveler snorted, tossed his head and danced sideways. She leaned forward, patted the arched neck. "It's all right, boy. Everything is all right." The horse calmed.

Emma gave him another pat and straightened in the saddle. How lovely it would be if there were someone to reassure her, to ease her fear. Disgust pulled her brows down, stiffened her spine. She had to stop this self-pity that eroded her courage and undermined her purpose. Still…

She halted Traveler and glanced over her shoulder.

Perhaps she should try once more—now that the time of departure was upon them—to dissuade Anne from going to Oregon country. Perhaps the reality of the leave-taking had softened Anne's determination. Perhaps. Hope she could not quite stifle fluttered in her chest.

Emma reined Traveler around, halted and stared as Anne, riding Lady, the bay mare William had bought for Caroline, emerged from behind her wagon. So Anne had, again, ignored her advice. She was supposed to be in the wagon. Abed.

Worry spiraled upward, crowded out every emotion but concern. Anne's face was thin and pale beneath the russet curls that had escaped from beneath the stiff brim of her black bonnet, her body frail and tense in her widow's garb. That she was in discomfort was obvious in her taut face and posture. If only she would give up this madness!

Emma tapped Traveler with her heels and rode to her sister's side. "Annie…" She frowned, changed her tone. She had tried pleading. "Anne, this is your last chance. It will soon be too late to change your mind. As your doctor, I am advising you to reconsider your decision to make this journey. You are not yet recovered from—"

"Do not say it, Emma!"

Anguish flashed across Anne's pale face. Emma's heart squeezed, her professional doctor's facade crumbled. "Oh, Annie, forgive me. I did not mean to—" She stopped, stared at the silencing hand Anne raised between them, the uncontrollable twitching fingers that were the outward sign of Anne's inward suffering. She reached out to touch her sister's arm. It was jerked away.

Emma pulled back. She stared at her younger sister, once so happy and loving, now so grim and distant, and closed her hand in a white-knuckled grip on the reins. All Anne had ever wanted was to marry and have children. But that dream was now as lifeless and cold as the stone that marked her loved ones' graves.

"I know you mean well, Emma. And I do not mean to be sharp with you. It is only—I cannot bear—" Anne's hesitant words stopped on a small gasp. She clutched her side.

Emma took note of Anne's closed eyes, the increased pallor of her skin, and clenched her jaw. She could not bring back Phillip and little baby Grace, but she could treat the physical injuries Anne had sustained in the carriage accident that had killed her husband and child. Only not here. Not on a wagon train.

Almighty God, if You can change the heart of a king, You can make Anne change her mind and return home to Philadelphia where Papa Doc and I can properly care for her—where the love of her family can help her over her grief.

Emma shifted in the saddle, closed her heart against the useless words. The prayer would only be heaped atop all the countless others she'd offered that had gone unanswered. She cleared the lump from her throat. "Annie—"

"No!" The black bonnet swept side to side. "I am going on, Emma. I cannot face the…the memories at home." Anne opened her eyes and looked straight into hers. "But I want you to go home, Emma. It is foolish for you to come along, to place yourself in harm's way so that you may doctor me when I no longer care if I live or die." Anne's voice broke. She took a ragged, shallow breath. "Turn around and go home, Emma. You still have your dream. And all you desire awaits you there."

Emma's vision blurred, her throat closed. She looked away from her sister's pain, stared at the wagons that had become the symbols of William's lost hope and Anne's despair—of her own thwarted ambition. *Why God? Why could not at least one of us have our dream?*

Emma huffed out a breath and squared her shoulders. Pity would help nothing. But the truth might help Anne. At least it would keep her from feeling guilty. "How I wish that were true, Anne. But though Papa Doc has taught me all he knows of medicine, his patients do not accept me as a doctor. And they never will." The frustration and anger she held buried in her heart boiled up and burned like acid on her tongue. "It is time for me to set aside my foolish dream. I will never be a doctor in Philadelphia or anywhere else. *Men* will not allow it. They will not permit me to treat them or their families. And who can be a doctor without patients?"

She lifted her chin, tugged her lips into the facsimile of a smile. "So, you and I will journey on together. And we had best start, or we will fall out of place behind our wagons and be chastised by the arrogant Mr. Thatcher." She urged Traveler into motion, gave an inward sigh of relief as Anne nudged her mount into step beside her. "What slow and lumbering beasts these oxen are. It will take us forever to reach Oregon country at this pace."

Anne stared at her a moment, then turned to face forward. "Forever is a long time to live without a dream."

The words were flat, quiet…resigned. Emma shot a look at Anne but could see nothing but the stiff brim of her black bonnet, the symbol of all she had lost. *Oh, Annie, you cannot give up on life. I will not let you!*

Emma set her jaw and fixed her gaze west, her sister's words weighing like stones in her heart.

Zach stopped Comanche at the edge of the woods, rested his hands on the pommel and studied the wagons rolling across the undulating plains. The line was ragged, the paces varied, but it was not bad for the first day. Too bad he'd had to scout out the trail conditions. Things would be better had he been around to run the practice drills himself. Still, Blake had done a fair job, but he was too soft on the greenhorns. They had to learn to survive, and there was more to that than simply learning a few new skills. They had to develop discipline, and a sense of responsibility to the group as a whole or they would never make it to Oregon country.

Zach frowned and settled back in the saddle. There had been a lot of grumbling when he pushed them to an early start this morning. The problem was the emigrants' independent spirit. They balked like ornery mules being broke to harness when given orders. It was certainly easier in the military where men obeyed and performed duties as instructed. But it was not as lucrative. And, truth be told, he had his own independent streak. No more fetters of military life for him.

"We are going to be free to roam where we will, when we will. Right, boy?" Comanche flicked an ear his direction, blew softly. Zach chuckled, scratched beneath the dark mane. Of course he had his ambitions, too. A trading post. One that would supply both Indians and army. And the fee for guiding this wagon train

to Oregon country, combined with what he had saved
from his army pay, would enable him to build one next
spring. The large bonus promised—if he got the emigrants to Oregon before the winter snows closed the
mountain passes—would buy the goods to stock the
place. He intended to earn that bonus. But in order to
do that he would have to drive these people hard and
fast. It snowed early in those high elevations.

Zach gave Comanche a final scratch and settled back,
his lips drawn into their normal, firm line. Too bad they
were not all reasonable men like Mr. Allen. It was obvious, even at his first meeting with the emigrants back
in St. Louis, that the man understood the need for rules
and limitations. Of course that wife of his was a different matter. She had no place on a wagon train with her
fancy, ruffled silk dress. He had learned in his days of
command to spot troublemakers, and Mrs. Allen spelled
trouble with her challenging brown eyes and her small,
defiant chin stuck in the air. She looked as stubborn as
they came. Beautiful, too. More so today, standing there
by the wagon in the soft, morning light.

Zach again crossed his hands on the saddle horn,
drew his gaze along the line of wagons. There she was,
riding astride, and looking at ease in the saddle. He
never would have thought it of her with her fancy gowns
and her city ways, but astride she was. Must have had
that outfit made special. He'd never seen anything like
it. She looked—

He frowned, jerked his gaze away. The woman's
beauty was but a shallow thing. He had overheard her
complaining to Allen of their wagon being too small
to live in. He shook his head, glanced back at the slen-

der figure in the dark green riding outfit. Coddled and spoiled, that was Mrs. Allen. But she was her husband's problem to handle, not his. And a good thing it was. He was accustomed to commanding men, not obstreperous women.

The lowing of oxen and braying of mules pulled him from his thoughts. Zach straightened in the saddle, stared at the mixed herd of animals coming over the rise behind the wagons. Those fool boys were letting the stock wander all over the place! And that bull in front looked wild and mean. If he caught a whiff of the river ahead and took it into his head to run—

He reined Comanche around. "Let's bunch up that herd, boy." The horse needed no further urging. Zach tugged his hat down firm against the wind, settled deep in the saddle and let him run.

Emma climbed to the top of the knoll, lifted the gossamer tails of the fabric adorning her riding hat and let the gentle breeze cool her neck as she looked back over the low, rolling hills that stretched as far as the eye could see. White pillows of cloud drifted across the blue sky, cast moving shadows on the light green of the new grass. It was a glorious day…except for the occasion.

She frowned, let the frothy tails drop back into place and turned toward the river. Her chest tightened, her breath shortened—the familiar reaction to her fear of water. She'd been plagued by the fear since the day William had pulled her, choking and gasping for air, from the pond on the grounds at their uncle Justin's home. She'd been reaching for a baby duck and—

"Randolph Court." Speaking the name drove the terror-filled memory away. Emma closed her eyes, pictured her uncle Justin's beautiful brick home, with its large stables where she and William had learned to ride along with their cousins Sarah and Mary and James. It was there her mother had taught her to ride astride instead of sidesaddle. A smile curved her lips. She could almost hear her uncle Justin objecting to the practice, and her mother answering, "Now, dearheart, if riding astride is good enough for Marie Antoinette and Catherine the Great, it is good enough for—"

"Lundquist, get that wagon aboard! Time is wasting! We have ten more wagons to ferry across before dark."

Emma popped her eyes open at Zachary Thatcher's shout. Was her wagon—"Haw, Scar! Haw, Big Boy!"— No, it was Ernst moving Anne's wagon forward. She held her breath as her sister's wagon rolled down the slight embankment toward the river. A figure, garbed in black, appeared briefly at the rear opening in the canvas cover, then disappeared as the flaps were closed.

Annie! What was she doing? She knew Mr. Thatcher had ordered that no one cross the river inside the wagons for fear they would be trapped if— *I want you to go home, Emma. It is foolish for you to come along, to place yourself in harm's way so that you may doctor me when I no longer care if I live or die.* A chill slithered down her spine. Surely Annie did not mean to— Her mind balked, refused to finish the horrifying thought.

The wagon halted at the edge of the riverbank. Men rushed forward to help Ernst unhitch the oxen. Others took up places at the tongue, wheels and tailgate. "No! Wait!" Her shout was useless, lost in the clamor below.

Emma yanked the front hems of her long skirts clear of her feet and raced down the knoll.

"The teams're free! Get 'er rollin'!"

The men strained forward, pushed the wagon onto the short, thick planks leading to the deck. Emma dodged around the wagon next in line and ran toward the raft.

"Sutton! Thomas! Chock those wheels fore and aft!" Zachary Thatcher grabbed chunks of wood from a small pile and tossed them onto the deck. "And see you set the chocks firm so that wagon can't shift or roll. There'll be no stopping her if she starts slipping toward the water." He turned toward Ernst. "Lundquist, you get those oxen ready to swim across."

Emma halted her headlong rush as the men, finished with their work, jumped to the bank. She stood back out of their way and stared at the raft sunk low under the heavy load. Only a few inches of the sides showed above the rushing water of the Kansas River. Every bit of courage she possessed drained from her. But Anne was in that wagon. Anne—who did not care if she lived or died. She drew a deep breath, lifted the hems of her skirts out of the mud with her trembling hands and ran down a plank onto the bobbing ferry.

"Mrs. Allen!"

The authoritative shout froze her in her tracks. Emma grabbed hold of the top of the rear wagon wheel, turned and looked full into Zachary Thatcher's scowling face.

"Come off the ferry and wait for your husband, Mrs. Allen. Everyone is to cross with their own wagon."

The ferry dipped, shuddered, slipped away from the bank. Muddy water sloshed onto the deck and swirled around her feet. Emma tightened her hold to a death grip on the wheel and shook her head. "My sister, Anne, is lying ill in this wagon, Mr. Thatcher." She instilled a firmness she was far from feeling into her voice. "I am crossing the river with her."

"Your *sister!*" Zachary Thatcher's face darkened like a storm cloud. "*What* sister? When did—"

"And I have no husband. William Allen is my *brother.*"

The ropes attached to the ferry stretched taut with a creaking groan. Emma gasped, turned and fixed her gaze on the men on the opposite bank hauling on the rope. Frightened as she was, the view across the water was preferable to the one of Mr. Thatcher's furious face. The raft lurched out into the river then turned its nose, caught the current and floated diagonally toward the other side. She closed her eyes and hoped she wouldn't get sick.

Chapter Two

"The last wagon is safely across, Anne. They are hitching up the teams to pull it up the bank." Emma hooked back the flap of canvas at the rear of the wagon to let in the evening light. "Perhaps now the camp will settle into a semblance of order."

"Perhaps. Please close the flap, Emma."

How she hated that listless attitude! Emma let the flap fall into place and fixed a smile firmly on her face as she stepped to the side of her sister's bed. "Would you care to take a short walk with me before the sun sets? I want to make certain Traveler and Lady swim across safely."

"No. You go, Emma." Anne lifted her hand and pushed a wayward curl off her forehead. "I am weary."

"And in pain." Emma dropped the phony smile and frowned. "You cannot move without wincing, Anne. I warned you riding would not be good for your injured ribs. It has irritated them. Your breathing is shallow. I will go get my bag and give you some laudanum to ease the discomfort." She stepped to the tailgate.

"Please do not bother, Emma. I want no medication—only rest."

"Annie—"

"I'll not take it, Emma."

"Very well." Her patience had run its course. Emma pushed the canvas flap aside, climbed through the opening then stuck her head back inside. "But I shall return when Mrs. Lundquist has prepared our supper. And you *will* eat, Anne. You are my patient and I shall not allow you to die—even if you want to!" She jerked the flaps back into place for emphasis, whirled about and headed for a spot beneath a tree to watch the men swimming the stock across the river.

A low hum of voices, broken by the shouts and laughter of children, vibrated the air. From the adjoining field came the lowing of cows and oxen, the neighing of horses and braying of mules. Chickens and roosters, imprisoned in cages lashed to the sides of wagons, cackled and crowed. Dogs barked and snarled at enemies real or imagined.

Such a din! Emma nodded and smiled at the woman and daughter working over a cooking fire and made her way to the outer rim of the men grouped around the lead wagon. Heads turned her direction. Faces scowled. Her steps faltered. She braced herself and continued on.

"Did you want something, Mrs…"

Emma met a thin, bearded man's gaze. The look of forebearance in his eyes caused a prickle of irritation that fueled her determination. "Only to be obedient to Mr. Thatcher's order to assemble."

"This meeting is only for the *owners* of the wagons. The heads of the families."

Emma glanced toward the condescending voice coming from her left, stared straight at the rotund, prosperous-looking man who had spoken. "Yes. That was my understanding."

A frown pulled the man's bushy, gray eyebrows low over his deep-set eyes. "Now, see here, young woman, we men have business to discuss. This is no time for female foolishness! Go back to your wagon and send your husband, or father, or—"

"My name is Miss Allen, sir." She kept her tone respectful, but put enough ice in her voice to freeze the Kansas River flowing beside their evening camp. "I have no husband. And my father is in Philadelphia. I am the owner of—"

"Impossible! I personally signed up every—did you say Allen?" The man's eyes narrowed, accused her. "The only Allen to join our train was William Allen and his *wife*."

The man had all but called her a liar! Emma forced a smile. "William Allen is my brother."

"Then your brother will speak for you, young lady. It is not necessary for you to attend this meeting."

Emma took a breath, held her voice level. "My brother's wife took ill and he was unable to make the journey. My sister and I have taken their place on the train."

"Two lone *women!*" The exclamation started an uproar.

"Gentlemen!"

The word snapped like a lash. Every head swiveled

toward the center of the group. Silence fell as those gathered stared at Zachary Thatcher.

"The trail to Oregon country is two thousand miles of rough, rutted prairies, bogs and marshes, quicksand, swift, turbulent rivers, steep, rocky mountains, perpendicular descents and sandy desert—most of the terrain seldom, if ever, traversed by wagon. Factor in thunderstorms, hailstorms, windstorms, prairie fires and—if we are too often delayed—snowstorms, and everything gets worse. You will never make it to Oregon country if you waste time arguing over every problem that arises. There will be legions of them. And this particular situation is covered by the rules and regulations settled upon by Mr. Hargrove and the other leaders of this enterprise before our departure. Now, to the business at hand. Miss Allen…"

A *problem* was she? Emma lifted her head, met Zachary Thatcher's cold gaze and traded him look for look.

"This meeting is about tending stock and standing guard duty. Each wagon owner must shoulder their share of the work. I understand your hu—*brother* hired drivers. As it states in the rules, hired drivers will be permitted to stand for wagon owners—in this instance, you and your sister. Therefore, Mr. Hargrove is correct—your presence is not required at this meeting." He turned to the thin man beside him. "Lundquist, your sons—"

The man nodded. "I'll fetch 'em in." He faced toward the river and gave a long, ear-piercing whistle.

She was dismissed. Rudely and summarily dismissed. Emma clenched her jaw, stared at the backs of the men who had all faced away from her then turned and strode toward her wagon. A *problem!* You would think she *wanted*—

Emma stopped, gathered her long, full skirt close, stepped around a small pile of manure and hurried on. Why was she so discomposed? Her demeaning treatment by the men was nothing new. She had become accustomed to such supercilious attitudes in her quest to be a doctor. Thank goodness Papa Doc did not share such narrow vision! Not that it mattered now. Her dream was not to be. Instead she was on this wagon train of unwelcoming men, headed toward an unknown future in an unknown, unwelcoming country.

Bogs, marshes and quicksand...swift, turbulent rivers...high, steep, rocky mountains... Emma shuddered, looked at her wagon. Her *home.* It was all she had. The reality of her situation struck her as never before. She sank down on the wagon tongue and buried her face in her hands to compose herself. Not for anything would she let Mr. Zachary Thatcher and those other men see her dismay.

Zach looked at the grazing stock spread out over the fields and shook his head. The men on first watch were taking their duties lightly, in spite of his instructions. But one stampede, one horse or ox or cow stolen by Indians, one morning spent tracking down stock that had wandered off during the night would take care of that. They would learn to listen. Experience was a harsh but effective teacher. So were empty stomachs. A few missed breakfasts would focus their attention on their duties. As for the camp guards—they, too, would learn to take advice and stay alert. Most likely when one of them was found dead from a knife wielded by a silent enemy. His gut tightened. He'd seen enough of that in the army.

He frowned, rode Comanche to the rise he had chosen for his camp and dismounted. He stripped off saddle and bridle, stroked the strong, arched neck and scratched beneath the throat latch. "Good work today, boy. If it weren't for you, those emigrants would have lost stock while swimming them across the river for sure. But they'll learn. And your work will get easier."

The horse snorted, tossed his head. Zach laughed, rubbed the saddle blanket over Comanche's back. "I know, they're green as grass, but there's hope." He slapped the spots decorating Comanche's rump and stepped back. "All right, boy—dismissed!" He braced himself. Comanche whickered softly, stretched out his neck, nudged him in the chest with his head then trotted off.

"Stay close, boy!" He called the words, though the command was unnecessary. Comanche never ranged far, and he always returned before dawn. And there wasn't an Indian born who could get his hands on him.

Zach smiled, then sobered. They were safe from hostiles for now, but once they moved beyond the army's area of protection it could be a very different story. Sooner, if one of these greenhorn emigrants pulled a stupid stunt that riled the friendlies. "Lord, these people are as unsuspecting of the dangers they're heading into as a newborn lamb walking into a pack of wolves. I sure would appreciate it if You would help me whip them into shape and grant them Your protection meanwhile."

He looked toward the red-and-gold sunset in the

west, took off his hat, ran his fingers through his hair, settled his hat back in place and headed for the wagons. There was one more piece of business to attend to before he turned in.

The small dose of laudanum she had finally convinced Anne to swallow had eased the pain. She would sleep through the night now. Emma pulled the quilt close under Anne's chin, climbed from the wagon and secured the flaps. It would be a comfort if Anne would consent to share a wagon, but she insisted on being alone. Not that it was surprising. She had resisted all physical contact, all gestures of comfort since Phillip and little Grace had died.

Emma sighed and looked around the center ground of the circled wagons, now dotted with tents. It was so quiet she could hear the murmurings of the few men and women who still sat working around cooking fires that had died to piles of coals. Traveler, Lady and a few other personal mounts were grazing in the center of the makeshift corral, their silhouettes dark against the caliginous light.

She walked to her wagon, lifted a lantern off its hook on the side but could find no means to light it. She heaved another sigh and looked up at the darkening sky. She should probably retire as others were doing, even if sleep eluded her. But to be alone in the wagon without light—

"Good evening."

Emma gasped and whirled about, the lantern dangling from her hands. "You startled me, Mr. Thatcher!"

She pressed one hand over her racing heart and frowned at him. "Is there something you wanted?"

"I need to know why you and your sister have joined this wagon train. What purpose takes you to Oregon country?"

His eyes were hidden by the darkness below his hat's wide brim, but she was sure he was scowling. She brushed back a wisp of hair that had fallen onto her forehead at her quick turn, then, again, gripped the lantern with both hands. "And how is that your concern, Mr. Thatcher?"

He tilted his hat up, stared down at her. "I am responsible for getting this wagon train to Oregon before winter, Miss Allen. *Everything* that can endanger that mission is my concern."

First he called her a "problem" and now he named her an endangerment! Emma lifted her chin, gave him her haughtiest look. "And how does our presence imperil your mission?"

"If you want me to name all the ways, you'd best let me light that lantern. We will be a while." He held out his hand.

Emma tightened her grip. "I think it would be best for you if I continue to hold the lantern, Mr. Thatcher. At this moment, you would not want my hands to be free."

Laughter burst from him, deep and full. Surprising. She had thought him quite without humor. Of course he was laughing at her.

"Now that erased one of the reasons on my list, Miss Allen. Seems you might not need quite as much protecting as I figured you would. All the same, I'll take my chances on freeing up your hands." He reached for the lantern.

This time she let him take it. She needed that lantern lit. Even more, she needed to know how he would light it. She watched as he walked to a nearby fire, squatted down and held a twig to one of the dying embers then blew on it. The twig burst into flame. Of course! She should have thought of that. He lit the lantern, tossed the twig on the embers and returned to her.

"Easy enough when you know how, Miss Allen. And that is my first reason." All trace of amusement was gone from his voice. His expression was dead serious. "If you do not know how to light a lantern out here in the wilderness, how will you manage all the other things you do not know how to do? You are a pampered woman, Miss Allen. Because of that pampering—and without a husband *or* brother to care for you—you are a burden and an endangerment to all the others traveling with you. And I assume it is the same with your sister. Only worse, because she is ill."

"My sister is not a *burden,* Mr. Thatcher! And she is my responsibility to care for, not yours or any other man's!" Emma snatched the lantern from his hand, held her breath and counted to ten as she adjusted the wick to stop the smoking. When her anger was under control she looked up at him. "What you say about me was true, Mr. Thatcher—until a moment ago. But I now *know* how to light a lantern here in the wilderness. And I will learn how to do all the other things I must know the same way. I will observe, or I will ask. I may be a pampered woman, but I am not unintelligent, only untaught in these matters. And I will rectify that very quickly.

As for my needing protection—do not concern your-self with my safety. I am an excellent shot with rifle or pistol. As is my sister. We will look to our own safety."

"And your wagons and stock?"

"We have drivers to care for them—as the rules per-mit."

His face darkened. "Accidents happen, Miss Allen! Your drivers can be injured or killed. And then—"

"And then I would be no worse off than a wife who has lost her husband." Emma lifted her chin and looked him straight in the eyes. "We have paid our money, and you yourself said we have met the rules and regulations set in place by Mr. Hargrove and the other leaders. My sister and I are going to Oregon country with this wagon train, Mr. Thatcher. Now I bid you good evening, sir."

He stared at her a moment, then tugged his hat back in place. "As you will, Miss Allen." He gave an abrupt nod and strode off into the darkness.

Emma turned to her wagon, packed and prepared by William for him and Caroline to live in on the journey. Everything had been so rushed after Anne's surprising announcement, only her own clothes had been added at the last minute. She should have spent some time at Independence exploring it, locating things. But she had stayed at the hotel caring for Anne.

A burden and endangerment indeed! She would show Mr. Zachary Thatcher how competent a woman she was! She set the lantern on the ground, untied the can-vas flaps, then reached inside to undo the latches that held the tailboard secure. Try as she might, she couldn't release them. Fighting back tears of fatigue and frustration, she grabbed up the lantern, walked to the front of the wagon, stepped onto the tongue and climbed inside.

Zach untied his bedroll, rolled it out and flopped down on his back, lacing his hands behind his head and staring up at the stars strewn across the black night sky. He was right. That woman was trouble. And stubborn! Whew. No mule could hold a patch on her. Spunky, too. She hadn't given an inch. Answered every one of his concerns. Even turned his own chivalrous deed of lighting her lantern back on him.

A chuckle started deep in his chest, traveled up his throat. Mad as she was at him, she'd have stood there holding that lantern all night rather than admit she didn't know how to light it. And that tailboard! She never did figure out how to open it. Must have spent ten minutes or so trying before she gave up and climbed in the wagon from the front. It had been hard, standing there in the dark watching her struggle. But she probably would have parted his hair with that lantern had he gone back to help her.

I think it would be best for you if I continue to hold the lantern, Mr. Thatcher. At this moment, you would not want my hands to be free. His lips twitched. She'd been dead serious with that threat to slap him. The spoiled Miss Allen had a temper, and did not take kindly to his authority over her as wagon master. He'd send Blake around with some excuse to examine her wagon tomorrow. He could show her how the tailboard latches worked.

He stirred, shifted position, uncomfortable with the thought of Josiah Blake spending time around Miss

Allen. That could be trouble. She was a beautiful woman. No disputing that. 'Course, he'd never been partial to women with brown eyes and honey-colored hair. He preferred dark-haired women. And he liked a little more to them. Miss Allen was tall enough—came up to his shoulder. But she was slender—a mite on the bony side. Though she had curves sure enough.

Zach scowled, broke off the thoughts. It was time to sleep. Tomorrow was going to be a rough day. Those greenhorns weren't going to like the pace he set. But he intended to break them in right. Which meant he would have them awake and ready to roll at the break of dawn. He chuckled and closed his eyes. Fell asleep picturing the pampered Miss Allen trying to build a fire and cook breakfast.

Emma used the chamber pot, dipped water into a bowl from the small keg securely lashed to the inside of the wagon and washed her face and hands with soap she found in a large pocket sewn on the canvas cover. There was a hairbrush in the same pocket. And a small hand mirror. She took them into her hands, traced the vine that twined around to form the edge of the silver backings. It was a beautiful vanity set. Caroline had excellent taste. Her fingers stilled.

Emma placed the mirror and brush on top of the keg, unfastened her bodice and stepped out of her riding outfit. Was Caroline's severe nausea improving? Was the baby she carried still alive? She untied her split petticoat, spread it overtop of the riding outfit she had laid on a chest. *Please, Almighty God, let William's wife and child live. Grant them—* Bitterness, hopelessness stopped her prayer. God had not spared Phillip and little Grace. Why would He spare Caroline and the unborn babe in her womb?

Emma pulled an embroidered cotton nightgown from a drawer in the dresser sandwiched between two large, deep trunks along the left wall of the wagon, slipped it on, then shrugged into the matching dressing gown. She took the pins from her hair, brushed it free of tangles and wove it into a loose, thick braid to hang down her back. From her doctor's bag she pulled her small crock of hand balm and rubbed a bit of the soothing beeswax, oatmeal and nut-butter mixture onto her hands, then smoothed them over her cheeks. A hint of lavender tantalized her nose. Papa Doc's formula. One he'd made especially for her.

Loneliness for her parents struck with a force that left her breathless. She stood in the cramped wagon, stared at the lantern light flickering on the India-rubber lined canvas that formed the roof over her head. What would she do without her family? Would she ever see or hear from them again?

A soft sound beneath the wagon set her nerves a tingle. She tensed, listened. There it was again—a snuffling. A dog? Or some wild animal that was drawn to the light of the lamp? She turned, reached up and snatched down the lantern hanging from a hook screwed into the center support rib but fear stayed her hand. If she doused the light she would not be able to see.

Something howled in the distance, then was answered by a frenzied barking beneath her feet. Only a dog, then. Still… Heart pounding, Emma put the lantern on the floor and tested the ties to make sure the ends of the canvas cover were securely fastened. Her hand grazed the top of the long, red box. She went down on her knees and lifted the wood lid. A fragrance of dried herbs, flowers and leaves flowed out. She caught her breath and peered inside—stared agape at the stoppered bottles, sealed crocks and rolls of bandages. Medical supplies! And a letter! In William's hand.

Tears welled into her eyes. She propped open the lid and lifted out the missive, held it pressed to her heart until she got the tears under control, then blinked to clear her vision, lowered the letter close to the lamp and read the precious words.

My dearest Em,

I know you think your dream is dead. But I believe it is God's will for you to be a doctor. I believe God placed the desire to help others in your heart. And I believe He will fulfill His will and purpose for you. Yes, even in Oregon country. The Bible says: "Delight thyself in the Lord; and he shall give thee the desires of thine heart. Commit thy way unto him; trust also in him; and he shall bring it to pass." I am praying for you. And for Anne. I know you will care well for her injuries, but only God can heal the hurts of her grieving heart. Remember that, Em, lest you take upon yourself a task no one can perform.

After Anne's startling announcement and your determination to accompany for her, I asked the local apothecary what you would need to ply your doctoring skills. I have done my best to procure the items he recommended in the limited time

available before your departure. I will bring more
when Caroline, our child and I join you in Oregon country. Until then, have faith, my dear Doctor Emma. And always remember that I am very
proud of you.
With deepest love and fondest regards,
Your brother, William

Her tears overflowed, slipped down her cheeks and
dropped onto the letter. She blotted them with the hem
of her nightgown lest the ink run and smear, then placed
the letter back in the box where it would be safe so she
could read it over and over again on the long journey.
A smile trembled on her lips. Even here in this cramped
wagon with wild animals howling and the whisper of a
river flowing by, William could make her feel better.

Weariness washed over her. She turned down the
wick of the lamp and stepped to the bed. It was exactly as William had designed it. A lacing of taut ropes
held two mattresses—one of horsehair, the other of
feathers—covered in rubber cloth secure inside a wood
frame that was fastened to the wagon's side by leather
hinges at the bottom and rope loops at the top. She unhooked the loops and lowered the bed to the floor. A
quilt was spread over the top mattress. A quick check
found a sheet and two feather pillows in embroidered
cases beneath it.

A horse snorted. A dog barked. In another wagon, a
baby cried. Emma shivered in the encroaching cold and
slid beneath the quilt, relishing the welcoming softness
of the feather mattress, wishing for secure walls and a

solid roof. Silence pressed, broken only by the whispering rush of the nearby river.

Commit thy way unto him.... If only it were that simple a thing. She stretched, yawned and pulled the quilt snug under her chin. Her eyelids drifted closed. William had such faith. But William was not a woman who longed with her whole heart to be a doctor. And he did not have to contend with despotic men like Zachary Thatcher. Nonetheless, for William...

She opened her eyes and looked up at the canvas arching overhead. "Almighty God, all of my life I have dreamed of being a doctor. That dream is dead." Accusation rose from her heart. She left the words unspoken, but the bitterness soured her tongue, lent acidity to her tone. "I have no other to replace it. Therefore, do with me what seems right in Your eyes. I commit my way unto Thee. Amen." It was an ungracious yielding at best. A halfhearted acknowledgment that God could have a purpose for her, should He care to bother with it. But it was the best she could offer.

She frowned and closed her eyes. It was not worth a moment's concern. Why did any of it matter? God did not deign to listen to her prayers.

Chapter Three

Emma lifted her face to the sunshine and breathed deep of the fresh, sweet fragrance the grass released as it was crushed under the wagon wheels.

Traveler snorted, tossed his head and pranced. She leaned forward and stroked his neck. "I know, boy. I am weary of this slow pace, too." She pursed her lips, glanced over her shoulder. Anne had yielded to her discomfort and exhaustion and taken to her bed in her wagon after their midday rest stop. She did not need her. And it was such a fine day. Surely it would not hurt to explore a bit. Perhaps ride out to see what was over that rise ahead on their right.

She shifted in the saddle, took a firmer grip on the reins. For over a week they had been plodding along, and she was tired of seeing nothing but wagons. She was longing for a real ride. And Traveler needed a run. Surely that was reason enough to disobey Mr. Thatcher's edict to stay by the wagons. *His* mount was being exercised. She smiled and touched her heels to the horse's sides.

Traveler lunged forward, raced over the beckoning green expanse toward the gentle swell of land. Emma let him have his head, thrilled by his quick response, the bunch and thrust of his powerful muscles, the musical drum of his hoofbeats against the ground.

Hoofbeats. Too many. And out of cadence.

She glanced over her shoulder, spotted a rider astride a large roan bearing down on her from an angle that would easily overtake her. A rider in faded blue cavalry garb and a wide-brimmed, once-yellow hat. She frowned, slowed Traveler to a lope. The roan's hoofbeats thundered close. Zachary Thatcher and his mount raced by her, wheeled at the top of the rise and stopped full in her path.

Emma gasped and drew rein. Traveler dug in his hoofs, went down on his haunches and stopped in front of the immobile roan with inches to spare. Fury ripped through her. She leaned forward as Traveler surged upright, then straightened in the saddle and glared at Zachary Thatcher. "Are you mad! I could have been thrown! Or—"

"Killed!" He jerked his arm to the side. One long finger jutted out from his hand and aimed toward the ground behind him. Or where ground should have been.

Emma stared, shivered with a chill that raced down her spine at sight of the deep fissure on the other side of the rise.

"This is not a well-groomed riding trail in Philadelphia, Miss Allen!" Zachary Thatcher's cold, furious voice lashed at her. "It is foolhardy and *thoughtless* for you to race over ground you do not know. There are hidden dangers all over these prairies. That is why I scout

out the trail. Now go back to the wagons. And do not ride out by yourself again! I do not have time to waste saving you from your own foolishness."

Emma fought to stem her shivering. "Mr. Thatcher, I—" She lost the battle. Her voice trembled, broke.

"I am not interested in your excuses, Miss Allen." He gave her a look of pure disgust, reined the roan around and thundered off toward his place out in front of the wagon column.

Emma stared after him, looked back at that deep, dark gape in the ground and slipped from the saddle. "I'm sorry, boy. I'm so sorry. You could have—" Her voice caught on a sob. She threw her arms around Traveler's neck, buried her face against the warm flesh and let the tears come.

The sameness was wearying. Day after day, nothing but blue sky, green, rolling plains and wagons. And slow, plodding oxen. Emma arched her back and wiggled her shoulders. She was an excellent rider, but though she was becoming inured to sitting on a horse all day, it still resulted in an uncomfortable stiffness.

"Whoa, Traveler." She braced to slide from the saddle and walk for a short while, heard hoofbeats pounding and looked up to see Zachary Thatcher racing back toward the train.

"Get to the low ground ahead on the left and circle the wagons! Lash them together! Move!" He raced on down the line of wagons shouting the order.

What—

"Haw, Baldy! Haw, Bright!"

Garth Lundquist's whip cracked over the backs of the

lead team. Cracked again. The oxen lunged forward. He jumped onto the tongue and grabbed the front board. Emma caught her breath, watched him climb into the wagon box even as the vehicle lurched after the wagons in front that were already bouncing their way over the rough ground. She sagged with relief when he gained his seat.

"Hurry on, Scar. Move, Big Boy! Haw! Haw!"

Ernst's whip and voice joined the din. Emma looked back. Anne's oxen teams were settling into an awkward run, the wagon jolting along behind.

Annie! That jarring was not good for Annie!

Emma halted Traveler, waited for the oxen teams to pass so she could tell Ernst to slow down. Wind rose, whipped the gauzy tails of her riding hat into her face. She brushed them back and turned to lower her head against the force of the blow, gasped. The western half of the sky had turned dark as night. Black clouds foamed at the edge of the darkness, tumbled and rolled east at a great speed. Lightning flashed sulfurous streaks across the roiling mass. Thunder rumbled. And rain poured from the clouds to earth in a solid, gray curtain.

The old terror gripped her, lessened in intensity from the span of eighteen years, but still there. She braced herself against the memory of lightning striking the old, dilapidated shed where she and Billy had lived with other street orphans—closed her mind to the remembered crackle of the devouring flames, the screams of Bobby and Joe who had been trapped inside. She heeled Traveler into motion, urged him close to her sister's wagon, then clapped her hand over her hat's crown and leaned toward the canvas cover as the horse trotted alongside. "Anne, there is a terrible storm coming. Brace yourself for a rough ride." The wind fluttered the canvas, bent the brim of her hat backward. She raised her voice. "Hold on tight, Anne! Protect your ribs! Do you hear me? Protect your ribs!"

"I hear—"

The iron rim of the front wagon wheel clanged and jerked over a stone. The wagon tilted, slammed back to earth. There was a sharp cry from inside.

"Anne?"

A sudden drumming sound drowned out any answer. Hail the size of a cherry hit her with stinging force, bounced off the canvas cover. Emma raced Traveler ahead, fell in behind her own wagon to gain some protection from the driving wind and pelting ice. The rain came, soaked her clothes. She lowered her head, hunched over and rode on, the hail pummeling her back.

Garth Lundquist guided the oxen toward the inside of the forming circle, stopped the wagon in place with the outside front wheel in line with the inside back wheel of his father's wagon that had stopped ahead of them. Emma sighed with relief, thought of the dry clothes awaiting her inside and would have smiled if her lips hadn't been pulled taut with cold and fear.

She glanced across the distance, watched as Ernst pulled Anne's wagon into place on the other side. Other wagons followed on both sides until the circle was complete. The enclosed oxen bawled, bugled their fear. Men jumped from their wagon seats and ran forward to calm their teams and lash the wagons together as ordered. Wagons rocked. Canvas covers fluttered and flapped.

Emma slid from the saddle, tethered Traveler to the back of the wagon then slipped through the narrow gap between the two side-by-side wheels. She skirted around her nervous, bawling oxen being calmed by her driver, and headed for Anne's wagon. Wind buffeted her, whipped her sodden skirts into a frenzy. She reached to hold them down and her hat flew away. Hail struck with bruising force against the side of her face. The rain stung like needles. She turned her face away from the wind and struggled on across the inner oval to the side of the wagon. "Are you all right, Anne?" The wind stole her words. She raised her voice to a shout. "Are you all right, Anne? I thought I heard you cry out." She cupped her ear against the fluttering onsaburg.

"I'm all right, Emma. Come in out of the rain!"

"I have to get out of these wet clothes. I will come back when the storm is over!" Water dripped off her flailing hair, dribbled down her wet back. Emma shivered and turned. A hand grasped her arm. She lifted her bowed head, looked into the fear-filled eyes of a sodden woman holding a folded blanket to her chest. The woman's lips moved. She leaned forward to hear her.

"Please, Miss. You were ridin'. Did you see my little girl, Jenny? I've checked with everyone and she's not here. She must of fell out of the wagon, and—" Lightning flickered through the darkened sky, streaked to earth with a crack that drowned out the woman's voice. Thunder clapped, rumbled. "—did you see her?"

"No. I am sorry, but I did not."

The woman swayed, sagged against the side of the

wagon. Her lips trembled. "You were my last hope. Oh, God…my baby…my baby…" She lifted her hands, buried her face in the blanket.

Emma's throat constricted. She put her arm about the woman's shoulders, though she wanted desperately to go to her wagon. "Please don't—there is still hope. My head was bowed, I was not looking—" She stopped. Closed her eyes. If the child had fallen out of the wagon she was probably injured, or worse. But if she did survive the fall, this storm… *The storm!* She took a shuddering breath and held out her hand. "Give me the blanket. I will go back and look for your daughter."

The woman lifted her head. Hope and doubt mingled in her eyes. *"Now?"*

Emma nodded, took the blanket from the woman's hands. "She will need this when I find her." *If I am not too late.*

She battled her way back to her wagon, climbed over the chains Garth had used to lash the wheels together and reached up to untie the back opening in the canvas. There was no time now to change out of her wet clothes, but she needed her doctor's bag. And Caroline's rain cape. She bit down on her trembling lips, tried to stop shivering and concentrate on her task. It was no use. The flapping had drawn the knots too tight—her chilled fingers could not undo them.

Lightning sizzled to earth with an ear-deafening crack. Emma cringed against the wagon, shivering and shaking so hard she feared her joints would detach. Hot tears stung her eyes. She tugged again at the knots, yanking at the bottom edge of the canvas when they did not yield. A spatter of water from the canvas was her only reward. A chill shook her to her toes. She sagged back against the wagon, ceding defeat.

The patient's welfare must always come first, Emma. A good doctor does not hesitate to sacrifice time or comfort, or to do whatever he must to save a life.

How many times had Papa Doc said that to her when they were called to a patient's side in the middle of the night? Strength of purpose flowed into her. "Thank you, Papa Doc." She shoved away from the wagon, unhitched Traveler and mounted. Coat or no coat, doctor's bag or not, she would go. The child did not have a chance of surviving the storm without her.

Please, God, let me find her soon. She cannot live in this storm. Emma lifted her lips in a grim smile. Why did she pray when she did not expect God to answer? Why did it make her feel better? It was foolishness.

Her teeth clattered together. She clenched her jaw, but could not sustain the pressure. She had never been so cold. But at least the hail had stopped and the wind was at her back. She tried to use her misery to block out her fear. It was impossible. Every time the lightning flashed across the sky and streaked to the ground with a thunderous clap that made the very air vibrate, she had to hold herself from screaming. She dare not let Traveler sense her terror. Thank goodness he was not a horse to panic at the flashes and rumbles.

"Good b-boy, Traveler." She patted the horse's neck, studied the ground in front of her. The rain and hail had beaten the grasses down so that it was difficult to make out the wagon tracks. If only the land were not all the same! Had she come far enough? Was this where they had started the wild run with the wagons? Was she even looking in the right place?

Almighty God, for that little girl's sake, guide me to her, I pray. She lifted her head and peered through the deluge, trying to spot something familiar. Something she had noticed earlier that afternoon. There had been a rise with a dip in the middle of the top. She had wondered if there was a pond....

Lightning glinted, turned the sky into a watery, yellow nightmare with a coruscating tail dropping to the earth. Thunder crashed. She rode on, topped the next swell and spotted the rise she was looking for off to the right. She had been going the wrong way. She slumped in the saddle, discouraged, frightened. What if she got lost out here? What if—

"Stop that this i-instant, Emma Allen! That little g-girl needs y-you!" She could barely hear her own voice above the pounding rain. But the scolding worked. She squared her shoulders, wiped the rain from her eyes and reined Traveler around. The wind slapped a long tress of freed hair across her eyes. She brushed it back, wiped the sheeting water from her forehead. She would surely find the wagon tracks now. Then she could line them up with that rise and backtrack. She rode down the other side of the swell into a broad swale, urged Traveler into a lope and came up the knoll on the other side. And there, lying on the sodden grass, was the child.

"Whoa!" Traveler danced to a stop. "Please G-God. Please l-let her be a-l-live." Emma slid from the saddle, led Traveler close and dropped the reins to the ground. *Please let him stand.* She grabbed the blanket she had been sitting on to keep it dry, knelt beside the child and touched a cold, tiny wrist. A faint throbbing pulsed against her fingers. Tears sprang to her eyes, mingled with the rain on her cheeks. She blinked her vision clear, leaned over the child to protect her from the bone-chilling downpour and began to examine the small body.

The storm had let up, except for the relentless rain. The occasional glimmer of lightning and grumble of thunder in the distance held no menace. Zach circled the herd of stock one last time. They were bunched and settled, the threat of a stampede past. The others would be able to handle them now. He slapped the water from his hat, peered through the rain at the wagons. Some had not moved, despite his relayed order. Must be there were problems Blake couldn't handle. He rode down into the shallow basin and headed toward the Lewis wagon.

"Be reasonable, Lorna."

"I'm not moving from this place without her."

"Blake said it's only a short ways. If she—"

"Don't say *if*, Joseph Lewis. Don't you dare say *if!*" The Lewis woman buried her face in her apron and burst into tears.

Zach scowled. This was no time for a domestic argument. "I ordered all the wagons moved to higher, dryer ground, Lewis. They'll bog here when the water soaks in. Unless you have a broken wheel or axle, get rolling."

"It's not the wagon, sir. It's—it's—" The man looked at his wife, cleared his throat. "Our little Jenny has come up missing. The missus asked all around for her and no one has seen her. We—we figure she fell out of the wagon during our run here. But I'll find someone to move the wagon while I go look—"

The wife jerked the apron from her face. "I ain't leaving this place 'till she comes back, Joseph Lewis! If this wagon moves, it goes without me. She'll come here, and I've got to know one way or…or the other."

"Hush, Lorna! I told you if Miss Allen—"

"Miss *Allen?*" Zach's scowl deepened. "What does Miss Allen have to do with your daughter?"

"She went to look for her."

Anger shot him bolt upright in the saddle. Fool woman! He'd told her not to go riding off by herself. Now he'd have two lost people to search for! At least she couldn't have much of a head start on him. His face tightened. "How long ago did Miss Allen leave?"

"Why, right away. When I was askin' round about Jenny. She said she would find her, and she got on her horse and rode off."

"During the *storm?*"

The woman nodded. Her lips quivered. "She took the blanket with her. To warm Jenny when she found her."

The fury of the storm was nothing compared to the anger that flashed through him. Zach stood in the stirrups, looked behind him. "Blake! Get these wagons moving! Every one of them!" He looked down at the man beside him. "Lewis, you move your wagon out with the others. I know this land, and if it's humanly possible, I'll bring your daughter back to you."

He glanced up at the misty light filtering through the rain. It would soon be night—and Miss Allen was out there searching unknown land with no trail experience to fall back on. *Fool women. May he be spared from them all!* He urged Comanche into a lope and started back along the wagon trail.

Chapter Four

Zach swiped off the water sluicing from his hat brim and squinted through the rain at the dark shape ahead. It was a horse, all right. One with an empty saddle. Where was the Allen woman? He scanned the area as far as he could see through the downpour. There was no sign of her. Had the horse been frightened by lightning and thrown her? Had he ridden past her unconscious, injured body in the storm?

He muttered a couple choice words he'd picked up in the cavalry and urged Comanche into a walk. If he spooked her horse, he might have to chase it for miles and he needed it to carry Miss Allen and the child back when he found them—no matter what their condition. His stomach knotted. He was used to handling injured or wounded or even dead soldiers—but a woman and child…

Zach shoved the disquieting thought away and focused on the job at hand. The first thing was to catch the horse. He reined Comanche to circle wide to the right, so the horse would not perceive them as a threat and bolt. He watched the horse, saw it lower its head and kneed Comanche left to move in a little closer. If he— *There she was!*

Zach halted Comanche, stared at the figure kneeling on the ground in front of the horse, head down, shoulders hunched forward, her back to the driving rain. It was, indeed, Miss Allen. And she was likely injured, else she'd be riding. He told the wind what he thought of foolish women, slid from the saddle and dropped the reins.

Water squirted from beneath his boots as he strode to Miss Allen's huddled body. Why was she holding that blanket instead of— *She'd found the child!*

"Miss Allen?" Zach touched her shoulder, felt the icy-cold flesh beneath the soaked gown, the shivers coursing through her. She lifted her head, stared up at him. Blinked. Her trembling lips moved.

"I f-found her."

He nodded, swept his gaze over her. "Where are you injured, Miss Allen?"

"Not inj-jured."

"Not—" Irritation broke though his control. "If you can ride, why are you *sitting* here?"

An expression close to disgust swept across her face. "Sh-she's injured. I c-can't mount."

Zach stared. Scowled. What was she planning to do? *Sit* here all night in the storm, shielding the child with her body? She could have— He squelched the thought. What did he expect of a greenhorn woman? "You can now." He leaned over and held out his arms. "Let me have the child."

She shook her head.

"Miss Allen! You and the child both need to get back to warmth and shelter. And I—"

"Have to...b-be careful. Her arm is broken...h-head injured. I will c-carry her. And we m-must walk horses."

"Walk them! But you need to get out of—" He stopped, stared at her lifted chin, the sudden set look of her face. "All right, Miss Allen, you will carry the child, and we will walk the horses. Now, give her to me, and let's get you mounted." He took the blanket-swaddled child, cradled her in one arm and held out his free hand.

Holding the child was a handicap. And Miss Allen was so stiff and sluggish with cold, so weighted down by her long, sodden skirts, it took him three tries, but at last he had her in the saddle. He handed her the reins, placed the child in her shivering arms and whistled for Comanche. The big roan came dutifully to his side.

"I'll have you warmer in a minute." Zach unlashed the bedroll from behind his saddle and yanked the ties. He shook out his blanket, tossed it over Miss Allen's shoulders and covered it with his India-rubber ground-sheet. He grabbed the flapping ends, crossed them over each other in front to cover the child and secured them to the saddle horn with one of the ties. It was the best he could do to warm and protect them.

"Th-thank you."

Zach looked up. Rain washed down Miss Allen's face, dropped off her chin onto the rubber sheet and sluiced away. She was shivering so hard he had doubts of her ability to stay in the saddle. He took off his hat and clapped it on her wet hair. It slid down to her eyebrows. "Keep your head down, we'll be facing into the storm on the way back. And hold on to that horn, I'll lead your horse." He took the reins from her and leaped into the saddle, started Comanche toward the wagons at a slow walk.

Rain drenched his hair, funneled down his neck to soak his coat collar and dampen his shirt. Zach frowned and hunched his shoulders as a drop found an opening and slithered down his back. It was going to be a long ride.

A pinpoint of light glowed in the darkness ahead. Only one reason for that. Someone had got a fire started. Zach stared at the welcome sight, a frisson of expectation spreading through him. That should cheer the Allen woman. It made him feel better. There was nothing like a fire when you were cold and wet and feeling miserable. Especially if there was a pot of coffee simmering on the coals.

Zach scanned the area as best he could through the rain, trying to spot the night guards. It wouldn't do to startle them. The greenhorns were liable to shoot before they were sure of their target. He looked back at the fire, close enough now that he could see the light flickering and make out the crude, canvas canopy someone had rigged. He hadn't expected any of the emigrants to figure a way to start a fire in a rainstorm, let alone know how to protect it. Likely it was the Lewises, guiding their way back.

The fire disappeared, blocked from his view by the wagons as they approached. He spotted it again through a gap between the bulky vehicles. Looked like Lewis had switched places with the Lundquists. Joseph Lewis and his wife were tending the fire. He could make out the two of them silhouetted against the rosy glow as he rode to the Allen wagon. They appeared to be the only ones about. Not surprising, given the late hour, the weather conditions and the hard day. But where were the guards? They should have challenged him on their way in.

He frowned, halted Comanche at the back of the Allen wagon, slid from the saddle and tethered the woman's horse. "We're here, Miss Allen."

"Yes."

She sounded about done in. Zach turned his head, raised his voice loud enough to be heard over the beating of the rain on that canvas canopy rigged to protect the fire. "Lewis, give me a hand. I've got your daughter and Miss Allen." He turned back, began to untie the rawhide thong holding the blankets to the saddle horn. "I'll have you free in—"

"My baby! Where's my baby?" Mrs. Lewis squeezed through the narrow space between the wagons' wheels, her husband right behind her.

"She's right here." Zach undid the last turn of the thong and threw back the edge of the blankets.

"Oh, give her to me!" The woman reached up for her child.

"Don't h-hug her." Miss Allen's teeth chattered, broke off her words. She threw him a look of appeal.

Zach stuffed the thong in his coat pocket, and gently lifted the child from her arms. "Your daughter has a broken arm and a head injury, Mrs. Lewis. She has to be handled careful."

The woman gave a little cry, sucked in a breath and nodded. "I understand."

Zach placed the swaddled toddler in her arms, turned back to remove his blankets and help Miss Allen from the saddle.

"T-take her into my wagon, Mrs. Lewis. I'll s-set her arm."

"You!" Joseph Lewis shook his head. "I'm right grateful to you for going to look for our Jenny, Miss Allen. But we need someone knows what they're doing to care for her. I reckon—"

"I know how to care f-for your daughter, Mr. Lewis. I'm a d-doctor."

A doctor! Zach froze, stared at Miss Allen—there was a look of grim forbearance on her face. He frowned and tossed his bedding over his saddle. A woman doctor. Judging from the argument going on between Lewis and his wife, it would cause a furor among the emigrants if she plied her trade. That was all he needed. Another problem to get in the way of his getting this train to Oregon country before winter hit the mountains.

He scowled, grasped the Allen woman around her waist and lifted her out of the saddle to the ground. Her knees buckled. She fell against him.

"S-sorry." She placed her trembling hands against his chest and tried to push herself erect.

Zach's face tightened as he steadied her. *Me, too, Miss Allen. Sorry you ever joined this train.* He leaned down, lifted her into his arms and stomped toward her wagon, heedless of the water in her sodden gown soaking through the wet sleeves of his coat.

* * *

The dry nightclothes and fire-warmed blanket felt wonderful. But it made her want to sleep. Emma swallowed the last sip of hot coffee and set her cup on the floor. She was losing her battle against the fatigue that dragged at her. Her eyes had closed again.

She forced her reluctant eyelids open, glanced at the child lying on the pallet made out of her feather pillows. Unlike her own still-damp hair, the toddler's had dried, and soft, blond curls circled the small face now pink with warmth. Jenny looked like any other sleeping toddler. Except for her splinted arm and unnatural stillness.

Emma lifted her gaze to Jenny's mother, sitting on the floor with her back against the long red box and holding her baby's hand.

"Jenny's got blue eyes. Like her papa's. I wishst she'd open 'em." The woman's chest swelled as she took a deep breath, sunk as she let it out again. "Will I ever... see her blue eyes again, Miss—Dr. Allen?"

Emma stiffened. That's what Anne had asked. Just before— She shoved the thought away, looked into the fear-filled eyes begging for hope and summoned a smile in spite of the bitterness squeezing her heart. "I cannot say for sure—such things are in God's hands—but I believe you will, Mrs. Lewis. Jenny's pulse is steady and strong, and that's a good sign." *Little Grace's pulse had been uneven and weak...*

The woman nodded, pulled the blanket draped over her shoulders closer together across her chest. "I've been prayin'." She looked up, and the lamplight glimmered on the tears swimming in her brown eyes. "I wasn't meanin' to make you uncomfortable, askin' you things only God Hisself can answer."

Yes. Only God, who had chosen to let little Grace die. "I understand, Mrs. Lewis." *If only she could.*

Silence fell. Rain pattered against the canvas cover. The faint sound of snoring came from the Lewis family's wagon. A child's yelp. And then— "Move over, Gabe! Yer pokin' me with yer elbow!"

The woman glanced that way, looked back and shook her head. "You were right to have Jenny stay here in your wagon. With four youngsters, things are a mite crowded in ours. Special with the Mister havin' to sleep inside 'cause of the rain. 'Tis mortal kind of you to let me stay here with her."

"Not at all. Jenny will want you when she wakes." *If she wakes.* Emma blinked and gave her head a quick shake, rubbed her hands up and down her arms beneath the blanket to ward off sleep.

"You've had a hard time of it tonight, what with going out in the storm after Jenny and all. Why don't you get some sleep, Dr. Allen? I'll keep watch over Jenny."

Emma stifled a yawn, shook her head. "Her condition could change and…"

"I'll wake you if it does." The woman's eyes pleaded with her. "Please, Dr. Allen. It would make me feel better for you to rest."

She was so sincere. Emma swallowed back her fear. Her being awake had not saved little Grace. She sighed and gave in to her exhaustion. "All right. But you must wake me the moment there is the slightest change, Mrs. Lewis. Any change at all. A whimper…or a twitch…

anything…" She stretched out on the feather mattress she was sitting on, pulled the quilt over top of the blanket wrapped around her and closed her eyes.

"Not meanin' to put myself forward, Dr. Allen. But I'd be pleased if you would call me by my given name, Lorna."

"Lorna…a lovely name." Emma tucked her hand beneath her cheek. Jenny had her pillows. "And you must call me Emma…"

"I'd be honored to, Dr. Emma."

Dr. Emma. The name echoed pleasantly around in her head. William had called her that in his letter. She snuggled deeper into the warmth of the quilt and smiled. If only she could…write William and…tell him she had a…patient…

"I gave the order to break camp, Lewis. Get this canopy down and your oxen hitched. We've wasted enough daylight. We move out in ten minutes."

Emma lifted her head at the sound of Zachary Thatcher's muffled voice coming through the canvas. She had been hoping for an opportunity to properly thank him for rescuing them last night. She pulled the blanket back over Jenny's splinted arm and turned toward the front of the wagon, paused to run her hands over her hair and down the front of her gown. The feel of the sumptuous fabric brought the memory of their first meeting leaping to the fore. She looked down at the three tiers of lustrous, rose-colored silk trimmed with looped roping that formed the long skirt and frowned. She could well imagine Mr. Thatcher's opinion of her inappropriate frock. But there had been no time to have gowns made after Anne announced her intention to take William's place teaching at the mission. With only two days of preparation time, the best she could manage was to purchase dress lengths of cotton and other sensible materials to bring—

"I ain't travelin' today."

Oh dear! Emma jerked her attention back to the conversation outside the wagon. Mr. Lewis sounded...truculent.

"What do you mean, you're not traveling today? You don't have a choice. Lest you want to go on by yourself."

And Mr. Thatcher sounded...adamant, to be charitable. Perhaps this was a poor time to—

"Tell that to that Allen woman what calls herself a *doctor!* She's got the missus all in an uproar over Jenny. Says Jenny can't travel, and the missus won't go without her. With three other young'uns that need carin' for, I—"

"You speak respectful of Dr. Emma, Joseph Lewis. She rode out in that storm and found your baby. Likely saved her life."

Lorna! Emma peeked outside. Joseph Lewis was glaring at his wife, who was glaring back at him from their wagon.

"*If* she lives, Lorna. We don't have a real doctor to—"

A *real* doctor! *Ohhh!* Emma hiked up her voluminous skirts, climbed onto the red box and reached to shove the front flaps of the cover aside. The back of her skirt snagged on the latch. *Bother!* She reached back.

"Don't you say *if,* Joseph Lewis! The Good Book says, 'According to your faith be it unto you.' And don't think I'm goin' to move one foot from this spot 'till Dr. Emma says it's safe for Jenny to travel, neither."

Emma freed her skirt and turned back. Lorna had climbed from their wagon and stood facing her husband. The sight of their angry faces turned her own anger to regret. She had not meant to set husband and wife at odds. But all was not lost. If Zachary Thatcher would agree not to travel out of consideration of the child's poor condition… She scooted out onto the driver's seat, cast a longing glance at her sodden, mud-stained riding outfit crumpled in the corner of the driver's box and stood. "Good morning."

All three people turned to look at her. Zachary Thatcher swept his gaze over her fancy gown and his expression did not disappoint her expectations. She abandoned the idea of relying on his understanding and sympathy. In the cold light of day, it appeared Mr. Thatcher did not have any. She looked down into his steady, disapproving gaze and stiffened her spine. "I regret the wagon train cannot travel today, Mr. Thatcher. But it would be dangerous for Jenny to be jolted and bounced around in her condition."

She watched his face tighten and stood her ground as he rode his horse close to the wagon and peered up at her. "I understand the child is ill, Miss Allen. But you must underst—"

"*Dr.* Allen, Mr. Thatcher."

His eyes darkened and narrowed. His lips firmed.

She was familiar with the disparaging expression. She had seen it far too often on the faces of her Papa Doc's male patients. Very well. If that was how it was to be. Emma trotted out her armor for the battle ahead.

"I am a fully trained, fully qualified doctor with credentials from a celebrated surgeon with the Pennsylvania Hospital—" she registered the growing disdain in his eyes and rushed on "—which I will produce if you doubt my word." Her challenge hit the mark. Anger flashed in those blue depths.

"This is not about your qualifications, *Miss* Allen. It is about getting this wagon train to Oregon country before winter snows close the mountain passes. To that end, these wagons will move forward *every day*—including today." He touched his hat brim and reined his horse around to leave.

Emma clenched her hands into fists. "Whether you acknowledge me as a doctor or not, Mr. Thatcher, Jenny Lewis is my patient. And I cannot—*will* not—allow her to be jostled around in a moving wagon. It could very well take her life."

Zachary Thatcher turned his horse back around, stared straight into her eyes. "And if this train gets caught by a blizzard in a mountain pass it could well cost us *all* our lives, Miss Allen."

"That is conjecture, Mr. Thatcher. Jenny's condition is fact. This wagon does not move until it is safe for her to travel."

Stubborn. He knew it the moment he set eyes on her. Stubborn and spoiled. But he never expected this. A doctor! And if this morning was any indication, one that would give him a good deal of trouble. Zach held the horseshoe nail against the hickory rib in front of him and lifted the hammer. "Ready, Lewis?"

"Hammer away!"

Zach hit the nail with such force the rib thudded against the sledgehammer Joseph Lewis was holding against it outside and twanged back. The nail was buried deep enough in the wood he didn't need to hit it again. "That will do it!" He tied a long, thick leather thong to the nail, tugged to make sure the knots would hold then picked up the oblong piece of canvas with the big knots on the corners and tied the other end of the thong around one corner and tugged. There was no way the thong could slip off past that big knot. He repeated the process with the other three thongs hanging from the nails he'd driven in other ribs, then gave the canvas a push. It swung gently through the air. There! That would take care of any jolting.

He gave a grunt of satisfaction, picked up the hammer and extra nails and leaped lightly from the wagon. "The bed is ready, *Dr.* Allen. Now tell Garth Lundquist to get your oxen hitched. Time is wasting!" He took the sledge from Lewis and strode off toward the Fenton wagon to return the tools to the blacksmith.

Emma stared after him, reading disgust and anger in the rigid line of his broad shoulders, the length and power of his strides. Her own shoulders stiffened with resentment. He made the word *doctor* sound like an *expletive.*

Joseph Lewis cleared his throat. "I'll go fetch Lundquist for you. Have him bring up your teams, Miss… er…"

Emma turned her gaze on him. He flushed, pivoted on his heel and hurried off.

"It ain't *Miss,* Joseph Lewis! It's *Dr.* Allen."

Emma glanced at Lorna Lewis. The woman was staring after her husband, her face as flushed as his. She tamped down her own anger. "Please, Lorna, do not trouble yourself on my behalf. I do not want to be the cause of discord in your household."

"Well, it ain't right, Joseph not givin' you your rightful due—an' Mr. Thatcher gettin' riled at you for holdin' up the train so's to keep my baby safe an'..." The woman's words choked off.

"And nothing, Lorna." Emma whirled around, her long, ruffled skirts billowing out then rustling softly as she climbed into her wagon. "I care not a *fig* for Mr. Zachary Thatcher's opinions or anger. And even less for his orders. As for Mr. Lewis's reluctance to name me a doctor...I am accustomed to that. Keeping Jenny safe is all that is important. And this wagon will not move until I am satisfied it will do her no harm. Now, give Jenny to me and climb in so we can see what sort of bed Mr. Thatcher has contrived."

She turned and carried the toddler to the canvas sling hanging lengthwise over the long red box just behind the driver's seat.

"Well, I never..." Lorna Lewis set the sling swinging.

"Nor I." Emma handed Jenny to her mother and examined the clever contraption from all angles. "I find no fault in this. It will make Jenny a wonderful bed." She lined the sling with her pillows, covered them with a blanket then gently placed Jenny on them and folded the sides of the blanket over her.

Chains rattled. An ox snorted, bumped against the wagon in passing, causing the bed to sway gently. "You want I should hitch up now, Miss Allen?"

Emma smiled and stuck her head out of the opening

behind the driver's box. "Yes, hitch up the teams, Mr. Lundquist. We will travel today after all. But drive the oxen carefully, mind you. No hurrying."

She ducked back inside, pulled a long scarf from a dresser drawer and held it out. "Wrap this twice around both Jenny and the sling, Lorna. Then tie it so Jenny cannot fall out. I will be right back." She climbed down, lifted the hems of her skirts above the still-wet ground and ran across the oval to check on Anne before the wagons began to roll.

Chapter Five

Emma sighed and clutched the edge of the driver's seat to steady herself as the wagon lurched over the rough terrain. And she thought she was uncomfortable riding Traveler all day. She could only imagine how sore she would be tonight from this day's continual bone-shaking travel. But at least her patient was being spared. The sling bed Mr. Thatcher had created worked perfectly. No matter how badly the wagon bucked, Jenny simply swung back and forth, the length of the leather thongs keeping the bed from too violent a motion.

Emma tightened her grasp against another lurch and grimaced. Too bad the driver's seat was not a sling. It would certainly make her ride more comfortable. She considered the idea a moment, then discarded it and resigned herself to endure the punishing jolts. A sling seat was not possible. The box beneath her held Traveler's feed.

The front wheels dropped into a rut and Emma glanced over her shoulder at Jenny. Her stomach—her personal measure of concern—tightened. The toddler looked perfectly normal. But if she did not wake soon…

Emma's face drew as taut as her stomach. She lifted her hands to adjust her scoop bonnet that had been jarred awry. The wagon ricocheted off some unforgiving obstacle, and she bounced into the air, then slammed back down onto the hard wood seat. "Ugh!"

A shrill whistle sounded ahead. Emma looked forward, saw Josiah Blake standing in his stirrups and circling his arm over his head, and heaved a sigh of relief. It must be time to rest and graze the stock. Which meant the buffeting would stop—at least for a while. And the break would give her time to check on Anne and ease her feelings of guilt for being unable to watch over her today. She would insist Anne come and ride beside her wagon when their journey resumed.

"Circle up!" The call passed from wagon to wagon, faded away down the line.

Emma frowned and worried her bottom lip with her teeth. Anne's pain had been worse last night and she was sure the wild ride in the wagon yesterday had re-injured her sister's mending ribs. Not that Anne had complained. As usual, she said nothing, simply endured whatever pain assailed her mending body. It was only an increased pallor, an involuntary wince and tightening of her sister's face that had alerted her to Anne's worsened condition.

Emma gripped the seat harder. Sometimes Anne's quiescence made her want to shake her. She and William, cousin Mary, even Mary's pastor had tried to reason with Anne, but none of them could sway her from her notion that her pain was deserved punishment for surviving the accident that had claimed the lives of her husband and baby. It made treating her more difficult. Anne did not want to get better.

Emma heaved a long sigh and released her grasp on the edge of the seat as the wagon followed the Lewis vehicle into the familiar circle and stopped. Across the oval, the source of her concern and frustration rode into view behind her halted wagon and dismounted, her movements slow and careful. Clearly riding was irritating Anne's injuries, but being tossed around in the wagon was little better. Oh, if only Anne had listened to reason, at this moment they would both be aboard one of their uncle Justin's steamboats on their way home to Philadelphia with William and Caroline! Home to the bosom of their family where Anne would receive the love and attention she needed.

A sick feeling washed over her. Emma swallowed hard, faced the thought that had been pushing at her all day. Perhaps she did not possess the skills needed to be a good doctor. She did not know what more to do for Anne. Or for little Jenny. Her learning was but a poor substitute for Papa Doc's medical experience, or her feisty temperament for their mother's patient, loving care.

"Mama? Maaaamaaaa!"

Jenny! Emma whipped around and scurried over the red box into the wagon, all speculation about her possible inadequacy forgotten at the toddler's frightened wail.

"Shhh, Jenny, shhh. Everything is all right." She smiled and patted the little blanket-covered shoulder. Round blue eyes, bright with tears, stared up at her. She studied their clear, focused gaze, held back the shout of relief and joy swelling her chest. The toddler's tiny lower lip protruded, trembled. She touched it with her fingertip and shook her head. "No, no. I will get your mama for you. But you must not cry, Jenny. It is not good for you to cry."

She turned and leaned out over the wagon seat. *"Lorna!"*

Lorna Lewis glanced her way, paled then sent a stern look toward her children standing by the wagon. "Don't you young'uns move from this spot 'till I say! Lily, you hand out the biscuits." She shoved a crock into her daughter's hands and turned, her movements stiff as she moved toward the wagon. "Is it—is Jenny—"

Emma smiled. "Jenny is *awake,* Lorna! And she wants her mama." She laughed her delight at the joy that spread across the woman's face and ducked back inside the wagon to untie the knot in the scarf that held Jenny secure.

"You must feed Jenny only broth, perhaps some thin gruel until we see how she tolerates food, Lorna." Emma smiled at the toddler resting happily on her mother's lap. "And keep her calm. Do not let the others overly excite her."

"C'n I ride in the swing bed, Pa?"

Oh dear! Emma turned around on her camp stool and looked up at the other Lewis children crowded together on the driver's seat watching Zachary Thatcher and their father hang the sling bed inside their wagon. Had she made a mistake suggesting the transfer of the bed? What if—

"You'll ride on that seat or walk same as you been

doing, Gabe. And that goes fer the rest of you, too. Jenny's bad hurt and this bed is special to help her get better. The rest of you young'uns ain't to be crowdin' round or hangin' on it. You hear me?"

"Yes, Pa!"

Emma smiled and let her worry drain away. Joseph Lewis's gruff orders and the children's chorused answer left no doubt as to Jenny's safety.

"Dr. Emma! Jenny's—her eyes closed sudden like."

The fear in Lorna Lewis's voice caught at her throat. *No! Not again! Please, not again!* Emma turned back. Jenny's color was good. She lifted the edge of the blanket covering her small patient and placed her fingertips on a tiny wrist. The pulse was strong and steady. "She's only fallen asleep, Lorna."

"Oh. Praise be to God. It was so sudden like, I thought…"

Emma nodded, closed her eyes against a surge of relief so strong she was lightheaded.

"Doctor?"

"Yes?"

"I been thinkin' on how we can pay you for savin' our Jenny. We ain't got much cash money. We put about all we had into outfittin' the wagon an'—"

"There is no charge, Lorna." Emma opened her eyes and smiled at the grateful mother. "I am pleased to have helped."

"All the same…" Lorna gave her a hopeful look. "Mayhap I can cook your meals?"

Emma shook her head. "That is a very generous offer. But I have engaged Mrs. Lundquist to prepare meals for my sister and me. And truly, you need not—"

Lorna's pointed chin lifted. "We pay our way. I'll think of somethin'."

"Miss Allen."

The deep voice brought a tautness to her stomach that had nothing to do with worry. Emma turned. Zachary Thatcher was striding toward her. She rose. "Is the bed ready for Jenny, Mr. Thatcher?"

"Yes." He stopped in front of her. "But what I wanted was to warn you *again* not to go off by yourself like you did last night. These foolhardy—"

"Foolhardy!" Emma glanced over her shoulder at the sleeping toddler, snagged her bottom lip with her teeth and flounced over to her wagon. She stepped into the shade on the other side and whirled to face the wagon master following in her wake. "I find your comment both inaccurate and insulting, Mr. Thatcher. I did not go for a *pleasure* ride in that storm. I went after a lost and, I assumed, injured child. And I found her!"

"Yes. By luck. It is certain it was not any measure of trailing skills on your part that led you to the child. All you did was endanger yourself."

Ungracious words. But true. Pride kept her back stiff. "I concede the danger, made greater due to my lack of frontier skills, Mr. Thatcher. I was aware of it last night. But I am a doctor. I could not leave that child to the mercies of that storm knowing she would likely die. I had to try and find her."

He shook his head. "No, you did not. That was my responsibility, Miss Allen. Or her father's." His gaze bored down into hers. "Given the gravity of the situation, Mrs. Lewis—or you—should have come to one of us. Had you gotten lost it would only have made the situation worse. I would have had two people to search for instead of one."

Emma clenched her hands, stared up into those unflinching, unforgiving blue eyes. The man had no understanding. No *compassion.* "Mrs. Lewis was trying to find her *child* while you men were busy securing wagons or herding stock. She needed help. Her *child* needed help. I provided it."

"Because of luck!" The words were all but snorted. Zachary Thatcher snatched his hat off, ran the fingers of his left hand through his hair, then slapped the hat back on his head. "Had I been informed of the situation, I would have found the child because of skill. With no danger to any other."

Emma raised her chin. "And would you have recognized and known how to treat her injuries, Mr. Thatcher? Are your *skills* equal to that? Jenny needed a *doctor.* I went to her then, and I will go to anyone who needs my help in the future—in spite of personal risk." His blue eyes darkened. She took a step back as he moved closer. He took another step, trapped her against the wagon.

"Have you no *sense?* That is feckless, thoughtless reasoning. You were fortunate this time, Miss Allen. The next time that may not be the case."

The words were chilling. More so because of the slow, quiet way he spoke them. They brought to mind that deep hidden chasm, the many dangers he had warned the emigrants about. She tore her gaze from his eyes, stared at a brass button on his shirt. "Then should I come to danger, it will be on my head. You, sir, are exonerated of all blame."

A strange sort of sound, not unlike a low growl, emanated from him. Emma jerked her gaze to his face. He opened his mouth, clamped it shut again, pivoted on his heel and strode away. She took a long breath, sagged against the wagon and watched him go.

Comanche's hoofs thundered against the ground, crushing the new grass, flinging small clods of prairie soil into the air. Zach leaned forward as they climbed a rise, urged Comanche to greater speed as they pounded down the other side. Stubborn! Stubborn! Stubborn! Downright mulish! That's what she was. The woman had no common sense! Standing there looking up at him with those big brown eyes and declaring he was exonerated of all blame if she came to harm. As if that was what worried him—being blamed. How did you reason with someone like that? "God, give me patience to deal with foolish women!"

Zach glanced up at the sun, frowned. Two hours' travel time left today, at best. Snows would catch them for sure if they moved at this pace. His frown slid downward into a scowl. It was early—little more than two weeks out—but the Allen woman was going to endanger them all if she continued to delay the train. Not to mention she would cost him his bonus, as well. He had to make her see reason. But how?

Zach lifted his head and sniffed the air, caught the scent of water. He slowed Comanche to a trot, headed for the slight rise on his left to look over the lay of the land and choose their camping spot for the evening. He had wanted to cross this stream today and camp on the other side, but the morning's delay had squelched that plan.

So what could he do? If she were a man, he would have no problem. He had dealt with insubordinate troopers. But he had no jail to throw her in. And he sure couldn't beat sense into her with his fists, though he was tempted to tie her up, toss her in her wagon and keep her there until they reached Oregon country! The woman was going to get herself hurt, or killed...or worse.

Memories of the mutilated bodies of settlers unfortunate enough to be caught in the path of angry hostiles flooded his head. His stomach knotted. By all that was holy, if it were not for her ill sister, he would throw Dr. Emma Allen over his saddle, heel Comanche into a gallop and not stop until they reached Independence where he would put her on a steamboat for parts east!

Emma walked beside the wagon, grateful to be spared the punishment of riding. Still, her legs were beginning to tremble in protest of the exercise. She sighed and swatted at the insects buzzing around her head. If only she could ride Traveler. But that was not possible without her riding outfit. She had no sidesaddle, and she certainly could not ride astride in this dress.

Her lips twisted in disgust. She was beginning to realize how very inappropriate her gowns were for her situation. The opulent skirts dragged against the grass, making walking difficult and tiring. And the shimmer and color of the silk seemed to attract insects. She waved her hand through the air in front of her face, putting a stop to the annoying buzzing and humming for a moment. When she stopped, the insects returned.

She sighed and trudged on. If only she had not lost her riding hat in the storm, she could have rearranged the gossamer fabric that formed the long tails into a protective veil.

"Oh!"

Emma stopped, glanced in the direction of the startled cry. A woman was struggling to rise from the ground, a small boy beside her. The woman gained her feet, took a step, cried out and fell forward. Emma grasped her voluminous skirts, lifted the hems free of her feet and forced her tired legs to run across the grassy distance. She pushed her skirts aside and knelt beside the woman seated on the ground holding her foot. "What happened?"

"I stepped in a hole and my ankle turned. My foot hurts… It's swelling."

"Yes, I see. I shall have to remove your shoe." Emma smiled reassurance, undid the laces and eased the shoe off to an accompanying hiss of sucked-in breath. "This will hurt a bit, but I must examine your—" The foot was drawn aside. She looked up. A flush crept over the woman's pale face.

"You're that doctor woman I've heard talk of, aren't you?"

Doctor *woman*. Emma's heart sank. She held her face impassive. "Yes. I am a doctor."

The woman nodded. "Thank you for the kindness, but I'll manage now."

"And how shall you do that, Mrs…?"

"Swinton." The flush deepened. The woman looked down and picked up her shoe. "Edward will help me. My husband said I was to have naught to do with you."

Would there ever come a time when those words did not hurt or make her furious? Emma nodded and looked at the boy. He was too young to send to the wagons for help. "I understand, Mrs Swinton. And I have no desire to force my ministrations on you. But I am afraid you are going to have to accept my assistance. Without examining you, I cannot tell if the injury is a break or a bad sprain, but the swelling tells me it is severe. You should not walk on it lest you do it further damage. And your son is not big enough to help you back to the train." She forced a smile and drove bitter words out of her mouth. "I am sure, under the circumstances, your husband will forgive you. You are not disobeying his edict. You have refused my doctoring skills. I will only help you back to your wagon, as would anyone. I am certain he would not want you left here helpless and in pain."

The woman looked toward the wagons filing by in the distance, pressed her lips into a firm line and nodded.

Emma rose and looked at the boy. "I shall need you to stand just here and help balance your mother for she must not put her foot down. Are you strong enough to do that?"

The boy gave an eager nod and moved into place.

Emma moved to the woman's side and bent to put her arm around her waist. "Now, Mrs. Swinton, place your arm about my neck and we shall rise together on the count of three. But do *not* put your foot down." She reached up to her shoulder, grasped the woman's wrist and braced herself to lift her. "Ready? One… two…*three*."

* * *

"These wagons give a very punishing ride. And they are so confining it makes me restless." Emma gave her sister a hopeful look. "Do you feel well enough to come outside and sit with me until nightfall, Anne? It is a lovely evening."

"Perhaps tomorrow, Emma. It has been a long, wearying day and I want only to retire." Anne reached to pull the pins from her hair, winced, gave her a wan imitation of her once-vibrant smile and picked up her brush.

"I shall leave a dose of laudanum should you need it to sleep." Emma pulled a tiny, cork-stoppered vial from her pocket, placed it on a trunk holding teaching supplies and climbed from the wagon. She closed and latched the tailgate, straightened the end flaps of the cover that fell into place. A canvas curtain that effectively shut her out of Anne's life. She sighed and turned away from the wagon toward the openness of the prairie. William was right. She could not heal Anne's grief. It was an impossible task. Yet she could not simply give up and let Anne perish of a broken heart. There had to be *something* that would make her want to live again. And she would not rest until she found that something.

She strolled on without direction or purpose, musing over possibilities, found herself near a thin band of trees, plucked a leaf from a low-hanging limb and absently shredded it as she worried over the problem. If only she could find some spark of interest in Anne for *something*. But she kept to herself day and night. Spoke to no one—

"Miss Allen."

Emma jumped, turned and stared at the stocky young

man striding toward her. "Good evening, Mr. Blake." She glanced toward the distant wagons. "Is there a problem?"

"Not if you turn back." A smile curved a line through Josiah Blake's dark, stubbly beard. "Night's about to fall and you're getting a mite far out for safety."

She glanced at the setting sun, the darkness under the trees beyond the reach of its gold-edged rose and purple-colored rays. A shiver slid down her spine. "Are you speaking of Indians?"

"Always a possibility. More so the farther west we travel. But there's other dangers—wolves and such."

Her skin prickled. Her imagination placed the beasts among the trees, skulking through the deep grass all around her. "Thank you for coming to warn me, Mr. Blake. I did not realize how late it is getting, or how far I had wandered." She started back toward the wagons, grateful for his presence as he fell into step beside her, but still frightened enough her feet itched to run. The band of trees along the stream now seemed a menace instead of a cool comfort from the sun.

"I was sorry to hear your sister's ill, Miss Allen. She's fortunate to have you to care for her. I mean, you bein' a doctor and all."

His words soothed the ache in her heart over her inability to help Anne out of her grief—eased her hurt from the Swinton rebuff earlier. She turned her head and gave him a grateful smile. "Thank you, Mr. Blake. You are most kind."

Zach watched Josiah Blake approach Emma Allen, saw them exchange words, then walk together toward the wagons. She would be safe now. Good man, Blake. Though his second-in-command had been a little too eager to accept the task he'd set him.

Zach scowled, edged through the trees and stalked back to the wagons to set the night guards. Emma Allen was a beautiful woman and that could become a major problem. There were quite a few single men on this train. What was she doing wandering off by herself this time of night anyway? Strolling around as if she was in some park back in Philadelphia without a care in the world.

He glanced back, saw Blake had escorted her safe to her wagon, caught the smile she gave him before he walked away. The second one. She'd never smiled at him.

Zach let out a disgusted snort. That could only be counted as a blessing. Emma Allen was nothing but trouble, and he'd wasted enough time watching out for her safety. He aimed for the herd and lengthened his stride. It would not happen again. He had enough work to do.

Chapter Six

Emma bunched her dressing gown to make a pad under her knees, pushed her long, thick braid back over her shoulder and delved into the trunk to sort through the material she had purchased for gowns before she boarded the steamboat and began this journey. She was *not* going to suffer another day of torment from those voracious insects. The veiling she bought to trim her hats would— What was that?

She slipped her fingers between the hard, smooth object and the pile of household linens it rested on, took a firm grasp and tugged it out from under the stack of fabric.

"Oh, my!"

Emma rested back on her heels, staring at the unearthed treasure in her hands. Light from the lantern flame danced in reflected golden luster across the waxed wood of the small lap desk. She placed it on her knees, ran her fingertips over the smooth, polished surface, felt the minor scar a sharp object had made in the wood.

A coyote howled, the sound mournful in the night stillness. Somewhere in the distance an owl hooted.

She rose, carried the desk to her bed, propped up her pillows and positioned herself with her back braced against the sidewall of the wagon. The circle of light from the lantern sitting atop the water keg fell across her knees. She raised the slanted top of the desk, touched the stationery inside, lifted a pen and swallowed hard as tears welled. How precious the most ordinary things had become. These were her connection with her loved ones at home.

A smile tugged at her trembling lips. She closed the desk and uncorked the inkwell that had been sealed with wax, then closed her eyes and thought about what she would write. Should she tell them of her aching loneliness for them? Yes. But nothing that would cause them worry or fear for her safety.

The coyote howled again. Another answered. She lifted her head, listened to the plaintive calls tremble on the air before the sad notes faded away, then dipped the pen and began to write.

My dearest William, Mother and Papa Doc,
How I miss you all. The coyotes are howling to-night, their sad, lonely song echoing what is in my heart as I take up my pen. Your pen, William. For I have found your lap desk in the chest of linens. A wonderful, precious treasure for it allows me to write you all, and thus, feel a bit closer to you.

Every day, every step carries me farther from you and my heart is burdened with sadness at day's end. It would be less so if Anne were improved, but she is much the same. She keeps always to herself. And the effort of riding Lady, or the constant jolting of the wagon delays her healing. I confess, Papa Doc, I do not know what more to do for her. She disobeys my instruction and refuses my medicines. I wish I had your forbearance, Mother. But alas, I do not. And at times I find myself quite out of patience with her. But I persevere. For I am determined to find that which will bring our Annie back to life. Back to us.

I am well. But though I ravenously partake of the meals Mrs. Lundquist prepares for us, the miles I travel each day have made me quite thin, though stronger. My gowns hang loosely upon my frame.

William, my dear brother, I know you are longing for news of our journey. I am told we shall reach the Big Blue River tomorrow or the day following. The river must be forded, for, as the dictatorial Mr. Thatcher says, there are no ferries here in the wilderness. As you will know, I am dreading that.

How I wish I could receive a letter from you. I have read your note over and over, William. It is a comfort to me. Thank you from my heart for the medical supplies, though I fear I will have little use for them. Still, your faith in my doctoring skills warms my heart.

My dearest love to you all, always,

Your Emma

She blotted the ink, blew on it to hasten its drying, then folded it to the inside, inscribed William's name and directed the letter to the Twiggs Manor Orphanage in Philadelphia. He would be back there teaching by now. Tears flowed. She swiped them from her cheeks, lifted the desk lid and took out the small candle of sealing wax and the little metal stamp. William's stamp, with its capital *A* for Allen.

The tears came again, faster. She placed the lap desk on the floor, lifted the chimney of the lantern, lit the candle and tilted it downward over the letter. The melting red wax dropped in a tiny puddle securing the loose edge to the letter body. She blew out the candle and pressed the stamp against the cooling wax, stared down at the *A* it imprinted. Would there be a way to send the letter home? Would they ever receive it and know how much she loved and missed them?

A sob broke free from her constricted throat. Another. And another. She grabbed a pillow, hugged it to her chest and threw herself on the bed to cry out her loneliness and fear.

"Follow us! Stay on our path!"

Emma turned her face from the river. Zachary Thatcher and Josiah Blake were leading the first wagon into the water and she could not bear to watch. She looked at the low hills in the distance, drew her gaze back to Garth Lundquist, thought of how odd it was to have him sitting beside her, and concentrated on the rumble of the wheels bumping down the sloping bank and the sound of the swiftly flowing water of the Big Blue.

"Gee! Gee!" Garth Lundquist cracked his whip in the air over the broad backs of the oxen. The teams plunged into the water, turned right, following the wagons ahead. The front wheels rolled into water, turned brown with mud churned up by hoofs, that splashed against the rims and rose quickly to cover the hubs.

Emma gripped the edge of the seat and stared down at the toes of her boots poking out from under the long, ruffled skirt of her watered-silk gown. An incongruous sight. But one to be preferred over watching the water rushing by beneath the floorboards. She stole a quick glance at the opposite bank. They were halfway there. *Please let us cross safely.*

The wagon dropped sharply to the right, jolted to a stop. Her grip broke. She slid along the canted seat.

"Haw! Haw!" The whip cracked. The oxen lunged. The wagon slipped farther right, sank deeper.

Emma threw herself toward the center of the seat, groped for a handhold to stop her slide, found only the smooth surface of the seat top, the protruding lip too small for her searching fingers to grasp. Fear squeezed her throat, froze her thoughts on the silky whisper of her gown against the smooth boards as she slipped toward the water waiting to embrace her.

"Hold those oxen, Lundquist!" An arm slid beneath her abdomen, plucked her from the seat, dragged her onto a saddle. The horn dug into her leg, water swirled around her feet, wet her skirts and boots. She twisted her torso, clutched hold of fabric and buried her face against a wool shirt that smelled faintly of horse, leather and man. The horse beneath her lunged. Water sloshed higher. She shuddered.

"Blake, get a rope around that front axle and hold her fast so she can't slip to the right! I'll get the back." Zachary Thatcher's deep voice fell on her ears, vibrated in his chest beneath her hands. "Let go of my shirt, Miss Allen. I have to tie my rope to the back axle." He loosed his arm from around her, withdrew the circle of safety.

Panic pounced. She pressed closer, held tighter. His muscles rippled. His strong hands gripped hers, tugged them from his shirt front, lowered them. "Hold to my holster belt." She seized the leather strap her fingers touched, felt him lean sideways and reach down. The saddle creaked. Cool air replaced the warmth of his body—emptiness stole her security. Panic gnawed at her nerves. She kept her eyes closed tight, fought the scream filling her throat, surging into her mouth.

Zachary Thatcher straightened, snagged her around the waist with his left arm, lifted her and held her tight against his chest. "Sorry, I have to snub the rope." He shoved aside her skirt, wrapped the rope around the horn and settled her back in place. "Lundquist, move those teams forward! And don't stop!"

Garth Lundquist's whip cracked. The wagon lurched.

"Back, Comanche!" The horse backed up, the wagon slid left, leveled out and rolled forward. "That's got it!" Zachary Thatcher urged his horse forward, leaned down and unhooked his rope, rode behind the moving wagon and up the other side. He spanned her waist with his hands, lifted her onto the wagon seat and rode away.

She sat gripping the sideboard and looking after him, fighting back tears and an unreasonable, overwhelming feeling of being abandoned.

* * *

"Now hold very still." Emma put fresh padding on Jenny's arm, added the splints and bound them in place, grateful for the need to think of something other than the terror of the fording—and the comforting strength of Zachary Thatcher's arms. "All done. You were a very good girl." She smiled at the toddler who promptly turned and buried her face against her mother's chest. Emma patted the child's back and looked up at Lorna. "Jenny's arm is healing fine."

The woman nodded. "Thank you, Dr. Emma. I watch her careful. An'…well, I been thinkin' whilst you was checkin' her arm. Like I told you afore, Mr. Lewis and I haven't got the cash money, but I can wash your clothes—an' your sister's—to pay for you takin' care of Jenny an' all. I got my water heatin' by the river. So if you'll fetch the clothes for me, I'll get Jenny settled and get to the washin'."

There was unyielding pride in Lorna Lewis's voice. Emma looked at her set face and nodded. "That is a very generous and welcome offer, Lorna. I will bring our clothes to you." She rose and started away, turned back. "Would you care to continue to take on that task while we journey? My sister and I will be happy to pay you." She gave a helpless little shrug. "I am afraid neither of us are trained in such skills."

Lorna studied her face for a moment then nodded.

"Wonderful! I shall tell Anne our laundry problem has been solved." Emma smiled and hurried to her wagon. She climbed onto the step attached to the tailgate and tossed back the flaps. If Lorna cleaned her riding outfit she would be able to—

"Pardon me, Miss."

Emma turned. A worried-appearing young woman holding a crying baby was looking up at her.

"Are you the doctor lady?"

The woman was close to tears. Emma nodded, gave her a reassuring smile. "Yes, I am a doctor."

Relief spread across the woman's face. "I need help, Doctor. It's Isaac. He won't eat nothing. And he won't stop crying. And he's such a good baby... It's been two days." Tears spilled down the woman's cheeks. "I've tried all I know, and what others have said..." She caught her breath. "My husband didn't want me to come, but I think Issac's fevered. And if he's sick..."

"Perhaps I should look at him." Emma stepped down and took the baby into her arms. "How old is Isaac?"

"A bit over a year." The woman wiped away the tears, stared at her child with fear-filled eyes.

Emma sat on the step, laid the baby on her lap, held his tiny, too-hot hands and swung her knees side to side, humming softly to calm him. There was a red flush on his chubby little cheeks, his eyes were squeezed shut. She let go of his hands, felt his forehead...*fevered*—gently probed the glands in his neck...*swollen*. She slipped her hands up and checked behind his ears...*nothing*.

"Is he...sick?"

Emma lifted the baby off her lap, held him in front of her and peered into his mouth when he opened it to squall his protest. The telltale spots were there on the inside of his cheeks. She snuggled the baby against her shoulder, rubbed his tense back, wishing with all her heart she had been wrong. She fixed a calm expression on her face and looked up at his mother. "Isaac is coming down with the measles."

The young woman's face blanched. "Measles?"

Every tale of every death caused by the disease was in the whispered word. "Yes. But Isaac looks to be a healthy, robust baby. And we will do everything we can to keep him that way." *Please, God, grant that it may be so.* She rose and gave the baby back to his mother.

The woman cuddled her son close, pressed her cheek against his soft curls, then looked up and squared her shoulders. "Tell me what I must do."

Emma looked into the determined face. The fear was there in the young woman's eyes, but the firm line of her mouth said she would not let it defeat her. And she had already defied her husband for her child's sake when she brought him to her. Isaac would be well cared for. "You must keep Isaac as calm and comfortable as possible. And keep him warm at all times—a chill will be very bad for him. And keep him inside the wagon. The bright sunlight will hurt his eyes." She had a momentary flash of Papa Doc closing the curtains on the window above her bed in the orphanage. "Encourage him to nurse as often as he will, and feed him only a thin gruel that is easy to swallow, for his throat is sore."

She looked up and met the mother's gaze. "What is your name?"

"Mrs. James Applegate...Ruth Applegate."

Emma dipped her head in acknowledgment. "And have you other children, Mrs. Applegate?"

"No...only Isaac."

Relief spread through her. Perhaps it was not too late to contain the spread of the disease. "If your husband will permit it, Mrs. Applegate, I will come to your wagon and check on Isaac every day. If he will not—" she reached out and touched the soft hair curling behind the baby's ear "—check here often. In the next day or two the rash will begin and it usually starts here, or on the forehead, then spreads. An oatmeal paste will help soothe the itching." She gave her another encouraging smile. "The disease will run its course in a week or so. But you must keep Isaac warm and quiet for several weeks after. Meanwhile, if he shows signs of distress, or develops a deep cough, send for me immediately."

The woman nodded, bit down on her lip. "Doctor, I…" A flush crept across the woman's cheeks. She lifted her head a notch. "My husband will give me no money to pay you. Have you any sewing or—"

"Sewing?" The pile of fabric tucked away in the trunk in the wagon flashed into her head.

"Yes. I was a dressmaker back home, before my marriage."

Zach stood beside Comanche and watched the emigrants herding the stock, settling them down for the night. Only a few animals had wandered into deep water and been forced to swim to the other side during the fording. He and Comanche had only had to save one milk cow. Everything considered, the greenhorns had done a good job today. Hopefully, they would do as well when they faced the whirlpools, swift water and quicksand in the rough river fords ahead.

He lifted his hat, ran his fingers through his hair then settled his hat back in place and tugged the brim low over his forehead. "Well, boy, there's no reason for us to be standing here. Let's get to camp so you can start grazing." Comanche twitched his ears, tossed his head. Zach gathered the reins, glanced in the direction of the wagons and frowned. Who was he fooling? He wasn't ready to turn in. There was a restlessness in him that wouldn't let sleep come easily tonight. And the reason was in that fourth wagon.

He turned away, yanked his hat down lower. What he needed was a hard run with Comanche's hoofs thundering against the ground. Or some combat with an Indian brave determined to have his scalp as a trophy. That would take his mind off the way Emma Allen had felt in his arms this afternoon. The way his heart had pounded when she grabbed his shirt and hid her face against his chest. He sure hadn't wanted to let her go when he put her back in her wagon. He'd wanted to pull her tight and kiss her. And now there was this sense of something unfinished inside him. He scowled, whipped around toward his saddle. "Let's make a final scout of the area before we go to camp, boy."

There was a whisper of sound behind him. He clasped the haft of his knife and pivoted, stared as Emma Allen stepped out of the shade of a tree into the soft, rosy glow of the setting sun. She glanced around and headed his way, a picture of beauty and grace. His heart kicked. He frowned at the involuntary reaction, grabbed Comanche's reins and strode to meet her. He had no idea why the woman would be seeking him out. But whatever the reason, he had already learned, if Dr. Emma Allen was involved, it spelled trouble for him. Whether it was as a doctor or as a woman, she was trouble for him.

Chapter Seven

"**M**easles." Zachary Thatcher removed his hat, ran his fingers through his hair, settled his hat back in place and frowned down at her. "You're certain?"

Emma stiffened at the implied doubt of her competency. "Yes, Mr. Thatcher, I am certain."

"But you say there's no rash..."

"The preceding signs are all there. The rash will appear sometime in the next two days."

He nodded, rubbed the back of his neck, stared off into the distance for a moment then blew out a long breath and again fastened his gaze on her. He looked as if he would like to shoot the messenger. "How likely is it to spread?"

Emma squared her shoulders. "Beyond doubt. All those who have been in contact with the Applegates are in danger of coming down with the disease. How far it spreads depends on you. Mr. Applegate has little faith in my doctoring skill—" she let her tone tell him she was aware that he shared Mr. Applegate's opinion

"—and, as he will not listen to me, you must tell him he and his family will be quarantined until—"

"Quarantined!" The frown on Zachary Thatcher's face deepened to a scowl. "This is a wagon train, Miss Allen."

"Yes." She fought down her impatience, held her voice calm and reasonable. "And unless you want this disease to run rampant through its members, you must quarantine the Applegates."

"And how do you suggest I do that?"

Emma clenched her hands, took a breath and forced herself to stand her ground instead of whirling about and walking away as she wanted to do. She was sick of fighting these battles with men who dismissed her doctoring ability simply because she was a woman. "You must have Mr. Applegate move his wagon a safe distance from the others and then *stay* with his wagon. And you must inform everyone they are not to go near the Applegates, nor their wagon, until they are able to rejoin the train and we travel on. Those who come down with the disease meantime, will be treated in the same fashion."

"Until we 'travel on.'" He fixed a withering gaze on her. "And when will that be?"

His voice had gone hard as stone. Emma put steel into hers. "When I pronounce the wagon train free of the disease."

His eyes darkened. "Now look here, Miss—"

"Doctor."

He stared at her.

She stared back.

He sucked in air, let it out. "These wagons roll west at dawn tomorrow, *Doctor. All* of them."

The words were final. The tone implacable. Emma opened her mouth, then pressed her lips together to hold back her retort. The bright blue eyes staring down at her had gone as flinty as the voice. Obviously, Mr. Thatcher would not be moved by her challenging him. She would have to take another path. "*Mister* Thatcher, I understand that, as captain and guide, it is your duty to get these wagons to Oregon country in a timely manner. But to travel when the Applegate baby is ill may well cause his death. If he is to have a chance to live, he needs to be kept calm and comfortable. He needs to sleep as much as possible and with the jolting of the wagon continually disturbing him—" She caught her breath, taken by the glimmer of an idea that could prove the resolution to their stalemate. "Have you had the measles, Mr. Thatcher?"

"I have." He eyed her as if she were a beaver trap ready to spring. "Why?"

"Because that means it is safe for you to go to the Applegate's wagon." She lifted her hand, tapped her lips with one fingertip and looked into the distance, feeling her way through the idea. "If you will make a sling bed for baby Isaac—as you did for Jenny—he will be warm and comfortable and able to sleep in the moving wagon." She brought her gaze back to meet his. "And if you will break your rule and allow some of the wagons to exchange places in the train, that will solve the problem. We can have a moving quarantine."

"A *moving* quarantine?"

Emma stared at him. It wasn't exactly a sneer, but it might as well have been. She stiffened.

"And how do 'we' accomplish that Miss Allen? It seems to me the idea defies the very meaning of the word."

"In ordinary circumstance, yes. But we have an extraordinary circumstance here." She plunged ahead, too desperate to find a solution to be deterred by his touch of sarcasm. "If you place the Applegate wagon in the rear with my wagon in front of it and Anne's wagon in front of mine, it will keep the Applegates separated from the others as we travel. Anne has had the measles so there will be no danger to her. When the train halts, we shall camp some distance behind it, thus maintaining the quarantine. That way I can care for both baby Isaac and Anne. And—"

"And what of you, Miss Allen? Have you had the measles?"

Surely that hint of concern was not for her? No, of course not. He was thinking of his wagon train. She gave a brisk nod. "Yes, I have. Anne gave them to me." A smile tugged at her lips. "*And* to William. *And* Mother, though she was only Laina Brighton to us then. *And* to a dozen or so of the other children in her orphanage. We were quarantined for *weeks* while Papa Doc treated us." She shook off the memories, sobered. "As I was saying, if any others come down with the measles they shall place their wagon in the rear behind the Applegates where I will be able to tend them also."

He shook his head. "I see you have experience with this quarantine business, Miss Allen, but, as you say, this is an uncommon situation. What you propose will not work. To place the wagons in the rear as we travel makes good sense. But to have separate camps at night is foolhardy. It weakens the train and puts us all at peril. Every day we travel takes us closer to the hostile tribes. I am hoping we will not have problems with them because of a show of force, and having a few wagons camped off by themselves, thus minimizing that force, is asking for trouble."

"As is a wagon train of ill or dying people, Mr. Thatcher." She clenched her hands, watched his frown return, brought back, no doubt, by the asperity in her voice. Well, she could not help it! Why could the man not see reason?

"True enough. But I cannot permit your plan. It's too risky. I haven't men enough to guard two camps."

Emma lifted her chin and looked him full in the eyes. "And how will you get this train to Oregon country if there are no men well enough to drive the wagons or herd the stock or stand guard?"

Zachary Thatcher didn't so much as twitch. He simply looked at her. But some change in his eyes made her suddenly feel crowded…threatened in the same way she had that day by her wagon. It was an odd sort of feeling that shortened her breath and brought heat to her cheeks. It made her want to turn and flee.

"And if the Lundquists have not had the measles and you and your sister are left with no drivers? Have you solved that problem also, Doctor Allen?"

His voice had softened, but the tone was still resolute. She stared up at him irritated by her sudden unease and nettled that he had found a weak spot in her argument for which she had no answer.

He turned away, took hold of Comanche's reins. "I'll give the matter some thought. For now, I will have a talk with Applegate and make that sling bed. Meanwhile, I suggest you return to your wagon." He touched the brim of his hat and walked away, the big roan with the dappling of spots decorating his rump plodding beside him.

The man was *insufferable!* Emma took a deep breath, unclenched her hands and turned back toward her wagon. Zachary Thatcher had said he would make the sling bed for the baby and talk to Mr. Applegate. At least that was something.

Emma lifted the lap desk from the trunk, set the lamp on the closed top and shifted her position to lean her back against the firm support. Her hands trembled as she took out the writing supplies and opened the inkwell. It was small wonder. If William was right, and it was God who put this desire to be a doctor and help others in her, why hadn't He made her a *man?* God was supposed to know everything. And if so, He had to realize there was no other solution to keeping her dream from being unfulfilled because of the small-mindedness of stubborn, arrogant men like Zachary Thatcher!

She scowled down at the blank paper in front of her, sorely tempted to write out her frustration. Instead, she took a deep breath and yanked her thoughts from her confrontation with Mr. Thatcher. She needed to write William, to feel close to him and his belief in her abilities, not spew her agitation into her letter and upset him. She relaxed her tense shoulders, adjusted the position of the desk on her lap and dipped the pen into the well.

My Dearest William,

How I wish you were here. I think of you often, knowing of your curiosity about the country and the animals so different from what we have known. The terrain is endless and bears a perfect resemblance to the waves of the sea. Antelope with their budlike horns, white throats and round black eyes peer at you from above the tall grasses. Wolves and coyotes howl at night. We do not see them by day. There are snakes in abundance. They slither from beneath the oxen's hoofs and the drivers kill them with their whips. Do not fear, for I stay close by the wagons, as ordered. Most annoying are the swarms of insects. I have attached veiling all around my wide-brimmed straw flat to keep them from my face and neck.

The weather is hot now. The sun blazes down upon us all day. And we suffer thunderstorms, unlike any I have before seen in severity. There is hail the size of the cherries that grow on the tree in the backyard of the orphanage. Do you remember, William, when I became so ill from eating the unripe ones?

I must tell you of my patient. A toddler who injured herself falling out of the family's wagon. I set her arm and continue to watch over her. Others reject me as a doctor. I fear there is a measles outbreak in the offing, but Mr. Thatcher ignores my warning and refuses a quarantine. In this, things are much like there at home.

I hope this finds you all well. It is distressing not knowing if Caroline's health has improved.

I comfort myself that Papa Doc is caring for her and the babe she carries. And that I shall have a niece or neph—

A fist thumped the side of the wagon. "There's a meeting called. Come to the head wagon!"

Gracious! Emma righted the desk that had tilted when she jumped, swallowed to force her heart down out of her throat back into her chest where it belonged and frowned at the ink blotch on the paper. She considered staying in her wagon to finish her letter, then sighed and rose to her feet. Most likely Mr. Thatcher was going to tell them of some obstacle ahead tomorrow. She had better go and listen to what he had to say.

Along the circle of wagons the dying embers of cook fires winked red into the dark night, appearing and disappearing as the men and women of the train crossed in front of them on their way toward the lead wagon. Zach watched them come, found himself searching for the slender, graceful figure of Emma Allen, frowned and squatted to add a broken branch to the fire.

It was only right he should look for her—she was the cause of this meeting. But the tense knot of anticipation in his gut told him that wasn't the only reason. He huffed out a breath, watched the dry bark smolder then burst into flames. The branch would soon be reduced to a pile of ashes and embers. He figured the same thing happened between a man and woman. Things burned hot for a while, then there was nothing left except the residue trapped within the circle of rocks that had walled in the flames. He wasn't looking for any walls.

Zach brushed the clinging bits of bark from his hands and rose. He wanted no relationship with any woman, let alone one as troublesome as Emma Allen. He intended to be free of all fetters, to roam where he chose, when he chose. That was the life he wanted. And it was the life he would have once the trading post he intended to build was up and running under a hired manager. But he needed the bonus for getting this wagon train to Oregon country to make that happen. And that meant they had to push forward every day in order to get through before the snow closed the mountain passes. There simply was not time for delays.

The murmur of voices, punctuated by the lowing of oxen or the neighing of a horse, disturbed the night's quiet. A wolf howled. A coyote yipped nearby. Zach tensed, listened, decided they were real and relaxed. He scanned the faces of the people gathering around the fire so unaware of the myriad dangers surrounding them. Moonlight silvered their features, revealed worry and concern, curiosity and puzzlement. Everyone was wondering what this hastily called meeting was about. He spotted John Hargrove hurrying toward him and stepped to meet him.

"What's going on, Thatcher?" The older man's bushy gray eyebrows fairly bristled with indignation. "What is the purpose of this meeting? And why was I not informed? As the one who formed this train I expect—"

"Calm down, Hargrove." It was the voice he'd used to deal with insubordinate soldiers and it had the same effect. John Hargrove looked angry, but he held his tongue. Zach threw balm at the resentment. "There's no need to get riled. I would have told you about the meeting had there been time. I appreciate your coming forward to stand with me. It's always good to show a united front."

"Indeed. Indeed." The eyebrows drew close over John Hargrove's deep-set eyes. "That, of course, is my purpose."

Zach nodded, swept his gaze over the assembled people, spotted the fire reflected in a shimmer of silk. She was standing off to one side, next to a wagon, her frilly dress incongruous among all the other plain, sensible gowns of wool or cotton. Another reason not to allow his attraction to Emma Allen free rein. The woman was totally unsuited to life on the frontier. He shifted his gaze toward the wagons, noted that there was no one else coming and stepped forward into the light of the fire. The murmuring stopped. An expectant hush hung on the air.

"I called this meeting because we have a problem that needs to be dealt with quickly."

"A problem... Must be Injuns... What kind of problem... Must be somethin' he discovered when he was scoutin' the trail... Is it Injuns..." The questions and speculations shouted out in dozens of voices collided in the air, made an undecipherable din. Zach gave a shrill whistle, held up his hands. The clamor stopped.

"The Applegate baby has the measles." The words hung in a sudden, dead silence. "You all know what that can mean. But with your cooperation we are going to do our best to head off an epidemic." He swept his gaze over the crowd. "First off, I want those of you who have had the measles to come to the left side of the fire, and those of you who have *not* had the measles to come to the right side. Mothers, some of your children may be too young to remember, so you help them get to the right place. And don't be concerned, you will not be separated from your family. This is only so we can know how to go on with our plan."

There was a general muttering. People exchanged glances. A few started to move. He looked at Emma Allen. She was frowning, looking perplexed.

"Hold on, Thatcher!" The words rang out. People froze in place and looked toward Tom Swinton. "My wife says she was holding the Applegate baby earlier, and he hasn't got any spots on him. How do you know he has the measles?"

"Dr. Allen examined him."

"That woman charlatan!" Tom Swinton snorted. "I'm not having any part of this, lest a *real* doctor says that baby has the measles. We're going back to our wagon. Come along—"

"That is your right, Mr. Swinton." Zach raised his voice to carry over the muttering that had started with Tom Swinton's declaration. "But if you take your family back to your wagon, you hitch up and move on. You will no longer be allowed to travel with this train." He looked out over the people. "And that goes for any of the rest of you, as well. Make your choice now." His tone left no doubt he meant what he said.

Emma Allen stared at him, her mouth agape. No one moved.

"Come with Mother, Edward." Pamelia Swinton's soft words carried clearly on the frozen silence. Zach fixed his gaze on the woman. She took her young son by the hand, grasped the limb she was using for a cane and hobbled toward the right side of the fire.

"Pamelia, I forbid—"

The woman stopped, drew herself up straight and faced her husband. "Not this time, Thomas. I obeyed your order to have nothing to do with Dr. Allen when I injured my foot and I still cannot walk on it. I will not take the same risk with our son's life, nor with the life of the babe I carry."

Her words galvanized the women in the group to action. In a flurry of movement they herded their children where they should be and took up their own places. The men exchanged looks with one another, shrugged and followed. Tom Swinton strode off to his wagon. Pamelia looked up at him. "Thomas stands on this side also, Mr. Thatcher."

Zach nodded, slewed his gaze to his left and took a head count of those that had already had measles. Twenty-five people—fifteen of them men or boys old enough to drive wagons, herd stock or stand guard. Garth Lundquist was not among them. He searched faces, settled his gaze on Josh Fletcher. The boy was young, only fifteen or so, but he was strong, sensible, and good with oxen and rifle. Better, perhaps, than Garth Lundquist with the rifle. He looked back to his right. Twenty vulnerable people, the majority of them children. Several of the families were split between the two sides, which complicated matters. He did some rapid calculating in his head, cleared his throat. *Make this plan work for their sakes, Lord.*

"As I said earlier, we have a plan. Dr. Allen proposed a way to quarantine the sick to protect the rest of you as best we are able while still continuing to travel. I concur. Therefore, there will be a change in the formation of the train tomorrow. Listen carefully for your new place. The two Applegate wagons will be in the rear. The two Allen wagons will be next in line so Dr. Allen can tend the sick. In front of them will be those families who have all had the measles and are in no danger. That would be the Hargroves and the Suttons. In front of them will be the Fentons, the Swintons, the Lundquists, the Fletchers and the Lewises. The lead wagon maintains its place. *No one* is to leave their assigned position."

He fixed his gaze on the burly young man standing at the back of those on his right. "Garth, you will stay with your family, help out with herding the stock of those who are in quarantine." He slid his gaze left. "Josh, you are to take over as driver for Dr. Allen."

The boy looked at his father, received a nod and squared his shoulders. "Yes, sir."

"What happens if one of us gets sick?"

Zach slid his gaze over the crowd, sought out the questioner. "If anyone in your family gets sick, your wagon goes to the rear of the train and the quarantine continues."

Axel Lundquist nodded. "Sounds like this thing might work."

There was a murmur of agreement.

"It will as long as you all stay in your own wagons with your own families until the disease has run its course and the danger passes. Of course, those driving for the owners of the wagons in quarantine will have to stay at the rear of the train. They will not be allowed to go to their family's wagon during the quarantine period. I will provide a tent for them." He allowed himself another glance at Emma Allen. She looked astounded. But there was a warm glow deep in her lovely brown eyes that made his heart beat faster in his chest.

Emma made a last pass with the strip of fabric under the arch of Pamelia Swinton's foot, brought it back over the top, wound it around the ankle again and tied it off. "That should help relieve your pain, Mrs. Swinton. But you must not put your weight on your foot until it is healed. When you use it, it sprains it all over again."

"Thank you, Dr. Emma. This time I shall heed your warning." Pamelia Swinton glanced up. "I'm sorry, I did not mean to sound disrespectful, Dr. Allen. I have heard Lorna Lewis call you Dr. Emma and it slipped out."

Emma laughed. "I like the sound of Dr. Emma. It is…friendlier than Dr. Allen."

Her patient smiled and reached for her stocking. "Then you must call me Pamelia."

Emma nodded and reached to help stretch Pamelia's stocking over the thick winding around her foot and ankle. "Pamelia, did your husband say at the meeting that you held little Isaac Applegate tonight?"

"Yes. He has been so fussy and fretful he is wearing Ruth out. She wearies quickly since she's been with child. And I was sitting resting my ankle anyway so—" She stopped tugging at her stocking and looked up. Her face paled. "*Edward.* Mr. Thatcher said there is to be a quarantine to keep us safe…" Tears glistened in her eyes. "Have I endangered Edward?"

Emma looked at the fear in Pamelia's eyes and

wished there were some way she could erase it. "There is no way to tell, Pamelia. But Edward is a fine, strong boy. I believe he will be fine if he does come down with the measles. He will be uncomfortable, but fine." She made her voice calm, reassuring. "Of course, you must let me know if he becomes fevered. Or if he has the sniffles, or a cough." She smiled and picked up Pamelia's shoe. "I am afraid this will not fit over the bandage. Have you some boots you can wear until your sprain is better?"

"Yes. And if they do not fit, I shall borrow one of Thomas's." She placed her hand on the edge of the tailgate and pushed herself upright, took a firm grip on her branch cane and reached for her shoe. "Thank you again, Dr. Emma. My ankle feels better already. I am sorry I cannot pay you now, but the money is in the wagon. I…I suppose now you shall have to wait for your fee until after the…the quarantine."

Emma nodded, placed her hand on Pamelia's arm. "Do not fret, Pamelia. Edward is a strong little boy, and he may not get the measles. The disease is a chanceful thing. Now, let me help you to your wagon."

"Thank you, Dr. Emma. You are very kind, but you had best not. Thomas is—you'd best not."

Emma stood and watched Pamelia hobble off into the darkness. The poor woman was so worried about her little boy she had not thought of the possible danger to herself and her husband.

Emma sighed. Sometimes it was difficult being a doctor. Still… *Dr. Emma*. It had a lovely sound. She smiled, picked up her lantern and headed for Anne's wagon to check on her and tell her all that had happened at the meeting. She was halfway across the inner circle when it hit her. Tonight these people, well…*some* of these people had accepted her as a doctor. Even Mr. Thatcher. Was it possible her dream was not dead? That it could still come true?

Commit thy way unto him; trust also in him; and he shall bring it to pass.

Could it be… She looked up at the star-strewn night sky, holding her breath, waiting for she knew not what—some sign? A sense of reassurance? There was nothing. Only the dark, and the sounds of the night. She raised the lantern and continued on her way. The truth was, she had a few patients because she was the only doctor on this wilderness journey, not because God had suddenly decided to answer her prayers. And Mr. Thatcher had acquiesced to her quarantine recommendation in order to keep the men healthy and able to work—not because he believed in her doctoring skills. Would she never learn to stop hoping for something that could not be?

Chapter Eight

~❧~

Emma ladled water from the barrel lashed to the side of the wagon into the wash bowl she now placed on the shelf beside it whenever the wagon train stopped. She lathered and scrubbed her hands with lye soap as Papa Doc had taught her to do whenever she treated the ill. Wonderful Papa Doc, who for many years had been scorned by his fellow physicians at Pennsylvania Hospital for what they called his "foolishness," his insistence on cleanliness during and after seeing patients or performing surgery. And for using alcohol to cleanse wounds and hands and instruments. That is, they had scorned him until they realized how many of his patients survived. Now most of them had adopted those same practices. But Papa Doc had been the first.

Thoughts of her adopted father brought tears to her eyes. She blinked them away, dumped the water on the ground then dipped her fingers into the small crock sitting beside the wash bowl and rubbed the balm he had formulated especially for her into her hands. She closed her eyes, wiped her hands over her cheeks then cupped her hands over her nose and inhaled. The fragrance of lavender tinged with a hint of soap transported her back to Papa Doc's office—to their discussions over his experiments, and those of the other doctors he exchanged letters with across the country, even across the ocean.

She sighed, tugged the long sleeves on her new, sensible dress of dark blue cotton back over her wrists and replaced the top on the crock. Would he write her of his findings about the medical use of sulfuric ether? She stared down at the crock, remembering his excitement when he had discovered the substance some of his pupils and their friends used to exhilarate themselves at parties rendered them insensitive to pain. He had pondered and mulled over possibilities for weeks. And then, two days before she left for St. Louis to visit Mary while William prepared for his journey to Oregon country, he had removed a tumor from Mr. Jefferson's back while the man smelled the sulfuric ether she had mixed and placed on a towel. Excitement tingled through her at the memory. Mr. Jefferson had felt *nothing*. He had not even made objection to her presence during the surgery. In truth, he had been most amenable while smelling the ether. A smile tugged at her lips, turned into a grin. Perhaps she should administer some ether to Mr. Thatcher.

Her amusement drowned in a wash of reality. She looked around the inner circle, then stared out at the wilderness surrounding the circled wagons. If Papa Doc wrote her, would she ever receive his letter? Would she ever again know of the new and exciting things he and his fellow doctors discovered?

Boots rasped against the sandy soil. "Dr. Emma, Ma says supper is ready."

She turned and smiled. "Thank you, Matthew. I'll be right there."

The tall, lanky young man nodded, stuffed the half a biscuit he held into his mouth and ambled off toward his wagon.

Emma brushed the wayward wisps of hair off her temples and forehead, tugged the button-front bodice with its high collar into place and smoothed down the long skirt of her new dress. It was the first of the two gowns she had commissioned Ruth to make for her. The woman had sewn it while sitting in the wagon watching over baby Isaac.

She looked down, ran her fingers over the rolled-ribbon trim at her narrow waist that was the dress's one vanity. The dress fit well. Ruth truly was a gifted seamstress. She was eager now for the other dress Ruth was making her to be finished. The dark red wool fabric would be welcome for the cooler weather of the mountains. She wiggled the toes of her shoes peeking out from under the hem of the long, full skirt and smiled. These gowns would not drag along the ground and snag on every little thing as she walked beside the wagon. And Mr. Thatcher would no longer look askance at those opulent silk gowns better suited for drawing rooms than rough trails and wilderness prairies. Not that she had seen much of Mr. Thatcher since the quarantine started. She seldom caught even a glimpse of him from here at the back of the train. He was always out front, scouting the trail for the best camping places, then leading the wagons to them. But he had kept his word and provided a tent for their drivers to sleep in.

Emma shrugged off the thoughts and turned her

mind toward supper. It would mean another battle to get Anne to eat. Well, so be it. She respected her sister's grief, but she refused to allow it to kill her. She placed her foot on the step, leaned into the wagon and took tin plates and flatware from the trunk beside the tailgate, hopped down and walked forward to the Hargrove's wagon.

"Good evening, Mr. Hargrove." The older man nodded and went on eating. He made no secret of his poor opinion of a woman doctor. Nor did he hide his displeasure with her for initiating the quarantine that kept everyone confined to their own wagons. But she did not expect he would change his mind about that. Mr. Hargrove liked to strut his importance as the organizer of the wagon train among its members and the quarantine made that impossible.

Emma turned from his frowning face and smiled at his wife. "Hello, Lydia. What have you for us tonight?"

The plump woman straightened from stirring the contents of one of the cast-iron pots sitting on the glowing coals of the cook fire, lifted the long skirt of her apron and wiped the perspiration from her face. "There's side meat and gravy, beans and stewed apples. And biscuits." She shot a pleased look at the pots. "Matthew found wood to make fire enough to cook us a satisfying meal. Those buffalo chips we've been using don't make coals for baking, so I made biscuits enough for tomorrow, too." Her lips lifted in a wry smile. "I never thought I would cook over such things! But when there's no wood..." She shrugged and held out her hand.

"You always make a good meal, Lydia." Emma smiled, handed her one of the plates then bent and spooned food onto the other. "I may be a doctor, but Anne and I would have perished of starvation over these last few weeks had you not offered to cook for us."

Lydia Hargrove laughed. "I figured as much when I saw you coughing and choking on the smoke rising from those potatoes you were trying to cook that first night of the quarantine. I never saw anything as burnt as those potatoes. They weren't good for anything but dumping into the fire for fuel."

Emma joined in her laughter. "I remember. I also remember how relieved and grateful I was when you came to my rescue."

Lydia Hargrove spooned food onto the plate she held and added a biscuit. "Truth be told, I enjoy cooking for you and your sister. It remembers me of before Sally and Ester married and left home." A frown wrinkled her forehead. "But I do wish I could manage something that would make your sister eat more. She looks mighty frail and peaked. But I suspect she will eat hearty again, once her grieving is done." She shook her head, stared down at the plate she held. "It takes the heart out of a woman to lose her husband and her babe. Takes time to get over a thing like that." The older woman lifted her head and Emma saw remembered sorrow in her eyes before Lydia smiled and held out the filled plate. "Listen to me, talking on and on, and keeping you here while the food gets cold. You'd best be on your way."

Emma nodded and hurried to Anne's wagon. The end flaps of the canvas cover were down as always. She sighed and stepped close. "Anne, I have your supper. And it will do you no good to tell me you have no appetite for you know I will simply come inside and pester you until—"

"Oh, Emma, why will you not let me be?" The flaps parted. Anne appeared against the dusky interior of the wagon, her black dressing gown hanging on her too-thin frame, her russet curls tumbling askew around her pale face. "Truly, I am weary and want only to sleep."

"After you have eaten, Annie." Emma kept her voice firm and pleasant. "I promise I will go away when you have eaten half of what is on your plate. But if you do not, I will stay and recite—"

"No, Emma. Truly I cannot eat any—"

She squared her shoulders and cleared her throat. "The sun had clos'd the winter day—"

Anne sighed. "Robert Burns, Emma? You know—"

"—The curlers quat their roarin play—"

"Enough, Emma! You *know* I cannot bear your atrocious Scottish accent." For a tiny moment Anne's voice seemed to lose its tone of grim bitterness, seemed to hold the merest ghost of her old humor. And then it was gone. She stepped back into the wagon. "Come inside. If it is the only way to silence you, I will try to eat."

Emma placed the cleaned dishes back in the trunk, turned on the tailgate step and looked out over the land. When they had reached the Platte River the prairies had given way to a wide valley. One with only occasional clumps of trees that rose like shadowed islands along the many ribbonlike streams that wound their way through it. They had crossed so many streams she had quite gotten over her fear of fording them. Now—

"Come down from there, Miss Allen!"

"Oh!" Emma whirled, lost her balance and fell forward.

Zachary Thatcher caught her in midair, lowered her to the ground. His arms were as strong, felt as safe as she remembered. She looked up, straight into those bright blue eyes. They held her gaze, then darkened. His arms tightened around her. Or did she imagine that? Warmth crept into her cheeks, spread to every part of her. She bowed her head to hide her flushed cheeks from him, stepped back and pressed her hand over the wild thumping at the base of her throat. "Forgive my clumsiness, but I did not hear you approach, Mr. Thatcher."

He cleared his throat, gestured toward his feet. "Moccasins. They are quieter than boots—better for tracking." A frown creased his forehead. "Come here, beside the wagon."

His voice held his normal, autocratic tone. For some reason it made her feel safer. She moved back to stand beside the water barrel, then glanced down at the leather moccasins that rose from his feet to cover his muscular calves. Leather thongs held them in place. "What are you tracking?"

"Whatever is needed. How are your patients faring?"

It was an evasive answer. She studied his face, could detect nothing from his expression. She formed a cautious answer. "Very well. Emily and Susan Fenton's measles are gone. And they are the last ones to fall ill. Two more days and the quarantine will be over. There is only—"

"The quarantine is over now." He turned away.

An owl hooted. Another answered.

"Mr. Thatch—"

His raised hand silenced her. Quick and quiet as

a shadow, he slipped into the narrow space between the aligned wheels of hers and the Hargrove's wagons and stood looking out into the distance. The soft light of dusk outlined his straight nose, his square jaw and strong chin. Something in the way he held his head sent a chill skittering along her spine—prickled her flesh. "What is it?" The sudden tautness of her throat turned the words into a whisper. She stepped close to him.

He pivoted, grasped her elbow and in two steps had her back behind the wagon. "Stay out of sight. There are Cheyenne out there."

"Cheyenne? You mean *Indians?*" Her jaw dropped, her eyes widened with shock.

He nodded, turned and strode to the Hargrove wagon. "John... Matthew... Get your rifles and assemble at the driver's tent!"

Before she could take a breath, he turned and headed for the Applegate wagons. What was he *doing?* These men were not yet recovered enough for...for *battle?* Emma made a valiant attempt to regain her composure, stepped away from the security of her wagon and ran after him, feeling the malevolent gazes of hundreds of savages fastened on her.

"James... Seth... Get your weapons and assemble at the driver's tent!"

The Applegate men scrambled for their wagons at his order.

"Mr. Thatcher! I must—"

He wheeled, scowled. "I told you to stay out of sight." He gripped her upper arms, stared down at her. "For once, will you do as you're told? Go back to your wagon and—"

"Not until I know—"

The muscle along his jaw twitched. "As you will. I haven't time to argue the matter." He released her and pivoted.

Hosea and Jasper Fenton were striding toward them, rifles in their hands. "We heard." Hosea jerked his head backward. "Nathan's gettin' his rifle, he'll be along." They swerved toward the tent. Carrie Fenton stood by their wagon, her body tense, her face pale. Nathan hopped down and loped off after his father and brother.

"Carrie, keep your girls calm and inside the wagon!"

It was all she had time to say. Zachary Thatcher was headed for the Swinton wagons. Emma ran and stood in his path. Ezra Beason, Thomas Swinton's hired driver, rushed by her, headed for the tent, rifle in hand. She took a breath to calm her racing heart. "Mr. Thatcher, I do not know what you want with these men. But whatever it is, you cannot involve Thomas Swinton. He was very ill and is not yet recovered. He could well die if he gets chilled or overtired."

Zachary Thatcher stared into her eyes, took a step toward her. She backed up.

"*Doctor* Allen, I have yielded to you as the medical expert on this wagon train to the point of allowing almost half of the able-bodied fighting men to be quarantined. But I *will not* cede you one iota of power beyond that."

He closed the gap between them. She tipped her head back, stared up into eyes that had darkened to the color of blue slate.

"The leadership and safety of the people on this train are my responsibility. One for which I am well qualified. Now do me the service of respecting *my* ability and get out of my way."

The last words were all but hissed. Emma caught her breath and shook her head. "I cannot. Not if it will mean Mr. Swinton's death."

Those blue eyes flashed. Zachary Thatcher made that sound low in his throat—the sound he had made that day by the wagon. He clasped her upper arms, lifted her aside and strode to the Swinton wagon. "Tom, get your rifle and come to the tent." He pivoted, and without so much as a glance in her direction, marched toward the crowd that had gathered. Thomas Swinton got his rifle and followed.

"What is it? What's wrong?"

Emma looked at Ruth climbing from the wagon with baby Isaac clutched in her arms, and gestured toward the tent. "Mr. Thatcher is telling them now." She hurried toward the people who had gathered, dimly aware that Ruth ran to walk beside her.

"—so I need you all to stay calm. Especially you men." Zachary Thatcher's gaze swept over the people, touched hers and moved on. "Things can get touchy when you are dealing with a war party."

War party! Emma heard a gasp, glanced at Ruth's stricken face and laid a comforting hand on her arm.

"—I don't think they intend us harm. I think they were out hunting Pawnee or other enemies, spotted our wagons and decided to come see what we are doing. That does not mean they will not attack if they feel the booty taken will be worth the battle. That is why we must appear strong. The main body has stopped some distance away, but their scouts are looking us over."

"How do you know?"

"They're talking to one another. That quail whistle you heard a minute ago was a scout giving his position. The owl you heard was another scout answering."

An image of Zachary Thatcher's intent expression as he listened to the owls earlier flashed into her head. Emma shivered, felt those savage gazes upon her again. How could he be so calm? There was such quiet strength in his face....

"—Indians are not troubled by the morals of white men. To them stealing is a virtue...especially horses. All ours are to be brought inside and tethered to the wagon tongues." His gaze pinioned two of the men in front of him. "Ezra and Matthew, you'll help with that. Saddle up and report to Blake."

Traveler and Lady! She had not thought—

"The river will protect our left, the stock is to be herded in close to the wagons on our right. They will serve as a barrier between the Cheyenne and the women and children and our supplies. They won't be able to rush the wagons. Ernst, Josh, Seth, you'll help herd them in."

The men named ran for their horses.

"The rest of you—"

Emma swallowed hard, looked at the people standing quiet and tense waiting to find out what their role would be.

"I'm setting a double guard around the camp and the stock tonight. I don't have to tell you what will happen to us if they get stampeded and run off."

Emma's heart thudded. She closed her eyes. *Please, God—*

"All of you men will be assigned a time and place of

duty. Stay alert. Indians are the best fighters you will ever encounter. They can hide behind a blade of grass, appear and disappear at will, move without sound. But they seldom attack a superior force, or one in a good defensive position. But bear in mind, when they do attack, they kill without compunction. For them, to kill an enemy is an honor." His gaze swept over them again. "You are their enemy. Don't forget it. Defend yourself. But I don't want any wild shots fired at something you hear or *think* you see. Be sure of your target. And remember, they yell like inhuman devils, but it's only noise to unnerve you and keep you from shooting straight and steady—ignore the yells. A bullet will kill them same as any other living creature. Now all you women go to your wagons and *stay there*. Should there be a battle, those of you who know how can load weapons or use them."

Once again Zachary Thatcher's gaze touched hers, slipped away. "John Hargrove, Tom Swinton—"

She stiffened.

"—James Applegate and Nathan Fenton. Your wagons are beside the river. You men will stay here and guard this area. If you spot any Indians approaching through the water, fire a shot to warn them off. If they turn back, let them go. Do *not* shoot to kill unless they keep coming. Keep a sharp eye out for diversions. Watch the water for Indians crossing while others draw your attention from them, and be ready to shoot. If they reach the trees along the riverbank they can sortie on the wagons from there and they will be hard to flush out. Hargrove and Swinton, you two take the first watch. Applegate and Fenton, rest while you can, but be ready. And douse this fire." His gaze swept over them once more. "You women, no lights in the wagons. An arrow can't find an unseen target. The rest of you men, come with me."

The women in attendance glanced at one another, then, faces set in grim acceptance of the situation, headed for their wagons. There was nothing to say. No comfort to offer. Things were what they were.

Emma watched Ruth Applegate hurry off beside her husband, baby Isaac clutched tightly to her chest. She looked at Pamelia Swinton hobbling along after Tom, young Edward beside her, and at Lydia Hargrove marching off beside John, at Carrie Fenton standing still as a statue beside her wagon. What would happen to all of them? And to all of the others on the train? What would happen to Annie? To her?

Annie. She had to protect Annie! Her stomach contracted. A quivering started in her legs and arms, spread to every part of her. She folded her arms across her torso to try and stop the quaking and peered into the dusky distance, fastened her gaze on Zachary Thatcher's rapidly disappearing figure. Somehow, though frightening, it had seemed everything would be all right until he strode away.

Chapter Nine

Zach edged up to the rock, molded himself to its form and studied the length of denser darkness on the ground ahead. Was it a ridge of stone—or a guard stretched prone on the ground? He scowled and edged a little closer. The darkness was an enemy that hid his foes. But the same darkness covered him. He stayed perfectly still, listened and watched a few minutes longer, then took a firmer grip on his knife, crouched low and inched his way toward the thick darkness near the top of the low, sandy rise.

Emma stared into the dark, listened to her sister's soft breathing. How could she sleep at such a time? It was worrying. Anne had not even been alarmed at the news of the Indians. Only irritated that she would not be left alone.

Emma released her grip on William's pistol, flexed her stiff fingers then reached up and rubbed her neck and shoulders. Never had a night been so long. Every muscle in her body was protesting her cramped position, demanding movement, but she dared not rise or stretch in the close quarters lest she bump something and knock it onto Anne.

She sighed and rested back against the side of the wagon, shifted slightly to ease the discomfort of the tense muscles around her shoulder blades, then wiggled her toes and feet to relieve the annoying prickles in her legs. The weight of William's pistol across her thighs hampered her movement. She lowered her hands, carefully felt for the weapon and again folded her fingers around the grip.

Hoofs thudded against the ground as the horses tethered to the wagon tongue changed position. Her heart lurched. Was an Indian stealing Traveler or Lady? Or had one crowded the horses over so he could climb into the wagon? She swallowed hard, lifted the heavy pistol with both hands and pointed it in the direction of the driver's seat. Should she issue a challenge to scare whoever might be there away? Or should she stay silent and shoot if someone tried to enter? *Could* she shoot? She supported her trembling hands with her raised knees and nodded. Yes. Yes, she could shoot someone to save Annie and herself. But then she would doctor whomever she shot.

Laughter bubbled in her chest, boiled up into her throat. The doctor in her recognized it as hysteria. She clamped her lips tight, fought the laughter down.

Some sort of night bird called. She held her breath and strained to hear if another answered. Oxen horns clacked together outside. She jerked her head in the direction of the noise, jerked it back toward the entrance over the wagon seat again at a soft whisper of sound. A horse swishing his tail? Or leather moccasins brushing against the wood? Tears smarted her eyes. Every normal night sound had turned into a threat. If only William were here. She so missed him and—

No! What a selfish thought. She did not want William to be in danger. And if he were here, he would be out there in the night doing whatever Mr. Thatcher told him to do. And Caroline and the babe she carried would be sitting here in this wagon with Indians prowling around outside.

Prowling around.

Moccasins are better for tracking. Her lungs seized. Is that what Mr. Thatcher had been speaking of? Tracking the Indians? Was he out there in the night sneaking up on the war party? An image of him as he'd stood listening to the Indians signaling one another by hooting like owls flashed into her head. There had been an intensity, a strength in his face that had both drawn and frightened her. What if— She shook her head, denying the thought. It was too terrifying. What would they do if something happened to Zachary Thatcher? Who would lead them to Oregon country? Who would get them safely across the mountains and rivers?

Emma shuddered, leaned her head back and closed her eyes, remembering how her wagon had slipped off the fording path in the Big Blue River and tipped sideways, how Zachary Thatcher had come and snatched her from the tilted seat as she was sliding toward the water. And of how safe, how *protected* she had felt with his strong arms holding her in front of him on his horse. And, again, earlier tonight, when he had caught her and kept her from falling. When he had looked down at her and his arms had tightened around her...

Suddenly, with her whole being, she longed to be in his arms again. What if he didn't return? What if she never saw him again? Tears slipped from beneath her lashes and ran down her cheeks. *Please, Almighty God, please. Do not let Mr. Thatcher be harmed. Please keep him safe for...for all our sakes.*

She wiped the tears from her cheeks with her free hand and opened her eyes. She could see nothing in the inky darkness, but it made her feel more vulnerable to have her eyes shut. Her chest tightened. She forced her lungs to draw a deep breath, then expelled it slowly. It was so hard to be brave, sitting alone in the dark with a pistol in her hand guarding Anne while evil crept through the night.

Zach stretched out along the length of the ridge of rock and peered around the end. Five small fires burned at the bottom of the swale, the warriors around them dark silhouettes against the glow of their flames. So the Cheyenne were being cautious, but did not feel threatened. If there were Pawnee or other enemy tribes close by they would never light fires. And they were not preparing for battle. So, barring some fool mistake by one of the greenhorns, they had no plans to attack the train.

Relief eased his tense muscles. An owl hoot from behind him on the right drew them taut again. He turned his head, spotted a returning scout loping toward the camp and hugged the ground. The warrior's footsteps vibrated through the earth beneath his ear. The whisper of moccasins against the sandy soil grew louder. The scout was not being careful, which meant he felt secure this close to camp and would not be so alert. Perhaps he would pass by without spotting him. And perhaps not.

Zach tightened his grip on his knife, tensed his muscles to roll aside and spring to his feet to silence the brave before he could give an alarm. Grains of sand skittered along the dry soil between the sparse blades of grass and pelted his hand. He held his breath—waited.

The scout loped by the end of the rocky ridge. Zach lifted his head enough to turn it and watch the warrior into camp. He drew his legs up beneath him, chose his path and got ready to run if the brave raised a cry.

All stayed quiet below. The Cheyenne gathered around the fires continued to eat, some were sleeping. He could make out their forms at the edge of the firelight. Near as he could see there were close to fifty braves in the war party. More than double the number of fighting men he could field. And of the men he led, most were unskilled and untested in warfare.

Zach scowled, studied the area behind him, slithered back from the top of the rise, then crouched and ran toward the cover of a nearby tree. Best not to return on the path he had used to come to their camp. He would take a roundabout route back to the river.

"There are so many of them!" Emma straightened, wiped her brow and stole another look at the Indians sitting on their horses, a short distance beyond the massed herd. "There must be at least fifty of them!"

"Mind your skirt!" Lydia Hargrove gave her a little

push back from the fire. "It's not Indians you'll be worrying about if you catch afire. And mind you don't burn that gruel. It needs stirring."

Emma nodded, bent and stirred the oatmeal bubbling in the iron pot over the coals. "How can you be so calm, Lydia? They look so…so…*savage!* Did you see their painted faces? And the feathers stuck in their hair? And they are fairly bristling with weapons." She straightened again. "Look at all those spears, and bows and arrows and shields! And now that the light is strengthening I can see hatchets dangling from their waists."

"Mayhap you would be calmer if you looked at what you are doing, instead of at the heathen. Remember, Mr. Thatcher said we are to act normal and not show fear."

There was tension in Lydia's voice, and her face was pale. She was not as calm as she pretended. Emma sucked in a breath and forced a smile. "I am acting normal. You are the cook, not I."

"True enough." Lydia laughed, but there was a strained sound to it. "That gruel is done."

Emma nodded, gave the oatmeal a last stir and pulled it off the fire. "What will happen to us, Lydia?"

"We will do as Mr. Thatcher says and break our fast as usual."

"And then?"

The older woman dumped the coals off the lid of the spider into the fire, lifted the pan out onto the grass and straightened. She wiped her hands down her apron and looked off toward the war party. "Most of our husbands and sons are shopkeepers or farmers, not fighters. What happens will be as God wills it."

The quiet words sparked a fire in her breast. Emma

looked at her wagon, at her doctor's bag and William's pistol resting on the shelf beside the water barrel where she had placed them and shook her head. "I am not as accepting as you, Lydia. Life is sacred. And I will fight to preserve it—with my doctoring skills, or with a gun."

"You may soon have the chance."

Emma jerked her gaze toward the Indians, spotted the lone figure riding out to meet them astride the large roan with gray spots decorating its hip. Her lungs froze. She opened her mouth to call Zachary Thatcher back, but no sound came out. She commanded her feet to stay put, to not run after him. *Please, God! Please keep him from harm. Oh, please keep him safe. Keep us all safe!*

Her pulse thundered in her ears, throbbed at the base of her throat. She closed her eyes, afraid to witness what might happen, then opened them again in case she was needed. He had covered half the short distance and stopped. An Indian was riding out to meet him. She looked at the garishly painted face, the spear clutched in a powerful hand, whirled and hurried to her wagon. If something happened she was too far away. She had to get closer. She snatched up her doctor's bag and William's pistol and, mindful of Zachary Thatcher's order, forced herself to maintain a moderate pace as she walked toward the other end of the circled wagons.

Emma wrapped the pistol in the oiled cloth, slipped it into its leather bag and placed it back in the chest. Weariness washed over her. She cast a longing look at the bed folded up against the wagon wall and sighed. She should try to sleep, but it was impossible. She was still too…unnerved. The Indians were gone. But so was

Mr. Thatcher. He had ordered the wagons to remain in camp until he returned, then rode off in the same direction the Indians had taken. What if— No. She would not think about that.

She lifted the lap desk from the chest and closed the top. Writing letters had become her escape, her comfort. She would use this time to write home and tell them about the Indians. But she must make the telling amusing. She did not want to cause her family to fear for her and Anne. Her lips twitched. She would tell them about the tobacco and beads.

Laughter bubbled up and burst from her mouth. She sat back on her heels, wrapped her arms about her waist and rocked to and fro with the false hilarity. It was only a nervous reaction to the long hours of tension and fear. She knew that. There was nothing funny about those savages. Or about Mr. Thatcher riding out alone to talk with them. She had been so frightened for him. But still—*tobacco and beads?* That was all that was required to make those fierce warriors go away. But now…

The laughter died. Now he was out there somewhere. Alone. And if something happened to him… If he were wounded or hurt…or worse, they would never know. She would not be able to help him and he might… Tears welled up, spilled over and ran down her cheeks. She wiped them away, tried to stop the sobs building up in her chest, but they demanded liberation. She crossed her arms on top of the chest, placed her forehead on them and released all of her worry and fear for him in a torrent of tears.

* * *

Zach peered over the rim of the ledge and watched Gray Wolf and the rest of the Cheyenne ride down the length of the wash below and disappear around the rock outcropping on the other side. If the war party had intended to ride ahead and set an ambush for the wagon train they never would have ridden so fast or taken that direction. The wagons could not follow their path. And they had not left sentinels to watch and report on the train's progress.

The tension across his shoulders eased. He rose and trotted back down the hill. "All right, boy. We have trailed them long enough. Time to go back and get the wagons moving." He swung into the saddle, reined Comanche around and touched him with his heels. The horse leaped forward, then settled into an easy, ground-eating lope.

Zach scanned the area ahead and resisted the impulse to urge Comanche to greater speed. The Cheyenne were far from their normal haunt. This was Pawnee and Sioux territory. And Arapaho and Comanche roamed these parts, as well. It didn't pay to get careless. Hopefully, Blake would remember that and keep the emigrant greenhorns alert and ready for an attack as he had ordered. But calm. They had to stay calm. His gut tightened. If other Indians happened upon the train before he got back, one foolish act, one careless shot on an emigrant's part could spark an all-out attack. And if that happened…

Images he didn't care to remember flooded his head. He thought about the women and children on the train, about Emma Allen. He clenched his jaw against

the memory of the sight of her when he had turned
back from meeting with Gray Wolf. He had ordered
the women to stay by their wagons, but there she was,
standing in the shadow of a wagon, watching the meeting, her face pale and tense, her doctor's bag in one
hand and a pistol in the other. And when their gazes
had met, he'd known from the look in her eyes and
the set of her shoulders she would have used both to
try and save him had he been in trouble. He had badly
misjudged her. Emma Allen may have led a pampered
life, but she had courage. And she took her doctoring
seriously. And he'd never seen a woman as beautiful.
If any harm came to her...

Zach shoved the thoughts away and again scanned
the area as he rode toward the pass that led back to the
river valley. It was dangerous to allow yourself to be
distracted when— His heart jolted. Five mounted Indians stood atop the low ridge on his right. He kept his
face straight ahead, watched them from the corners of
his eyes. They turned their mounts and started down the
hill on an intercepting path. He loosened his sidearm in
its holster and judged the distance to the pass against
the angle of the Indians' approach. It would be a close
thing. Too close. Even with Comanche's speed. It would
be better not to run and excite them with the chase.
"Ease up, boy. We'd best meet these braves head-on."

*Be with me, Lord. Give me wisdom. And, if need be,
make my shots true.* He reined Comanche around to
face the Indians and halted. They galloped toward him.
He leaned forward and patted Comanche's neck. "Be
ready, boy. We may have a run ahead of us yet. But at
least it will be a fair one with a chance you can win."

The horse flicked his ears back, then forward again, tossed his head.

Zach straightened in the saddle, lifted his right hand palm out, and pushed it forward and back. The Indians slowed, trotted their horses a little closer and stopped. He could see them clearly now. Pawnee. And they were not painted. But that did not mean they would be adverse to a little "sport" with a white man. He fastened his gaze on the brave in the lead, raised his hands and locked his forefingers together in the gesture of friendship.

The Indian returned the sign.

But more than one soldier had died because of an Indian's treachery. Zach cast another swift glance over the surrounding area. He saw nothing alarming. "Okay, boy, let's go." Comanche snorted and walked forward. The brave walked his horse out to meet him.

Zach looked into the warrior's dark eyes. Their expression was wary, but not angry. "Do you speak my tongue?" There was no answer. He tapped himself on the chest, pointed at the brave and again linked his forefingers in the sign for friendship. The brave did not move aside to let him pass.

Zach again tapped himself on the chest, made walking motions through the air with his fingers, then drew his hand across his arm in the signal for Cheyenne and pointed behind him. The brave stiffened. Quickly, Zach, again, slashed his hand across his arm, then lifted his fisted hand to his forehead and turned it back and forth in the signal for anger. He held his hands forward and spread the fingers wide, clenched them, then repeated the process four more times. He pointed down to Comanche's tracks, then swept his arm back and pointed his finger. "Cheyenne war party...fifty strong."

The brave turned, shouted a guttural command. The other four Indians rode forward, one galloping off along his back trail. In minutes he reappeared, signaled the others to come. The four warriors raced off. Zach let out a long breath, heeled Comanche into a lope and headed for the pass. Things were happening too quickly. He had to get back to the train.

Chapter Ten

My beloved family,

I take up my pen to write you of the odd thing that has happened. Mr. Thatcher, being accosted by five Pawnee warriors, warned them of the presence of a large Cheyenne war party nearby. I believe this saved his life, for it seems though they are wild and savage, as evidenced by the bloody scalps dangling at their waists when they suddenly appeared at our wagon train a few days later, these Pawnee have their own code of honor. Those five warriors have escorted us safely through what Mr. Thatcher calls Sioux territory. During the past weeks, they rode ahead of us to discover the best path for our wagons, and to warn of any Sioux close by. And though we all were wary and distrustful of their intent, they proved to be excellent guides. They led us to the safest fording places and helped us to cross our wagons. We did not, during their time with us, lose one animal to the wilds or to ravening beasts thanks to their prowess.

There is so much I wish to share with you all. I have seen my first buffalo. Swarms of them! At the meeting of the North and South Platte rivers, the horizon was black with the beasts as far as the eye could see. There are elk there, also.

I do wish you could see this country. We have traversed plains, valleys and now hills that come down to the banks of the river and oblige us to climb the heights then curve around and again descend to the river below.

It is now late July, and tomorrow we will reach a place called Fort William where, Mr. Thatcher assures us, we shall stop for a day to wash, bathe, purchase available supplies, repair wagons, doctor ill or hurt animals and trade with Indians. Having brought us here, the Pawnee have now left us to return to their homes.

I am well. Anne is healed of her injuries but remains distant from everyone. How I wish I had news of you all. My concern grows for Caroline and the baby.

As ever, I am your devoted,

Emma

Emma addressed and sealed the letter, placed it atop the others she had written and rose to put the lap desk in her wagon. Dusk had chased away the sunlight and mellowed the heat of the day. A breeze played among the trees strewed along the riverbank and carried the voices of mothers calling to their children. She lifted her head and listened to the squeals and laughter of the playing youngsters echoing off the rocks behind the camp then smiled and returned waves as they came running in obedience to the mothers' summons—Gabe and David Lewis dragging in last, as always. The clamor quieted, stopped. From the direction of the river, a harmonica began a soft, languorous lament.

Emma glanced toward the herders bringing in the grazing stock and searched out the wiry form of the small, dark-haired man riding in a wide loop around the animals in the water to turn them back to land. Charley Karr said the beasts calmed when he played. But the music always brought an ache to her throat. She glanced toward Anne's wagon, noted the canvas flaps tied closed and sighed. It would be so lovely to have someone with whom she could visit while the other emigrants settled in for the night. Would Anne ever get over her grief?

A vague sense of failure gnawed at her. Had she left anything undone that might help her sister? She sighed and retrieved the oatcake she had saved from supper then headed for the horses grazing at the far end of the inner oval, mentally reexamining her treatment of Anne. She could think of nothing to do but continue to love her, even if she wanted to be left alone. Loneliness washed over her, creating a longing in her heart, a hollow feeling in her stomach. If only Mother and Papa Doc were here. Or William. They would know what to do for Annie.

Emma came out of her musings, stared at Traveler. He was growing gaunt since they had left the good grass of the prairies behind. And his feed was gone. Would he survive the arduous trek ahead over the mountains? Or would it destroy him? Tears stung her eyes. "I brought you an oatcake, boy." She fed him the treat and finger-combed snarls from his forelock and mane as he munched, noted the dull, lusterless condition of his coat and wished she had saved the other oatcake for him instead of eating it herself. Tomorrow she would—

"Sharing your supper?"

Emma jerked her head up, stared across Traveler's back at Zachary Thatcher. How was it possible a man of his size could move as silent as a shadow? She nodded. "A bit of it. I wish I had more to give him."

Understanding flashed in those bright blue eyes. He stepped closer, ran his hand over Traveler's proudly arched neck. "A journey like ours is hard on the stock. Mules fare better than horses. Especially when the good grass gives out when they are climbing the mountains."

That was not what she wanted to hear. Especially not with the sympathetic undertone of warning his voice carried. Would she lose Traveler? Her throat tightened so she was afraid to try and speak. She clenched her jaw and stared at Traveler's shoulder, fighting the urge to lean her head against him and cry.

"I saw you writing earlier and thought you might like to know if you leave your letters at the fort tomorrow, when someone passes through, headed east, they will most likely carry them with them."

She lifted her gaze to his face. "To St. Louis?" She snagged her bottom lip with her teeth to stop the trembling.

His eyes darkened, the rugged planes of his face softened. He reached out his hand, lowered it to Traveler's back, close to where hers rested. So close she could feel the warmth radiating off it. "That is the end destination, yes. If they are not going that far they will pass the letters on to someone else." His thumb moved, brushed against the side of her palm, stayed.

She glanced down, fought the urge to slip her hand sideways, to know the feel of the warmth and strength of his hand covering hers. A strange reaction to his accidental touch, yet it remained. Grew. She moved her hand before she yielded to the temptation.

Zachary Thatcher stepped back and cleared his throat. "There is no guarantee the letters will make it back, you understand. There is a lot of rough, wild and dangerous territory they must pass through on the way."

She looked up, felt that same, strong draw when their gazes met and curved her mouth into a polite smile to hide behind. "Yes, I know, Mr. Thatcher. I have just come through that rough, wild and dangerous territory."

He nodded, held her gaze a moment longer then looked away. "So you have, Miss Allen, so you have." He touched his hat brim and walked off.

Emma stood and watched him go as silently, as quickly as he had come, feeling somehow cheated. It was only when the darkness swallowed him she realized night had fallen. Traveler nibbled at something and moved on. The horse's plight settled like a stone in her heart, drew her thoughts from Zachary Thatcher. What was she to do about Traveler? What *could* she do? "If I had known about the grass failing, I never would have brought you, boy. I am so sorry."

Tears blurred her vision. She blinked them away and walked to the closest wagon she could see then made her way slowly along the circle toward her own in order not to startle the animals in the wagon corral. A spot of light flared ahead, steadied to a soft glow. She paused and stared at the small beacon, then moved forward more surely, guided by the light, trying to ignore the feeling of warmth stealing into her heart. She could be wrong...

She approached her wagon, looked around. There was only the empty night, and the welcoming light of her lantern. She picked it up and again searched the darkness, considered calling out to thank him in case he were near. But how foolish she would appear if she were wrong. Still...no one else knew she was out there in the darkness, alone.

Alone. But not as lonely as before. He had lighted her lantern and placed it on the water barrel shelf to see her safely to her wagon. The warmth around her heart grew. It was silly of her to feel so...so *cared about.* She was certain Mr. Thatcher would do the same for any of the emigrants on the train, but still... She climbed into her wagon, placed the lantern on top of the red box then pulled the canvas flaps into place and tied them closed.

She was safely inside. Zach stepped away from the rock he was leaning against and jogged off toward his campsite, the moonless night no challenge to his skill. Something he refused to identify coursed through him, bathed his heart in unwelcome warmth. She had smiled when she picked up the lantern. A small smile to be sure. One that merely played at the corners of her rose-colored lips. And it had not been directed at him, as she had smiled at Josiah Blake. No, she had smiled *because* of him. And that was better. There was no danger of his emotions becoming entangled that way. And there was a danger of that. No sense in fooling himself about it. There had been a moment tonight when she had looked at him....

Zach scowled, spotted the deep black of the fissure in the rock face and climbed to his bed on the shelf above. He had wanted to leap right over that horse and take her in his arms. He had touched her hand, hoping. But she had moved hers away. And that was for the best.

He stepped to the edge of the shelf, stood listening to the night, absorbing the normal sounds of the area so his senses would warn him if danger neared the train. Tonight had been a close thing. Too close. Dr. Emma Allen was like a magnet to him. He needed to keep his distance.

Chapter Eleven

"Annie, please come with me to visit the fort. I am certain you will find—" Emma stopped, stared at the russet-colored curls set swaying by the negative shake of her sister's head.

"You go, Emma. There is nothing of interest to me there. I shall stay here and rest."

Emma lifted her chin. "I will not go without you, Anne! There are Indians camped nearby and—"

"And Mr. Thatcher has set guards over the wagons and the stock. I shall be fine." Anne turned, focused her gaze on her. "I am not being difficult, Emma. I cannot—the children...the families..."

"Oh, Annie." Emma reached out her hand, took a step forward. Anne shook her head and turned away. Emma stopped, lowered her hand to her side. "All right, Anne. I will go without you. I must inquire as to getting my letters carried back to St. Louis." She cast a hopeful look at her sister's back. "Have you any letters—"

"No. None."

Anne's curt tone told her not to inquire further. She

held back a sigh. "Very well. I shall return shortly." She lifted her skirt hems out of the way and climbed from Anne's wagon, let the flaps fall into place.

"We're goin' to the Injuns' camp, Dr. Emma!" Gabe Lewis raced by, wheeled and ran back. "Pa says maybe I c'n trade my marble fer a bow and arrow!"

"Me, too!" Little David Lewis, never far behind his older brother, held out his hand and unfolded his pudgy fingers. A large amber-colored marble resting on his palm winked in the sunlight. He grinned up at her.

"Oh, my, that is a lovely marble!" She returned his grin, looked over at Gabe. "I wish you well in your barter." He flashed her a grin and raced off, David close on his heels.

"Gabriel and David! Do not go outside this wagon circle without your pa!" Lorna Lewis looked up at her and shook her head. "Those boys will be the death of me. Always runnin' off and gettin' up to some mischief!" She glanced toward the closed wagon flaps. "I come for your sister's laundry—sent Lillian to fetch yours. My wash water is heatin' down beside the river."

Emma ducked inside the flaps and drew out a pillowcase stuffed full of Anne's laundry. "Is Jenny using her arm normally, yet?"

Lorna chuckled and shook her head. "She's still tellin' the other kids it's her 'special hurt' arm. The little minx uses it to get her own way."

Emma laughed. "Very clever of her."

"Except she forgets now and again when they get to playin', so the kids are on to her high jinks."

"Will you be taking her and your other girls to the fort?"

Lorna glanced toward the palisade, then looked back at her and shook her head. "Mr. Lewis will buy what we're wantin' in the way of supplies. I aim to get the wash done, and the wagon emptied out and put to rights. Those young'uns make an awful mess of things. And then I mean to bake bread and biscuits enough for a week whilst there is light to see and wood to make a good fire. After that, I aim to bed down the children and enjoy the pleasure of sittin' still." She laughed and took the pillowcase from Emma's hand. "Tell Lillian to hurry on."

Emma nodded and headed for her wagon.

Emma stared at the fort. Indians roamed around the area, going in and out of the fort at will. So many Indians. She flicked her gaze toward the conical skin shelters dotting the grassy field. At least they were on the opposite side of this tongue of land formed by the Laramie and North Platte rivers. She drew her gaze back, lifted it skyward to the guardhouse overhanging the wide, gated entrance in the palisade wall. Surely they would watch and see her safely across—

"Dr. Emma! Dr. Emma!"

Emma whirled about. Mary Fletcher was running toward her. "What is it, Mary?"

"Ma says come quick!" The young girl clutched her side and drew in a ragged breath. "Daniel cut himself bad…with the hatchet!"

"Where is he?"

"They're bringin' him…to…yer wagon."

"Stay here until you catch your breath!" Emma lifted the hems of her skirts and ran back across the inner oval toward her wagon. Charley Karr was climbing the slope from the river, young Daniel draped across his arms. Hannah Fletcher walked at his side, holding her son's hand. There was a bloody gash in the calf of the boy's leg, a gash so large it was visible even over the distance. She scrambled up to the driver's box of her wagon, gave a hard shove that folded the collapsible canvas overhang back against the first rib of the wagon body. Sunlight poured down on the driver's seat. She climbed over it, scooted across the red box behind it and yanked a sheet out of the chest.

"Where do y' want me to put him, Doc?"

"Here—on the driver's seat." She flapped the sheet open and spread it over the tops of the seat and red box.

Charley Karr hopped up onto the wagon tongue. "Y' might want to take that there sheet off, Doc. He's bleedin' pretty bad."

"I know, Mr. Karr. Please put him down."

The man shrugged, leaned forward and placed Daniel on the seat then stepped down.

Emma glanced at Hannah Fletcher. The woman's face was pale, but her grip on her son's hand was firm. "Please come up into the box, Mrs. Fletcher. I may need your help."

The boy bit down on his lower lip, stared up at her out of hazel-colored eyes that were clouded with pain and fear. The freckles marching across his nose and cheekbones stood out in stark contrast to the pallor of his skin.

Emma smiled, then fisted her hands, placed them on her hips and shook her head. "You are supposed to use the hatchet on firewood and trees, Daniel—not on your leg."

"I k-n-now, Dr. Emma. It s-slipped."

She glanced at his calf. "That's a nasty wound. I shall have to clean it, then stitch it up." The boy's face turned pasty white. He swallowed hard. She patted his shoulder. "But I promise you, you shall not feel it." She glanced up at Mrs. Fletcher, read the disapproval in her eyes.

"Daniel is eleven years old, Dr. Allen. He's old enough to know the truth."

"That *is* the truth, Mrs. Fletcher. Now, please sit down and let Daniel rest his head in your lap while I get things ready." She opened the red box, took out various stoppered bottles, a shallow bowl, suturing equipment, a pile of clean rags and a bandage roll. *Thank you, dearest William, for these supplies. And for your faith in me.*

She closed the top of the box, smoothed the sheet, placed the shallow bowl, the rags and bandage roll on top of it. The rest of the items she placed on top of the water keg. It gave her an excuse to turn her back so Daniel could not see her thread the needle. When she finished she placed the suturing material in the shallow bowl, opened one of the stoppered bottles and poured alcohol over it, then set the bottles on the box. *Almost ready.* She turned back to the keg and frowned. There was no time to heat water. Cold water would have to do. She dipped some water into her washbowl, pushed up her sleeves and scrubbed her hands and wrists with lye soap. *Thank you, Papa Doc, for teaching me to be a doctor. I wish I had more practice at this next part.*

Emma put on the long doctor's apron Ruth Applegate had made her, climbed from the wagon, walked to the front and climbed into the wagon box. Her patient looked up at her, his eyes dark with fear. She smiled down at him. "Do you remember I promised you you would not feel me stitching up your wound?" He bit down on his lip and nodded. "Well, this is the reason." Emma reached across him to the equipment on top of the red box, poured some alcohol into a small vial, opened one of the stoppered bottles and added some of the heavy, oily liquid to the alcohol. "This will put you to sleep. And when you wake up, it will all be over."

The boy's eyes widened. "For true?"

Emma grinned at him. "For true. Are you ready?"

He looked at his mother, then nodded.

"Good." Emma picked up one of the rags, looked at Mrs. Fletcher. There was fear and skepticism in her eyes. "I shall need your help, Mrs. Fletcher. I am going to pour this ether on this rag and hold it under Daniel's nose where he can breathe it. When he goes to sleep, I shall need you to hold the rag. If he starts to awaken before I finish stitching his wound, I want you to hold the rag back under his nose, until he again falls asleep. Can you do that?"

Mrs. Fletcher's face tightened. She looked at the rag. "It won't hurt him none?"

Emma shook her head and smiled. "I promise you it will not."

The woman looked down at her son, took a deep breath and nodded.

"All right then. I shall begin."

Emma poured the ether on the rag and held it under Daniel's nose. He took a tentative sniff, looked up at her and grinned. "It smells—" he took another, deeper sniff "—smells...kinda...funnnn..." His eyes closed, his body went slack.

"Well, I never seen the like!"

Emma smiled and handed his mother the rag. "There's no need to whisper, he cannot hear you. No!" She grabbed Mrs. Fletcher's hand and pulled it away from her face. "Do not sniff it. You will go to sleep, and I need you to watch Daniel." She reached for the alcohol, splashed some on her hands then poured some onto the cut, doused one of the rags and began to wipe the blood from his leg.

The day had slipped away. Emma frowned and placed her hand on her stomach. It still quivered with nerves. Not surprising as it was the first time she had used the ether on her own. Or on a child. She had thought it was safe. But she could not know for sure.

She took a deep breath, let it out slowly and blotted the notes she had made on Daniel's treatment. Her stomach added hunger pangs to the quivering, reminding her she had not eaten supper. Though she had watched the boy carefully all day, had stayed with him while he ate his supper and could detect no sign of any ill effects from the ether, her own stomach had rebelled at the thought of the meal Mrs. Fletcher offered.

She shook her head and tucked her medical journal back in her doctor's bag. In this instance, the patient had fared better than the doctor. Daniel had eagerly told his tale and showed off his bandage to all who had come around. Indeed, he felt so well, it had been difficult to make him stay quiet until he was settled for the night. She, however, had not enjoyed being the center of the excited furor that rose over her treatment of Daniel when the emigrants who had finished their work, or returned from the fort, gathered at the Fletchers' wagon. Not all of them were favorably impressed. Especially Mr. Hargrove. And she had little to offer them by way of explanation. There had been moments when she had wished for Mr. Thatcher's presence—when she would have welcomed his authoritative way. She latched the black bag, rested her hands on it and stared off into the distance. If anything should go wrong with Daniel's healing...

No! She would not think such things. She would write Papa Doc a report on Daniel. He would understand she had done what she thought best for her patient, and he would be thrilled to know the ether worked so well.

If he ever received the letter.

Emma looked out at the fading light, then glanced at the pile of letters on the dresser. She did not have enough courage to cross that broad expanse of field to the fort in the growing darkness. Tears welled into her eyes. She *so* wanted to send her letters on their way to her family. It would ease some of her loneliness for them by sharing a small part of what she was experiencing on this journey—by letting them know they were always in her thoughts and in her heart. The disappointment brought a choking lump to her throat. Perhaps Mr. Thatcher would grant her time to go to the fort and inquire about someone carrying the letters back to St. Louis before they started out in the morning. If not... well, Papa Doc would be proud of her. He always said a good doctor puts his patients first, before his own wants or needs.

Neighing and snorting and pounding hoofs intruded on her thoughts. She glanced up, saw the tossing heads and flowing tails of the horses the men were herding into the wagon corral where they would be safe from theft by the Indians. She wiped the tears from her cheeks and opened the crock of dried apples she had found when she was searching among the stores in Anne's wagon for something to feed Traveler and Lady. There was still light enough to visit the horses. She felt close to William when she was with his horse.

Emma climbed from her wagon and stood on the step looking over the corralled stock. Cold air touched her face and neck and hands. She shivered and started toward Traveler at a brisk pace. If the temperature dropped so quickly here along the river when the sun went down, how cold must it be in the mountains? She lifted her gaze to the massive wall of stone that barred their way west. The mountains looked cold, gray and impenetrable in the shadowed light of dusk. How would they ever get their wagons over them? It seemed an impossible task. But Mr. Thatcher had ridden off this morning to check the trail conditions for tomorrow's journey. Pray God, he returned safe. Myriad possibilities for harm to him flooded her mind. Fear knotted her already unsettled stomach. *Please, Almighty God, keep him safe.*

Emma yanked her gaze from the mountains, strode to Lady and fed her two of the dried apple slices then moved on to Traveler. The horse accepted her offering, then lowered his head to graze. She stroked his neck and listened to him chomping on the rich, thick grass. *A journey like ours is hard on the stock. Mules fare better than horses. Especially when the good grass gives out when they are climbing the mountains.*

Emma clenched her hands and took a deep breath. Zachary Thatcher had been warning her. But she would not lose Traveler. She would not! There had to be—

"Miss Allen…"

Emma whirled. "Mr. Thatcher! You are returned *safe.*" The words burst out of their own volition. Heat spread across her cheeks as she looked up at him. She had not meant to sound so…joyous. "I mean—I was looking at the mountains, and they seem so formidable…"

"They are that, Miss." A small, wiry-looking man, dressed in fringed leather, stepped out from behind Zachary Thatcher. "But Zach, here, is equal to 'em. He saved my bacon today! Them Blackfeet had me fer sure." The words were accompanied by a hefty thump on Zachary Thatcher's shoulder. "This the lady you was tellin' me about, Zach?"

Emma stared at the man's weathered and bearded face, looked into his alert, dark eyes. Why would Zachary Thatcher discuss her with him? She shifted her gaze back to Zachary Thatcher, let her eyes convey her puzzlement, but read reassurance in his.

"Miss Allen, this is Jim Broadman. One of the best mountain men in the country. He has business back East, and has agreed to carry your letters to St. Louis." A slight frown puckered his brow. "If you haven't made other arrangements, that is."

He had remembered about her letters! Emma's

breath caught. "I have not. Thank you for your thoughtfulness, Mr. Thatcher." She smiled at the mountain man, who promptly yanked his stained and battered hat off. "How kind of you, Mr. Broadman. Thank you for—"

"No need fer thanks yet, Miss." The man frowned and clapped the dirty felt hat back on his head. "Them Blackfeet shot my horse plumb out from under me today. I can't go east 'till I get me another mount." He gave Zach a wry smile. "One that knows how to *run*. Not some sad excuse of a…er…of a horse like I had." He glanced back at her. "I'll get on over t' the fort an' see can I find—"

"No. Please wait, Mr. Broadman." She swallowed hard, glanced at Zachary Thatcher then looked toward the west, toward those high, rugged mountains. *A journey like ours is hard on the horses.* She lifted her chin, placed her hand on William's horse. Zachary Thatcher did not make a sound. He did not move a muscle. But, for some reason she could not define, she was certain he understood what she was about to do, and it gave her strength. She stroked the horse's shoulder, fought to keep her voice even. "This is Traveler, Mr. Broadman. I—I want to return him to my brother. Traveler is a swift runner, and I will loan him to you for your journey. In exchange, you must agree to deliver both Traveler and my letters to Mrs. Samuel Benton at Riverside, upon your arrival in St. Louis." She squared her shoulders and turned. "Do you find that agreeable, Mr. Broadman?"

The man nodded, stepped forward and ran his hand over Traveler's back. "He's a fine horse, Miss." His gaze locked on hers. "I'll take good care of him. Y' have my word on it."

Emma nodded and turned away. Zachary Thatcher stepped up beside her.

"Broadman, you go on to the fort. I will get the letters and bring them to you."

"And William's saddle." Her voice sounded odd, sort of tight and small, but she got the words out.

"As you wish. Now, come along, Miss Allen, there is no reason to delay."

Zachary Thatcher gripped her elbow with his strong hand and propelled her toward her wagon. She did not object. For once, she was thankful for his autocratic ways. And for the strength and warmth of his hand that supported and guided her.

Chapter Twelve

Wind rippled the canvas. Rain hammered on it with deafening force. Emma shivered and closed the dresser drawer, caught her breath as the yellow light of lightning flickered over the watery surface of the cover and flashed its brightness through the wagon. Thunder crashed, its fury vibrating the boards beneath her feet.

That strike had been close! Emma snagged her lower lip with her teeth and glanced down at the garment dangling from her hands. Perhaps she should stay in the wagon. "And then who would get the fresh water you and Anne need, Miss Coward? Garth Lundquist? He must keep the oxen calmed. Put on the cape!" Her voice was all but drowned out by the pounding rain.

She frowned, swirled the India-rubber cape around her shoulders and fastened the ties. How long ago the comfort of her life in Philadelphia seemed. Now there was nothing but storms and mountains and walking, walking, walking. "And do not forget being reduced to talking to yourself, Emma Allen."

She heaved a sigh, flipped the hood up to cover her

head then pulled the empty water keg to the back of the wagon and slipped the knot that untied the flaps. The wind tore them from her grasp, sucked her skirt hems out into the rain with such force she grabbed hold of the canvas to keep from being pulled after them. She turned and backed down the steps, wrestled the keg to the ground.

Water blew off the fluttering canvas and spattered against her face. She turned away from the wind and hurried toward the rock cliff beside her wagon, dragging the keg after her. Rainwater flowing off the rim of a deep ledge jutting out from the cliff formed a waterfall in front of her. She ducked her head and dashed through the deluge, the water splashing on her back chilling the India-rubber of the cape and making her shiver. The beating of the rain on her hood ceased. She shot a grateful glance at the ledge of rock that now formed a roof over her, then shoved the keg beneath the stream of water gushing out of a fissure in the rock wall and shook the raindrops from her hands.

Lightning sizzled and snapped. Thunder clapped and rumbled. She flinched, stepped closer to the wall of stone and looked around. The curve of the cliff and the overhanging ledge made a shelter of sorts, protecting her from the rain and the worst of the wind. What of the others? The storm had struck so fast it had caught the wagons ahead of hers strung out in a line along the ridge they were crossing. What if lightning struck one of the them? Or stampeded the oxen? And what of those behind her? Was Anne all right? She closed her eyes, tried to will away the frightening thoughts but they slipped into her mind like the cold, damp air creeping beneath her cape. What if night fell before the storm stopped, and they could not reach a place where they could camp and circle the wagons? There had been Indians watching them from the hills yesterday. Blackfeet, Mr. Thatcher had called them. Did Indians attack during rainstorms?

A shiver raced down her spine. She wiped the moisture from her face and stared toward her wagon but could see nothing through the pouring rain, could hear nothing but its drumming against earth and stone. It was as if she were alone in the watery world.

She drew her hands in through the slits in the cape and rubbed them against her skirt to warm them. Since they had entered the mountains, every day had become more difficult. In the broken terrain of the foothills, the grass had given way to sage and greasewood. Then the streams had turned bitter with alkali, making it hard to find a camping area. The poor animals bawled, neighed and brayed their misery throughout the nights. And every day the way became steeper and more rugged. Today's misery was the storm with its relentless, pouring rain. But, at least, she was able to catch the runoff gushing from the rocks. She would have sufficient good water for the oxen and Lady tomorrow if the alkali problem continued. Of course, tomorrow could hold a new trouble.

Take therefore no thought for the morrow: for the morrow shall take thought for the things of itself. Sufficient unto the day is the evil thereof.

Emma snorted, hugged herself against another chill. "I hear you, William, even if only in my memory. But

I doubt you would quote that scripture so glibly, were you standing here with me."

Lightning threw flickering light on the water flowing off the stone ledge above her. She gathered her courage, drew the hood of her cape farther forward and grabbed hold of the filled keg and tugged. Water sloshed out and wet her shoes. She scowled, tipped out some of the water, then took a tighter hold and dragged the keg out of the sheltered area to the other side of her wagon. Rain pelted her, stung her face. She yanked the slipping hood back in place and bent to lift the keg. It did not budge.

"Hold on there, Miss Allen!"

Zachary Thatcher appeared like an apparition out of the watery gray. He slid from his saddle, hoisted the keg and dumped it into the large water barrel lashed to the side of her wagon.

She held on to the hood and tipped her head back to look up at him. "Thank you, Mr. Thatcher." The words were barely audible. She raised her voice to a shout. "I guess I overfilled the keg for my strength."

He nodded and leaned closer. "Where did you get the water?"

"There is a stream spurting from that wall of rock. I think it is overflow from the rain. Thank you again." She reached for the keg. He hefted it to his shoulder.

"Show me."

She led the way, conscious of him moving up to walk beside her, blocking the wind. And of his horse trailing behind. Surely the horse would not— She ducked under the water sheeting off the rock and turned. He would. Comanche followed his master into the sheltered area. At least he came as far as possible. The water off the rock hit his broad rump and splashed every direction. Zachary Thatcher seemed not to notice. He carried the keg to the gushing fount.

"Here, boy." Emma took hold of the horse's bridle and turned him sideways, then stroked his wet, silky nose. "You are a very smart horse to come in out of the rain." She laughed and crowded back to give him room, bumped into Zachary Thatcher and bounced off. She might as well have hit the mountain for all the give there was to the man. She looked up, and the apology on her lips died. He was staring down at her, an odd expression on his face. "Is something wrong?"

"No…" He shook his head, frowned and removed his hat, slapped the water off it and settled it back on his head. "Comanche has never let anyone but me touch him."

"Oh." She looked back at the horse. "Perhaps it is because of the storm. He wants to please me so I will share my shelter." She smiled and ran her fingers through Comanche's mane, stroked his hard, heavily-muscled shoulder. The horse did not seem to suffer from the lack of good grass. "Why is Comanche not growing gaunt like the other horses, Mr. Thatcher?"

"He's a Western horse. And, as you said, a smart one. There are small patches of grass around little pockets of sweet water in these mountains. Enough for one or two animals. I set him free to roam at night and he finds his own grass and water."

She glanced up at him. "You do not worry he will get lost?"

He shook his head. "He doesn't range that far. He is always back before dawn."

"Truly? My, you *are* smart, Comanche!" The horse flicked his ears and tossed his head. She laughed, then sobered and lowered her hands to her sides. Zachary Thatcher's boots scraped against the stone. His bulk loomed beside her.

"Jim Broadman will take good care of Traveler, Miss Allen. His life depends on it."

There was sympathy in his voice. Zachary Thatcher was a perceptive man. Too much so at times. Emma nodded and straightened her shoulders. "I do not regret my decision, Mr. Thatcher. I am glad Traveler is being returned to William. I did not want to see him suffer. But I cannot deny I miss him."

"And your brother."

If that was an attempt to change the subject to make her feel better, it failed miserably. "Yes… And Mother and Papa Doc, also." Her throat thickened. She dipped her head, pointed. "The keg is full."

Zachary Thatcher nodded, grabbed Comanche's reins and dropped them to the ground, then turned and hoisted the filled keg to his shoulder.

She started for the wagon. His hand clamped on her shoulder.

"You stay here with Comanche, Miss Allen. No sense in us both going out in the storm."

She watched him go, grateful for the opportunity to get command of her emotions. She pushed the hood off, smoothed the wet strands of hair back off her forehead then put it on again and shook out her long skirts. The horse snorted. She laughed and did a slow pirouette. "I know…it is all foolishness. But it makes a lady feel better to look her best. Even in the midst of a storm."

"Talking to yourself or Comanche, Miss Allen?" Zachary Thatcher swiped water off his face and gave her a crooked grin. "It usually takes longer than a few weeks in the mountains for that to happen. Besides, you've no need to be worrying about such things. I've never seen a time you didn't look pre—fine." He stepped past her and shoved the keg back under the spouting water.

What was she supposed to say to that? She ignored the warmth his comment spread through her and turned her back and braced a hand against Comanche's shoulder. Zachary Thatcher's grin was having a queer effect on her knees. "Thank you for your kind words, Mr. Thatcher."

"It wasn't kindness, it was the truth."

The softness in his deep voice stole the remaining strength from her knees. She grabbed for the saddle horn.

"This Papa Doc? Is he the one that taught you to be a doctor?"

"Yes." She took a breath, launched into the safe subject. "Billy...William...was run over by a carriage when we were orphans and lived on the streets in Philadelphia. Mother, well, she was not our mother then, of course, she adopted us later. Anyway, Mother and Papa Doc saw the accident and took us to her home. Billy had a broken leg and a head wound." She stared at the rain, remembering her fear when her big brother would not wake up and talk to her. "Papa Doc treated Billy's injuries. He made him better." Something of the wonder she had felt then returned. She smiled, stroked Comanche's neck. "That was the beginning of my desire to be a doctor. I loved Mother, but I adored Papa Doc. I followed him all around the orphanage when he came to treat the other children." She gave Zachary Thatcher a sidelong glance. "Mother turned her home into an orphanage. And then, when she and Papa Doc married, they took William and me and Annie to live with them in Papa Doc's house." Her throat tightened again. She drew a deep breath.

"He must have been a good teacher. I've never heard of a doctor putting someone to sleep before working on them the way you did Daniel Fletcher. I'm sorry I missed seeing that."

His quiet, matter-of-fact tone drove the threatening tears away. Was he approving of her work? Or merely curious about the ether? She looked up. Their gazes locked, held. Rain fell outside the small, sheltered area. Lightning flashed and thunder crashed, but, suddenly, it did not matter. Something in his eyes made her feel safe. And more. She lowered her gaze and stared at his boots, wishing he would take her in his arms. The boots moved toward her. She caught her breath, looked up, lost it again. His eyes had darkened to the color of blue smoke. Something flickered in their depths. He sucked in air, pivoted on his heel and stepped over to Comanche.

"It seems everyone who comes out to Oregon country has a dream, Miss Allen. I'm guessing yours is to be a doctor." He looked down, swiped water off his saddle.

Heat burned in her cheeks. Obviously, that moment had not shaken him as it had her. She drew her hands inside the cape and pressed them against her stomach to stop its quivering. "You have guessed wrong, Mr.

Thatcher. To be a doctor *was* my dream. I have learned that is impossible. Men want a male doctor to care for them and their families. And no one can be a doctor without patients."

"You have patients."

"For now...yes. But I do not delude myself. The men on the wagon train permit me to treat their families only because there is no male doctor available. And there are those who still refuse to acknowledge my skill." The old bitterness rose. Zachary Thatcher was one of those men. The thought steadied her when he again looked her way. "It is not my dream that brought me on this journey, Mr. Thatcher, it is Anne. You see, William was to teach at the Banning Mission in Oregon country, and when his wife became too ill to make the journey, Anne declared she would take his place. As she had been recently injured in the carriage accident that killed her husband and child, I could not let her make the journey alone and without care."

Her words called forth a vision of her empty future with disturbing clarity, and suddenly, she knew what she would do. "Oregon country holds nothing for me. When Anne is settled at the mission, I shall travel on to Oregon City and take a ship for home." An unexpected sadness washed over her. She forced a smile. "And what dream brings you west, Mr. Thatcher? Do you hope to found a town and build an empire?"

He shook his head, threw the trailing reins back over Comanche's head. "Like you, Oregon country holds nothing for me. I'll leave the founding of towns and empire building to Hargrove and Applegate and the others. It is these mountains that call to me. All I want is to be to be free and unfettered to roam them as I will."

She nodded, smiled through an unreasonable sense of loss and disappointment. "I wish you well in your travels, Mr. Thatcher."

He looked at her.

Her smile faded. That queer weakness overtook her again. She grabbed for the saddle horn and found his hand waiting. His fingers curled around hers, rough and warm and strong. That smoky look returned to his eyes. Her heart faltered, raced. She stared up at him, shy and uncertain, unable to breathe as he stepped close, lowered his head. Rainwater dripped off his hat brim. His lips, cool and moist, touched hers. She closed her eyes, swayed toward him. His arm slid around her, crushed her against him. His mouth claimed hers, his lips heated, seared hers. And then it was over. He released her, stepped back.

She stared up at him, her heart pounding.

"I've wanted to do that since the day you stood on the deck of that ferry, fear and fury in your eyes, and told me you had no husband." His voice was husky, ragged. "Now it's done." He turned, hoisted the keg onto his shoulder, ducked under the water and headed for her wagon. Comanche plodded after him.

His words were as rough against the exposed tenderness of her heart as his work-hardened hands had been against her skin. Emma touched her fingers to her lips. She drew a deep breath, lifted her hands and yanked her hood up, then squared her shoulders, ducked her head and walked out into the wind and rain, defying her emotions that were as raging and turbulent as the storm.

* * *

Fort Hall was a disappointment. The few log buildings hiding behind the high log wall enclosure had no windows, only a square hole cut in each mud-covered roof. And in the bastion were a few portholes large enough for guns only. But, as the captain explained, it was not meant for comfort. Its purpose was to afford the inhabitants protection from the frequent attacks by hostile Indians.

Emma pushed her bonnet back to allow the breeze to cool her face and looked up at the hill above the path the wagons were obliged to take to cross over the waterfalls below. Blackfeet Indians had been watching them every day. And they made no effort to hide the fact. Whenever you looked up, they would be there. It was unnerving. They put her in mind of a cat stalking a mouse.

She stepped around a rock following the ruts the wagons ahead were cutting into the ground, then stopped and looked back. Anne was riding the mule that had belonged to the captain's wife at Fort Hall. The woman had been happy to trade the mule for Lady. Emma sighed. Another connection to William was gone. But it was for the best. There was abundant grass at the fort for Lady, and the mule seemed docile enough. Even if it were not, it would find its match in her sister. Anne was an excellent rider, with gentle hands and a firm seat.

Emma grinned. It had not always been so. Annie had often been thrown from her pony. But one day after Pepper threw her, she had stood up, dusted off her skirts, gripped Pepper's reins and led him back to the mounting block, her russet curls bobbing with her every determined step. Anne had never been thrown from a horse again. Mother insisted it was the red curls.

Emma stared at Anne, her faltering hope for her sister strengthening. Anne still had red curls. She would get over her grief. She only needed something to rouse her strong, fighting spirit. Perhaps Anne would find that something when she began teaching at the mission.

Emma faced forward and started walking again. When Anne was settled, she would be free to return home and…and what? Content herself to help Papa Doc? It was as close as she would come to her dream of being a doctor. Tears stung her eyes. Anger drove her up the steep grade. If God did not want her to be a doctor, the least He could do was take this desire to be one out of her heart and give her a new dream!

The storm, the half cave and Zachary Thatcher's kiss slipped into her mind. She set herself firmly against the thought. That was no dream! The kiss had meant nothing. He had told her his dream was to be unfettered and free to roam the mountains at will. The kiss had only been something he had to do, like…like when she had jumped off the roof of Uncle Justin's stable onto the hay pile. The idea had taunted and tempted her. But once she had made the jump, it was done. She had never been tempted to do it again. And that is what Mr. Thatcher had said, "Now it's done." And so it was. And she was not foolish enough to think or hope otherwise. She had only reacted so strongly because she was lonely and frightened of the storm. Zachary Thatcher had offered a moment of safety and comfort. That was all.

She huffed the last few steps to the top of the hill, stopped to catch her breath and look at the small valley a short distance below. There was a meandering stream, trees scattered here and there and grass for the animals. It would be a good camp tonight. She sighed, shook her head and started down the descent. How strange life was. Everything she had known had been stripped away from her. Her comfort, her *life,* now depended on those three things—water, wood and grass.

"Dr. Emma!"

Emma lifted her gaze from the stony ground and looked down the hill. Mary Fenton was running toward her, waving her hand in the air. The girl stopped and cupped her hands around her mouth. "Miz Hargrove says can you come, she needs you. She says hurry!"

Lydia? Had there been an accident? Emma lifted the front hem of her skirt and ran.

Chapter Thirteen

❧

"I am here, Lydia!" Emma put her foot on the bottom step, stopped and stared as Lydia Hargrove shoved aside the canvas flaps over the tailgate of her wagon. "What is wrong? Are you—"

"I'm fine, I—"

A moan, quickly broken off, came from the wagon's interior. Emma glanced toward the sound, then looked back up at Lydia Hargrove.

"It's Ruth Applegate." The older woman's voice lowered. "I thought it best to keep her here 'till Mary found you." She climbed out of the wagon, turned and held out her arms. "Come to Auntie Lydia, Isaac." She lifted the toddler out, held him close. "Time for me to start the cook fire. I'll keep Isaac with me while you talk with his mama."

Emma nodded, read all the things the woman left unsaid in her expression and climbed in the wagon. Ruth Applegate was sitting in Lydia Hargrove's small rocking chair, clutching her abdomen. The young woman's face was pale, her mouth compressed into a thin line.

Emma picked a path through the various trunks and household items and knelt in front of her. "Are you in pain, Ruth?"

The young woman nodded, gave a soft hiss and rubbed her hands over the fabric covering her stomach.

Emma watched Ruth's eyes close, noted how she clenched her jaw to hold back an outcry. "Is the pain constant? Or does it come and go like cramps?"

"Like cramps." Ruth released a breath and opened her eyes. "I—I think it's the baby. It feels like when Isaac started to be born."

Emma nodded, kept her expression serene. "When did the cramps begin?"

"Not long ago. When I was carrying Isaac up the grade. The pain doubled me over and I had to put him down. Lydia saw me when their wagon came by and they stopped. She took Isaac and bid me sit in her chair. I asked her to send someone for you." Ruth's eyes filled with tears. "I don't want to lose my baby, Dr. Emma."

Emma reached out and squeezed her hand. "I cannot promise that will not happen, Ruth. Babies have a way of choosing their own destinies. But I will promise you I will do everything I know to help you." She looked the young woman straight in the eyes. "Will your husband let me come to your wagon to care for you?"

Ruth looked down at their joined hands on her stomach and shook her head. "I'm sorry, Dr. Emma. You saved Isaac when he had the measles. And even told me what to do for James when he got them so bad, but he—he won't..."

"I understand, Ruth. Here is my first instruction." The young woman's gaze shot to her face. Emma smiled. "Do not distress yourself. It is very bad for the baby. We shall manage." *But how?* She thrust the worry aside. "My second instruction is this...no more work."

"But—"

"There can be no buts, Ruth. You must go to bed and rest. You will do no more cooking, no more walking. You cannot lift or care for Isaac."

Ruth's eyes filled with tears. "Dr. Emma, that is impossible. James will nev—"

"Nothing is impossible, Ruth. It may be difficult, but not impossible. I will give it some thought and—ah!" Emma clapped her hands together and smiled. "Olga Lundquist prepares my meals and Anne's. I will simply give her more supplies from our stores and have her cook them for your family." *And increase her pay.*

"And I will care for Isaac." Lydia Hargrove stuck her head and shoulders into the end of her wagon and grabbed hold of a large iron spider.

"Oh, Lydia, I cannot—" The tears slipped down Ruth's cheeks. "Isaac is getting so...rambunctious." There was worry, but also a touch of pride in her words.

Lydia snorted. "I'm not so old I can't handle a toddler. He's settin' out here, quiet as you please, diggin' in the dirt with my spoon. The matter is settled. Caring for your little one pleasures me. And I will cook your meal tonight."

"Oh, but I—how will I ever repay you both!" Ruth covered her face with her hands and sobbed.

"Bosh!"

Ruth jerked her head up.

Emma gaped at Lydia.

"You stop that nonsense, Ruth Applegate! Our husbands drug us along on this journey, and it's up to us to help each other survive it! There'll be no talk of repayin'!" She withdrew her head and shoulders and disappeared.

Emma laughed, she couldn't help it. Lydia Hargrove looked as if she would like to use that spider on her husband and James Applegate, instead of cooking with it. If only Ruth had some of that spunk. She turned back to her patient.

"All that remains is to get you to bed."

Ruth put her hands on the rocker's arms and started to rise.

Emma shook her head. "I said no walking. I will go find your husband."

"And everything will be all right if Ruth goes to bed?"

Emma met James Applegate's skeptical gaze. "I did not say that, Mr. Applegate. But she will almost surely lose the baby if she does not."

"Almost." The man's brows drew down into a frown. "How long does she have to stay abed?"

"I cannot answer that question with any certainty."

"Seems there's not much you *can* say for certain. Too bad there's not a *real* doctor here."

Emma clenched her hands, fought to keep her voice calm and pleasant. "Not even a man doctor could answer your questions, Mr. Applegate. These things are a matter of nature."

"Not havin' a man doctor handy, it's hard to know the right of that." He raised his hand and stroked his beard, looked off to the west. "With these steep climbs, the extra weight will be hard on the teams." He looked at her again. "She can stay abed three days."

"Three—"

"But if the way gets too steep, an' the teams start to struggle, she will have to walk."

Emma clenched her hands, fought to keep her voice even. "If you are agreeable, Mr. Applegate, there may be a solution to your problem. Ruth can stay in my wagon, where I can watch over her." She tried to hold them back, but the words popped out anyway. "My brother bought extra teams."

She need not have worried about her acerbic comment. He merely nodded and stroked his beard. She could almost see him weighing his dislike of her against his team's well-being. At last, he lowered his hand and deigned to look at her. "All right. I will be along shortly to carry Ruth to your wagon."

Emma lifted a small pile of clean rags out of the red box, closed the lid and turned to look down at her patient. "Are you more comfortable now?"

"Yes. The cramps have stopped." Ruth gave her a hopeful look. "Perhaps I should go back to my wagon."

Emma shook her head. "I do not want to dishearten you, Ruth, but I also do not wish to give you false hope. It happens this way sometimes. The cramps stop, and then start again. I am hoping that if you stay abed for a few days, things will be fine."

Ruth nodded, fingered the ribbon adorned with embroidered rosebuds that separated the bodice from the skirt of the nightgown she wore. "This is fine work. Too fine. My shift—"

"Is not warm enough for these cold nights. I do not want you taking a chill." Emma placed the rags on the dresser to have close at hand should they be needed for spotting, then set a pail close by for discards. "You should cover up."

Ruth pulled the blankets and quilt that covered her legs up to her chin. "It sure feels strange goin' to bed without cleanin' up supper and puttin' Isaac down to sleep. I hope he don't give Lydia trouble. He can be stubborn…"

"I am quite certain Lydia is equal to the task."

"Yes. I'm sure she is…"

Emma studied Ruth's unhappy face and reached for her wrap. "I am going to see if Anne needs anything before I retire. I shall check on Isaac on my way." She gave the worried mother a smile and glanced toward the tailgate. She could not get by the bed to open it. She stepped to the front of the wagon, scooted across the lid of the red box and climbed out onto the driver's seat. Moonlight flooded the world in silver. A shiver coursed through her. The night air was cooling fast.

She closed the flaps tight, then climbed down and hurried toward the Hargrove wagon. She was almost there when Zachary Thatcher came striding out of the night toward her. Her stomach fluttered. She stopped and pulled her wrap more tightly around her shoulders, ignoring, as best she could, the betraying quickening of her pulse at the sight of him. He stopped in front of her, dipped his head in greeting.

"Matthew Hargrove said you wished to speak with me, Miss Allen."

"Yes." She braced herself for his reaction. "Ruth Applegate is with child and a problem has developed. She is in danger of losing the baby." She gave him an imploring look. "She must have rest, Mr. Thatcher. We cannot travel tomorrow. Or—" She stopped, stiffened at the shake of his head.

"I'm sorry, Miss Allen. But the wagons form up and travel on tomorrow at dawn, same as always."

Emma stared at him, disappointment and anger churning in her stomach. "Mr. Thatcher, as a *doctor,* I am telling you that being bounced and jolted by that wagon will almost certainly cause Ruth Applegate to lose her baby. Perhaps even her life. I am asking you—"

"Have you seen the Indians on the hills, Dr. Allen?"

She stared up at him, taken aback. "The Indians? Yes. But—"

"There are over three hundred of them. There—" he jabbed his finger in the air to their right "—there—" another jab behind them "—and there."

The last jab was to their left. She peered beyond the circled wagons into the darkness, her heart pounding.

"They surround our camp every night. The only way open is west."

The quiet, factual way he spoke was terrifying. She shuddered, looked up at him.

"They do not attack the train because I have assured them we are only passing through their territory. They are watching to see if what I say is true." He stepped closer, locked his gaze on hers. "If these wagons do not roll west tomorrow morning, Dr. Allen, Mrs. Applegate, her baby and every other member of this wagon train will be in grave danger. If we travel on, at least she and her baby have a chance. Now, if you will excuse me, I have guards to post." He touched the brim of his hat, turned and walked off.

Emma stared after him until he disappeared, then looked around the inner oval. The animals were settling down for the night. Here and there the red embers of dying cook fires shimmered against the dark, or a lantern showed as a dull circle of gold on the canvas of a wagon. Voices, muted and indistinct, floated on the air as men and women finished chores and bid one another good-night. Did any of them know of the danger that lurked out there in the night, waiting to pounce on and destroy them?

There was no lantern light showing in the Hargrove wagon. Little Isaac was asleep. And little Jenny… and Gabe and David… Mary… Emily and Susan and Amy… So many children.

Emma turned and forced her trembling legs to carry her back to her wagon. Ruth was waiting to hear about Isaac. Ruth, who was in danger of losing her unborn baby and, perhaps, her life. And she was helpless to do anything about it.

She climbed to the driver's box, took a deep breath and fixed a smile on her face. Ruth must be kept calm. She could not let her guess… She ducked beneath the canvas flaps to tell Ruth Isaac was sound asleep.

Zach moved from guard to guard under the cover of the darkness, checking their positions, making sure they were alert without alarming them. Thus far the Blackfeet had kept their word, but their presence was a constant threat—one that weighed heavily on his shoulders. He had not told Emma Allen the whole truth.

He scowled, detoured around a rock outcropping and headed for the far side of the herd. The hard truth was, the Indians were driving them the same as they were driving these oxen and mules and horses. And if they did not move, that open-ended circle would close about them, they would be overrun by the multitude of fierce warriors and his few unskilled, untrained fighting men would die quickly in battle. It would be different for the women and children on the train. His gut knotted. It had been bad enough seeing the horrors visited on women and children he did not know. To think of Emma Allen and—

Emma. She was so beautiful standing there with the moonlight bathing her face. And the way she had looked at him as he walked toward her... For a moment he'd thought...

The knots in his gut twisted tighter. Zach took a firmer grip on his knife and slipped through the night toward his camp. What he had thought had no bearing on the truth. Or on his job. He had to keep this train moving. Now more than ever.

Chapter Fourteen

"Ugh!" The jolt slammed her back against the dresser, her breath gusting from her lungs. Emma clamped her lips together to stop a moan, pushed herself back onto her knees and resumed her gentle kneading of Ruth's abdomen. The baby was lost, but the bleeding had not stopped, and she refused to lose Ruth, too. She simply *refused*.

Ruth's sharp intake of breath alerted her. The flesh beneath her hands went rigid, relaxed, went rigid again. *Please!* Emma stopped the kneading, checked the rag between Ruth's legs. At last! She folded the rag over the expelled birth matter, slipped a clean rag in its place, then dropped the dirty one in the pail. The tension in her shoulder muscles eased. Ruth should be all right now. If… No! She would not think that way. *Sufficient unto the day...*

"The bleeding should stop now, Ruth." She pulled the nightgown back down over Ruth's legs and tugged the covers up over her. "I want you to stay well covered. You have lost blood and will take a chill easily." She sat back on her heels and looked down at her patient. "I am sorry about the baby, Ruth."

"I know you tried your best, Dr. Emma. And you were right. The cramping and spotting did stop after I went to bed last night." Ruth turned her face away. "It was the bouncing around this morning that started it again."

"Yes, but—" Emma raised her head. "Listen!" Chains rattled, hoofs stomped. The very distraction she needed for Ruth. She looked back at her. "Mr. Lundquist is unhitching the oxen. We must have reached our camping spot. It seems dusk comes earlier every day, and our travel time grows shorter and shorter." She rubbed her upper arms, chilly now that she had stopped working on Ruth. "But it is good that you will be able to have a long night of rest."

Ruth nodded, plucked at the quilt. "James worries about the weather. It is already so cold at night ice forms on the water in the barrel. He's afraid snow will catch us in the mountain passes."

From the sound of Ruth's voice, James was not alone in his concern. In truth, she had thought about that possibility herself. How could she not with Mr. Thatcher issuing dire warnings of such an occurrence, or of Indian attacks, whenever she asked him to have mercy and stop the train for her patients' sakes. Emma shoved away thought of the Indians and gave Ruth a wry look. "I am sure the snow would not have the temerity to defy Mr. Thatcher. He will bring us safely through to Oregon country."

The comment brought forth the smile she was seeking, albeit a weak, listless one. She pushed to her feet and slipped by the bed to peek out of the tied flaps.

"What do you see?"

"We are stopped on a low plateau, very near a river below. I suppose it is still the Snake River." She undid a tie and tugged the flaps farther apart. The cool September air rushed in. She shivered, closed the flaps and turned back to Ruth. "There are three islands in the river, side by side. Rather like this..." She folded her index finger down with her thumb, spread her extended fingers and held out her hand where Ruth could see it.

"That should make James happy. It will mean plenty of good water, and maybe grass, for the stock."

"The islands are too small and rocky for grazing. But they are almost on a level with the water. It should make things easier if we are to ford across tomorrow."

"Dr. Emma..."

"Yes?"

"Where are my clothes, please?" Ruth boosted herself to a sitting position. "I'm grateful for all you've done, but there is no reason for me to stay now. I would like to go back to my own wagon." She swallowed, cleared her throat. "I want to see Isaac. And I—I have to tell James about the baby."

Emma bit back her objection and lifted Ruth's clothes off the top of the chest and handed them to her. "You must go right to bed, Ruth. Do not lift or carry Isaac, and do not get chilled."

"I'll be careful, Dr. Emma. I'll keep Isaac in bed with me." Ruth stood, removed the nightgown and pulled on her shift. "James will not—" She looked away, put on her dress and busied herself with the buttons. "I will be happy to sew you another dress to pay you for all you have done for me."

"Another dress would be wonderful, Ruth. You do lovely work." Emma smiled and helped Ruth into her shoes. "We will talk about it when you are stronger." She picked up a blanket and handed it to Ruth. "Put this around your shoulders while I untie the flaps and open the tailgate, and then I will help you to your wagon." *And see you settled in bed.*

"But Isaac—"

Emma shook her head, untied the flaps and slid back the latches on the tailgate. "I will go and get Isaac from Lydia, *after* I help you to bed. Now, take these rags for the spotting, and let me help you down these steps."

Things had quieted. The children had been called to their wagons for the night. Emma turned her lantern low and peeked out of the flaps. There were no curious youngsters running about who might follow her. She put on her wrap and picked up the small, towel-wrapped bundle she had put on the floor beside the chest out of Ruth's sight. An image of the tiny baby, of her minuscule hands and feet, filled her head. She forced the image away, put the bundle in the empty pail and climbed from the wagon. Her flesh prickled. She scanned the area ahead as she walked away from her wagon, visions of wild savages with feathers in their hair filling her head, fear quickening her steps.

Moonlight lit her way to the spot she had noticed earlier. She went down on her knees, placed the tiny bundle in the small hollow at the base of the large rock, then gathered up nearby stones to seal off the opening.

The smooth cold surfaces numbed her fingertips as she wedged the stones firmly in place.

There. It was done. She dusted off her hands and rose to her feet, then stood looking down at the rock, unable to simply walk away. "I wish you were here, Mother. You would know the right words to say." She sighed and closed her eyes. "Almighty God, this baby did not grow to know life on this earth. May it know eternal life with You. Amen."

There was a soft, rustling sound. Her heart lurched. She snatched up the pail and ran for her wagon.

"...that current is mighty swift."

"The rain has swollen the river, but we should make it across all right. If need be, we will lash the wagons together..."

Emma jerked to a halt. That was Zachary Thatcher talking with Axel Lundquist. He must be making his nightly round of the wagons. Had he discovered her missing? She frowned and headed toward the other end of her wagon. Zachary Thatcher was the last person she wanted to see at—

"Miss Allen..."

Too late. She turned. He was coming toward her, a scowl on his face. "You know the rules, Miss Allen. No one is to go off by themselves at night. Especially a woman."

Emma lifted her chin. "Yes, I am aware of your rule, Mr. Thatcher, but—"

"There are no exceptions, Miss Allen." He glanced down at the pail dangling from her hand and his scowl deepened. "You were dumping trash? Why didn't you do that with the others earlier, when it was safe?"

She clamped her jaw together and moved to the tailgate of her wagon. His hand closed on her arm, preventing her from climbing the steps—bringing back the memory of being in his arms.

"You cannot put the other members of this train in danger because of your whims, Miss Allen. From now on—"

She jerked her arm free and whirled about. "It was not a *whim* that took me off by myself, Mr. Thatcher, it was a *baby*. A tiny, little baby girl that will never know life because I could not save her! The least I could do was bury her." Her voice broke. She whipped back toward the tailgate. His hand closed on her arm again. She braced herself against his touch.

"If there is fault to be borne in this circumstance it is mine, Miss Allen." His deep voice flowed over her, bringing the tears she was struggling to hold back dangerously near to flowing. "I am the one who ordered the wagons to move on in spite of your warning as to the likely consequence. I am sorry for the outcome, but—"

"The fault is not yours, Mr. Thatcher." She turned and looked into his eyes. "As guide and leader of this wagon train, your task is to keep its members safe. You succeeded. As a doctor, my task is to preserve life. I failed."

"Miss Allen—"

She shook her head. "Please, do not say more." She looked down at his hand still holding her arm and took a breath to steady her voice. "Please release me, Mr. Thatcher. I would like to retire."

He didn't move.

She stared at his hand, afraid to look at him, afraid

to say more for fear the tears that were so close would escape her control. She willed herself to wait, to stay still, when everything within her yearned to step into his arms and cry out her despair in the one place she had felt safe since this wretched journey had begun.

His fingers flexed, lingered. She heard him draw in a quick breath, and then he released his hold.

Cold replaced the warmth where his hand had been, traveled deep inside her. She stepped to the water shelf and hung the pail on the hook on the underside hoping he would not notice the trembling in her hands. When she returned to the back of the wagon he was gone.

Emma gripped the sideboard of the wagon and stared at the roiling, foaming water in front of the oxen. The three fords of the swift-flowing water in the channels between the islands had been frightening. *This* was terrifying! She looked from Garth Lundquist, who was calming the nervous beasts, to the two wagons that had already made it through the maelstrom to the opposite bank of the river and sucked in a deep breath. William's wagon was well built and Garth Lundquist was an excellent driver. She would be safe. And Anne. *Please let Annie be safe.*

Wind flowed down off the surrounding mountains and whipped across the river valley, its cold breath stinging her face and hands. She drew her wool wrap closer about her shoulders, then wiped her clammy hands on her skirt. Her wagon was next.

She took another, firmer grip on the sideboard and watched the pantomime of motions as Zachary Thatcher spoke to Josiah Blake and John Hargrove. The wagons moved away from the riverbank, then, once again, Zachary Thatcher rode upstream and urged Comanche back into the river. The horse struggled against the strong current, his head bobbing on the water, his tail floating at a downstream angle from his body as they drifted diagonally toward the island. When they reached the solid ground at the upper point of the island, man and horse surged free of the water.

Emma focused her attention on the roan, and, less obviously, on his rider. Zachary Thatcher's belt encircled his neck and one broad shoulder, his holster rested high on his chest. His boots, pants and the lower half of his tunic were sodden. He leaned forward and stroked Comanche's neck, his mouth moving, his words swallowed by the roar of the rushing water. After a minute or two, he straightened in the saddle. Her stomach flopped. It was time. She faced front, her heart pounding.

Comanche's hoofs beat against the stony ground, drew closer. Zachary Thatcher rode by on the other side of the wagon and took up a position to the left front of the oxen. Garth Lundquist talked with him a moment, then nodded and ran back, climbed into the seat and took up his whip. He snapped it over the oxen's broad backs. Comanche plunged into the foaming water, the oxen lunging after him. The wagon lurched and rolled off the island, the roiling water swirling around the floorboards, washing up against the sides and splashing over the sideboard to soak her skirts. She gasped at the touch of the frigid water against her skin. Zachary Thatcher must be—

A rush of water hit them, swept over the oxen. The wagon quivered and slewed sideways. Zachary Thatcher urged Comanche close, plunged his hand into the water then straightened in the saddle, pulling the lead ox's head up out of the water by a horn. The beast lurched forward, the other oxen following. The wagon straightened, shook and shuddered, buffeted by the water. The old fear rose, clutching her throat, squeezing her chest.

The lead oxen's shoulders cleared the water, step by plodding step they rose slowly out of the water. They were through the maelstrom! They were safe.

She took a long, slow breath and released her death grip on the seat and sideboard as the wagon broke free from the sucking water and rolled up the sloping bank.

Zachary Thatcher waved them on toward the other wagons, then rode off upstream.

What a mess! Emma swept her gaze around the circled wagons. Women and children were carrying barrels, boxes and cloth bags of food stores, mattresses and bedding, chests, trunks and household items and clothes out of the wagons to dry. The canvas covers on several of the wagons were rolled up on the sides to let the wind blow through and perform the same service. The frosty wind that made wet or damp clothing torture. There would be colds and sore throats, frostbitten fingers and toes to treat from this day's work. Thank goodness William had purchased all those medical supplies.

She slid her gaze to her wagon, then brought it to rest on Anne's. Guilt nudged her. For no good reason. It was not their fault William had the wagon beds shiplapped and caulked so watertight the only place river water had oozed through was around the tailgate. It was their blessing. Still—

Lydia Hargrove chuckled. "Stop borrowin' trouble, and give these pots a stir, Emma. Making soup to feed everyone was a good idea, but the soup won't be any good lest you rile the pots every once in a while. Too bad we don't have one big enough pot!"

"How do you know I was 'borrowing trouble,' Lydia?" Emma smiled at the older woman. "Perhaps I was daydreaming."

"No, you was borrowin' trouble. You had your doctor face on."

"My *doctor* face? Gracious, I was not aware I had one! I shall have to be more careful." Emma laughed, lifted her arm to protect her face from the smoke and swirled the liquid in the pots with the wooden spoon. In spite of her precaution she got a strong whiff of smoke and started coughing.

Lydia Hargrove straightened from dividing the dried green beans young Amy had brought as the Fletchers' contribution among the four large iron pots hanging close over the flames and wiped the tears from her eyes. "It's sure tryin' to cook on a fire with the smoke blowing in your eyes an' makin' them smart so as to blind you."

"And while shivering so with the cold it's hard to hold on to things." Olga Lundquist dipped a cup into the bag at her feet and scooped out rice to add to the pots.

"That is the reason for the soup, Olga. It will help warm everyone." Emma squinted her eyes against the smoke and leaned over to peer into the pots. "Should I get you more bacon?"

"No. You brought a good, generous chunk."

Emma nodded, pulled her wool wrap higher up

around her neck and smiled at the young girl running toward them. "Hello, Susan."

"Hello, Dr. Emma. Ma sent some carrots, and Mrs. Applegate give me some onions to bring for the soup." Susan Fenton handed the small sacks of desiccated vegetables to Lydia Hargrove, then hunched her shoulders, wrapped her arms around herself and turned her back to the wind. "Ma says do you need me I can stay an' give ya a hand. She's sortin' through the stuff the water soaked to dry it out."

Lydia shook her head. "You go back and help your mother, Susan. We have already sorted out and repacked our wagons. It's—"

"Dr. Emma! Y' gotta come quick!" Nathan Fenton ran up and skidded to a stop beside the fire.

Emma's stomach flopped. She dropped the spoon and hurried toward him. "What is it?"

"Edward Swinton fell in the river. Mr. Thatcher got him out, but he's not wakin' up."

No! Not another child! Emma lifted her skirt hems and ran toward the river, Nathan running along beside her. *Please let him be alive, please—*

"Dr. Emma, help me!" Pamelia Swinton sat on the ground beside the river, holding Edward and rocking to and fro and sobbing.

Emma dropped to her knees and reached for the little boy's wrist. A slow throb pulsed against her fingers. Too slow. His flesh was icy cold, his skin blue. *What should she do? How could she—*

"Thomas and Mr. Thatcher got the water out of him, but he—" Pamelia's voice choked "—he won't wake up.

So they sent Nathan for you. Edward's dead, Dr. Emma! But they have to get the wagon out—The Indians—"

Emma grabbed Pamelia's shoulders and gave her a quick shake. "Stop it, Pamelia! Listen to me! Edward is *not* dead. He is only cold." *Too cold.* "We must get him *warm*. Help me get these wet clothes off him." She jerked the shoes and socks off Edward's small feet, started tugging at his sodden pants.

Pamelia released her hold on Edward and yanked at his shirt.

A whip cracked. Hoofs thumped the ground behind her. Edward's pants came off in her hands. Emma threw them on the ground, grabbed the hem of Pamelia's skirt and folded it up over Edward's legs and feet. "When you get Edward's shirt off, wrap him in this." She yanked off her wool wrap and dropped it beside Pamelia. "I will be right back." She stood and raced to the wagon being pulled up the riverbank. "Mr. Swinton, I need a blanket for your son. Hurry!"

The man looked down at her, turned and dived into the wagon.

She looked out at the river and froze. Zachary Thatcher was back in the water, swimming Comanche toward the stock bunched at the opposite riverbank waiting for the herders to start them across. She stared at the wet hair clinging to his bare head, the soaked tunic stretched across his broad shoulders and her heart trembled with fear for him. In this frosty wind... *Please*— She lifted her gaze upward, gasped. The plateau behind the herders was covered with Indians sitting their horses and watching. So many Indians. Hundreds of them. Watching. If they attacked while the men of the train were split by the river… While Zachary Thatcher was caught in between—

"Here!"

She shifted her gaze, caught the blanket Thomas Swinton threw her, stole another quick glance at Zachary Thatcher then ran back to Pamelia and Edward. She was a doctor. She could do nothing about the Indians or the weather or any of the other terrible, frightful hazards of this journey. But she might be able to save young Edward's life.

For how long?

Emma set her jaw, dropped to her knees. She wrapped the doubled blanket around Edward, took him into her arms and started up the slope. *For as long as I am alive to fight!*

Pamelia scrambled to her feet and reached for her son.

Emma shook her head. "I will carry him, Pamelia. Your gown is soaked from Edward's clothes, you will wet his blanket. Run ahead to the fire and dry your clothes before you take a chill." She glanced at Pamelia's face and firmed her voice. "Do not waste time in argument, Pamelia. Edward needs you well to care for him." Thought of the Indians watching from the plateau sent a shudder through her. A silent prayer rose from her heart. *Please, Almighty God, grant that it might be so.*

Chapter Fifteen

Emma propped her pillows against the sidewall, placed the lantern on the water keg and quickly withdrew her hand. Everything was cold to the touch! She snatched up the extra blanket and draped it around her shoulders, then lifted the covers and sat on the bed, tucking her dressing gown around her legs and pulling the covers over them. The toes of her stocking-clad feet ached from the chill of the floorboards. She wiggled them deep into the downy softness of the feather mattress and leaned back.

Cold air, radiating off the canvas, sent a shiver down her spine. She jerked forward, tugged the blanket around her shoulders higher around her neck and rested back against the pillows again. What would it be like when they reached those snowcapped elevations? It seemed every day's climb brought colder weather. And the days were growing shorter, the cold nights longer.

She frowned, picked up the lap desk and put it on her legs. She was beginning to understand why Mr. Thatcher had been pushing them so hard and fast. And why he found her an…annoyance. But she had to fight for what was best for her patients, even if that ran afoul of his wishes.

She looked down, absently ran her fingertip over the small scar on the desk, then sighed, blew on her cold hands, rubbed them together and lifted the top. The letters she had written since leaving Fort William stared up at her. Had her other letters reached home yet? Traveler was a strong, fast horse, and Mr. Broadman would not be slowed by traveling with a wagon train. How excited Mary would be to receive them. She smiled, arranged things to her satisfaction and dipped her pen.

My beloved family,
I pray this finds you all in good health. Anne is still withdrawn, but we are both well. The weather is deteriorating. Many of our fellow travelers have colds, coughs and sore throats from the wetting they received during our fording of the Snake River. I wrote you of that eventful day. Little Edward is recovered from his near drowning, though he must still be protected from the cold.

We passed Fort Boise today without stopping, as our path was a long, steady climb that took until nightfall to accomplish. Our camp is by the Powder River. The Indians that have been trailing us left us today as we approached the fort. There is great relief among us all.

Mr. Thatcher has been pushing us to greater effort than before. Not that we see him. He rides off at dawn to discover our path for the day and choose our next camp. Mr. Blake now makes the nightly rounds of the wagons and relays Mr. Thatcher's orders. We are approaching the Blue Mountains, and the air grows more chilly with every climb. Do not be concerned, Mother. I have my winter cape.

I would be remiss, William, if I did not tell you that your wagons are holding up admirably to the journey. Neither Anne nor I have been troubled with the need for repairs. And our wagons do not leak when fording the rivers, save for a little water coming in at the tailgate. That is a blessing that Caroline will be truly grateful for, should you continue to pursue your dream and someday make this journey. I warn you, it is arduous beyond belief! Yet, Anne and I fare well.

My dearest love to you all,
Emma

Emma slipped the letter back into the desk, corked the ink bottle and set the desk aside. She would take care of it tomorrow, when it was warmer.

She tugged the blanket off her shoulders, shivered at the rush of cold air and hurried to spread the blanket over the bedcovers. Her fingers prickled. She cupped them over the lantern chimney a moment, relishing the heat, then extinguished the flame and crawled under the covers, curling up in the warm spot where she had been sitting. Mr. Thatcher had no wagon. Where did he sleep? Most likely out in the open on the hard, cold ground. He seemed impervious to things like weather and frigid water.

She frowned, burrowed her head deeper into the

feather pillow and covered her exposed cheek and ear with the edge of the blanket. He had been thoroughly soaked diving in the river to rescue little Edward Swinton, yet, in spite of the biting wind, he had continued to work to get the stock and herders across safely. She had feared he would sicken, but he was working harder than ever. He no longer came near the wagons, but spent all his time in the saddle searching out their best route. Or was he roaming the mountains "free and unfettered"? And why should she care? It was good that someone should achieve their dream.

She yawned, turned her thoughts from Zachary Thatcher and determinedly focused them on her plans to travel on to Oregon City and take ship for home. Anne's injuries were healed and she neither needed nor wanted her now. There was no reason to stay....

The fatigue dragged at him. His legs felt wobbly as a newborn foal's. Zach mustered determination in place of his usual strength and slid the saddle from Comanche. Whatever was wrong with him was getting worse. Fear flashed through him. He scowled, tamped it down.

Maybe Miss Allen would have some medicine— something to make him feel better, stronger. He rested a moment, then removed the saddle blanket, draped his arms over Comanche's broad back and leaned against him trying to absorb his body heat. He couldn't go to Miss Allen. The woman would probably demand he stop the train and rest! He couldn't do that. There wasn't time. He could smell snow in the air.

The fear pounced again, stronger. He had to get these people out of these mountains before the snow started.

He *had* to! Or they would die. He lifted his shaky hand and wiped a sheen of moisture from his forehead. At least the Indians had kept their part of the bargain he had struck with them and left when the train reached this valley. 'Course, that was not to say they wouldn't be back. A frown creased his forehead. He couldn't be sick! He had to fight his way through this weakness. Maybe if he rested...

"No rubdown tonight, boy." He took a breath to ease the growing tightness in his chest, coughed at the rush of cold air then winced at the stabbing chest pain the cough produced. Chills chased one another through him. He forced himself erect, stepped back and went to his knees.

Comanche tossed his head, gave a soft nicker.

Zach waved his hand in the air. "Go on, boy. Dismissed!" He reached for his bedroll. A fit of coughing took him. The pain in his chest stabbed deeper. He braced himself with his hands on the ground, hung his head and struggled to breathe. The moonlit earth whirled. *Give me strength, Lord. Help me. These people need me.* He dragged the saddle blanket to him, dropped onto it, grabbed the edge and rolled. It wasn't big enough to cover him, but it would have to do.

Comanche plodded close, lowered his head and snuffed. The horse's breath was warm on his face. And then there was only the darkness...

"Dr. Allen!" A heavy fist thumped the side of the wagon. *"You awake?"*

Emma dropped the lap desk, jerked upright and bumped her head on the lid of the chest. It slammed closed as she bolted to her feet. "I am coming!" She grabbed her wrap and shoved open the canvas flaps above the tailgate, stared down at Josiah Blake and Charley Karr. "What is it?"

"Somethin's wrong with Zach. We need you to come with us."

Her heart lurched. Bile surged into her throat. Charley Karr was leading a horse. She swallowed and nodded. "Lower the tailgate. I will get my bag." *Please, please let him be all right!* She whirled, grabbed the black leather satchel off the dresser, turned back and climbed from the wagon. "Where is he?"

"Up there." Josiah Blake gestured toward a small rise to the left of the circled wagons and started walking.

It was too far. What if they did not reach him in time? What if she were not a good enough doctor to help him? The thoughts tumbled through her head in time with the half-running steps she was taking to keep up with the men's long, determined strides. She looked at the horse and the rifles, at the men's grim faces and the bile surged again. *If a bear, or wolves, or—* "Has Mr. Thatcher been attacked by an animal? Do you have to kill—"

"His horse."

No! Horrid pictures flashed into her head. "Comanche is…injured?" *Could she help him?*

"No." Josiah Blake shot her a sidelong look. "The fool animal won't let us near Zach. Just keeps circlin' him and gnashin' his teeth at us, like some mare with a colt. Ain't never seen anything like it! We gotta put him down to get to Zach."

"Oh, no, Mr. Blake! Mr. Thatcher would never want that."

The man's face tightened. "We got no choice."

Comanche has never let anyone but me touch him.

Until that day in the storm. Her pulse raced. "Let me go first, Mr. Blake." She shot him a pleading look. "Let me try to calm Comanche."

He stopped, faced her and shook his head. "No tellin' what that fool horse might do. He might come at y', Dr. Allen."

"I am not afraid of that, Mr. Blake. Please, for Mr. Thatcher's sake, let me try."

He frowned, rubbed his thumb back and forth on the rifle barrel. She held her breath. Finally, he nodded. "All right, Dr. Allen. We'll stay out of sight. But we'll be ready, should you need us. You'll see the horse when you get up top. Zach's on the ground beside him."

"Thank you, Mr. Blake." She took a deep breath and ran ahead. The climb was steeper than it appeared. She breasted the top of the rise and stopped, her heart leaping into her throat. Zachary Thatcher was sprawled on the ground, a horse blanket half covering him. Her body twitched with the desire to run to him. She made herself concentrate on the horse standing beside him. "Hello, Comanche. Remember me?" She started forward.

The roan tossed his head, thudded his hoof against the ground then trotted around his master.

She stopped. *Don't do this, Comanche! Please! Let me pass.* "You do not mean that, boy." She held her voice low and calm, took a slow step forward. "You know me." Comanche's ears flicked. Was that a good sign? She took another step. "And you know all I want is to help your master. I love him, too." She jolted to a stop, stunned by what she had said. Could that be *true?* Of course not. It was ridiculous. She pushed the thought aside and took another step. "Please, boy, let me help him." She stretched out her hand.

The roan gave a low whicker, tossed his head and stepped toward her. "Good boy, Comanche." She rubbed his silky muzzle, then rushed to Zachary Thatcher and dropped to her knees beside him. His wrist was cold, his pulse rapid but strong. She placed her hand on his forehead. Hot—in spite of the cold weather. A chill shook him. She jerked off her wrap to cover him, then spotted his bedroll a short distance away and jumped up to get it. One quick yank on the leather thongs and the ground-sheet and blanket unrolled on the ground beside him. She dropped to her knees, reached over and gripped the front of his tunic and tugged with all her strength. On the third try, she rolled him onto the bedding.

He coughed, winced and opened his eyes. "Troops, *dismissed!*"

Comanche wheeled and thundered off.

The men ran up to stand beside her.

"Heard him yellin' about troops. He must be 'dreamin'"

She shook her head. "No, Mr. Karr, he is delirious." She grasped the edges of the bedding and covered him. "I can do nothing more for him here. We must get him to my wagon."

"I'll get my horse."

Emma nodded, watched Charley Karr run to get his mount and sat back on her heels, holding back tears.

* * *

How would she get him warm? She had every blanket and quilt in the wagon piled on him, but he needed to be warm *now*. Emma jerked open the chest that held the linens, dropped to her knees and pawed through the piles of towels and sheets. There had to be a bed warmer…or a soapstone…or a—

A stone!

She bolted to her feet, glanced at Zachary Thatcher then scrambled over the red box and ducked through the canvas flaps onto the wagon seat. Josiah Blake was standing by the fire, talking with the men of the train. He looked at a loss. She cupped her hands around her mouth. *"Mr. Blake!"*

He looked up. There was something close to panic in his eyes. He ran to her wagon. "Is he…"

"He is the same, Mr. Blake. But I must get him warm. Please have some of the men gather flat stones and warm them in the fire, then bring them to me. And hurry!" She didn't wait for his answer. She turned and crawled back into the wagon, grabbed the iron teapot from her medical supplies in the box, added some herbs then closed the box, set the teapot down and placed a pile of towels beside it. *Please let it work—*

"Squad, right!" Zachary Thatcher jerked upright, coughed.

"Lie down, Mr. Thatcher! You must stay covered." Emma grabbed his shoulder.

"They're coming around our flank!" He shoved her hand away, tried to rise and fell back, his entire body shaking with a chill. He coughed, coughed again. His face went taut with pain. His eyes closed, and he went still.

She pulled the covers back over him, tucked them up around the sides of his head, his face hot against her hands. His breath wheezed from his lungs. She brushed the damp hair off his forehead and her doctor's mien crumbled. If only she had seen him during the past few days, she could have— Her breath caught. She stared down at him and pressed a hand against the sudden sick feeling in the pit of her stomach. Was that why he had not come around the wagons? Because he was ill and wanted to avoid *her?* Did he think that little of her skill? Or was it her personally he derided?

"Dr. Emma… I have stones for you. Ma had some at the edge of her fire."

Emma blinked tears from her eyes and turned back to peer out the front of the wagon, once more the doctor. "Please bring them up to the driver's seat, Matthew."

The young man hopped up onto the wagon tongue, leaned down and lifted a pailful of the heated flat rocks to the seat, then leaned down and lifted another.

"Thank you, Matthew." Emma dumped the stones out of the first pail onto the lid of the red box, tossed in the iron teapot and the bags of herbs and reached for the other pail. "I shall need more when these cool."

He nodded. "They're gatherin' 'em now. I'll bring 'em soon's they're hot." He grabbed the pails and hopped down.

"And Matthew, please tell your mother and Olga Lundquist I need some good, strong meat broth for Mr. Thatcher. And also, some summer savory and sage tea. The herbs are in the pail." Emma closed the flaps, covered one of the stones with a towel and carried it to the bed. She lifted the covers, tucked the wrapped stone next to Zachary Thatcher's shivering body and hurried back for the next one. *Please let this work. Please...*

The prayer rose in a continual stream from her heart as she concentrated on wrapping the heated rocks and placing them around Zachary Thatcher as quickly as possible, her ear tuned to the sound of the air whistling in and out of his lungs, his hard coughs and his feverish mutterings. She closed her mind to the word pressing against her will. Not even in her thoughts would she admit Zachary Thatcher had pneumonia. Or that it might already be too late to save him.

Chapter Sixteen

Emma glanced up at the sound of someone climbing to the wagon seat, caught a glimpse of Lydia Hargrove's face, then skirts being shaken into place. She smiled when Lydia poked her head through the opening of the canvas flaps.

"Here is the tea, Emma." She set the towel-wrapped iron teapot on the lid of the box and started to climb in.

"No, Lydia, do not come in!" Emma scurried from her place on the floor beside the bed to stop the woman from entering. "Mr. Thatcher is contagious, and I do not want you to sicken." She grasped the teapot and placed it on the top of the dresser out of the direct draft. "Thank you for making the tea so quickly, Lydia." She poured a bit of the hot liquid into a cup.

"It's little enough to do. The broth is cooking." Lydia glanced at Zachary Thatcher. "How is he?"

Emma hesitated, then took a breath and shook her head. She could not lie. "He's not well."

"His breathing sounds labored."

"Yes."

Lydia fastened her gaze on her. "He looks fevered."

Do not make me say it, Lydia! She nodded, went to her knees on the floor and set the cup down to lift Zachary Thatcher's head and shoulders. He was too heavy for her. She could not hold him *and* the cup. Tears smarted at the backs of her eyes. She bit her lip to keep them from flowing, and tried again. Fabric rustled. Lydia Hargrove's skirts appeared, ballooned out as the woman knelt beside her and slipped her arm beneath Zachary's raised head and shoulders. "I'll hold him. You give him the tea."

Emma shot her a grateful look, grabbed the cup and raised it to Zachary Thatcher's mouth. He turned his head away, rolled it side to side. "Draw sabers!" He jerked his arm from beneath the covers, raised it. "Charge!" His arm dropped to the bed, and he went limp.

She touched the cup to his mouth again. "Drink this, Mr. Thatcher. It will help your cough and your fever." There was no response. She tipped the cup so the tea touched his parched lips. They parted. She poured a little of the liquid in his mouth and he swallowed, then swallowed again, and again. He burst into a fit of coughing, grabbed at his chest. "Lift him higher, Lydia!" She put down the cup and rubbed his back as Lydia raised his shoulders. When the paroxysm passed, she fluffed his pillow, piled the extra pillow on top of it and they lowered him to rest against them. He was shaking with chills. She tucked his arm back under the covers and pulled them up close around his head.

"How long has he been like this?"

Emma looked at Lydia, then averted her gaze.

Knowledge of Mr. Thatcher's dire condition was in the woman's eyes. "I cannot say. He was like this when they found him this morning." She rose, stepped to the keg and ladled some of the cold water into the wash bowl.

"Fool man! Why didn't he come get help when he come down sick?"

Because of me. The pain stabbed deep. She had fought him for her patients' sakes, and because of that Zachary Thatcher was...was— Emma swallowed hard, tossed a cloth in the water, wrung it out and folded it. Fortunately, judging from the tone of her voice, and the look of disgust on her face, Lydia was not expecting an answer. She fixed her professional doctor's expression on her face and carried the cloth to the bed and laid it on Zachary Thatcher's forehead. He muttered something unintelligible and turned away.

"Ain't a man born got the brains God give a goose when it comes to takin' care of hisself!" Lydia frowned down at Zachary Thatcher, then lifted her gaze. "I expect that's why God made us women. Though it sure is worryin' for us."

It is indeed.

"I'd best be gettin' back to help Olga with the broth an' such." Lydia fixed an assessing gaze on her. "We'll send along some good, nourishing soup an' biscuits for you. You're lookin' a mite peaked." She rose and stepped to the red box.

"Lydia..." The woman looked back at her. "My Papa Doc taught me to always wash my hands when I left a patient. He said it keeps the illness from spreading." She smiled at the older woman. "Thank you for your help. You will find soap and hand balm beside the washbowl."

* * *

The day passed in a blur of worry and work. Emma wrapped heated stones, coaxed spoonfuls of soup and swallows of tea into Zachary Thatcher and searched her memory for every tiny crumb of information Papa Doc had given her on treating someone with his disease.

She remembered Papa Doc's story of how he had discovered the benefit of fresh air for the patient with straining lungs while he had been caring for the then Laina Brighton, and dived into the dresser to find her Augusta spencer in bottle-green velvet. She put the short jacket on beneath her doctor's coat, tucked the covers more snugly around Zachary Thatcher and opened the canvas flaps a bit to let the brisk September air blow through the wagon.

She folded her extra sheets into a bundle, enlisted Matthew's help to lift Zachary Thatcher's head and shoulders, and slipped the bundled sheets beneath his pillows to further elevate his torso and stretch his chest to aid the expansion of his lungs.

Nothing helped. In spite of all she did, Zachary Thatcher's condition worsened. During the night his fever climbed. His cough deepened. His chills became so severe they shook his entire body, and his lungs rasped and wheezed with his efforts to breathe.

She tried to maintain a professional detachment, but with every passing minute her fear increased. She was losing the battle. Zachary Thatcher could die, and it would be her fault. She was the reason he was so sick, and she was not a good enough doctor to save him. Guilt warred with reason. Fear undermined determination. And finally, tears overcame her will. She buried her face in her hands and sobbed out her misery. "Oh, Papa Doc, I wish you were here! If only you were *here*."

We are doctors, Emma...not God. Never forget that. And never fail to pray for your patients.

Anger shook her. She jerked her head up and swiped the tears from her cheeks. "I *prayed* for Annie's baby, Papa Doc. I did! I begged God to let her live, but she died. Little baby Grace died in my arms! And I prayed Caroline would get well so William could have his dream of coming to Oregon country. I prayed and prayed, but she did not. I prayed Annie would get over her grief. She has not! I—"

Trust Me.

The words rang through her spirit. Emma caught her breath, clenched her hands and stared at the canvas arching over her head. "No, God. Not anymore. I am afraid to trust You."

Zachary Thatcher coughed, coughed again. He arched his back, his lungs struggling to draw in air, then went limp.

She leaned over him, clutched his shoulders and gave them a violent shake. "Mr. Thatcher! Mr. Thatcher, *breathe!*" Her lungs strained to suck in life-giving air for him. His remained silent, deflated. Panic took her. She collapsed to her knees, sobbing into her hands. "Oh, Heavenly Father, there is nothing more I can do. You are the source of life. Please...*please* breathe for him..."

A soft, rasping whistle broke the silence. It was the most beautiful sound she had ever heard. She held her breath, listened. It came again. She lifted her trembling hand and placed it on Zachary Thatcher's blanket-covered chest, felt the slight rise and fall as his lungs filled to their impaired capacity then emptied. She did not know if it were answered prayer or mere coincidence. But she knew what William and their mother and Papa Doc would say…and do. She closed her eyes, allowed her heart to open to her shattered faith. "Thank You, Heavenly Father. Thank You." Peace washed over her. A peace she had not felt since she turned away from God in anger.

She stayed there a few minutes watching Zachary Thatcher breathe, then lifted the cloth from his fore-head and wiped the sheen of sweat off his face. His skin was cooler against her hand. His shivering abated. She studied his face. He was sleeping normally. The crisis was over.

If a patient with pneumonia survives the crisis, it is most likely that, with proper care, he will live.

With proper care. She would see to that…somehow. In spite of Zachary Thatcher's disdainful feelings to-ward her. She rose on her shaky legs and stepped to the front of the wagon to tell the others she would need no more heated stones. Dawn was lightening the east-ern sky.

Emma shifted the pail to her other hand and made herself slow her steps. Lydia was with him. He was sleeping normally. He would be all right. Unless he did something foolish and caused a relapse.

She sighed and smoothed the tabs at the hem of the spencer over her knotted stomach as she started up the rise. This urgent need to be with Zachary Thatcher, to reassure herself he was still alive and on the mend, was foolishness. But it had been such a close thing she still could not believe it. And telling herself it was so did not help. But her feelings and needs were not important. The best thing she could do for Zachary Thatcher right now was to take care of Comanche.

She smiled and looked down at the pail as she crested the low hill. How fortunate that William loved oatmeal with honey for his morning meal. She had found a large bag of rolled oats and a sealed crock of honey among the food stores in Annie's wagon. Comanche should—

A low nicker greeted her. She looked up, relief making her knees go weak. She had not realized until that moment how afraid she was that the horse would not have returned. "Hello, Comanche. I brought you a treat." She held out the pail.

The horse stretched his neck, snuffed then drew back and tossed his head.

"Ah, so you want to be coaxed, is that it?" Emma laughed and tipped the bucket toward him. "You know you want the oats and honey. You might as well give in."

The roan snuffed, drew his head back and thudded his hoof against the ground.

"Hmm, stubborn are you? All right. I will set the bucket down. But I will not go away." She placed the pail on the ground at her feet. "If you want the treat, you must come get it."

The horse jabbed his nose toward her, then stepped back, dragging his feet.

"I know…you want me to leave, but I am staying right here." She sobered. "You cannot outwait me, Comanche. You are too important to your master. You might as well make friends."

The horse flicked his ears, took a step forward.

"Good boy, Comanche." She kept her voice low, confident. "Take another step."

The roan stepped toward her, stuck out his head and snuffed at the bucket.

She stood perfectly still.

He stuck his nose in the pail, then lifted his head and crunched the mouthful of sweetened oats. A minute later, he shoved his nose back in the bucket.

"Good boy, Comanche." Emma lifted her hand and stroked the horse's hard, heavily muscled shoulder. His flesh rippled beneath her hand, but he did not move away. She slid her hand up. "You have got tangles in your mane." She scratched beneath the long, thick hair, then ran her fingers through it. Comanche crunched on. She smiled and began finger-combing out the snarls.

Zach came awake, his heart pounding. Something was wrong. He felt as weak as a new fawn. He stayed perfectly still, listening, smelling, assessing his situation before he moved. Had he been wounded? He mentally searched his body for pain, found nothing but the incredible weakness. And thirst. His mouth felt dry as dust, and his body was screaming for a drink of water. He ignored the need. The greater need was to know what had happened to him. Where he was.

There was a hint of golden light against his eyelids. A lantern turned down low? So it was night. A soft breathing to his right alerted him to the fact he was not alone. He pressed his fingers down slightly, expecting hard earth, finding a yielding softness. Soft weight held him in a cocoon of warmth. Where was he? Wind moaned. There was a sound of fabric rippling. He inched his hand to the side beneath the warm weight, found cold wood. Floorboards? He was in a wagon. Whose? And how had he gotten here?

Zach opened his eyes a slit, waited. When they had adjusted to the dim lantern light he slid his gaze to the right. His heart jolted. Emma Allen was sitting on the wagon floor, leaning against a pillow that was propped against a dresser. She was wrapped in a quilt, only her head showing. Her long lashes lay like smudges against her skin. Her lips were parted slightly in slumber, and tresses of her hair trailed along her cheek and curled onto the quilt. Emma Allen. *Doctor* Emma Allen. Memory flashed. Yes. He had been sick. *Very* sick. That would explain the weakness. And the tiredness. And the doctor. And— It was *her* wagon! He should not be here. Did the woman give no thought to her reputation?

Zach scowled, considered waking her, but the exhaustion overrode his need for answers. Tomorrow would be soon enough. For now he would go to his camp. He shoved against the floorboards, found no strength in his arms. He lifted his head, tried again. The effort exhausted him. He dropped back against the downy pillows and closed his eyes to rest and gather strength for another try.

Emma took another peek from under her lashes. Zachary Thatcher had succumbed. His eyes were closed, his face relaxed. The rise and fall of his chest under the blankets was slow and even. The weakness from the pneumonia had defeated him. He was fast asleep.

She frowned and fully opened her eyes to study him. What was the man thinking, trying to get up and leave?

In the cold of the night? To go where? Back to his camp to roll up in a horse blanket? He could relapse and die. Why would he do such a thing? Was his desire to avoid her that strong?

Hurt washed over her. She called up anger to fight it. Zachary Thatcher was an arrogant, stubborn, ungrateful man! Yet her fingers itched to touch him, to take his pulse, to feel his forehead and be certain he was all right. Perhaps that made her a good doctor, but it also made her a very foolish woman.

Chapter Seventeen

Emma had not stomped her foot since she was a very young girl, but she was close to doing so now. She looked at Lydia Hargrove for support, read the "let it be, they will not listen" look in her eyes and took a calming breath. "Mr. Thatcher, you are not a well man. You need rest and—"

"And this wagon train needs to get moving." His voice was quiet, implacable. But not nearly as strong as normal.

She watched him set his breakfast plate aside and stand, did not miss the shiver he tried to hide, nor his careful movements that betrayed his weakened state. At least there was no sign of recurring fever. She clenched her hands at her sides to keep from placing one on his forehead to be sure. She looked at his set jaw and turned to the others. "Mr. Hargrove, you are the leader of this wagon train. You can order—"

"Thatcher has full say. And he is right. The train has to keep moving. We've already lost a full day's travel and more." The older man gave her a piercing look.

"You don't understand the importance of our decision, Miss Allen, and—"

"Mr. Hargrove, I fully understand the import of your decision." She looked straight into the portly man's deep-set eyes. "It is you, sir, who do not understand. Tell me—" she swept her gaze over Joshia Blake, Charley Karr and back to John Hargrove "—who is going to lead us out of these mountains if Mr. Thatcher has a relapse and dies? Do any of you know the path we must take to reach Oregon country?"

She swallowed back the lump of anger rising to clog her throat and looked at the subject of her fear. There was no sign of yielding. "Will you at least wear a coat and do all in your power to keep yourself from taking a further chill, Mr. Thatcher?" She jutted her chin in the air. "I assume you have a coat as you are so concerned about the snows in the mountains! I can only hope your concern for the welfare of these people lends itself to your deigning to obey my instructions that far!"

She pivoted on her heel and stormed off toward her wagon, too furious, worried and afraid for Zachary Thatcher to watch him leave camp.

Zach guided Comanche through the stand of pitch and spruce pine at the foot of the hill, choosing the best path for the following wagons, snapping off branches to point the way when he changed direction. The wagons would have a hard time of it coming down that steep descent. It had taken all his strength to stay upright in the saddle. He rode out into the open, shivered as the air sinking off the mountains touched his neck with its icy fingers and chased down his spine.

He reached up and pulled the collar of his sheep-skin-lined buckskin coat higher. He hated to admit it, but Miss Allen was right. He was not well. He was still weak and easily chilled. He frowned and tugged his shrunken hat down lower on his forehead. His body had betrayed him. He had figured he would get stronger as the day wore on, the way he always did. The opposite was true. Fatigue such as he had never known pulled at him. He found himself slumping in the saddle. But the air smelled of snow. He had no choice but to push on. If the wagons were caught here in the mountains…

Who is going to lead us out of these mountains if Mr. Thatcher has a relapse and dies?

Zach deepened his frown to a scowl. Emma Allen had struck straight at the heart of the matter. The choices were the same as always—stop and rest for her patient's sake, or push on. But this time there was a huge difference. *He* was the recovering patient. And if she was right and he sickened and—

Zach gave his head a sharp shake, glared up at the darkening, overcast sky. He wouldn't die. He couldn't. These people's lives depended on his staying alive. He leaned forward and patted Comanche's neck, shifted his gaze to the lofty snowcapped heights that surrounded the circular Grande Ronde plain. There was not time enough to continue on today. Those mountains were the worst of the journey. They would likely have to double the teams to haul the wagons up, maybe use block and tackle…and again to hold them back on the steep descents. As weary and worn as the animals were, that forced rest because of his illness might have been a fortuitous thing. And an early stop tonight would help, as well.

He straightened in the saddle and glanced around. There was dried grass and a good mountain stream for water. Plenty of large timber for wood. They could camp here tonight and make the long climb out of the plain tomorrow when the animals were fresh off a night's rest. When he had rested.

He scanned the surrounding mountain walls, found what he was looking for and urged Comanche forward.

The spot was perfect. The stone curved along the narrow ledge, providing protection from the worst of the wind. He glanced up at the slight overhang above him. It was deep enough to shield him from falling snow if he crowded his bed close against the rock wall. He turned in the saddle and looked out over the basin below. There was a clear view of the entire area, he would be able to see if trouble threatened. If the Blackfeet returned.

A flash of white through the cluster of pines on his back trail caught his eye. Josiah Blake rode into view, followed by the first wagon. Zach gave a shrill whistle, waited until Blake spotted him on the ledge, then stood in his saddle, lifted his arm and circled his hand over his head. Blake turned toward the following wagons and repeated the signal. The first wagon entered the plain and swung out to the right.

Blake could handle things now. Zach urged Comanche over to the rock wall and slipped from the saddle. He removed his gear, brushed the saddle blanket over Comanche, then stood back and slapped the spots on the horse's rump. "All right, boy, our work is done. Dismissed!"

The horse tossed his head, nudged him in the chest and trotted off. Zach dropped to his knees, yanked the ties and spread out his bedroll. He would rest until the wagons were circled and the herd massed. Time enough then to go down and set the guards in place for the night. He placed the extra blanket he had taken from the supply wagon on top of his groundsheet and stretched out on it, grateful for the added barrier it provided between him and the cold stone. The other blanket brought a warm comfort to his chilled legs.

He closed his eyes, let his mind drift. That feather mattress had sure been warm and comforting last night, not like the stone beneath him now... He shifted his weight, tugged the hatchet at his belt out from under him. Not as comforting as Emma Allen's hand on his forehead though. Or the quiet prayer for his healing she had been whispering. She certainly had soft hands. And a gentle touch. He hadn't wanted her to move her hand. Had stayed still, barely breathing, until she moved away. A man could get used to that kind of thing. And to the soft yielding of her lips beneath his, the way she felt in his arms...

A gust of wind whipped around the stone barrier, picked up dust and dirt off the ledge and swirled it through the air. He frowned, tugged the collar of his coat higher around his ears. That kiss had been a mistake. A big mistake. He had thought it would satisfy him to hold her, kiss her. Instead it had made it worse. Emma Allen was a woman from a wealthy family who had stated her desire to return to the pampered life she had always known. And she was a doctor. She cared for all her patients. He'd seen that. The gentleness in her touch meant nothing special. Nothing at all. Nor did he want it to. He wanted no ties to her or any other woman. He had valleys to roam and mountains to explore. Still…

He scowled, rejecting the thought, tried to summon a vision of the valley where he wanted to build his trading post. But all he could see was the look of hurt and anger in Emma Allen's eyes when he had refused to rest as she advised. He had no need to worry about an entanglement with her. She wanted no part of him. But all the same, he'd never seen such beautiful eyes…

Every ridge had gotten higher, steeper and more difficult to climb, every chasm deeper and more frightening to descend. And the trees! So many trees the men had to cut a way through them. But it was over now. Emma donned her blue wool cape, climbed from her wagon and walked toward the group gathered around the fire by the head wagon. Zachary Thatcher was there. She had seen his tall, gaunt frame from her wagon. He had lost weight since his illness. He should—

She frowned, broke off the thought, ignored the worry and fear that haunted her for him. Zachary Thatcher did not want her advice…or anything to do with her. He had made that abundantly clear. And in a few more days he would be out of her life forever. If he accepted her offer to take Anne to the Banning Mission and then escort her on to Oregon City.

That sick, hollow feeling struck the pit of her stomach again. She paused, took a deep breath, and then another to gain control. It would not do to let her emotions show. The last thing she wanted was for Zachary

Thatcher to guess how she felt about him. What was wrong with her anyway? Why was she so foolish, always desiring what she could not have? And why should she care so deeply about someone so arrogant, so... So competent and brave. And right.

She looked up at the falling snowflakes, sparkling like diamonds in the moonlight. If he had agreed and halted the wagons for the quarantine, or the other times she had asked, this snow would have caught them deep in the mountains. And she knew now how terrible and costly that could have been. The snow and ice on these dreadful, twisting trails was dangerous. But deep drifts in those narrow gaps would have trapped them...

She shuddered, started walking again. It did not matter now. Soon they would make the last mountainous descent to the Columbia River Valley. Then the emigrants had only to choose the place where they would begin building their town. She and Annie would travel on. Annie to the Banning Mission, and she to Oregon City to board a ship for home. Tears stung her eyes. She would miss these people she had grown so close to over the past months. The hardships they had endured together had formed a closeness she had never known in her friendships at home. Lydia and Pamelia and Olga and Lorna and— She would never see little Jenny and Edward or the other children grow. She would never know if Pamelia's baby—

She stopped again, blinked the tears from her eyes. She must focus her thoughts on family and home. But they seemed so far away... And Annie would be here. And if William brought his family to Oregon country next year, she would be on one of Uncle Justin's ships docking at Philadelphia when he was starting out from St. Louis. She would not see him, or Caroline or their baby if— *Please, Heavenly Father, let William's baby live. And please watch over these people. Please keep them safe and—*

"Dr. Emma! Joseph was about to come fetch you. Come join us."

Dr. Emma. She would never be called that again. She looked across the remaining distance at Lydia, swallowed the lump in her throat and hurried to the fire, automatically scanning faces for signs of illness, looking for any visible injury. "Is there a problem?"

"Yes." John Hargrove cleared his throat, glanced around the people assembled then fixed his gaze on her. "We have been discussing our new town and the needs—"

"Fire that bullet straight, Hargrove—'for the target in yer sights gets away!"

There was a roar of laughter at Axel Lundquist's taunt. Emma shot a glance at him. The grizzled farmer winked. She stiffened, shocked to her toes. She looked at Lorna Lewis who wore a huge grin. And Pamelia—

"We have taken a vote, Miss Allen, and—"

"Oh, for goodness sake, John! We want you to stay and be our doctor, Emma! The men will all help build you a cabin. And our boys will keep you supplied with firewood. We'll all share our garden bounty with you." Lydia rushed around the fire to her. "Will you?"

Emma stared, her mouth gaping open. Then all of the women were crowding around her, urging her to say yes. She looked from their anxious faces to the men. Axel Lundquist winked again and nodded. Joseph Lewis gave a sheepish nod. Thomas Swinton actually smiled and nodded. And the others—they had voted for her to stay. Her heart swelled. She kept her gaze from straying to Zachary Thatcher. He had no part in this request, or her decision. He would be off roaming the mountains…free and unfettered. That thought stole her elation.

"We should like an answer, Miss Allen."

Emma looked over at John Hargrove, took in his frown. Poor Mr. Hargrove, obviously he disapproved. But the others… She cleared her throat and nodded. "Yes. My answer is *yes*."

"I told them you would!" Lydia gave the other women a smug smile. "They were afraid you would say no, seein' as how we haven't much to offer you." The women, who had stood silent and staring, broke into speech.

"Hush, ladies! We have business to conduct." John Hargrove glared across the fire at them. "Your chattering will keep us all standing out here in this snow! Now then—" He turned toward the men. "Thatcher, we can't offer much by way of recompense, but we want you to stay on, as well."

Hope surged in her, vibrant, intense, unbidden. Emma caught her breath, lifted her hand beneath her cape and pressed it against the sudden, wild throbbing at the base of her throat. She turned and looked Zachary Thatcher's way. He turned his head. Their gazes met. She lifted her chin and turned away for fear he could read her desire that he stay in her eyes.

"—At least until we get the town built up and are settled in. You know how to deal with Indians. And we'll need your skills to lead hunting parties. We're running low on supplies."

"I appreciate the offer, Hargrove. But my job was to bring you to Oregon country. I'll be moving on."

His deep, rich voice killed her hope. She lowered her hand to press against that sick, emptiness in her stomach, looked at the women and forced a smile. "If you will excuse me, ladies, I want to go tell Anne what has happened." She hurried away, refusing to let her emotions overcome her.

Chapter Eighteen

My dearest William, Mother and Papa Doc,
I write exciting news. We have arrived in Oregon country! I confess there were times I did not believe we would make it here as the journey is fraught with dangers, not the least of which is making almost perpendicular, snow-and-ice-covered ascents and descents such as we experienced on our last days in the Blue Mountains. At Mr. Thatcher's direction, the men hitched up extra teams and used block and tackle attached to trees to help the poor teams that were struggling to maintain their footing haul the wagons uphill, then slowly played out the rope to keep the wagons from sliding forward and overrunning the teams going downhill. It was harrowing and frightful, especially when there were no trees near. The men would then hitch teams to the back of the wagons, and, often, themselves grasp hold of the ropes to hold the wagons back. It was very treacherous footing and many took hard

falls, including the women and children, who, of course, could not ride in the wagons because of the danger. Hannah Fletcher fell and broke her wrist. Thankfully, the break was in a fortuitous position and I was able to splint it.

I can never adequately thank you, dearest William, for the medical supplies you provided. Or for praying for me. God has heard and answered your prayers. The emigrants have asked me to stay with them and be their doctor! My dream is coming true, as you said it would. I believe the Lord will bless you and make your dream come true, as well.

We are encamped by a river at the base of the Blue Mountains on a range of small, low hills covered with a growth the farmers among us call bunchgrass. They say it will provide excellent grazing and help the weary, trail-worn animals quickly regain their strength. Beyond these hills, as far as the eye can reach, are plains and mountains. Timber, well suited for building, is in abundance on the mountains. Mr. Hargrove says many back East are desirous of moving West and a town situated to "welcome" them to Oregon country will prosper. The women simply want to have this journey end. Several of the men are exploring today in hopes of finding the most advantageous location for our town. Wherever the town is placed, its name will be Promise.

Anne does not wish to tarry until the town's location is settled. Mr. Thatcher, too, has no desire to stay with our company. He will take Anne on to the Banning Mission. I shall miss her.

Emma stared down at the words, blinked to clear her vision. And Mr. Thatcher. She would miss Zachary Thatcher. She took a deep breath against the heaviness in her chest, wiped the nib, stoppered the inkwell and set aside the lap desk. It was time. But she had promised Anne...

She rose and climbed from the wagon, brushed the hair back from her face, shook the long skirt of her red wool gown in place and looked toward her adopted sister's wagon. Anne was on the driver's seat facing straight ahead, her slender frame draped in her black widow's garb. Zachary Thatcher was hitching Comanche to the rear of the wagon. She lifted her chin, turned and started up the low rise behind her wagon. She had promised Anne she would not come and say goodbye, but she would not simply let her ride away.

The sound of mules braying and wagon wheels rumbling spurred her on. She reached the top of the rise and turned. Zachary Thatcher sat beside Anne, the reins held in his hands. Hands that had once held hers. She swiped at her tears, wrapped her arms about her torso and watched the man who held her heart drive her adopted sister away. She watched until the hills hid them from her sight, and then she turned and started back down the hill, a horrible empty ache where her heart had been.

"Look what I found, Dr. Emma!"

She started out of her thoughts, looked down at David's pudgy hand and forced a smile. "What a lovely stone, David."

"Yeah, it looks kinda like a heart." His hand lifted. "You c'n have it, Dr. Emma. I'll find another one." He thrust it into her hand and raced off.

Emma opened her hand, looked down. A stone heart to replace the one she had lost. She lifted her gaze to David, who now squatted beside his brother, examining something on the ground in front of them. *Dr. Emma.* She was a doctor. Her dream had come true. It was enough. She would *make* it enough. She blinked, blew out a long breath and continued down the hill.

Emma pulled the desk onto her lap and unstopped the well. She had to hurry now. The men would be leaving soon. She kept her gaze from the words she had already written, dipped the pen in the ink and continued the letter.

> I have learned much and, I pray, gained wisdom on this long, grueling journey. I believe I am the stronger for it. I know my faith has grown. How could it be otherwise? God has answered my prayer to be a doctor in a way I could not imagine.
>
> A few of the men are going to ride to Fort Walla Walla and there hire Indians with canoes to take them down the Columbia River to Oregon City for needed supplies. They will carry with them my small bundle of letters to send on their way to you. I wonder often if Mr. Broadman carried my first bundle of letters safely to St. Louis. I hope that my letters have reached you and that

Traveler is safe and well and waiting for you, dear William, at cousin Mary's. Shall I confess to you the terrible selfishness I have discovered in my heart? Having made this long, punishing journey, and thus being well acquainted with the deprivations and dangers thereof, my heart still longs for you to come to Oregon country next year. I do not, for one moment, wish you or yours harm, and my best advice would be that you stay home. But, what joy it would give me to see you again!

Now I must close for the men are ready to leave. I pray one of Uncle Justin's ships will have reached port during our long journey and there will be letters from you all waiting for me. My heart aches with loneliness for all of you. I long to receive news of you.

My dearest love always,

Your Emma

Emma addressed the letter, affixed the wax seal and placed it with the others. A length of narrow blue ribbon from the dresser tied them into a neat bundle. All was now ready for the men's departure. She placed the lap desk back in the chest and climbed from the wagon.

Controlled chaos greeted her. Once again, the women were taking advantage of the day off from traveling to clean their wagons, their clothes and bedding. Washtubs steamed over fires strung out along the river. Furnishings, clothing and food supplies littered the area around each wagon.

Except for hers.

She glanced at her wagon and an odd sort of dissatisfaction, a sensation she had never before experienced, gripped her. The extent of her cleaning was the quilt and blankets she had hung out to air over the boxes, crates and barrels of supplies off-loaded from Anne's wagon and stacked in the driver's box. A woman alone did not require the prodigious amounts of supplies and possessions that cluttered and crowded the wagons of those with a family. A woman alone did not make a mess. And a woman such as she did not know how to clean, or cook, or do the wash or any of the other myriad tasks these other women, some much younger than she, did so effortlessly.

She frowned, wrapped her arms about herself and stared at the other women. She had agreed to stay and be the doctor in their town. And she was alone. She had better learn how to take care of herself. Because, other than her doctoring and shooting skills, she was useless here on the frontier.

I will observe, or I will ask. I may be a pampered woman, but I am not unintelligent, only untaught in these matters. And I will rectify that very quickly.

The words she had spoken to Zachary Thatcher the night he had pointed out her ineptitude for life on the wilderness journey brought a flush to her cheeks. They were brave, challenging, *empty* words. She had not tried to learn the skills she needed for survival on the journey or here in Oregon country. She had merely paid others to care for her and Anne, the same as the servants at home had done for them all their lives. No wonder Zachary Thatcher found her worthy of...of disdain.

Emma squared her shoulders and scanned the women. Zachary Thatcher was out of her life, but she still had her pride! And a need to survive. *Cooking first!* As soon as she gave her letters to Josiah Blake she would go to Lydia and ask her to teach her.

Zach tightened his grip on the reins of the packhorse he was leading and urged Comanche to a faster walk. He wanted to be out of these rolling hills and into the Blue Mountains before nightfall.

He topped a rise and scanned the surrounding area, searching for the wagon train as Comanche crossed the elevation. He didn't want to come upon them accidentally. He had made a clean break and he wanted to keep it that way. His last job was done. He had escorted Anne Simms to the Banning Mission four days ago. There was no need for further involvement with the emigrants. He had his fee and his bonus money, less what he had spent on supplies for wintering in the mountains. He was free. And he intended to stay that way.

There was no sign of the wagons. He stopped Comanche, took a closer look around. Nothing. A thread of worry wormed its way into his thoughts. He had told them to keep close by the river. Of course, they could have followed the north branch. Perhaps he should ride over that way and—

No. The emigrants were no longer his concern. Not... any of them.

Zach frowned, forced the image of Emma Allen from his mind and guided Comanche on a straight path to the thick growth of pine at the base of the mountains. There was no need for caution now, and he had no time to waste. If he pushed forward every minute of daylight of every day, he could reach the valley where he wanted to build his trading post before the blizzards started.

He slowed Comanche, peered into the dusky light beneath the trees then ducked beneath a feathery branch and began to wend his way up the wall of mountain. He had it all planned. He and the horses would live in that huge cavern he had found. And he would spend the winter cutting down trees and trimming and notching logs. In the spring he would start building...

Emma poured the saleratus into the palm of her hand, dumped it onto the flour in the crockery bowl, stirred it in and added a wooden spoonful of lard. "Tonight, Lydia, my biscuits will be as light and fluffy as yours."

"Not if you use that spoon. You work the dough overmuch."

"Is that what I am doing wrong?" Emma dropped the spoon on top of an upturned barrel serving as a "table," lightly fingered the mixture until the lard was well distributed then added a small amount of potato water to make it all hold together.

A cloud of smoke rose from the stone-encircled fire and made her nose burn. She wiped her tearing eyes with the back of her hand, scooped up some dough and gently patted it into a circle. She would need eight of them to fill the spider she had greased with lard. "Do you expect Matthew and Charley with a load of logs for your house tonight? Or are they staying on the mountain to fell trees with the others?"

"They'll stay the night." Lydia carried her filled spider to the fire, grabbed the small iron rake and pulled a pile of hot coals forward. She sat the spider over half of them, and used the rest to cover the rimmed lid. When she finished she stepped back and fanned her heat-reddened face with the long skirt of her apron.

Emma lifted her gaze to the Blue Mountains, raised it to the snow-whitened pinnacles. Was he up there? Alone? Was he ill or injured or— Her finger poked a hole in the last biscuit. She pushed the edges together and put it in the spider, carried the heavy, iron frying pan to the fire and put the coals under it and on the lid to start the biscuits baking.

"Here's more wood fer your fire, Mrs. Hargrove. Mrs. Lundquist and Ma have got all they need." Daniel Fletcher grinned and dumped a bucket of large wood chunks on their already big pile. "Ma says Pa and Josh are choppin' the notches out of the logs fer houses so fast she an' Mary an' Amy are gettin' buried by 'em!" The young boy's chest swelled. "Pa and Josh let me help."

"Well we need every hand if we're to get our homes built before winter sets in."

The boy nodded. "Pa says it don't take long to get the houses up when everyone helps. I got to get back to work!" He ran off.

Emma stared after him, listening to the sound of the bucket bumping against his leg as he ran, of axes biting deep into wood. Was Mr. Thatcher close enough to hear the men cutting down trees? Or was he already high in the mountains on his way to his valley? The memory of those treacherous ice-covered slopes lifted her gaze toward the sky. *Please keep Mr. Thatcher safe, Almighty God. Please keep him healthy and safe.* She picked up the spoon and stirred the soup simmering in the iron pot hanging over the fire. Bits of browned bacon floated among chunks of potato and diced onion and corn. The men here would be eating good, hot food tonight. What would Zachary Thatcher eat?

The fish was good. He would save what was left for his breakfast. Zach moved the pan and added another piece of broken branch to the fire. He would not be able to do that much longer. He was almost to Indian territory. He leaned back against a rock, tipped his hat low over his eyes and listened to the tethered packhorse grazing. Were the emigrants adding to their dwindling supplies by fishing? Had they settled on a site for their town yet? Had they started building their homes? Emma Allen's home? They'd better. If winter caught them…

He frowned, watched the fire flare as the branch broke apart and fell against the hot coals. How cold did it get in Oregon country anyway? Did they have blizzards? Or ice storms? If they did, and Emma Allen was still in her wagon…

Zach surged to his feet, yanked off his hat, ran his hand through his hair and tugged his hat back on. The sun was setting, hiding its face behind the tall mountain peaks, shooting warm, red-and-gold streaks into the western sky. He should get his bedroll. He turned, faced east. The sky was a cold gray with black encroaching along the far edge. He stood and watched the sky growing darker by the minute, feeling the cold seeping into his heart and spirit.

What was he doing? Why was he riding toward that darkness? There was nothing for him there. There was no excitement, no anticipation to this journey. He had been forcing himself to go on each day. His dream of building a trading post, then roaming the mountains free and unfettered was as cold as that eastern sky. That life had no appeal for him now. Everything he wanted was back at the wagon train, wrapped up in one feisty, slender, blond-haired, brown-eyed woman. Somehow, somewhere along the way on their journey west he had fallen in love with Emma Allen.

But what was he to do about it? She was a doctor and he had withstood her every request, effectively destroying any personal regard she might have held for him. Of course, he was a soldier. And if there was one thing he knew how to do, it was to win a battle...

Chapter Nineteen

"I got me a bad hurt, Dr. Emma!"

Emma set aside her writing desk, rose and peered over the side of the driver's box. Gabe Lewis looked up at her and held out a bloody forearm for her inspection. David was at his side, as always. The boys could have been twins but for their age difference. Both had black curly hair, dark blue eyes and grins that made you want to hug them, no matter what mischief they had been up to. She nodded and stepped back. "Perhaps you had better come up here and let me look at your arm."

Gabe flashed one of those wicked grins at David and both boys charged for the wagon tongue, Gabe a half step ahead. Before she could even turn around he was scrambling over the front board into the box. Obviously, the wound was not causing him great pain. He inched toward her, making room in the box for his brother. She planted her feet more firmly and motioned David onto the seat.

The five-year-old hopped up to the spot she indicated, then dropped to his knees, peering at her lap desk. "What's this thing?"

"It is a lap desk."

Gabe turned and looked at it. "What's it for?"

"It is for writing letters and other things. Such as accounts and party invitations."

Gabe stretched out his hand to touch it, stopped and put his hand behind his back instead. "That what you was doin' when we come?"

His voice reflected the wonder in his eyes. Her heart squeezed. She should have thought— "Yes. I was writing a letter to my brother. He lives in Philadelphia." *Perhaps she could send one of the men to the mission to get a few slates and readers...*

"That one of them big, back East cities with people crowded all over one another I heard about?"

Her lips twitched at his description, but she managed to stem the smile. "Yes. Philadelphia is a very large, important city. It is where the Declaration of Independence was signed."

Both boys frowned, swiveled their heads in her direction, their eyes alight with curiosity. "What's that?"

William, my dear brother, how you would love this moment. She sought for an explanation they would understand. "Well...a 'declaration' is when you state something very firmly."

"Like Ma telling Pa he ain't goin' to smoke his nasty-smelling pipe in her clean wagon?"

So that was why Joseph Lewis sat outside by the fire alone at night! Emma coughed to control the laughter bubbling up into her throat at Gabe's example. "Yes. That is correct." The boy's face lit up as if she had given him a piece of candy. She smiled down at him. "And 'independence' is—" *Oh, my. This could be dangerous, heady information for a seven-year-old.* "—it is when one is *old* enough and *wise* enough to manage one's own affairs."

The boys looked at one another, gave sober, sage nods. "Like Pa tellin' Ma he'll have the say of where he smokes his pipe."

Oh dear. Emma cleared her throat. "Let me see your arm, Gabe." It was covered in both fresh and drying blood. "I shall have to cleanse that before I can see what harm has been done." She picked up the lap desk. "Sit down. I will get my things."

A conspiratorial look flashed between the boys. Gabe grinned and plunked himself down on the seat. *What was that look about?* Emma tied the canvas flaps back, set the desk on the red box, slid it out of the way and climbed inside.

Gabe twisted around, perched on his knees on the seat and looked at her. "Are ya gonna give me some of that sleepin' stuff an' stitch me up like ya did Daniel?"

Ah! So that was it. "I will not know if your wound requires me to put you to sleep while I make the stitches until I clean the blood away. I will make my diagnosis after I see the wound." She bit down on her lower lip to keep from laughing and dipped water out of the keg into the washbowl. Now to teach these little schemers that doctoring was not for fun. She set the desk aside, opened the red box and removed a bottle of alcohol, the shallow bowl, her suturing equipment and a roll of clean, narrow cloth bandages. She placed them all in full view on one end of the red box, then donned her doctor's apron, tugged the cork from the bottle of alcohol and splashed a little into the water, enough to cleanse with only a little sting. She wanted to teach him a lesson, not torture him. "I believe I am ready now."

Gabe did not look quite so happy about the situation as he had a few moments ago. She fixed a sober look on her face, tossed in a clean rag and handed him the washbowl. He scooted back off the seat out of her way and she climbed outside, took the bowl. "Sit down, Gabe."

The boy swallowed hard, did as she bid. David's eyes looked wider, rounder…scared. She wanted to hug him. Instead, she placed the bowl on the seat beside Gabe, squeezed out the cloth and began to gently clean away the dried blood. It was only a surface abrasion. With bits of bark clinging to it.

"You have been climbing trees again." One glance at his sheepish face told her she had made a correct diagnosis. It was also the most likely reason he had come to her, instead of going to his mother, who was continually warning the boys to stay out of trees. He did not want to give her proof of her warnings. She was quite sure the "being put to sleep" idea was an afterthought. She rinsed the rag and began again. What would it be like to have sons like these? Adorable boys, full of curiosity and energy, that explored the world with such enjoyment and zest. Zachary Thatcher would father such sons.

The thought brought heat rushing to her cheeks, tears welling into her eyes. She blinked the tears away and continued her work. She would never know if that were true. Zachary Thatcher wanted only to be free of all entanglements. Most of all he wanted to be free of *her,* and her stubborn insistence on having her advice for her patients obeyed. He had been gone almost three weeks. Had he reached his valley?

She fixed a smile on her face and looked up at her young patient. "This will not need to be stitched, Gabe. It will heal fine if you will only keep it nice and clean." She dropped the cloth into the water, spread some salve on the scrape and wound Gabe's arm with the clean bandage.

A good doctor puts his patients first, before his own wants or needs.

How many times had she heard Papa Doc say those words? How many times had *she* said them? Sincerely, but blithely said them. She tied off the bandage and patted Gabe's hand. "I am finished. You may go now. But you come back if your arm turns red or starts to hurt you. Promise?"

He grinned up at her, nodded then climbed over the side of the driver's box, dropped to the ground and ran off. David followed.

She lifted her hand and rubbed to try and ease the pressure in her chest, but there was nothing she could do to make it stop. It was her heart that hurt. And only having Zachary Thatcher's love could stop the ache. Zachary Thatcher...who was lost to her because of her calling to be a doctor. She threw out the bloody water, pushed the bowl through the opening and climbed inside to take care of her things. Tears slipped down her cheeks as she went down on her knees, opened the red box and placed the alcohol and her suturing equipment inside. She stared at all the bottles and crocks and herbs and bandages, then slowly closed the lid, sat back on her heels and covered her face with her hands.

"I did not know, Lord." The hot tears ran down her fingers, mixed with the soft sobs, the warm, hesitant breath carrying her words, and dripped off her wrists onto the red wool covering her lap. "I truly did not know how much being a doctor could cost...until now."

"I cannot thank you enough, Mr. Thatcher, for your consideration in taking the household furnishings and the apple seedlings off of my hands. I have no desire to stay in this wretched backwoods country without Mr. Canfield. Indeed, I had no desire to come here at all. But Mr. Canfield fancied himself a nurseryman of great talent. A woman's lot is a hard one." The Widow Canfield sniffed delicately into her embroidered lace handkerchief, stepped closer and looked up at him from beneath her lashes. An extremely coy look from a woman so recently bereaved.

Zach took a step back and gave a small, polite bow. "I am sure it is the Lord's hand that has made your need to leave Oregon country, and my need to stay here, meet in such a fortuitous way, Widow Canfield. I wish you a safe and pleasant journey." He turned away from the cloying woman and gripped the hand of the big, white-haired man walking with them toward the ship waiting on the Columbia River. "And to you, sir, I offer my sincere thanks for agreeing to store the furnishings here at Fort Vancouver until my home is built. I give you my word it will be a matter of a few months only."

"'Tis not a problem, Mr. Thatcher. There is no need to be rushing the building. We have plenty of room here for storage of such items." The chief factor of the fort lifted a big hand and clapped Zach's shoulder. "Welcome again, to Oregon country. I'll look forward to hearing how those apple trees fare, when next you come to visit."

"I shall do all in my power to make that report an excellent one, sir."

Zach turned and headed for the barn, his steps long and eager. All he had set out to do had been accomplished. And without traveling all the way to Oregon City as he had thought would be necessary. He shook his head, smiled. *Those apple seedlings...* A turn he had not planned or expected. Surely God was blessing his endeavor. He entered the dusty, dusky barn and marched to the far stalls.

Comanche neighed, bunched his shoulders and hopped then lowered his head and kicked the back wall of the stall.

Zach stepped to the door, reached across and scratched under Comanche's dark forelock. "I know, boy. I'm sorry I had to put you in here. Let me get this travois packed and we will be on our way."

The roan whickered his displeasure. Tossed his head and pawed at the door with a front hoof. "At ease, Comanche!" Zach gave him a last pat, stepped to the back wall and knelt down to load the apple tree seedlings onto the piece of canvas stretched between the two long poles leaning against the wall.

He pulled the first crate toward him and carefully lifted out the fragile seedlings to pile them on the travois. Each had a narrow blue ribbon tied around them. The corresponding blue crate was labeled Sheepnose. He grouped them together and reached for the red crate labeled Winesap. The last group had green ribbons on them and were labeled Pippen. They might better have said Blackfeet, Sioux and Comanche. He would have understood that.

He stood, moved to the corner and picked up the large piece of burlap he had placed there last night. He spread it overtop the apple seedlings and tied it in place with leather thongs to hold the seedlings secure on the long ride, then stared at his handiwork. Was that the right thing to do? Would it hurt to cover them? It was the only way he could think of to protect them. He removed his hat, shoved his hand through his hair and scowled down at the bundled sprigs. "I sure hope I'm right and this is Your plan for me, Lord, because I know nothing about growing apples!"

He tugged his hat back on, leaned down to pick up his packs and noticed a small, green-covered book in the blue crate. He picked it up, thumbed through it and grinned. It was full of information about growing apples, written in a neat, careful hand. Seemed as if everything was working out fine. He chuckled, a low, confident sound that came from deep in his chest, lifted the book toward the ceiling and snapped off a sharp salute. "I hear You, Lord."

He stood there for a moment in the quiet, then tucked the book in one of the packs and carried them to the opposite stall to load on the packhorse. He had his battle plan and his weapons. And he was certain now the Lord was blessing his efforts. He couldn't wait to get back and lay siege to Emma Allen's heart!

Emma threw off the covers, sat up and pulled the quilt around her. She could not sleep. She felt hemmed in, restless. How wonderful it would be to have someone to talk to when worry stole your sleep, and your peace. She stood and stepped to the front of the wagon, listened for any unusual sounds. Anything that might indicate danger. All she could hear was the river's whisper as it brushed along its banks on its way. She untied the end flaps, peeked outside. Bright moonlight lit the landscape, turned the distant mountains silver.

She gathered up the dragging edge of the quilt and crawled outside to sit on the driver's seat. The air was frosty. It nipped at her cheeks, her ears and toes. She drew her feet back under the quilt's protection, folded the top edge high on the back of her neck, then grabbed both front edges and tucked her covered hands under her chin. They were well into October now. How long before winter would arrive? How would it come? With snowstorms? Ice storms? Or would it be gray and overcast and soak them with frigid rain? It was strange not to know what sort of weather to expect.

She lifted her chin, blew out a long breath and watched the small gray cloud appear. The air touched its cold fingers to her exposed throat. She shivered, tucked her chin back into its warm spot between her covered, fisted hands and looked toward the mountains.

The highest peaks were white with snow. Was it so deep it had closed off those narrow passes? Not that it mattered. She knew he wasn't up there. He would have traveled beyond that distance long ago. Still, she liked to look at the mountains. It made her feel close to him. Fear clutched at her heart. She hoped he had an extra blanket.

* * *

It was done. Zach smoothed the rough edges where his knife had gouged the board, blew off the tiny bits of wood and slowly ran his hand over the surface to test for slivers. There was no roughness anywhere. He turned the board this way and that studying his work in the moonlight, then smiled and shoved the board in his saddlebag. Time to sleep.

A sharp yank on the ties freed his groundsheet and blanket. He stretched out and spread the cover over his legs. Cold air kissed his cheek. He frowned, looked up at the streaming moonlight. It was a clear night with a chill in the air. It could get down to a frost level before morning. He shoved off the blanket and put more wood on the fire, gathered up a few more pieces littering the ground under a nearby tree and carried them back to have close at hand. He didn't want anything happening to those apple seedlings. He took hold of the double poles and pulled until the loaded end was near the fire. That should protect them.

He stretched out again, linked his hands behind his head and stared up at the sky. Where were the wagons? If he knew where Hargrove and the others had located their town, he could figure the best place to plant his orchard. And build the cabin. A nice one with two rooms, a lean-to kitchen and a loft. And a stone milk house. That would do for a start. He would build her whatever she wanted later on. There was plenty of timber on the mountains. And rocks for chimneys.

A frown drew his brows together. Would it be good enough? She was from Philadelphia. And judging from her clothes, and her sister's and the way her brother had outfitted his wagons, they were wealthy. What if she refused him?

He scowled, flopped onto his side and closed his eyes. That was enough of thinking. No soldier should ever go into battle thinking he was going to be defeated. He would win Emma Allen's heart. Nothing less was acceptable.

Chapter Twenty

Emma put her plate, cup and flatware in the small chest, tossed out the dishwater and set the small tub back on the shelf that had held the water barrel. That item, no longer needed with the river only a few steps away, had been upturned to use as a "table." She dipped her fingertips into the small crock beside the chest on the shelf and rubbed the soothing balm into her hands, then lifted them and stroked them over her cheeks. The hint of lavender scent made her smile. In her next letter she would ask Papa Doc to send at least a dozen crocks of the hand balm with William—if he decided to come to Oregon country next year.

She frowned at the rush of hope and excitement that thought caused her, removed her long apron and hung it on the nail by the shelf. She had not yet overcome her selfishness in wanting her brother to make that dangerous journey; the loneliness made it difficult. And it was harder than ever with Annie gone to teach at the Banning Mission and the emigrants all spread out on their selected parcels of land. She had become accustomed to having the children racing around the wagons playing games and getting into mischief, and now they had new homes and this vast land to explore. And the women—

Stop! You are being pathetic. Emma made a wry face and walked to the fire to place the iron pan in which she had cooked the piece of beef that, along with yesterday's cold biscuit, constituted her supper, onto the hot coals to clean. One small piece of beef cooked by herself, *for* herself, on her own small fire *was* pathetic.

The sound of children's laughter floated to her from the direction of the Lewis family's new home. No doubt Gabe and David were up to some high jinks. If so, there was a good chance she would see them soon. They were her most frequent patients. She laughed, grabbed her wrap off the sideboard of the driver's seat and walked beyond the front of her wagon toward the plains so she could see beyond the Hargrove and Swinton homes to where the river emerged from the rolling hills. Joseph Lewis had decided to build there so the fall of water coming out of the hills would drive the blades of his sawmill.

She walked a few steps farther and peered through the dimming light. Yes, his wagon was standing outside their front door, waiting for tomorrow's leave-taking. What a blessing it would be for everyone if he found the ship carrying his saw blades had arrived when he reached Oregon City. Everyone was hoping and praying it would prove to be so. They were all eager to have cut boards available to finish their homes. They were using split logs now for the roofs. She frowned and pulled her wrap closer about her against the growing chill. It made her wince every time she saw them lifting those heavy logs into place. If one of those ropes broke—

She shuddered and shifted her gaze higher. Black dots that were the emigrants' oxen, mules and horses grazed on the rolling hills under the watchful eyes of the night guards. It would not be so when barns were erected.

She shook her head and looked again toward the river. Change had come so rapidly. The men had divided into crews, some to fell trees on the mountains and cut them to the needed lengths, others to haul them to town and still more to trim and notch them. All worked together to raise the houses. Even the children, who were so eager to help, had been given tasks according to their abilities. She had written a long and careful accounting of the building to William, had even drawn a map of the homes' locations.

The first, up against the rolling hills, was the Lundquist farm. Soon to be two farms when Garth's betrothed arrived next year. And standing on the riverbank, the Lewis home and the spot where the sawmill would soon stand marked by wooden stakes. Next—she shifted her gaze down the silvery ribbon of water—the Applegates' home and cornerstones for the future mill. And then—again, a short distance downriver—the Fentons' home and blacksmith shop.

Her gaze drifted over the empty space left for a schoolhouse and any businesses that might come to their town, skimmed over the Swintons' combination home and general store, the Hargroves' combined home and bank, and stopped on her wagon. Beyond that, at a distance too far to see in the deepening dusk, was the Fletcher farm. And then the Suttons' and Murrays'. Those three families were still in wagons. But the Fletcher cabin was to be raised tomorrow.

She glanced up at the darkening sky, rubbed her chilled hands together and walked back to light her lantern. She knew how now, thanks to Mr. Thatcher. She pushed the thought of him away, placed the end of a long, slender twig against the dying coals of her fire, blew gently and when it burst into flame, held it to the wick in the lamp. She adjusted the flame, set her clean iron pan up on the surrounding wall of stone and rose.

A tiny thrill of anticipation zinged through her. This was where her home and doctor's office would be. Soon. After the homes of the Fletchers and Suttons and Murrays. She had insisted her home be the last one built. She did not have a husband or children to make a home for, and the wagon was sufficient for a woman alone, though it would be wonderful to have walls and—

A slow rhythm, so scarce she wasn't sure she heard it, echoed faintly through the night. Horse hoofs. More than one perhaps... *How far away?*

Her heart lurched. She held the lantern close, spun down the wick to extinguish the flame and turned toward the west, every fiber of her being straining to detect the sound she had heard in the distance. It came again, the sound of hoofs striking against rock. Slow, steady... Closer now. Indians?

Her mouth went dry. The dark pressed in on her. She pivoted and swept her gaze toward the emigrants' homes. Without glass windows for candle or lamplight to shine through, they were invisible in the dark. Her fire! Had the stones hidden it from view? She snatched up the small hoe and dragged dead ashes over the glowing coals.

The hoofbeats had stopped. She cast a longing glance toward the Hargroves' log cabin, torn between her desire to run to them for safety, and her need to stay outside and listen so she could give warning should danger come their way. Would any hear her cry? She tightened her grip on the iron hoe and inched her way back toward her wagon. She would go and alert John Hargrove. But if danger rode at her out of the night, she wanted William's pistol in her hand.

Zach slipped from the saddle, let Comanche's reins dangle to the ground then led the packhorse to the river and tethered him to a tree. That was lantern light he had seen ahead. He was sure of it, though it had been quickly extinguished. He shoved the travois beneath the low, feathery branches of a pine for protection, lifted off the packs and hurried back to Comanche. A quick dip into his saddlebags produced his moccasins. He tugged off his boots, laid them across his saddle and laced the moccasins on.

Comanche turned his head and nudged him in the chest.

"Sorry, boy, but I can't let you roam until I know what's out there." He gave the strong shoulder a commiserating pat and jogged off into the night, following the river.

The smell of a smoldering fire led him to them. He stared across the river at the wagon cover, a leaden gray in the lightless night. The log cabin black beside it. And there was another. He'd found them.

He stomped down the impulse to splash across the river, find Emma Allen and kiss her senseless. That day would come. First, he had to show her that his opposition to her advice on the trail was of necessity, not desire. He had to convince the woman of his respectful regard for her position as a physician. Because any man that wanted to marry Emma Allen had to court the doctor, too. That much he knew for a certainty. The woman was a she-bear when it came to fighting for her patients. It was one of the reasons he loved her. He had to convince her of that. And he would start tomorrow. He grinned, turned and loped back the way he had come.

Emma dried her face, smoothed on some cream and scowled at herself in the small mirror. She had made a fool of herself last night, rushing to the Hargroves' with a pistol in her hand and warning of "hoofbeats" in the night. Mr. Hargrove had warned the others and set guards, but it had all come to naught. And now John Hargrove thought her "hysterical." And several of the men thought the "hoofbeats" she heard were only in her imagination.

Emma sighed, brushed a tendril of hair back off her forehead and pulled her Augusta spencer on over her red wool dress. The velvet fabric gave warmth without the bother of a wrap. And she wanted to look her most sensible and efficient after last night's disaster. The frown reappeared in the mirror. She shoved the mirror back in the pocket on the canvas cover and climbed from the wagon. She had been *sure* she heard hoofbeats!

Like now.

Emma turned toward the sound, stared through the

morning mist along the river at the imposing figure atop a roan with distinctive spots on its hindquarters. Her heart stopped, lurched into a wildly erratic beat.

Mr. Thatcher had returned.

No. That could not be. Perhaps she *was* imagining things. She closed her eyes, took a deep breath and opened them again. The man wore a fringed buckskin shirt. And he was leading a packhorse. But there was no mistaking that erect posture and those broad shoulders. It was Zachary Thatcher.

He rode closer, began to wend his way through the trees along the river.

Emma pressed her hand over the throbbing pulse at the base of her throat and stepped out of sight behind her wagon. She couldn't let him see her. Not like this. Not while she was so…undone.

He stopped, tethered the packhorse to a tree branch then guided Comanche into the river. Water splashed around the big roan's hoofs, rose to his knees, his belly then dropped again. Man and horse surged up onto the bank, headed her way. She stood frozen, willing Zachary Thatcher to not see her, begging God to blind his eyes to her presence. He looked straight at her, impaled her on the gaze of those bright blue eyes that peered out from beneath his broad-brimmed hat. Eyes that looked straight at a person, noticed everything about her— She squared her shoulders, lifted her chin.

He stopped, smiled. "We meet again, Miss Allen. Could you tell me where I might find Mr. Hargrove?"

She nodded, found her voice. "That is his cabin next door."

He dipped his head, touched the brim of his hat and rode off.

She sagged against the wagon and watched until he disappeared around the corner of the Hargrove's cabin.

"Haw! Haw!" A whip cracked, cracked again.

Matthew Hargrove! The first load of logs for the Fletchers' cabin was on its way. And she had not even started her cook fire. She pushed away from the wagon, walked to the fire and used the hoe to scrape the ashes off the banked coals. A few handfuls of dry pine bark and some gentle blowing brought flames leaping to life. She added some small chunks of wood from her pile and went to the wagon to get the things she needed to start a pot of soup.

Zach stood in the doorway of the Hargrove cabin and watched the wagon come. He looked over his shoulder at John Hargrove who was pulling papers from a small chest. "Matthew is coming with a load of logs." He couldn't resist the temptation to bait him a bit. "You adding on to this cabin already?"

"No, no." Hargrove shook his head and spread one of the papers out on the top of a dresser. "Those logs are for the Fletcher cabin. He's downriver. Figures the plains will be good for farming. The Suttons and Murrays are downriver, too."

Zach nodded, turned to face the dim interior of the cabin. "And Miss Allen's cabin? Will she be next to you? Where her wagon now sits?"

"That's right. Though I wish it were not! I dislike hysterical women." The older man smoothed out the creases in the paper. "Now here—"

"Hysterical?" Zach frowned. The word had come out a bit too sharp. Lydia Hargrove had stopped making biscuits and looked at him. He slouched back against the wall.

"Yes. As hysterical as I've ever seen!" John Hargrove's gray, bushy eyebrows drew together in a deep frown. "Last night, she came running over here in the middle of the night carrying a pistol and raving about some imagined 'hoofbeats' she heard coming our way. Got everyone stirred up."

"It was not the middle of the night, Hargrove." Zach gave him a cold look. He did not care for men who exaggerated the truth. "And it was not 'hysteria.' It was me."

"You!"

"That's right. I camped a short way downriver last night. But even if it hadn't been me, Miss Allen did the wise thing in raising an alarm. Had it been someone bent on evil, delay could have brought disaster. It's better to lose sleep than your scalp." He gestured toward the dresser. "Is that the map you were looking for?"

"Yes. If you will show me the land you are interested in, I'll mark it off as taken."

Zach nodded, strode to the dresser, looked at the map and pointed. "That's the section I want." *The one behind Emma Allen's lot. Where she will see me every day.*

"Across the river?"

"That's right. From this bend in the river all the way to the Blue Mountains."

The banker gave him a sharp look. "That's a big parcel, Thatcher."

"I've got big plans, Hargrove. Mark it as taken."

* * *

"The men got the Fletcher cabin well started today."

Emma glanced over at Lydia and nodded. She didn't feel like chatting. She was exhausted from being around Zachary Thatcher. She had tried her best to avoid him, but every time she carried water to the working men, he called for a drink. And he had been in her line when she had ladled out her soup. And...and every time she saw him or heard his voice she tried to think why he had returned. And to prepare herself for his leaving. Her breath caught. He could not possibly be intending to cross those mountains now, could he? Not after all the warnings he had given them about the snows closing the mountain passes and trapping you— Is that why he had that packhorse and that—that *trundling* thing it was pulling? Were all those supplies in case—

"Emma! I asked you a question."

She stopped, looked at Lydia. "I beg your pardon. I—"

"Was not listening to a word I said." Lydia gave her a searching look. "Are you feeling all right, Emma?"

"I am perfectly fine. Only a little weary." She turned away from Lydia's perusal and started walking. "What was your question?"

"I want to know if you will come by in the morning and help me make dried apple dumplings for tomorrow's meal for the men? Olga and Hannah are making stew."

Tomorrow. How would she face tomorrow? If he were here, it would be torture to be around him. And if he were gone— Yes. It would be easier if he were gone. The emptiness would be unbearable. But at least she would not have to pretend she did not love him. She looked down to hide her face from Lydia, stared at her empty hands and flexed her fingers. He had offered to carry her kettle home for her, and when she had made an excuse to linger, he had smiled and taken it from her anyway. Oh, yes. It would be much easier if Mr. Thatcher were gone tomorrow.

"Of course I shall help you, Lydia. I will come by first thing in the morning." She fixed a bright smile on her face, lifted her hand in farewell and walked to her wagon. She climbed to the driver's seat and went inside. She did not want to see where he had put her kettle. She did not want to look across the river to see if he was still there. She *would* not!

Her resolve lasted until she had prepared for bed. By then she could resist no longer. She turned the lamp down low, braved the cold to open the back flaps a crack and peered out. There was enough moonlight to spot the grazing horses immediately. And then she saw him. What was he— He was digging for something. It looked as if there was a *hole*—

He stopped, leaned on the shovel and looked her way.

She jerked her head back and snapped the flaps closed. Surely he had not seen that tiny crack of light? But then, with that penetrating gaze of his bright blue eyes, perhaps he had. She dared not look out again.

She shivered her way to the bed and crawled under the covers. He was not gone. She sighed and closed her eyes. *Almighty God, please exchange my weakness for Your strength. Please help me to be strong and hide my love for Mr. Thatcher if he is still here tomorrow. Or help me to accept the emptiness that will be in my heart if he is gone. Amen.*

* * *

Zach stared at the wagon cover. The slit of lamplight was gone. She had closed the flaps up tight. Had it been an accident they had been open a crack? Or had she been looking out? At him? He smiled and turned back to his digging. There was no way he could know for certain. But the possibility that his plan was working gave him pleasure enough to warm his heart all night. If Emma Allen was curious enough to spy and try and see what he was doing, she must care about him. At least a little. He would do his best to make her curiosity and her caring grow.

Chapter Twenty-One

Her cheeks and nose were red from the cold. Emma flexed the stiffness from her fingers, pushed the combs into her hair then tied the length of dark blue ribbon around the base of the thick coil at the crown of her head to hold the tendrils from escaping. Her hands shook from the shivers coursing through her as she put away the hairbrush and mirror. The nights had been growing steadily colder, but last night had been frigid! No matter how many blankets she had piled on, she could not get truly warm. How she had longed for the fireplace that graced her bedroom at home in Philadelphia!

She frowned and drew her thoughts away from the past. She must look to the future. She would have her cabin soon. There would be no cold air slipping beneath a canvas cover to nip at her exposed skin then. No floors from which the cold rose to chill her limbs in spite of the extra wool petticoat she wore. She would have a fireplace that would warm her as she performed her morning toilette, and warm water always ready on the hearth.

She glanced at the water in the washbowl, shivered at the memory of its frosty touch. There had not been ice on the water in the keg, only the thin skin promise of the winter yet to come. She must remember to write and warn William and Caroline of the weather. If her ink wasn't frozen!

She stared in disgust at the small crock she had opened. Her hand balm was hard. She loosened a bit with the tip of her scissors, then held it in her palm to soften before she rubbed it in. Her Augusta spencer added warmth her blue wool dress alone could not provide. But even it was not enough this morning. She put on her long apron, then lifted her fur-trimmed wool cloak out of a dresser drawer and swirled it around her shoulders, tugged the hood in place. The fur lining of the hood felt wonderful against her cold ears and cheeks.

She reached up to the lamp that dangled from a hook in one of the hickory ribs that supported the wagon cover and extinguished the flame, then stepped to the front of the wagon and untied the canvas flaps. Cold air rushed at her. She glanced at the Hargroves' chimney. There was smoke rising like a gray column toward the lightening sky. She secured the flaps, climbed from the wagon and hurried toward the warmth of their cabin.

Not once did she allow herself to look across the river. She reached to pull aside the blanket that served as the Hargroves' door, heard a deep, rich voice and jerked her hand back. *He was there.* She spun about to go back to her wagon.

Who shall abide in the Lord's tabernacle, children? He that sweareth to his own hurt and changeth not. If you make a promise, you must keep it.

Lydia was expecting her. Emma clenched her hands and gritted her teeth. Why had her mother been so diligent in teaching them God's Word? Why could she not ignore it? She took a deep breath, turned back and stepped inside. The fire was burning. But it was the look in Zachary Thatcher's eyes as he looked her way and rose to his feet that brought warmth to her. She was suddenly thankful for the cold that had turned her cheeks red. It would mask the blush that was making them burn. She lifted her chin.

"Come in, Emma. I have already started soaking the apples."

"Coming, Lydia." She glanced at John Hargrove, who, as usual, did not bother to hide his displeasure at her coming. "Forgive me if I interrupted your conversation." She stepped into the room, gave a polite nod of greeting in Zachary Thatcher's direction and removed her cloak. She hung it over the back of Lydia's rocking chair and joined her friend. "What shall I do, Lydia?"

"You can help me make the dough to wrap the apples in." The older woman dumped some flour in a large crockery bowl and reached for the saleratus. "That other bowl is for you to use."

"—Fletcher cabin will be finished today, Thatcher. It's taking longer because it's a big one. The Sutton and Mur—"

"Make the dough the same as for biscuits, Emma. Only use a bit more lard."

She nodded, turned her back toward the men and dumped some flour in the bowl, trying not to pay attention to their conversation, but unable to avoid hearing bits and snatches of it in the close quarters of the room.

"—my guess is six or seven days. We can start on yours—"

Her hand jerked. *"Yours?"* The word escaped. There was no choice but to turn and face him. "I could not help but overhear, Mr. Thatcher—though I believe my ears deceive me. I thought I heard Mr. Hargrove say you were going to build a cabin. A strange occupation for a man who wants no *fetters*."

His gaze held hers. "As is making biscuits for a doctor, Miss Allen."

"You've got a mite too much saleratus in there, Emma."

She turned around, saw Lydia's curious gaze and looked down. "Yes. I—it was an accident." She picked up a spoon and scooped out some of the saleratus to save for the next batch of dough. Zachary Thatcher's deep voice rumbled in the background. She abandoned politeness and tilted her head to better hear.

"I'm not sure I want—"

"We'll be rolling it out thin."

Oh, Lydia, please do not talk!

Lydia grabbed a handful of flour, sprinkled it on the table, then scraped the dough out of her bowl on top of it. "Joseph Lewis made this table out of our wagon's tailboard and some sturdy pine limbs. You should have him make one for you when you are in your cabin, Emma. It works fine."

"—to Fletcher's and start working." Zachary Thatcher's voice raised. "I will look forward to eating some of those apple dumplings at supper, ladies." There was a soft swish and a draft of cold air as he lifted the blanket and stepped outside.

The conversation was over, and still she did not know

if he would stay or go. He had not answered her query. She dusted the table with flour, dumped out her dough, made a fist and thumped it—hard.

She was so beautiful. His heart had almost stopped when he looked up and saw her standing there in that fur-lined cloak. Zach frowned, wrapped the rope around the split log and tied it off. He had almost blurted out the truth right then. But he had caught himself in time. Still… "Haul away!" He stepped to the side and prepared to steady the log as Nathan Fenton urged the oxen to pull. Something of what he was feeling must have shown on his face the way her eyes had widened, and that proud little chin of hers had lifted. She had been more cool than normal to him after that. Still, she was curious as to his intent. Perhaps more than curious. He had seen her back stiffen when Hargrove mentioned him building a cabin. And he had seen the flash of frustration in her eyes when he evaded answering her query. But there had been a challenge in her question— and hurt. It was not time to declare himself openly. He would continue working his plan until— "Whoa! That's far enough, Nathan!"

Zach slid out on the ridge beam, yanked on the rope end to undo the knot and dropped the rope to the ground. It took a little maneuvering but he finally got in position to wrap his arm about the half log and lift the end enough he could slide it into the notch. That was the last one. They could put the roof planks on now. Then tomorrow they could start building the Sutton cabin. It could not be soon enough for him.

He slid back off the ridge beam and went hand over

hand down the climbing rope to help get the first roof plank in place. Tonight, he would finish planting his apple seedlings. And tomorrow night he would show her he was a man with a future.

"Is there something wrong, Emma?"

"Wrong?" Emma lifted the last apple dumpling in the pan onto the large ironstone platter and shook her head. "No. There is nothing wrong. Why do you ask?"

"You seem quiet, but…touchy." Lydia fixed an assessing gaze on her. "Like you were when you were around Mr. Thatcher yesterday."

"Why, that is—" She looked at Lydia's raised eyebrows and gave a little laugh. She could not let her guess how she truly felt about Zachary Thatcher. She did not care to be an object of pity. "All right, I confess. I find Mr. Thatcher's low opinion of me…annoying." She pushed the emptied pan to Lydia's side to be refilled with the raw dumplings they had made and piled in the middle of the table. Now for another. She grabbed the hem of her long apron, leaned down and removed the lid from another pan on the hearth to see if the dumplings were done.

"Hmm. He's mighty quick to speak up for you for someone who holds you in low regard."

"Whatever are you talking about?"

"I'm talking about yesterday, when John named you 'hysterical' to Mr. Thatcher. He told him how you come runnin' over here in the middle of the night carryin' a pistol and ravin' about imagined 'hoofbeats' and gettin' everyone all stirred up."

Emma drew up straight as an arrow and looked at the older woman. "It was *not* the middle of the night!"

Lydia grinned. "That's what Mr. Thatcher told John. And he told him you weren't hysterical either." She nestled the raw dumplings close together in the pan, poured in a bit of boiling water from her iron teapot. "He said it was him you heard riding in. And that you were wise to raise an alarm, 'cause it was better to lose sleep than to lose your scalp." The lid of the iron spider clanged against the rim of the pan.

Emma stared at her, the dumplings she'd been checking forgotten. "He said I was wise?" She frowned when the older woman smiled and nodded. "Well, I cannot imagine *why*. He certainly did not think I was wise when we were coming west! He opposed my every request for my patients."

Lydia nodded, glanced down. "The dumplings in that pan done?"

Emma flushed, put down the lid she held and lifted the pan to the table. "It was obvious that Mr. Thatcher shared most men's disdain for women doctors." The spoon clanged against the pan as she lifted out a dumpling to put on the platter.

"Or that he was only trying to do what we hired him to do, keep us all safe." Lydia raked a fresh batch of coals out onto the hearth, set the refilled spider on them and covered the lid with more coals. "If I recollect right, when little Jenny Lewis injured her head so severe you said the joltin' around of ridin' in a wagon would kill her, it was Mr. Thatcher that come up with the idea of that 'swing' bed that made it possible for her to ride without being hurt."

Emma stared at her. "I—I had not thought of it that way. I thought…"

"That Mr. Thatcher was fightin' you because of you bein' a woman doctor."

"Yes."

Lydia wrapped her apron hem around her hand, reached across the table and pulled the iron pan to her side of the table. "It appears to me, he respected your doctorin' skills so much he figured out a way to follow 'em and still move the wagons forward like needed to be done."

Could that be possible? Emma searched her memory, trying to find a flaw in that argument.

"Same as when baby Isaac come down with the measles, and Mr. Thatcher held that meetin' tellin' everyone about your idea for a movin' quarantine to keep people from gettin' sick." Lydia lifted a dumpling to the platter, scooped up another. "When Tom Swinton challenged your sayin' Isaac had measles when he didn't have spots, Mr. Thatcher told him that him and anyone else that didn't believe you had to leave the train and not come back. And he was right rigid about enforcing that movin' quarantine. Seems to me he wouldn't have done all that if he didn't respect your doctoring."

Yes, but the moving quarantine was because he would not stop as she—

"Seems to me, you two worked hand in hand to make that whole nasty situation come out right well."

Hand in hand. A sick feeling hit the pit of her stomach. *Had she been so angry and close-minded because of the way men sneered at her for being a doctor, she hadn't seen the truth?*

"You gonna let them dumplins burn?"

"What?" Emma looked down at the pan Lydia was refilling. *The dumplings!* "No. No, of course not." She whirled to the hearth, snatched hold of the end of her apron and lifted a lid from one of the pans.

Emma cut the pans of corn bread into generous squares, then placed the knife on the table and walked away. The preparation for today's supper was finished, and she needed to be alone.

She hurried up the path being worn into the grass-covered plain. By the time the Sutton and Murray cabins were finished, the wagon wheels and the people's footsteps would have turned the path into a road, one that sandwiched the cabins between it and the river. Already it had the look of a village.

Promise.

But perhaps not for her.

Tears stung her eyes. She blinked them away and hurried on to her wagon, went to the stone circle that held the banked coals. She needed the comfort and warmth of a fire to chase away the shivers that trembled through her.

Could she have been so wrong? Had she seen Zachary Thatcher's actions through the haze of past disdain and scorn, through the hurt of rejection? Had she unwittingly destroyed any personal regard he may have felt for her by her stubborn insistence on having her doctoring skills acknowledged? Had her calling as a doctor cost her the possibility of a shared love?

She went to her knees, heedless of the fine dusting of gray ash on the ground beneath her, and breathed the fire to life. She fed the flames wood until they leaped with unrestrained joy and threw sparks of celebration into the growing dusk.

She stared into the flames and shivered. What was she to do? Every time she saw Zachary Thatcher the ache in her heart grew more acute. And now, it seemed, he was going to stay in Promise. He was going to build his own cabin, on his own land.

I'll leave the founding of towns and empire building to Hargrove and Applegate and the others. It is these mountains that call to me. All I want is to be to be free and unfettered to roam them as I will.

She rose and looked across the river to the plain where his packhorse grazed, then turned and looked up at the rugged Blue Mountains. What had changed? Why had he returned? Why—

The thud of Comanche's hoofs against the ground warned her.

She closed her eyes and clenched her hands. There were miles and miles of river. Why must he cross here? She squared her shoulders, arranged her features into a cool, polite expression and turned.

He had dismounted and was standing behind her. So close. If she lifted her hand she could touch him. Her fingers twitched with the memory of clinging to his shirt when he saved her from sliding into the river, of the feel of his hand holding hers. Her heart raced with the knowledge of the warmth and strength of his arms holding her close. She swallowed the swelling lump in her throat and blinked her eyes.

Comanche gave a low nicker, stretched his nose toward her. She reached out and stroked his velvet muzzle, turned to slip her hand beneath his dark mane. *Bless you, Comanche. Bless you for giving me a reason to turn away.*

"He likes you. He's never been like this with anyone but me."

Zachary Thatcher's deep, rich voice flowed over her. She took a breath to steady her own. "He likes the oats and honey I fed him when—" *Oh dear!* She swallowed again. Took another breath. Kept her face turned toward Comanche's side. It didn't work. He walked around to Comanche's other side, rested his hand on the saddle. She could feel his gaze on her face. She did not dare look up.

"When what?"

"When you were ill."

"You did that?"

She nodded, dredged up a smidgen of courage and looked up at him. Her knees slacked with that odd weakness at the blue, smoky look in his eyes. She grabbed the edge of the saddle.

"Why?"

The word felt like a caress. "Because I—" She stopped, horrified by what had almost slipped out. She gave a small shrug. "You had told me Comanche grazed on his own, but always returned to you. I was responsible for your not being there. I wanted to give him a reason to keep coming back so he would be there if—when—you returned." *Dangerous ground. Do not speak of that time.* "The oats and honey were a bribe."

"I don't think the oats and honey are what brought him back. He let you pet him when we were getting water during that thunderstorm on the mountain."

She looked up, saw his eyes were darker still and jerked her gaze away. *Do not think about that day. Do not think about those moments—*

"He trusts you."

"I shall try to be worthy of his trust."

"You already are."

She could take no more. She had to stop this. Send him away. She drew on all of her professional training to mask her emotions. "Mr. Thatcher—"

"I gave him one of your apple dumplings."

She was so shocked by the rapid change of subject and tone she lifted her head and stared at him. He grinned. A slow, lopsided grin that had her clutching the edge of the saddle again.

"He liked it. So did I." He tipped his hat back, crossed his arms on the saddle and rested his chin on them, gazing down at her. "I didn't know you could cook like that."

"I learned."

He grinned.

She lifted her chin. "I did not know you could build log cabins like that."

His grin widened. "*I* learned."

She caught her breath, thrown off guard by this teasing, charming side of him she'd never seen before. "Mr. Thatcher—"

"I know how to carve things, too."

"I am certain that is very useful, but—"

"I made you a present."

"Me?" He had done it again. Thrown her completely off balance. She hoped her lack of equilibrium did not show.

He nodded and walked around Comanche to stand

beside her. He reached in his saddlebag, pulled out a good-size piece of wood and handed it to her. "For your cabin door."

Her fingertips felt ridges and grooves on the underside. She turned the board over.

Doctor Emma.

"Oh." Tears welled. She blinked and blinked, ran her fingertip over the letters, the vines that curved around each corner. "Thank you, Mr. Thatcher. I—I will treasure this always. But...I do not understand."

His fingers curved beneath her chin, lifted. She had nowhere to look but at him, unless she closed her eyes. Her heart lurched at the memory of what had happened the last time she had done that. She swallowed and met his gaze.

"We had some rough times over your patients on the journey here. I wanted you to know that I never doubted your doctoring skills...Dr. Emma." He leaned down, touched his lips to hers then turned, swung into the saddle and rode off.

She stood there staring after him, feeling the warmth of his mouth on hers, long after the sound of Comanche splashing through the river had faded away.

Emma washed and creamed her face and hands, brushed her teeth, then donned her rose-embroidered cotton nightdress and dressing gown. She removed the combs and brushed out her hair, let it fall free around her face and shoulders for warmth, then slid under the covers and picked up Zachary Thatcher's gift. Her movements were all slow and deliberate, because she felt brittle. As if a quick movement would make her break.

She ran her hand over the beautifully carved sign, then pulled it beneath the covers and hugged it to her chest. The question she had been asking herself since talking with Lydia this morning had been answered. Lydia was right. She was wrong. Zachary Thatcher had respected her as a doctor from the beginning. She held the proof of that in her hands. But what did that quick, gentle kiss mean? Was she wrong in her thinking there, also? Did he hold her in high regard as a woman, or not? Perhaps so. But that was not what she wanted from Zachary Thatcher. Not anymore. She wanted his love.

Heaviness settled over her, drove her deeper under the covers. But there was no place to hide from the pain. She had said yes when the emigrants asked her to be their doctor. She had "sworn to her own hurt." Because Zachary Thatcher did not return her love was not a reason to break her word. She would have to stay in Promise and pray she did not see him often.

God had answered her prayer. He had given her her dream. She simply had not realized what her dream would cost.

Chapter Twenty-Two

"Can you open your mouth and stick your tongue way out for me, Edward? Like this." Emma looked down at young Edward and stuck out her tongue and crossed her eyes.

Edward giggled and tried to mimic her. He broke into a barking cough, struggled to catch his breath. His eyes widened with fright. He began to wheeze.

"Let me help you sit up, Edward." She slid her arm beneath the little boy's shoulders and lifted him to a sitting position. "Now, do as I say. Breathe very… slowly…" She smiled and gently rubbed his back. He calmed. His breath came easier. "There, you see. You need not fight to breathe. You are all right. Now, let me put this pillow here—" she propped it against the wall "—and you lean back and rest."

She rose and smiled down at him. "I am going to give your mama some things that will help you feel better. I want you to do as she says." She walked to the front of the room.

"What is wrong with Edward, Dr. Emma?"

"He has the croup, Pamelia." She glanced back at the little boy. "He should improve in two or three days. Meantime, it is frightening for him because he feels he can't breathe. I want you to keep him calm and help him to relax when he has a coughing attack, as I did. Keep him sitting up, it makes it easier for him to breathe. And give him some sage and savory tea regularly. A warm poultice on his chest may help." She took a tighter grip on her bag. "His condition will worsen at night, so be prepared by resting during the day. I do not want you becoming ill. The croup is very contagious, so please do not let others come to see him, especially children. And wash your hands every time you take care of him."

"I will do as you say, Dr. Emma." Pamelia smiled. "And this time Thomas told me he will come to your office and pay your fee." She laughed. "I believe that means your wagon."

Emma smiled. "For a few more days. They are cutting the logs for my cabin today." She stepped to the blanket that covered the doorway. "Send Thomas for me if you are concerned for Edward."

"Yes. Thank you for coming, Dr. Emma."

She nodded, swept the blanket aside and stepped out into the sunshine. It was a lovely day, surprisingly warm after the cold weather they had suffered. She hoped it lasted until her cabin was built. And her fireplace. Carl Sutton and Luke Murray were adding fireplaces to the cabins that were being raised so quickly. The Hargroves' fireplace had been the first.

She glanced at the wide stone base that tapered upward to the narrow chimney as she walked by the Hargroves' cabin. Their fireplace was lovely and warm on cold days. She wanted one like it. And a table made from her tailgate. She would ask Joseph Lewis to make her one the next time she saw him. She would need a good, sturdy table for any operations. And a cupboard to hold her medical supplies. And a door. She was tired of canvas flaps and blankets. Could Joseph make her a door from the wood of the wagon? And perhaps shutters for windows? How lovely it would be to have windows again! Where did one purchase glass in the wilderness?

He will come to your office. She sighed and turned into the open area where her wagon sat. Perhaps one day she would have an office. For now, people would come to her home. She *did* have her first furnishing for the office. She had a sign. Her Doctor Emma sign from Mr. Thatcher. She would use it always.

She stood looking at the open area where, tomorrow, her cabin would sit, then looked down at her feet and smiled. Someday, this would be a wooden sidewalk. Or, perhaps, brick or stone. Someday.

She walked to the wagon, climbed to the wagon seat, pushed the flaps out of the way and crawled inside. Yes. It would definitely be lovely to have a door again! She put her doctor's bag on the dresser and looked around. There was not much to furnish her cabin.

The mattresses were in a good, sturdy wood frame. Perhaps Joseph Lewis could make legs to raise it off the floor. And she had the dresser. And the chests. And the long red box. She would keep that always. It had held so many treasures for her on the long journey. And the sign. Her symbol of success as a doctor, and failure as a woman. Which would become more important as the years went by?

She drew a long breath and stepped to the rear of the wagon, opened a slit between the canvas flaps and looked out across the river to Zachary Thatcher's land. He would build his cabin there. Perhaps that had something to do with his mysterious digging. They would be neighbors. Every time she looked out her windows, or walked outside, or went to the river, she would see his home. And she would wonder.

When would he bring a wife there? For surely that would happen. How would she bear meeting her, seeing her around town over the years? How could she bear watching her grow large with his children? And then see them playing and exploring, hear their shouts and laughter? How could she bear watching him grow older and never share his joys and sorrows? Would this feeling of fragility, of…shattering frailty…lessen? Would she ever stop feeling empty inside?

"Dr. Emma?"

She dropped the canvas, whirled, her heart pounding. She had not heard him come.

"Dr. Emma?"

Finally. The acknowledgment of her doctoring skills she had sought. But it was not the name she wanted on his lips when he called to her. "Yes, I'm coming."

She wiped the tears from her cheeks, hurried forward and climbed out into the driver's box. He had dismounted, and was standing beside the wagon, Comanche behind him. She could see him out of the corner of her eye. She shook the long skirts of her red wool dress into place, arranged her face in her "professional doctor's look" and gathered her courage to look at him. "Is something wrong?"

"No." He tipped his hat back and took her gaze prisoner. "I have something I want to show you. Will you come with me?"

To the ends of the earth. "Yes. Of course."

He held up his hands.

Her heart stopped. *She couldn't...shouldn't...* She moved to the side of the seat, felt the strength of his hands circle her waist and leaned forward to place her hands on his hard, broad shoulders.

She never touched the ground. He lowered her until her waist was level with his chest, turned her back to him and caught her against him with one strong arm. He swung into the saddle and urged Comanche forward still holding her tight against him. The way he had held her once before. He had saved her then. She was dying now.

Comanche splashed through the water, surged onto land and walked to the small copse of trees that clustered on the riverbank. His camp was there, hidden from view. A stone fire circle, the packhorse equipment and a small tent. He dismounted and grasped her waist, lifted her down, looked at her. She turned and hid her face from him.

"Is this what you want to show me?"

"No. It's this way." He gestured toward the open plain.

She nodded and started walking toward nothing, needing to put space between them. He moved up beside her, adjusted his long stride to match her shorter one.

"Over here." He took her elbow, turned her to the left, walked forward a few feet and stopped. There was a small circle of disturbed soil with a long, skinny piece of twig sticking out of it. He touched the twig and looked at her. "This is an apple tree. A Winesap apple tree. There are twenty of them here." He swept his hand forward.

She saw them then. All the small circles of raw soil with twigs sticking out of them. "This is what you have been digging!" She glanced up at him for confirmation, saw his smile and knew her error. She had just admitted she had been watching him. Heat crawled across her cheekbones. She ducked her head, touched the twig. "It looks dead."

He chuckled, a low, manly sound that made her want to turn and step into his arms and place her head against his chest to hear the rumble of it inside, before he set it free.

"I thought the same when I first saw them, but they are only dormant, ready to wait out winter and grow in the spring."

She looked up at him, the question in her eyes.

"I've been reading up on growing apples. Over here—" he led her to another twig "—are twenty Sheep-nose apples. And there—" he gestured farther to their left "—are twenty Pippen apples."

"You must like apples." It came out more droll than she intended. He threw back his head and laughed and the sound brought joy bubbling into her heart. She turned and looked up at him and his laughter died to a grin.

"I like apple dumplings."

Oh dear. She whipped back around toward the open plains. "Are there any more dormant twigs out there?"

"No. But there is space for more, if these do well. And on the left, all the way to the rolling hills, there is space to grow grain to sell and to feed the cattle and horses that will graze those hills. I figure the world can use more Comanches." He stepped up beside her, pointed to one of the lower, flatter hills close to the plains. "I see the barn right there."

There was an odd, fluttery feeling, a *knowing,* growing in her stomach. She took a deep breath and looked up at him. "I thought your dream was to roam the mountains free and unfettered."

He nodded, took her gaze captive. "A man can change. *Hearts* can change. When I left here, I started back to my valley to build my dream. But every step I took got harder to take. Every mile became a chore. There was no excitement, no anticipation, no pleasure in the journey and I knew, I wasn't riding *toward* my dream, I was riding *away* from it." His voice grew husky, his eyes turned the gray, smoky-blue of the mountains behind him. "Those mountains hold no dreams for me now, Dr. Emma Allen. My dream—all I want—is standing right here in front of me. I've shown you my future. I want you to share it with me. I love you, now and forever. Will you marry me?"

She nodded and stepped into Zach's arms, joy flooding her heart. "Yes. Oh, yes, I will marry you. I love you, Zach—"

He caught her to him, drew her against his hard chest, his lips covering hers. A kiss like she remembered, only so much more.

She opened her heart, parted her lips beneath his and gave all her love in return.

Epilogue

Emma rose from her chair, rested her hands on her swollen abdomen and walked out onto the porch. A smile touched her lips. Every time she came outside and looked over the budding orchards she was more thankful she had won the argument over where they should build their home. Zach had wanted to build in town, next door to the Hargroves', in the lot where her wagon had sat, so she could be near her patients. But she had wanted their home here on the plains, by the barn, so she would be near Zach while he tended the apple orchards and watched over their cattle and horses.

She turned and looked across the river at the sturdy iron rod with a bell on the top, and a side arm from which dangled a hand-carved sign that read Doctor Emma. She smiled and rubbed her hands over the bulge beneath her skirt. Zach had promised the bell was loud enough to be heard over the clamor of any and all future children. And the neighing and snorting of Comanche's get.

She sank down onto the porch swing Zach had hung so she could sit and look toward the fields and barns while she waited for him to come to the house at the end of the day. Things had worked out so well. And, looking back, she could see God's hand clearly guiding them and blessing them. The furniture Zach had purchased from the Widow Canfield was enough for all five rooms, with some left over for expansion. Those items, awaiting the births of future little Thatchers, were in the loft of the second barn they had built by the house for storage of apples.

Emma sighed, pushed her toes against the porch floor and set the swing in motion. This was her favorite spot. Would the baby she carried like to sit and swing here with her? She laughed and pushed harder. Probably not, if they were the energetic, adventurous sons she hoped for. As soon as they could walk they would be off exploring their land, learning to ride Comanche's colts and fillies. Of course, she could have a little filly of her own. The daughter Zach wanted...one, he said, who would look like her and be just as stubborn. Tenacious, she always corrected, because she loved to hear him laugh.

She heard the thunder of hoofs, looked up and saw Zach riding Comanche across the field, heading home. To her. Her heart filled. How blessed she was. She stopped the swing and closed her eyes. "Thank You, God, for leading me on the path to Your blessings. For fulfilling my dream of being a doctor, and giving me so much more than I even knew to ask for."

The hoofbeats pounded close, stopped. She smiled,

rose from the swing as Zach swung from the saddle then hurried forward to step into her husband's strong, loving arms.

* * * * *

Pamela Nissen started writing her first book in 2000 and since then hasn't looked back. Pamela lives in the woods in Iowa with her husband, daughter, two sons, a Newfoundland dog and cats. She enjoys scrapbooking weekends with her sister, coffee with friends and running in the rain. Having glimpsed the dark and light of life, she is passionate about writing "real" people with "real" issues and "real" responses.

Books by Pamela Nissen

Love Inspired Historical

Rocky Mountain Match
Rocky Mountain Redemption
Rocky Mountain Proposal
Rocky Mountain Homecoming

Visit the Author Profile page
at Harlequin.com for more titles.

ROCKY MOUNTAIN MATCH

Pamela Nissen

Having the eyes of your hearts enlightened,
that you may know what is the hope to which
he has called you, what are the riches of
his glorious inheritance in the saints.
—*Ephesians* 3:18

For my lovely daughter, MaryAnna,
whose strength and perseverance inspires.
You are a heroine in the very truest sense of the word.

Acknowledgments

Thank you to my friends and family: your
encouragement has carried me through seasons of
doubt. And to Melissa and the Steeple Hill family,
thank you for believing in me and loving my
characters as much as I do. Sincere gratitude goes to
my amazing critique partners: Diane, your words
and friendship are life-giving; Jacque, your tenacious
loyalty is comforting; and Roxanne, your gentle
expertise coaxes me out of my comfort zone. To my
wonderful children, MaryAnna, Noel and Elias:
thank you for being so supportive, and for tolerating
more than one "cold cereal dinner" on this journey.
And special thanks go to my husband, Bill, who,
when I couldn't get these characters and story line
out of my head, said, "Why don't you write a book?"

Chapter One

Boulder, Colorado—1890

Inky darkness crowded Joseph Drake from every side. It shrouded him like a thick coat, with power so substantial that it was almost suffocating. Its bleakness mocked his vulnerable state, sending humiliation barreling through him with avalanche force.

He hated this. Every bit of it. He could barely stomach the thought of asking for help or being pitied. And he loathed the idea that those helping him would be monitoring his each and every pathetic move.

Drawing in a steadying breath, he braced himself against the pitch blackness as he sat on the edge of the feather mattress, clutching the thin sheet in his hand. He was so dizzy. His head swam and his ears rang incessantly, deepening his bad mood. He couldn't have imagined how unsettled he'd still feel after being on bed rest for three weeks. Raising his hands to his head, he slid his fingers over the fresh bandages shrouding his eyes.

How he wished he'd just wake up and find that his accident in the woodshop had been a horrible nightmare.

"God, please," he pleaded, his throat thick with emotion. "I need my sight back."

When Ben, his older brother by two years and a doctor in Boulder, had removed the wraps yesterday, Joseph had been confident that he'd be able to see again. But that confidence had vanished like some taunting wraith as he'd frantically grabbed for any image through the thick, dark cloud.

He'd tried to stay calm, but deep down he'd felt a crumbling begin at the very base of who he was. All along he'd minimized his injury. After all, it could be too soon to tell any permanent outcome—and Ben was new to doctoring. The thought had crossed Joseph's mind more than once that maybe Ben was a little green around the edges and lacked experience.

He'd reasoned it all, but the prospect of being permanently blind staked out his soul like a dank, stony grave marker. And the huge furniture order he'd taken on just days before his accident lay like dead flowers crushed into the fresh turned dirt. He'd cushioned the deadline when he'd signed the contract, but with his brother, Aaron, being the only one working in the woodshop for the past three weeks, the padding had been jerked away hard and fast.

Fighting to remain hopeful, he pushed himself off the bed, his cracked ribs protesting with the movement. He inhaled sharply, digging his toes into the rag rug's nubby texture.

His jaw ticked with instant irritation as a distant chorus of giggles wafted through his open window. It didn't take much to conjure up the origin of the twittering noise. He could see it now…a cluster of bonneted women standing in front of the hotel. Lined up like flowers for the picking, just another batch of mail-order brides brought in to help populate the west.

It was downright demeaning, in his book, the way they'd set themselves on display like that.

When a knock sounded on his front door, he startled. Clad in just underclothes, he lurched forward, struggling for balance as he probed for the wall where his clothes were hung.

Ben's strong urging that Joseph gradually ease back into life on his own whipped through his mind like a warning knell. But bandages over his eyes or not, Joseph was a twenty-seven-year-old man, and like a caged animal, he craved independence and freedom. Privacy.

"I'll be right out," he yelled after another knock sounded.

His fingertips brushed against sturdy cotton fabric and he sighed with relief. He pulled on his britches and boots, then shrugged into his shirtsleeves, although a new level of frustration assaulted him as he intently focused on lining up the five wooden buttons with buttonholes.

Eight years ago he'd built his own home, but now he could barely dress himself. He shuffled out of the bedroom, galled at having to give such simple routines a second thought. Groping along the wall, his breathing grew shallow as each awkward step echoed over the hardwood floor—a mocking reminder of his vulnerable state.

When his leg knocked hard into something, Joseph

flinched, reaching down to steady the imposing piece of furniture. His hands careened into the small table and tipped it over, sending a loud bang reverberating throughout the quiet house.

"Joseph? Are you all right?" Ben rapped at his door again.

He stooped to right the piece. "I'll be right there," he shot back through tightly clenched teeth.

Hands quivering, he felt the satin-smooth finish. He'd always prided himself in this well-known trademark, but now he wondered if he'd ever be able to resume his profession.

And his plans to marry and have a family… None of that was certain now. If his vision didn't return, there was no way he'd saddle any young woman to life with a blind man.

Humiliation cloaked him soundly and offending images of himself stumbling through life alone and without sight intensified his bad mood.

When Joseph finally reached the front door, he fumbled for the handle, then eased it open. A gust of fresh air hit him square in the face, reminding him just how long he'd been down.

"Mornin', Joseph!" Ben clapped him on the arm. "Sorry. I didn't mean to hurry you, but you said you didn't want me barging in anymore, but then when I heard…" Ben's voice trailed off. "I see you made it up and about."

"Were you expecting something else?" Joseph retorted.

"Not exactly, I guess."

Joseph tried to push aside his sour mood as he caught

the rumble of a buckboard rolling slowly by in front of his house. "What brings you over? I thought you gave me a clean bill of health yesterday." Sliding a hand up the front of his shirt, he checked for misaligned buttons.

"How are the ribs? Are they giving you much trouble?"

"I feel fine," he lied, ignoring the constant dull ache and the comment he could swear he overheard from inside the wagon, regarding his bandages. His accident had probably been the talk of the town for the past three weeks.

"Well, your color is better. Not bad for a man who's been through what you have. Are you sure you're feeling strong enough to tackle things today?"

"I said I'm fine." Joseph furrowed his brow. "But if I didn't know you better, I'd think you were expecting me to trek up the Flatirons with you. That's not likely to happen."

"Believe me, a quiet day in the mountains sounds great after visiting with ol' Donovan Grimes. The fellow's hearing must be just about gone, the way he shouts. My ears are still ringing." Ben shifted his booted feet on the porch floor. "By the way, Aaron said that Ellie had planned to bring dinner tonight, but she's not feeling well. I'm going to check in on her after this."

Joseph grew immediately concerned for his sister-in-law. She was having a difficult time of this first pregnancy and he knew it weighed on his younger brother Aaron. Especially now that he was carrying double the load in the woodshop with Joseph being laid up.

"Tell you what, I'll just have the hotel diner make you up a plate and deliver it to you. How's that sound?"

Joseph balled his fists. "I said yesterday that I'd take it from here."

"I'd accept the help if I were you," Ben urged. "Soon enough you'll be begging us to have a little pity on you and bring over some good, home-cooked meals again."

"What's that supposed to mean?" Stepping outside, he closed the door behind him so Ben wouldn't get any ideas of staying for a visit.

Ben cleared his throat, a trait Joseph had begun to recognize over the past three weeks as a nervous gesture. "Remember when we talked, shortly after your fall, about getting you training in case you don't—"

"Whoa. Whoa." He swiped beads of perspiration forming on his brow. "*We* talked? I think you mean *you* talked. I didn't agree to anything."

"I know how adamant you are about being independent—I want that for you, too. But you'll get there quicker with training," Ben finished as though racing to get it out.

Gritting his teeth, Joseph plastered himself against the door. He'd prove to his older brother that he could make it on his own, but he couldn't even seem to move his feet enough to turn and stalk back inside. Truth be told, he was scared to death to take a step forward into the darkness.

And he'd never been afraid of anything.

"What are you getting at, Ben?" A bout of light-headedness assaulted him and he struggled to keep his balance as he stood to his full six foot, three inches. "What's going on?"

Ben sighed. "Promise me you'll hear me out before you go jumping down my throat, all right?"

"I'm not promising you anything." Joseph tightened his fists. "Just tell me what you did. Now!"

"I—I arranged for a teacher to come out from Iowa."

"You did what?"

"I arranged for a teacher to help you," Ben declared with a little more firmness. "I know you don't want to do this, but you need to give it a chance."

"It's a waste of time. My vision is *going* to return."

"I hope you're right. You know that I've read everything I can get my hands on. But like I told you yesterday, the more time that passes with no change, the less chance there is for restoration," Ben said, his voice tight. "I know this has to be hard, but if your vision doesn't return, what then?"

That question had staked out territory in Joseph's mind for the past three weeks. That his entire life could be permanently altered infringed on his well-planned life like some dark omen.

In a softer tone, Ben continued. "Will you refuse help even when it could make things easier for you?"

Every muscle shuddered with anger. "I—don't—need—help!"

Even as the declaration crossed his lips he knew he might be deceiving himself. But the thought of being trained in the simple aspects of life rankled like nothing else. He'd always been self-sufficient. Always.

Joseph forced himself to stop shaking. "Wire the man and let him know he doesn't need to waste a long trip like that."

Awkward silence draped heavily between them, making Joseph's skin prickle and a foreboding creep down his spine.

Ben sighed, slow and heavy. "I—I can't do that."

"You can't send a telegraph wire?" His pulse pounded in his ears. "Why not? It's not that hard."

When his brother stepped back, Joseph loosened his fists, unfurling them one finger at a time. Ben could be stubborn, but so could Joseph—and he had a long history of winning arguments.

"Miss Ellickson," Ben called out toward the street. "Why don't you come on up."

Joseph froze. "Tell me what's going on," he demanded, his heart slamming against his chest. "I mean it, Ben."

Ben came to stand directly in front of him now, so close that Joseph could smell his brother's subtle, clean scent. "Your teacher arrived by stage two days ago."

Hearing the faint clicking of boots across the boardwalk, a trembling shook Joseph to the core. Unbidden, he pictured an old schoolmarm clad in a dowdy brown dress, a severe knot of mousy-brown hair clinging to the back of her head and rimmed glasses perched on her long nose.

His jaw muscle ticked. "Why wasn't I informed? This is *my* life we're talking about here."

"You'll probably never forgive me for this. And I knew that you'd refuse, no matter what sense I tried to talk into you. You're stubborn, Joseph, too stubborn for your own good. As your brother and doctor, I made the decision for you."

"That's just great! I get to have my life planned by you now." Joseph gave a mock laugh. "I may have lost my vision for a while, but I haven't lost my mind. Send the woman back!"

Just shy of Joseph's height, Ben leaned closer, his

voice dropping to a stern whisper. "I also knew that as a perfect gentleman, you wouldn't give this dedicated *young* woman a hard time."

The distinct sound of the front gate clicking shut and the woman's slow, light steps coming from the walkway sent Joseph's heart racing inside his chest. His breathing grew ragged.

"Listen, Joseph, she comes highly recommended, with a glowing letter sent by the school she's been working at for the past five years. She's Sven and Marta Olsson's niece," Ben added as though that tidbit of information would make him agree.

Well, he was anything but agreeable. The last thing he wanted was some teacher coming in and watching him stumble around his own house.

He tensed, only faintly aware of his sore ribs. "It's a waste of her time," he said in a harsh whisper.

Ben firmly gripped Joseph's shoulder. "Whether you gain back partial vision or no vision, she can help you right now. She's used to this."

"Used to what? Seeing someone make a fool of himself?"

The soft treading of the woman's shoes up the stairs sent a quaking through Joseph's entire being. Beads of sweat trailed down his forehead, soaking into the bandage.

"I wouldn't be so quick to make a judgment," Ben urged. "You never know, she might just be the answer to your prayers."

The answer to his prayers? Katie mused silently. Clutching her instruction books tight against her chest, she stepped up to the porch and stared at Mr. Drake who stood legs braced wide, fists clenched at his sides and his chin set in stubborn defiance. She slid her gaze up, noticing that even though bandages shrouded his eyes, they couldn't hide the fact that he looked none too happy. An unmistakable, aggravated scowl creased his forehead.

The answer to his prayers… I'm probably more like his worst nightmare, she admitted, swallowing hard.

Hope had bloomed on the long journey from Iowa to Colorado, but now uncertainty choked out eager anticipation like a dense thicket of weeds invading tender spring flowers. Never had she questioned her ability to teach and certainly she'd never shied from taking on a challenging student, so why should she now?

"Miss Ellickson, I'd like to introduce my brother, Joseph Drake." The twinkle in the doctor's gray-blue eyes belied his simple brown attire and had put her at ease when she'd met him yesterday, but now he appeared anything but confident.

Slipping her fingers over each fine pearl button trailing down her powder-blue waistcoat, she grappled for confidence. "Good morning, Mr. Drake. I'm pleased to meet you."

When she reached for his tight-fisted hand, he drew back as though she'd seared him with a hot iron. His mouth was set firm and hard. He shifted his weight from one foot to another, his leg muscles bunching beneath camel-colored britches. And as he drew his shoulders back, his chest stretched wide, revealing a well-defined muscular build beneath a white cotton shirt.

Embarrassment flushed her cheeks and she quickly

averted her gaze to the fresh coat of dark gray paint that gleamed like icing on the porch floor.

"You may not feel ready for it, Joseph, but Miss El-lickson is prepared for a full day's work." The doctor gave her a lame look of encouragement, then shifted a wary gaze to his brother. "I know you're probably mad enough to spit nails, but give it two weeks. At least until you see the doctor in Denver."

While he continued with a halfhearted pep talk, Mr. Drake remained grim. His commanding presence filled the small porch, sending a quiver of unease down her spine. And a brief, unwanted flash of fear through her mind.

Nervously she smoothed back wispy strands of blond waves, wondering when the unbidden memories from the past year would stop haunting her. When would she be free of her attacker's vile grasp? Even months later, she could still feel his hands pinning her down to a dire moment in time that would never end.

Her chest pulled tight, the same painful questions swirling through her mind.... Where was God then? Why hadn't He helped her? Why hadn't He protected her?

She wanted to trust God, wanted to rest knowing that He was watching out for her. But it seemed a mountain of anguish stood in her way of finding the childlike in-nocence she'd once had.

Squeezing her eyes tight, she refused to let her past get in the way of this new job assignment. When Uncle Sven had wired her about this opportunity, it was like a thousand Christmases all wrapped into one. This was a chance to start fresh, far away from the continuous reminders. A chance to distance herself from the constant threat she felt back home.

Squaring her shoulders, she studied the man before her.

Stubborn. She'd seen it more than once while working at the Braille and Sight-Saving School, but she'd never encountered someone so dead set on refusing help. His imposing stance spoke far louder than the words of protest she'd overheard as she'd waited on the boardwalk for the doctor to summon her.

"I won't keep you two any longer." Dr. Drake's voice broke into her thoughts. "If you need anything, Miss Ellickson, please don't hesitate to let me know."

Nodding, she smoothed a hand down her full damask skirt, pasting on a tranquil smile in spite of feeling as if he was leaving her to one mean, hungry wolf. "We'll be just fine."

She watched the doctor's long strides take him down the walk and almost wished she could follow. Scanning the tidy yard surrounded by a white picket fence, she experienced a measure of safety. But as she slid her gaze to the rugged Rocky Mountains, she felt a tangible unease at the untamed land.

While she turned to face her new student, she braced herself before she spoke. "I can understand your discomfort, Mr. Drake, if my presence here doesn't sit well with you. If it eases your mind at all, I can assure you that you will get neither pity nor charity from me," she stated simply, hoping to allay such fears.

"Quite honestly, you'll get as much out of this as you're willing to put in," she added, unsuccessfully trying to gauge his response. "And if you readily embrace a challenge as your brother says you do, I think that you'll be pleasantly surprised at the outcome."

From the stoic stance he'd demonstrated so far, she'd obviously underestimated the doctor's claims that he was stubborn. Had Uncle Sven not vouched for Mr. Drake's stellar character and assured her safety with him, she might just turn and leave for good. Which was exactly what he wanted right now.

And precisely what he didn't need.

Firming up her wilting strength, she made a desperate grasp for boldness as she stood directly in front of him. "Mr. Drake, you need me. And I'm prepared to give you my all to help you gain independence. So perhaps we should begin our first…"

The words died on her lips as a low, deep growling sound came from the porch's dark shadows. Her breath caught in her throat. Hair prickled on the back of her neck. She flicked her gaze to where a mound of black fur lumbered into the sunlight.

"Bear!" Stifling a scream, her books dropped to the porch floor. "Quick! Get inside! He's coming!"

She lunged for Mr. Drake and wedged between his large frame and the clapboard house. Fear gripped like a vice, clamping down with brutal force as she wrapped her arms around his broad chest and tried to tug him toward the front door.

"Mr. Drake, please. We must—get to safety!" she grunted, struggling in vain to move him.

Peeking around him, she could see the hulking black bear closing in on her, its wide boxy head hung low, thick shoulders bearing its lumbering mass, and its long fluffy tail…

She froze. Grasped his chest tighter as waves of prickly heat spread through her. *Bears didn't have tails. Did they?*

Narrowing her gaze, she braved another glance around Mr. Drake's chest, all firm and muscular beneath her tight hold, to see a huge dog with a head the size of a barrel staring at her with big brown, expressive eyes. The dog dropped to the edge of the porch with a weighted thud and bored sigh, looking up at her as if to say it had been mortally wounded by her accusation.

"Miss Ellickson, that is a dog, not a bear," he said, prying her hands loose from his chest.

Katie let out an unladylike whoosh of air. Utter embarrassment at her impropriety overwhelmed her as it dawned on her how close she was to Mr. Drake. Her cheeks flamed hot and she wiped a quivering hand over her lips.

She slipped out from behind him. "I—I apologize."

Tugging at her waistcoat, she smoothed back her hair, grateful he couldn't see her crimson cheeks. He could probably hear her heart pounding in her chest, though. "How foolish of me. It's just that with the shadows I thought—"

"Perhaps it's not me who has less-than-perfect sight," he cut in without even the hint of a smile. "Colorado is no place for the faint of heart."

Flames of anger nipped at her composure, but she quickly snuffed them out. "I'm sure it's not—and I regret my outburst. I suppose I'm just leery of the wilds of Colorado," she admitted on a shaky sigh. Even though she was a little more than leery of him right now, she was determined to remain professional. "Is this your dog?"

"Boone's a Newfoundland, and he wouldn't hurt you for anything," he said as Katie stooped to pet the dog. "Unless he senses that I don't like you."

She pulled her hand back and passed a wary glance from the dog to him. "Well, then, I guess you'd better change your mind about me—or your dog will be having me for lunch."

Chapter Two

Was she friend or foe?

That question reverberated through Joseph's mind as he sank deeper into the chair across from where Miss Ellickson sat on the sofa. The faintest scent of lilies, pleasing and natural, drifted from her direction and he took a long, measured breath.

Since meeting her this morning, he'd been cross. He didn't want her here, but felt trapped because his brother had set things up in such a clever way that Joseph wouldn't have a choice but to slap his jaws shut and suffer through.

He'd entertained illusions of the woman taking off like a scared rabbit. Instead, she'd seemingly marked her territory and called him to climb this uphill battle—and he never backed down from a challenge.

He could hardly blame her if she'd chosen to leave because he wasn't exactly Boulder's idea of a welcoming committee. He was sour, indifferent and unfriendly, and he knew it.

Reaching down next to his chair, he found Boone's

head, soft and furry beneath his touch. He gently stroked the dog's thick coat, acutely aware of Miss Ellickson's presence.

Rivers of wounded pride coursed through his veins at his predicament. This woman may have come highly recommended and be competent, but she couldn't give him what he wanted most... His vision.

Slumping deeper into the cushioned chair, he pressed the pads of his fingers over his bandaged eyes, something he often did hoping the pressure would somehow produce a change. He'd do most anything if it meant regaining his sight, but nothing seemed to make a difference. Strong will and hard work had always been his friends, but now it was as if they were bound on the sidelines while he stood alone in the midst of a raging battle.

Joseph held out hope that in two weeks, when he'd travel to see the doctor in Denver, he'd find more encouraging news. If so, he'd never take another day of blessed sight for granted.

Raking his fingers through his thick hair, he shifted uncomfortably in the chair, knowing that until then, this woman would witness each humiliating attempt to do things right.

Would she laugh? Turn away in embarrassment? Pity him?

He loathed not seeing! And was determined not to be a burden. But remembering how meager tasks such as dressing or walking through his own house took every bit of concentration he could amass, he wondered if things would ever come easy.

"Yoo-hoo... Joseph?" Julia Cranston's high-pitched

voice jerked him from his thoughts as the front door creaked open. "Are you home?"

Joseph briefly recalled the day of his accident when Aaron had found another love note from Julia at the door. She'd sealed it with red wax.

"Kinda bold, don't ya think?" Aaron had jibed.

Joseph had glanced warily at the heart-shaped seal. He'd gone on a few innocent outings with Julia, but had no plans to go running down the aisle yet.

"Whatcha' waitin' for?" Aaron had asked. "If you're holdin' off till all your ducks are lined up, you'd better get movin' fast or they're gonna go line up in somebody else's pond."

At the time he'd thought little of Aaron's prodding, figuring he had plenty of time to set in place that part of his life. But just minutes later his whole life had changed. A single moment, a careless movement on a ladder, had altered his entire life. Now he could only hope that God would answer the barrage of petitions he'd made for healing.

Hearing the door rattle again, he realized that Julia hadn't visited for a week. Now that he was up from bed rest, he felt acutely aware of his inadequacy because a woman like Julia, delicately beautiful and refined, was used to being pampered. She'd sat by his bedside a few days since his accident, spending most of her time relating the latest news of Boulder's upper crust, rarely inquiring about his injury.

"Come on in." He stood and struggled for balance.

"Oh, there you are! I'm so glad to see you up," Julia crooned as she beelined toward him, her skirts swishing and heels clicking across the wood floor.

The overwhelming powdery perfume she wore preceded her in a thick cloud, triggering the sudden need to sneeze. He raised a hand to his nose and warded it off as her light footsteps came to an abrupt stop in front of him.

"I—I thought you were going to be through with those silly old bandages," she bleated, her excitement suddenly deflated.

He could almost feel her piercing hazel gaze bearing down on him. "Ben put new ones on to give my eyes more time."

"More time? Whatever for? You said that you were going to be as good as new when those awful wraps came off."

He swallowed hard. "My eyes need more time to heal."

Julia gave an exaggerated whimper. "Well, that ruins positively everything! I had a very special surprise for you today, but now you won't even be able to see it."

"What was the surprise?" he asked, his jaw clenched tight.

"My dress, of course." Stiff fabric rustled at her touch. "I just came from the dressmaker's and I was going to surprise you. Daddy *insisted* I have a new dress made for the Glory Days celebration in a few weeks. It's simply the most beautiful cobalt-blue taffeta you've ever seen," she announced. After another long whimper she added, "Now you can't even see it to tell me how stunning I look."

Miss Ellickson cleared her throat from the sofa.

"Why, Joseph!" Julia perched a hand on his forearm. "I didn't realize you had company."

"Julia Cranston, this is Miss Ellickson." He felt Julia stiffen, as though some invisible rod just shot up her back.

"Good morning, Miss Cranston," his teacher said.

Julia threaded an arm through his. "Miss Ellickson, you say? I don't recall the name from around here."

He could only imagine the confused look on her face. Even though her family had arrived just months ago from Boston, she was already familiar with everyone within twenty square miles.

"You must be new to the area," Julia finally conceded.

"I arrived just Saturday," Miss Ellickson answered stiffly.

"Miss Ellickson is here from Iowa. Ben sent for her to—to carry out some training I may need." The admission needled him.

"Whatever would you need training for, Joseph?" Julia sidled closer, her voice rising in pitch. "Uncle Edward says you're the finest craftsman this side of the Rockies."

He sighed. "Not training in carpentry. Training in case my sight doesn't return—right away." *Or at all,* he thought, the very prospect making his stomach churn.

"This certainly is a shock!" She hesitated, then patted his hand. "Well, you poor thing, Joseph, looking pitiful in those wraps the way you do. Maybe you should be back in bed?"

He winced at her choice of words. He didn't want to be pitied. "I'm fine. Really. What brings you here, anyway?"

"I stopped by the shop thinking, of course, that you'd

be there working your little heart out after being in bed for so long." Her voice was loud enough to call in cattle. "You can imagine my surprise when Aaron said you were still at home."

"My eyes are bandaged, not my ears." He dug his fingers into the chair's thick stuffing. "I can hear you just fine."

"Of course. As I was saying," she continued, the pitch of her voice showing no noticeable change. "I brought you a most wonderful meal. I'm quite certain you'll be very pleased."

A tantalizing aroma wafted to his senses, penetrating the cloud of perfume. He tried not to show his surprise at her sudden display of domestic prowess. "Did you make this yourself?"

"Well, I...not exactly. But I gave Cook *very* specific instructions. She absolutely puts me to shame, Joseph," she simpered, then whisked out of the front room toward the kitchen. "I am simply dreadful in the kitchen."

"Don't be so hard on yourself. You probably do a fine job," he called after her, but remembering the sawdust taste of the cookies she'd made last week, he was pretty sure that wasn't true.

"You're a dear to say so. But I dare say that I won't be winning any first-place ribbons in the pie-baking contest at the town celebration." Julia's high-pitched laughter shot through his house like bolts of lightning. "Come and eat, Joseph."

Vile fear wrapped around him when the almost twenty feet he had to go suddenly felt more like a mile. Perspiration beaded his forehead and a slow trembling coursed through his body like deadly venom. His pulse pounded in his head, throwing off his concentration. He gritted his teeth. Drew in a shuddering breath. Just as he started forward with his hands outstretched, he felt a light touch on his arm.

"Mr. Drake," Miss Ellickson whispered beside him as she gently guided his hand to her elbow. "Would you be so kind as to escort me to the table?"

He jerked his head down to her, ready to refuse. But the overwhelming relief he felt as she led him with steady measured steps to the kitchen brought his protest up short.

"You must be positively famished," Julia gushed.

When Miss Ellickson placed his hand on the back of a dining chair, he whispered, "Thanks."

Bracing his hands on the chair, he willed the trembling to stop. "So, what do we have here?"

Over a deep sigh, he could hear Boone's lumbering gait coming toward him. Joseph could just see the dog throwing his tail lazily from side to side as he swaggered across the room.

"Oh no, Joseph! Are you going to let that horrid animal sit here while you eat? God only knows where she's been." No doubt Julia's pink lips were pursed tight, her small nose wrinkled in disgust. She never did like Boone and wasn't shy about saying so. "I don't see how you can stand having Bongo in your house like you do."

"Boone," he corrected, irritated that she could never seem to get his dog's name right. "And 'she's' a 'he.'"

"Boone, Bongo, he, she…it matters not to me. The beast is just so uncouth. Mother would surely faint if she could see it in your house. Why, that creature is nearly a horse."

"He's a dog, and he's fine. *He* minds his manners."

Lowering himself to the long trestle table, he trailed his fingers along the sturdy walnut's smooth finish, remembering when he'd crafted the piece. He'd built it, eager for the day when his wife and children would be seated here with him.

Julia clanged silverware against a plate, jerking him out of his reverie and invoking a fast-building sense of dread. That anxiety multiplied by ten as he realized that this would be the first time since his accident that he'd sat down for a meal.

"Everything is all set for you, Joseph. You can eat now."

He swallowed hard. Clenching his fists in his lap, he wondered what *everything* was…pork and beans, soup, chicken? He had no idea what she'd laid out or where it was located on the table. Beads of perspiration formed on his brow, his pulse pounded a deafening rhythm in his head.

"I wasn't planning on joining you, but maybe—"

"No, that's not necessary," he quickly cut in.

"Honestly, I did have plans to have tea with Colleen Teller, the *senator's* daughter," she twittered. "Of course, I'd have to go home and change. It would simply be unacceptable if she were to see me wearing my new dress today and then again for the celebration. Don't you think?"

He offered a hearty nod, thankful she had other plans.

"Well, then, by all means let me see you out, Miss Cranston. You won't want to be late," Miss Ellickson clipped off.

"That's completely unnecessary. I can see myself

out." Julia clutched his hand and leaned closer, her perfume nearly choking him. "Maybe I should stay. What do you think, Joseph?" A whine of regret laced her whispered words. "I suppose I could reschedule with Colleen. Her agenda is busy, but I'm sure—"

"Please, go. Have your lunch with Colleen. I'd rather eat alone." He braced his elbows on the table and steepled his fingers under his chin. "Miss Ellickson, you can take a dinner break, too. There's a good diner just down the road—have them put your bill on my tab."

"I'll be joining you here. Thank you all the same," she responded quietly.

Julia's sharp intake of breath wasn't lost on Joseph. She grasped his shoulder. "Miss... Miss Ellington—"

"Ellickson." Joseph shook his head.

Her nails bit into his flesh. "Miss Ellickson, perhaps you didn't hear Joseph. He said he'd rather dine alone. If you—"

"Julia, I can handle this," he ground out, disgusted at her steely tone. Although he'd taken her on a few outings in the past two months, he didn't fancy being treated like some possession of hers. "Miss Ellickson, you're probably in need of a break. I'm sure I can handle it on my own."

"I can understand your hesitance, Mr. Drake. Believe me, I do." Her voice trembled.

Tension chorded his body as he wondered why everyone couldn't just let him make his own decisions. If he wanted to eat alone, shouldn't he be afforded that one small courtesy?

"I'm sorry." Miss Ellickson's voice was soft and even,

coming from the chair to his left. "But I'm here to—to teach you. Not to coddle you."

Julia withdrew her hand from his shoulder, mumbling as her booted heels clicked loudly across the floor. When she slammed a plate down on the table, he nearly jumped out of his skin.

He swallowed hard, trying to control his mounting frustration. "I didn't ask you to coddle me, Miss Ellickson."

With a harrumph, Julia plopped down in a chair across the table from him. "Oh for goodness's—"

"You've made that quite clear," Miss Ellickson continued as if oblivious to Julia's presence. "But as with all my students, I'm here to instruct you in how to get along on your own, and that's what I'm going to do—starting with dinner."

"Joseph has been eating dinner for twenty-seven years, Miss Eberhard," Julia informed on a nervous laugh. He could hear her dishing something onto her plate. "He can get along just fine. Can't you, Joseph?"

"Just drop the subject." He grasped at his fading calm.

"Fine, I see the way of things." Julia gave her napkin a swift snap and a puff of air fluffed over to him. "You have never had a problem doing things on your own," she reminded him, the shrill sound of her voice contrasting sharply with the delicate chorus of birds outside. "I realize that when you were laid up flat on your back you needed assistance. But now—"

"But now, with these bandages on, I still can't see." Raising his focus to where she sat directly across from him, he wished he could see, but he couldn't even open his eyes through the thick bandages. "And there's a slim chance that my vision might not be what it was."

He swallowed against the admission. If his sight didn't fully return, he'd have to find independence as soon as possible or he'd never be able to stomach himself.

"Oh, Joseph, don't be silly. You're going to be fine," Julia dismissed, then took a bite of something that crunched.

Awkwardness flooded his resolve. He could hear Miss Ellickson arranging things on the table, even dishing items onto his plate while he sat rigid as a board, every muscle in his body stiff and unyielding to the internal cry to relax. All he wanted was to be left alone, but Julia was being unusually possessive and Miss Ellickson was intent on doing her job.

A job he didn't even hire her to do!

"Your plate is in front of you," Miss Ellickson began, her voice low and measured. "Now, like numbers on a clock face, there's a thick wheat roll at nine o'clock, mashed potatoes at twelve o'clock, cooked carrots at three o'clock and roast at six o'clock. If you'll raise your hands to feel for your plate," she directed, pausing as if waiting for him to follow her lead, but he couldn't seem to move his hands from where they were tightly fisted in his lap. "You'll find your fork to the left of your plate, spoon and knife on your napkin to the right. And your glass of grape juice is about three inches to the right of your plate, at two o'clock."

From across the table, Julia's sharp scrutiny bore down on him like a locomotive. He tried to ignore it. The aroma rising from the food normally would've made his mouth water, but instead his stomach churned. His discomfort could reach a swift end if he insisted they leave, but at this point he was too stubborn to give in.

"Shall we give thanks?" Miss Ellickson asked.

The distinct air of vulnerability in her voice pricked Joseph's heart, but he quickly brushed it aside as though it were a pesky bug. In spite of his surging anger, he bowed his head as Julia's utensils clanked to silence against her plate. Truth be told, over the past weeks he'd spent more time telling God what to do than talking with Him or thanking Him. Had God heard his plea for healing? Or had He passed him by for good?

On a long sigh, he began to pray. "Lord, thank You for this meal. Bless the hands that prepared it." Remembering his sister-in-law's tenuous health and the certain stress Aaron had to be under, he added, "And be with Ellie and the baby. Keep them safe."

"Amen," Miss Ellickson whispered after a long pause.

With a curt nod, he sat in the offending darkness, trying to ignore the daunting insecurity as he struggled for self-control. Pulling his sagging shoulders back, he braced himself, unwilling to look like a helpless excuse for a man—especially in front of Julia.

Crisp, metallic sounds from her silverware sounded against her plate. She hadn't uttered one word in the past moments, but he knew she must be closely monitoring his every move. Her sharp inspection pierced like tiny shards of glass.

Could he do this? With his head bowed, Joseph tried to picture the things set before him. He slowly slid his hands up to the table, probing for his knife and fork.

Once he'd located his utensils, he raised them to the plate.

"Now, when you've located your fork and knife—"

"I've eaten without help in the past, Miss Ellickson," he cut in, knowing even as the words formed on his lips that he should just swallow his pride. "And I can do it now."

Joseph fought to still his trembling hands. As he made a stab for the meat to cut it, the supple chunk seemed to dodge his effort, sliding away from him. His fork fell from his grasp, clanking loudly against his plate.

He couldn't miss the small gasp Julia gave. "Oh, no, Joseph, you dropped your fork," she announced loudly.

"Really?" Fumbling for his fork, he put it to the plate again while inside tremors of fury thundered. When he couldn't locate the piece of meat with his utensils, his agitation increased.

"Here you are, Mr. Drake. The roast is back on your plate," his teacher spoke evenly.

The roast had flown off his plate?

Steeling himself, he struggled to gather his composure as he repositioned his fork toward the carrots. With intense focus, he tried to recall where she'd said they were—three o'clock or ten o'clock? Framing one side of the plate with a hand, he set his fork to the plate, succinctly stabbing one long spear and cutting it in two. A small sigh of relief passed his lips as he opened wide and directed the carrot in. It brushed his lips, tumbled down his shirt, then fell to the floor with a moist thud.

He gritted his teeth as Boone immediately shifted across the floor and sniffed at the vegetable. Joseph's breathing came heavy, labored. The loud rushing in his ears grew almost deafening.

"It's all right." Miss Ellickson's tone was low and even.

He slammed his fist on the table to ward her off. He would do this alone or drown in a pool of humiliation.

"If you'll put your fork to the plate," she offered, forced patience lacing her words, "and first gauge where the food—"

"*I* will do it!" Joseph interrupted angrily, acutely aware that not one morsel of food had made it to his mouth yet.

Humiliation ricocheted in his mind like a shotgun blast in an underground cavern. Groping for his knife, his hand careened into his glass of grape juice. It tipped, the glass clinking on the solid wood.

"Oh, my new dress!" Julia yowled, her chair scraping away from the table. "My beautiful new dress! It's ruined!"

Joseph sucked in a shaky breath. He stood, knocking his chair over with the back of his legs and sending Boone scurrying away, toenails scratching across the floor as the loud crash reverberated throughout the house.

Hearing the frantic sound of Julia wiping at her garment, Joseph brought his hands to his head, threading trembling fingers through his hair. "I'm sorry," he forced on a broken breath.

"Please don't worry, Mr. Drake. Accidents happen," Miss Ellickson responded quietly as she rose and crossed to the sink. "I'll get it cleaned up."

He drew quivering fingertips over the bandages covering his eyes, failure's evil taunt screaming through his thoughts. He was sickened at his stubborn pride. Balling his fists firmly at his sides, he clenched his teeth tight. Even if he couldn't see, he should be able to make it through a meal.

Simple things were now difficult. Difficult things, seemingly impossible. When he'd been released from bed rest, he thought he'd feel more comfortable, more capable. Instead, he felt more like a prisoner than a free man.

He jerked suddenly at Miss Ellickson's light touch on his arm. "I didn't mean to startle you. I just wondered what you'd like for me to do?"

Julia huffed. "Isn't it *obvious* that you've already done quite enough? Just look at the mess he's made," she hissed. "Poor Joseph obviously isn't ready for this. I'm certain that you can't be doing him a bit of good by pushing—"

"Stop!" he growled. "Just leave, now."

A moment of crushing silence was followed by the whoosh of Julia's skirts as she walked toward the front door. "I can tell when I'm not wanted," she spat, her voice laden with unveiled disgust as she stormed out, slamming the front door behind her.

"Mr. Drake? I'm terribly sorry about all of that." Miss Ellickson slid her hand off his arm. "I'll understand if you want to call it a day."

Tilting his head down toward her, he wished he could see her. He just wanted one glimpse. From the moment they'd met this morning, she'd seen him at his worst, with behavior he didn't even know he was capable of. She'd taken his rude, unyielding responses with a stiff upper lip. Why? Who was this woman who would sacrifice her own comfort and willingly endure the ugliest part of him?

Chapter Three

Unadulterated fear had shown like gaping holes in Mr. Drake's stony wall of composure. From five years of experience working with the blind, Katie had learned to recognize the sure signs. And she'd never seen such desperation. All morning she'd witnessed it in his tensing jaw, tight fists and grim expression. She was worn out just watching him work so hard to fortify himself against the fear.

She stood for several moments on his porch, her legs weak as she clutched her books to her chest. He'd said that he'd lost his appetite. That he needed some time to think. And she knew when to let up a little. After all, this was all so very new and painful for him.

Breathing deep, she welcomed the soothing west wind filtering through her skirts, cooling her skin. For over three hours she'd remained stalwart in spite of his unyielding behavior, though she'd nearly bit her tongue in two when Miss Julia Cranston had shown up. It wasn't Katie's business who that woman was to Mr. Drake, but whatever her relationship, Miss Cranston wasn't taking into account his vulnerable state. And for that Katie felt fiercely protective.

Compassion for him tugged at her heart. It was clear that this man of strength and self-sufficiency had been dealt a very difficult hand in life. Things were horribly unfamiliar to him. Maybe for now, anyway, he felt like a shell of what he had been.

Still, Katie could see an iron will there—and a fortitude that perhaps he didn't even realize existed. He was unlike anyone she'd worked with. Decidedly stoic, yet beneath that stony exterior, a vulnerable man, scared to death. And she wanted to do everything she could to give him back his life.

Squaring her shoulders, she struggled to gather her wits before walking the distance back to Uncle Sven and Aunt Marta's. She'd never hidden her feelings well. No doubt they'd worry if she showed up looking as distraught as she felt.

Brushing wisps of hair from her face, she started down the three steps, but came to an abrupt halt when Mr. Drake's voice penetrated the solid walnut barrier.

"Why? Why me?" he choked out, his halting footsteps shuffling from the area of the kitchen where she'd left him, toward the front room. "How could you do this to me? What did I do to deserve this?" Mr. Drake's voice rose in volume, twisting her heart with its mournful, almost terrorized sound. "Why, God? Why me? You have to let me see again!"

His deep, raw cry sent shivers down her spine and a piercing sword to her heart. When she heard him knock something over, her breath caught in her chest.

"Oh, God! You—*promised!*" Heaving sobs broke his words.

A heavy object slammed against the door.

Swallowing hard, she blinked back hot tears stinging her eyes. She could try to comfort him right now, but he'd reject it. She could do everything she knew to aid him in gaining physical freedom, but only God could heal his wounded heart.

Lifting a trembling finger to her face, she swiped a tear sliding down her cheek as she remembered his awkwardness this noon when he'd prayed. She didn't need eyes to see that his relationship with God was being sorely tested. How well she knew that reality— her own trust in God had been pulled up painfully short in the past year.

"God, please help him," she whispered. "Help me."

From behind the door, Mr. Drake's breathing came in audible gasps. "God, You pr-promised you wouldn't forsake Your own!"

"Go ahead, Joe-boy. Hit me as hard as you can," Aaron provoked, his words sounding more like he was offering to loan Joseph his boots, rather than his face.

"Hit all three of us till you can't pull another punch if it makes you feel better," Ben added in complete earnestness. "You need to do *something*. You're about ready to explode."

Joseph balled his fists and sucked in a slow breath, trying to hold his mounting frustration at bay. Since yesterday he'd felt like a tightly coiled spring begging for release. The reality of his inadequacy had hit him full force, and since then he'd been fighting just to stay clear of the bitter rage that nipped at his heels. In the past if he were angry, he might've laid a well-aimed ax to logs, splitting wood till he dropped, but now he couldn't even seem to make it around his house without knocking something over or bumping into a wall.

Last night he'd successfully warded off his brothers when they'd shown up on his doorstep. But this morning they wouldn't be put off. For the past thirty minutes Ben, Aaron and Zach had been trying to get him to talk about yesterday. They'd said that Miss Ellickson wouldn't divulge a thing, but that Julia had given away plenty. She'd been loose-lipped all over town.

If he needed a reason to be mad, that definitely could've been it, but for some reason he didn't really give a coyote's hide. Whatever she'd said was probably true. He could hardly blame her for spouting off. Had he insisted that he be left alone to eat his meal, then she wouldn't have had a thing to talk about.

Julia's stories were to his benefit anyway. His blessed privacy would be ensured this way. No one would brave visiting if they knew how uncomfortable they'd be.

"Come on, Joe-boy, swing at one of us," Aaron urged. "We're standing right in front of you."

"This is your chance, big brother," came Zach's low voice. At twenty, he was the youngest of the Drake brothers and had been striving to sow something other than wild oats. "I reckon you've probably been wantin' to do this to me more than a time or two."

"Ha! Are you giving us the opportunity, too?" Aaron guffawed. "Line on up, boys! Maybe we could knock some sense into Zach—keep him from making any more dirt-poor choices."

Joseph could hear a scuffle in front of him and figured that Aaron was probably ruffling Zach's hair or faking a punch. Like a couple of playful bear cubs, they were always messing around, but he knew it wouldn't amount to much. Zach had made some bad decisions— decisions that had almost landed him in jail. They were just glad he was finally holding down a job as a ranch hand, and hadn't gone the way of the third brother, Max, who'd taken off eight years ago with his inheritance and then some, and was living on the run.

"You two yahoos cut the bantering! We're not here about Zach, we're here about Joseph," came Ben's firm warning. "Come on, Joseph. We're not kidding. Let loose—it'll do you good."

Joseph gave a low growl. "Would you three knock it off?"

Shaking his head, he pushed between them and with hands outstretched and clumsy, shuffling steps made his way to the dining table. He grasped the top rung of a chair, leaning heavily into it. "You might as well stop this charade. I'm not going to hit any of you. Never have, never will."

Aaron came to stand beside him. "Maybe you *need* to haul out and hit us. We know you enough to see that you're about ready to blow. I've never seen you so dog-gone angry."

"I'm not allowed to be angry?" His jaw muscles tensed.

"No. It's not that," Aaron answered. "We can't blame you at all for being angry. Can we, Ben?"

"Absolutely not." Ben's long strides brought him to flank Joseph's other side, followed by Zach. "You've been calm and collected since your accident—handling things better than most people would. Believe me, I've seen folks go through far less, only with a mountain of ill-tempered attitude. I'm just glad to see you finally showing some kind of emotion."

Pushing up to his full height, Joseph raked his fingers through his hair. "Well, then, what is it? Would you do me a favor and clue me in on what you're getting at here, because so far you're not making a lick of sense."

After a long moment of silence Aaron spoke up. "Flat out, Joseph...we're worried."

"Worried? About what?" Shoving his hands on his hips, he shook his head. "If anyone should be worried here, it's me. The three of you are acting like you just got kicked in the head by a horse." Waving his hand in the air, he yelled, "Quick! Get a doctor!" Then he knocked the side of his head with his hand. "Oh wait! You *are* the doctor."

"Don't try to dodge the attention like you always do," Ben retorted, clearing his throat. "Now listen, we're here, in part, because we're worried about Miss Ellickson."

He jammed his hands on his hips and furrowed his brow. "Miss Ellickson?"

Just thinking about the mess he'd made of dinner yesterday sent shame, thick as mud, coursing through his veins. But then like a flag of warning, concern for Miss Ellickson rose inside him. "What about Miss Ellickson? Has something happened?"

"She'll be here any minute now. And Ben, Zach and I—we're here to make sure you plan on being civil to her."

He gave a short harrumph. "You don't think I will?"

"I don't know. You tell me," Ben answered in a no-nonsense tone. "Like I said yesterday, you've always been a gentleman in the past, but as angry as you are, we don't want you scaring her off. She's come a long way to work with you."

Another day with her definitely didn't sit well with him. Not at all. Last night he'd barely gotten a wink of sleep thinking about her. He'd been bracing himself for her return and now here his brothers were, showing more concern for her than loyalty to him.

He felt trapped. Trapped in his home. Trapped in his body. Trapped in a fear so unfamiliar.

Taunting disorientation blanketed him and he struggled to steady himself against the unnerving effects. "What would make you think that I'm going to scare her off, anyway?"

Ben slid a chair over the hardwood floor and sat down with a weighted thud, Zach and Aaron following his move. "Oh, you wouldn't intentionally do that—I don't think, anyway. But believe me, you can be intimidating even when you're not angry."

"Yeah. It's like the Red Sea parting every time you walk through a crowd," Aaron quipped with a chuckle. "Wish I had that effect."

Joseph tightened his grip on the chair. "I'm not the one who invited her here. When you mentioned the idea in the first place, I made it clear how I felt. But then you showed up with her in tow, pushing me into this whole thing. I went through with it yesterday and I'll do the same again today, but I'm telling you, I'm just going through the motions."

When Aaron reached over and grabbed Joseph's arm, Joseph flinched at the unexpected touch. His brothers meant well—Ben had gone above and beyond in his care of Joseph. Aaron had been carrying twice his usual load in the shop, and Zach had risked losing his tenuous position as a ranch hand to help out. They were doing so much, but nothing they could do right now would make him feel better. True, he could batter them bloody, but somehow he knew it wouldn't touch the strange bitterness and pain that had settled deep in his heart.

Ben squeezed Joseph's forearm. "You don't have to like the training and you don't even have to like Miss Ellickson. All we're asking is that you be *civil* to her and give her a chance."

Oh, he'd give her a chance all right. He'd suffer through two more weeks of this. She might even show him something that could make the time bearable. But if he had his way, she'd be gone after he returned from Denver to see the doctor. It didn't matter where she went—she could even stay in Boulder for all he cared— he just didn't want to need her.

Joseph lowered himself to a chair, set on hiding his raw emotions from his brothers. "All I can say is that I hope she's not disappointed when I don't need her after all. Seems like an awful long way to travel to work for only a couple of weeks."

When he heard Ben clear his throat, his pulse began a rapid beat in his ears. He could imagine what Ben would say next, so he quickly added, "And you can breathe easy. You have my word… I'll be on my best behavior. I'll be a veritable welcome wagon from here on out."

* * *

Mr. Drake stood in front of Katie, his tall, tightly muscled frame filling the doorway. "Come in."

Come in? Katie silently mouthed as she peered up at him to see one of his hands hooked over the top of the door, the other gesturing for her to enter. Since yesterday she'd prepared for a goodbye fare-thee-well, sure that he would refuse further training, but now he'd invited her to—to come in?

She'd prayed all night long that he wouldn't give up, and if he did, she'd try to persuade him otherwise. Terrified of going home, she needed a reason to stay here in Colorado. But also, after meeting Mr. Drake yesterday, she wanted desperately to help him find freedom again.

"Thank you," she said, her voice steadier than she felt.

With an armload of books, she squeezed by him, acutely aware of his solid form so near hers. When she removed her pale straw bonnet and hung it on a coat hook, her attention was drawn to the floor where a Bible lay sprawled open. Her breath caught as she remembered hearing something crash against the door yesterday. She tenderly scooped up the Bible, its cover worn with the passage of time and its pages yellowed and frayed from use. Carefully cradling it against her chest with the other books, Katie steadied her wavering emotions. "Your Bible. You must have dropped it."

Without a word, he quietly latched the door.

"I'll just put it over here on the mantel for you." After she'd laid it on the beautifully crafted mantel, she turned and noticed Boone lying beside one of the wingback chairs. "Well, good morning, Boone. How are you this fine morning?" Kneeling beside his massive head, she held out her hand to him.

Katie smiled as he pressed his big, wet nose into her palm and stared up at her with expressive brown eyes. After giving her a wet kiss, he flopped his head down on the wood floor with a dull thud. She smoothed the unruly hair on top of his head. "I certainly hope this means we're on friendly terms."

Still smiling, she rose and returned to where she'd left Mr. Drake standing. She nervously fingered the row of silver buttons trailing down her high-necked white blouse. "And how are you today, Mr. Drake? Are we on friendly terms, too?"

He pushed away from the door, a smirk lifting the corner of his mouth. "I suppose you were wondering if I'd call it off?"

"To be perfectly candid, the thought had crossed my mind." Threading her fingers together in front of her, she added, "I was very much hoping you would continue with the training."

He jammed his hands into his pockets, his jaw muscle ticking. "I don't quit things that easily, but even if I did, I have three brothers holding my feet to the fire."

"They must care a great deal."

When he just nodded, she walked to the kitchen where the bold scent of fresh coffee met her squarely. Setting her books on the table, she smoothed her pale yellow cotton skirt. "Smells like you made coffee. Do you mind if I help myself?"

"Go right ahead." He shuffled to the table, his hands splayed in front of him. "My brothers were over earlier this morning and Ben made a pot." Reaching for a chair, he added, "I'm warning you, he makes it strong enough to wake the dead."

"Perfect. I didn't get much sleep last night. I must not be used to my new surroundings yet," she half lied. In truth she'd lain awake thinking of how she could best help him.

And how she could keep this job.

She couldn't bear the thought of going home already—too many dark clouds threatened on the horizon there. Here, she had hope that the sun's warmth would shine on her face again. With or without a job her aunt and uncle would welcome her to stay, but Katie would never think to impose on their goodness overly long, especially if she wasn't earning her keep.

"Mr. Drake, could I get you a cup, too?"

He shifted nervously, then reached out to his adorable dog who sauntered up beside him, his big, furry feet sweeping across the wood floor as though he wore heavy boots. "Sure. Thanks."

As she scanned the cupboard shelves for two mugs, she wondered what had come over Mr. Drake. The contempt he'd readily shown yesterday was barely visible today—in fact, she might even go so far as to say that he was congenial.

Spotting a row of mugs on the third shelf, she said, "They're a little out of reach."

He stood, quirking one brow. "What?"

"The mugs… I'm not tall enough to reach them."

Lifting his head in silent recognition, he moved toward her, his movements jerky and uncertain. When he'd pulled them from the shelf, he turned, almost knocking into her.

"Here you are," he said, holding the mugs out to her.

Katie squeezed back against the counter as he towered over her. An eerie chill crept up her spine as she struggled to block out the haunting memories that assaulted her. But the way Mr. Drake stood over her, trapping her and closing her in like he was, she wanted to scream and escape from the suffocating confinement.

Gulping back the bile that rose in her throat, she snatched the mugs from him with trembling hands. "Thank you."

She slipped around him and crossed to the stove. As she steadied her hands enough to pour the steaming liquid, she willed her heart to stop pounding. Setting the pot back on the burner, her brow beaded with a cold sweat and her vision narrowed. She fought to even out her short gasping breaths, clutching the stove handle as though it were some lifeline.

Katie reminded herself over and over that he was not Frank Fowler, the man who'd set into motion a year of turmoil that she could share with no one. She'd had to carry the burden alone and at times it threatened to shatter her under its weight.

Frantically grasping for some thread of hope, she struggled to drag herself away from the edge of despair. Like a faint, saving call, she could hear a comforting voice, reminding herself that she was safe now. Hundreds of miles away from Fowler and from the wicked sneer that would stretch across his face each time he'd see her.

Squeezing her eyes shut against the images, she felt her stomach tense. She'd thought that putting distance between herself and home would eliminate moments like this, but the miles had done nothing. The memories were stronger than ever. The fear, consuming. The images had struck with the force of a landslide, unearthing every raw emotion she'd attempted to bury.

"Miss Ellickson?" Mr. Drake's tentative voice broke through her swirling thoughts.

Rising above the fray of images barraging her mind, Katie slowly spun back around. "Here you are." Her voice was thin and strained. Her hands still quivered as she set down the cups of coffee. "Here's your coffee— be careful, it's hot."

She lightly grasped his hands and directed them to the stone mug. His hands, large and work-worn in hers, felt strong enough to ward off any enemy, yet gentle enough to soothe a baby.

And brought an immediate, tangible calm to Katie.

The fear that had mounted so quickly, rocking her off kilter, dispelled just as fast. A shaky sigh escaped her lips.

"Miss Ellickson?" His brow furrowed. "Are you all right?"

Sinking into a seat across from him, she took a slow sip of coffee. "Yes, I'm fine."

"Are you sure? I'd get you something to eat," he said, gesturing toward the cupboards, "but I'm not sure of what's here anymore. If you can find something…"

"Thank you, but Aunt Marta made sure I ate this morning," she managed, cupping her hands around the warm mug and staring at him from over the rim. She noticed, for the first time, how his deep chestnut hair hung in playful waves across the white bandages on his forehead, and the way a stubborn cowlick kicked a thick clutch of hair to the side, giving him an innocent look.

Something about him was so captivating, intriguing, almost demanding of her attention. Was it the confidence he exuded in spite of his fear? Was it the way he filled the room with his strong, quiet presence? Or was it his undeniable good looks?

Eager to distract her thoughts, she looked away, noticing a long cane leaning in the corner. She hadn't seen it there yesterday, but then with all of the commotion she easily could have missed it. "I see you have a cane?"

When he paused, she couldn't miss the way he turned his head away from the object as though it were an offending image in his home. "Ben brought it by this morning."

Her heart pulled tight. "Well, if you're up to it, maybe the best use of our time today would be to help you get more comfortable around your home. We'll count out steps between rooms and furniture—that sort of thing."

Bowing his head, he fingered the edge of the mug. "So the walls and furniture don't find me first?"

"Exactly."

He raised his chin. "We might as well get it over with."

Although resignation hung heavy in his voice, Katie could hardly believe he'd so readily agreed. She stared for a long moment, not quite sure how to take his co-operative agreement.

"You're awfully quiet. Are you still there?" He traced his fingertips slowly over the table's smooth surface.

Katie shook off her surprise, then pushed up from the

table. "I'm sorry. I apologize if my mind is elsewhere this morning."

Nodding, he rose from the table.

"We'll begin at your front door, counting steps from there first. You can use the cane for—"

"For *firewood,* maybe." He threw a scowl her way, then shuffled toward the door.

"Well, now, that's not a very agreeable thing to say," she threw back at him.

"That's because I'm not feeling overly compliant, Miss Ellickson." He leaned a shoulder against the door. "At least not as far as that thing goes."

"Using that *thing* might prevent you from a mishap." She perched her hands on her hips, surprised and strangely relieved at his show of stubbornness. "Back at the school we liken a cane to eyes. It will help you see where you're going."

He gave a sarcastic laugh. "Well, we're not at the school and I don't plan on being this way forever, thank you."

Crossing her arms at her chest, she eyed him. "Stubborn, aren't you?"

Her heart squeezed at his insistence that things were going to change for him. She hoped, for his sake, they would.

He raised his chin the slightest bit. "So I've been told."

"Then you can take my elbow, like we did yesterday. It's the preferred way to navigate as opposed to holding one's hand or being pushed along. But if you use the cane, as well," she added, hoping to appeal to his greater sense of reason, "you'll be able to tell what might be lying in your path."

"No, thanks." His curt response and the way his jaw tensed left her void of any argument.

"Why don't you tell me about the layout of your home? Don't be vague about where your furniture is located, so that you'll have a clear picture in your mind."

With a slow exhale, he made a detailed description, his tone reminiscent at times as he described his home to a T.

"Perfect. Now, try to relax and walk at a normal pace and I'll match your stride." When she gently guided his hand to her arm, a tingling warmed her skin. She fought to ignore the sensation, resolute in her desire to remain professional. "I'll do the counting and make sure you don't run into anything."

He tensed beside her, his grip tightening slightly. "All right. But I'll warn you that I'm a little shaky on this."

"You'll do fine. Trust your instincts. If you're aware, you should be able to sense when something is in your way."

Cautiously he took a step while she began counting. Then with each step following, his grip tightened as though she alone kept him from falling off a steep precipice. His hand trembled. His breathing grew shallow.

At eighteen steps and just inches from the back door, she stopped. "Now, use your hand that is outstretched to see how close you are."

Perspiration beaded above his full lips. With one hand he clutched her arm, with the other he tentatively reached out, groping for the unseen. When his trembling fingers brushed against the wall, he exhaled a broken sigh.

Covering his hand at her elbow, her heart squeezed at seeing how much this had cost him. She peered up at Mr. Drake, taking in the stark change in his demeanor from just moments ago, when stubbornness waved like a proud battalion flag, to now, when raw fear weighed his shoulders and head down low.

She swallowed past the lump in her throat. "Very well done. Your pace was just fine."

He slid quivering fingers over his lips, then raised a fist to his bandaged eyes. "You'd think I could make it across the room without breaking a sweat," he ground out. "I may as well have been scaling a mountain."

"Don't be discouraged." She squeezed his hand. "It takes time getting used to all of this."

"It's my own home. I should be able to walk across the room without trembling in my boots."

"You're doing just fine—especially since you've only been up for a couple of days." She turned to face him. "Taking everything into account, you're doing very well."

His face softened some, the corner of his lips lifting slightly. "You're Little Miss Sunshine, aren't you?"

A warm blush crept up her cheeks. She smiled at his comment, surprised once again by his congeniality. "Better that than gloomy."

"Far as I can tell, you could never be accused of that," he replied, his hands still trembling some.

"There's a bright side to everything."

"What could be positive about this?" He gestured to his bandaged eyes.

Hugging her arms to her chest, she stared at him, the way he wore frustration like an unwanted old coat, and desperation like an acquaintance of ill repute. "You're right, Mr. Drake. Your injury is not something easily reckoned with. Not having your sight is certainly nothing short of difficult, and I'm sure you wouldn't wish it on anyone. Even an enemy." Katie tried to steady the quiver in her voice. "But even as uncertain as things are right now, you can focus on where you've been or on where you're going."

His lips formed a tight, distressed line. "I wish I could. But taking a step forward when I can't see where I'm going…it scares me to death."

At his admission, sadness rose within Katie. She was shocked at the tiniest crack he'd allowed into himself, an opening that gave a glimpse into his silent battle.

Threading her fingers together in front of her, she searched for the right words. "I know this isn't easy. In fact, I'm not sure how I could face such a thing. If you don't regain your sight, there'll be challenges. It won't be easy, but I promise you it will be rewarding." Katie gathered a bit more boldness, then added, "And if you'll allow me, I'll be here beside you to help you find your way to the other side."

Chapter Four

Embarrassed once again, Joseph's face flamed hot. He was sure he'd suffered more humiliation in the past five days than he had his entire life.

He bit back a groan, trying to ignore his frustration. Having worked with Miss Ellickson for almost a week, why was he having such a hard time doing a simple task like pouring water from a pitcher? If he didn't fully regain his vision, how would he ever be able to work in the shop again, handling sharp tools?

"Here, let me help you," Miss Ellickson offered, the quiet calm in her voice beckoning him like a peaceful stream. "Sometimes trying too hard makes things more difficult. Now, lightly grasp the glass like this." She gently positioned his fingers around the glass, her touch soft and soothing. As she slipped his forefinger at the last knuckle over the rim, she said, "Don't hold too tight. Keep a light touch. Remember how that feels and now find the pitcher."

Deeply concentrating, he was determined not to spill again as he slid a hand along the counter to find the pitcher. When his fingers connected with the stone pitcher, he noticed how it was beaded with perspiration from the hot August day.

"Got it," he confirmed.

Once he'd painstakingly set the lip of the pitcher over the rim of the glass, he poured the water. And when the cool liquid reached his finger, he pulled the pitcher back and sighed.

"There you go, that was perfect! Not one drop spilled." The reassurance in her voice brightened his gruff mood enough that he even relaxed a little. "See? You can do it."

He angled his head down to Katie. "Thanks, Sunshine." Joseph smiled at her, hoping that she noticed, because so far this week it seemed as if all he'd done was scowl. In turn, she'd never once gotten impatient or cross with him. "Always the encourager, aren't you?"

"You deserve it. You're working very hard."

When she gave his hand a light squeeze, he couldn't help but wonder what she looked like. "You know, I figure that if I was a cat, I'd be dead."

"What?" she asked on a laugh.

"I'd be dead from curiosity." Raising his brows, he took one step closer to her. "You see, Miss Ellickson, you're the only new person I've met since my accident. And your appearance—I mean the way you look—is still a mystery to me."

The air seemed to grow warm and thick between them. His entire being hummed in full awareness of her presence beside him.

"Good thing you're not a cat, then," she finally responded, her voice sounding tight, strained.

Joseph gave an almost imperceptible nod, wishing that his brothers would indulge him with a few words about her physical appearance. They'd sure been vocal about him treating her well, and being a man of his word, he'd been on his best behavior. Although at this point he didn't really need encouragement to do that—Miss Ellickson was easy to like.

He decided that when he returned from Denver with his vision intact, she was the first person he wanted to lay eyes on. If her appearance mirrored at all what he'd grown to understand of her character, he was sure she'd be beautiful.

Wouldn't that be the irony of it all...a beautiful woman watching him stumble through simple things.

Leaning back against the counter, he momentarily cringed. "So, what next, Sunshine?"

When she stifled a laugh, his lips curved into a smile again. For some reason, the sound of her light laughter warmed his heart and made him want to make her smile again.

"Is this your name for me? Sunshine?"

"If the shoe fits." He recalled different moments throughout the week when her encouragement had been the balm he'd needed to keep going. To keep moving forward toward normalcy, however meager it was compared to independence.

"You're very kind, but I hardly think I warrant anything quite so grand." He could hear her gathering some papers on the table.

Four steps and Joseph had crossed to the table, noticing for the first time how much less halting his footsteps sounded compared to just a few days ago. "Why don't you let me be the judge of that?"

Unbidden, a deep fondness for her rose within him, and that unnerved him. Because somewhere along the line he'd missed how attached he was becoming to her. Was it because she'd given him hope at a time when things were bleak? Was it because she was so selfless in her work with him? It was just a job for her, wasn't it? Maybe she had this effect on other students, too.

Or was it something more?

If so, he'd have to guard himself. She didn't deserve his strained indifference, but he couldn't let himself grow any fonder of her. If he didn't regain his sight, his future as a single man would be irrevocably sealed because he wasn't about to burden anyone with his blindness.

Her voice finally broke through the raw, unsettling revelation. "Well, Mr. Drake, why don't we—"

"If it's all right with you, would you mind calling me Joseph?" Guarding himself or not, he couldn't stand another day of being addressed as Mr. Drake. He jammed his hands into his pockets and stood tall. "Mr. Drake is, well, it's just too formal for my liking."

She paused for a brief moment. "All right, then. Joseph it is—if you'll call me Katie."

Or Sunshine, he thought, helpless to keep his emotions from running away.

If Joseph had been planted on the pulpit with flowers growing out of his Sunday clothes, he wouldn't have felt more conspicuous than he did right now.

He shifted uncomfortably in the wooden pew, wishing he'd just ignored Ben's challenge for him to attend church. Each step away from his cocooned world and nearer the church building had brought him closer to people's stares, even if he couldn't see them. Having arrived a few minutes before the service started, he couldn't avoid being a sideshow for curious onlookers or a conversation piece walking in with a bandage wrapped around his head.

He sat stock straight in the second row of pews, the back of the bench hitting well below his shoulder blades. Even though Ben's tall frame was close to him and he'd kept a steady flow of whispered small talk going since they'd sat down, Joseph might as well have been alone. Inky darkness seemed to enfold him, isolating him in a room crowded with friends and acquaintances.

He shrugged off his uncertainty as faint comments regarding his attendance wafted to his ears. Joseph gritted his teeth. There was certainly nothing wrong with his hearing.

As much as he wanted to remain inconspicuous, he'd always seemed to attract attention in a room, especially that of women. It sure wasn't something he set out to do. Julia had been no different. She'd sidled up to him like moss on a log as soon as she'd met him. But since his accident, certain little things, like her high-pitched voice, grated on his nerves.

Thoughts of seeing her again settled on him like cold rain. She'd not stopped by since that first day he'd worked with Katie, and Joseph wasn't surprised. He hadn't needed to see Julia that day to know that she was madder than a hornet. He could hear it in her sharp tone, the swish of her skirts and the brisk clip of her heels.

A few times when he lay awake listening to all the sounds of the night, he'd think about his relationship with her. Would she want to see him again if he didn't gain back total sight? And sight or no, did he even want to pursue anything other than friendship with her? He just couldn't ignore how ill at ease he'd felt with Julia in the last three weeks.

When he'd first met her, he'd been intrigued by her vivacious, flamboyant ways. Maybe it was an eastern air about her, or maybe it was just Julia. Whatever the case, it was as though he could see what she was really like, now that he couldn't see her. And he wasn't sure that he liked what he saw.

Shrugging off his glum musings, he focused on the sun's warmth pouring through the row of tall windows to his left. Thoughts of Katie filtered into his mind, spreading calm through him like warm honey. He couldn't deny that he missed her presence by his side today. She'd given him a tangible confidence in moving about his home, eating without incident and even doing some cooking.

Was it her expertise she'd been so eager to give him that made him feel alive again? Or was it something more?

Katie's heart clenched tight inside her chest when the pastor spoke in his sermon about trusting God. Like a broken-down wagon ransacked along a trail, she was almost empty of trust. Could she ever get beyond feeling like she alone must protect herself? It seemed as though God hadn't protected her, but instead had allowed the vilest of things to happen to her—and by a man who claimed to serve God!

She'd trusted and been betrayed. Offered goodwill and been preyed upon. She'd been wounded to her core and endured it alone in shame for all of these months.

When Uncle Sven had wired her about coming out here, she'd jumped at the chance to leave Iowa—leave her past behind. And after meeting Joseph, she knew she'd made the right decision.

As the service concluded with a familiar hymn, Katie rose from the pew and stood beside Ellie and Aaron. She felt a pull at her heart, thankful for the quick friendship that had developed with Ellie. From the moment she'd met the young woman a week ago, they'd bonded like blood sisters.

Although Katie joined in the hymn, her focus was constantly drawn to Joseph. He stood taller than those around him, his chestnut waves stirring in the warm breeze that blew through the tall windows. His shoulders impressed her with their broad and sturdy strength. On occasion she even glimpsed the resolute set of his jawline.

The pastor's voice finally broke her reverie. "I want to remind everyone of the Glory Days celebration in three weeks. Mrs. Duncan is in charge of it again this year," he announced, gesturing to the round-faced woman who stood waving to the congregation as though she were on parade. "So, if you'd like to volunteer, talk with her after the service."

Katie sensed an excitement stirring in the room as the parishioners began filing out of the white clapboard church.

Edging her way out to the narrow aisle, she glanced at Joseph one last time and her stomach dropped. Miss Julia Cranston stood gazing up at him, her silky dark tresses and striking smile punctuating the room with icy elegance.

A stab of protectiveness shot through Katie's heart. Was Miss Cranston saying thoughtless things yet again? Katie couldn't imagine that the woman set out to be hurtful, but some people just had a knack for saying the wrong things.

Watching the interaction, she wanted to shove her way between the young beauty and Joseph, but she restrained herself. Clutching the pew in front of her, she felt almost giddy when the woman gave up with a shrug after just a few moments.

Inordinately relieved, Katie exited the church with Ellie.

"Did you see how Ethan Hofmann looked at you, Katie?" Ellie inquired, her cheeks flushed pink, matching the tiny rosebuds dotting her simple white cotton dress.

Katie stopped at the bottom of the steps, waiting for Ellie to catch her breath. "I'm not sure what you're talking about. Who's Ethan... Hofmann?"

Ellie's hands went to her stomach and gently held the swell. "Ethan Hofmann. The blacksmith's son. He was sitting to your right, several rows up, and he spent the entire service staring back at you." Her crystal blue eyes grew wide. "His neck will be giving him fits tomorrow—and it serves him right!"

An icy quiver traveled down Katie's spine. Over the past year, she'd received bone-chilling stares in her church back home. It was almost as though Frank Fowler, a well-respected deacon, innately knew when no one was looking, when his leering gaze and snapping black eyes wouldn't set gossipy lips flapping.

She pushed aside the unwelcome memories and gave a weak laugh. "I don't even know the man, Ellie."

"That young man didn't even have the decency to hide his infatuation. He was way too bold, if you ask me," Ellie insisted as she steadily beelined for a towering pine tree, its tall, weighted branches stretching wide. Cautiously sidestepping exposed roots, she turned and leaned heavily against the trunk, her cheeks flushed as though she'd just walked miles.

"Miss Ellickson, is my wife fussing over you like an old mother hen?" Aaron teased from behind her.

She turned to see an amused, boyish grin plastered across Aaron's face. Bowing her head, she took in the invigorating scent of fresh pine needles beneath her feet. "She's just keeping a watchful eye on things."

"I'm not the only one keeping an eye on things." Ellie hooked an arm through her husband's, snuggling up next to him. "Darling, you're going to have to speak with Ethan Hofmann. He's acting like a foolish schoolboy. He could hardly take his eyes off Katie during church." When she hooked Katie's arm also, Katie couldn't help but smile.

Aaron winked at her as he patted his wife's hand. "I'm sure Katie can take care of herself."

Katie swallowed hard and schooled her expression. Had Aaron known how brutally untrue those words really were he never would've said them. She'd tried to fight Frank Fowler off, but her meager five feet four inches was no match to Frank's size and his evil determination.

"But if you ever do need help or have any concerns, Katie, just let Ben, Zach or me know. Joseph, too. He may not be able to see right now, but he's always had a way of bringing order to things without bruising a single knuckle. People around these parts think twice about crossing him."

Ellie sighed, slumping her shoulders. "Well, I still think you should talk with Ethan about this. After all, Katie's a young, beautiful *unmarried* woman. The single men around here seem to lose all common sense when it comes to someone like her."

Giving Ellie's hand a warm squeeze, Katie pulled away. "It's fine. I didn't notice the man."

That was true. She hadn't noticed him because she couldn't seem to take her eyes off Joseph.

Glancing momentarily back at the church, she spotted him standing alone, and her heartbeat quickened inside her chest.

"Ellie-girl, I think you've about worn yourself out for one day," Aaron cautioned in a most gentle and loving way. "I'm gonna get you back home where you can rest. And don't you go arguing with me either." Katie turned to see Aaron wrap an arm around his wife's slight shoulders, then gently settled her back against the tree. "Stay here while I check on Joseph, then we'll be on our way."

"I'd be glad to do that," Katie offered, noticing, too, how Ellie appeared nearly spent. Her face was flushed and her brow beaded with perspiration. "Really. It's no trouble at all."

"Are you sure? I just want to make sure he's all right."

Aaron glanced around the churchyard. "I thought Ben would be out here by now."

Katie gave Ellie a quick hug, then turned to Aaron. "Just get Ellie home. I'll check in with Joseph."

"Good enough." Aaron nodded.

"We'll have you out for supper some night this week," Ellie offered as her husband swept her up in his arms. She hooked her arms around her Aaron's neck, her laughter resounding like a bird's joyous spring song as he carried her toward their wagon.

Smiling, Katie waved. "I'll look forward to that."

Walking toward Joseph, she stared through a shimmer of tears, wishing that she, too, could know that kind of love.

But who would ever want her the way she was... used?

That horrifying reality never seemed to lose its sharp sting. Her heart clenched with overwhelming sadness, but she couldn't give in to it.

Ignoring the old familiar dirge, she glanced up to see Joseph sitting on the steps, his hands clasped in a tight ball between his knees. He was probably trying not to be noticed, but there was nothing inconspicuous about him. Like honey to a bee, he drew every bit of her attention with his commanding, masculine build encased in a stark white shirt and dark bronze britches, and his chestnut hair hanging loosely about his head. She barely took notice of the air of discontent tainting his features.

"Good morning, Joseph." She slowed to a stop in front of him. "It's a splendid morning, isn't it?"

"Miss Ellickson?" He stood and clung to the railing.

"Thought you could get rid of me for the weekend, did you?"

His face relaxed ever so slightly as he slid his hands off the rail and tucked them in his pockets. "Well, not exactly. I just didn't know you were here this morning, that's all."

"I was sitting in the back with Ellie, Aaron and my aunt and uncle."

"Oh." Was that a tinge of disappointment she heard in his voice? "I—I was sitting with Ben."

"Yes. I noticed. Are you still waiting for him?" She briefly scanned the yard for Ben.

"Actually I was hoping to find Aaron. Ben's inside meeting with Mrs. Duncan about the upcoming celebration. He said it might be a while, so I told him I'd get Aaron to walk me home. Or Zach if I can round him up."

Katie hugged her arms to her chest. "Ellie wasn't feeling well, so Aaron took her home. But if you don't mind, I could walk with you."

He shook his head. "No, that's all right. You don't need to do that on your day off."

"It's no problem at all. I'd be glad to walk with you. Besides, it's such a beautiful day." Holding her elbow out in front of him, she offered, "Here's my arm. You just set the pace." When he reached out and found her arm, his touch sent stirring warmth through her.

He started forward at a leisurely pace. "It galls me how tired I am from just this one outing."

"Don't be so hard on yourself. It takes a great deal of mental energy to do what you've done today."

"Well, I can tell you one thing, Tuesday of next week can't come fast enough. When I get these bandages off and can see again, I doubt I'll close my eyes for a week straight."

She hoped that he was right. That he would see again.

Noticing the curious stares of a few of the church folks who still lingered on the grounds, she asked, "You don't think people will talk, do you?" She stepped around a bed of fragrant lavender. "I mean, with me walking you home?"

He came to a stop and tilted his head down at her. "I'm sure that by now they're aware that you're my instructor. Word gets around fast here. But if it's uncomfortable for you, I could just wait for Ben."

"Oh, no," she said, a little too eagerly. "I mean, of course it's not uncomfortable."

With a smile tipping the corners of his mouth, he nodded, then continued an even stroll toward his home.

"Joseph. Katie, wait up!" a voice called from behind them.

Katie turned to see Ben jogging toward them.

"Sorry about leaving you stranded." Ben clapped Joseph on the arm and pulled in a long breath. "I got tied up with Mrs. Duncan and you know how that can go. Pastor Winters almost paid a hefty ransom to free me. At the rate she's going, you'd think she was planning a presidential inauguration."

"Mrs. Duncan isn't a woman to miss details," Joseph said, leaning slightly toward Katie.

"That's very diplomatic of you, Joseph. Personally, I'd rather strain at gnats all day than iron out details with that woman." Ben gave a wide-eyed look. "I hope you're in for a fast walk, Joseph, because I've got to hightail it out to the Randalls' place. Jeb laid an ill-aimed ax to his leg yesterday and I just got word that it's not looking too good."

Katie winced. "That sounds bad."

"When I left him late last night I said I'd be back later this afternoon, but I'd feel better if I got out there as soon as I can. Besides that, I've just acquired a couple of stray kittens that showed up in my barn yesterday."

"Your newest four-legged patients?" Joseph asked.

"Yep. And they're in need of round-the-clock attention right now. I have them bedded down in a crate beside my bed."

Joseph smiled and focused down at her. "Ben's always taking in strays and doctoring them back to health."

"Aww…"

"I can't help it. They just show up."

"That's so sweet of you," Katie said, her throat going tight with instant emotion. She loved animals.

"Yeah, well, what else is a fella to do?" Ben remarked as if he were trying to step out of the focus.

"Go on ahead. Katie said she'd walk with me." The sideways grin Joseph gave her set her pulse skittering. "That is, if you still don't mind?"

She shook her head. "Not at all."

"Good, it's settled." Ben clapped his hands, then came forward and gave Joseph's arm a quick squeeze. "Thanks again for coming with me today."

Joseph nodded. "By the way, you sent the wire for my appointment in Denver Tuesday, right?"

Ben passed a wary glance to Katie and her heart instantly squeezed with compassion for Joseph.

"Nine o'clock Tuesday morning," Ben confirmed.

A tightness strained Joseph's features. Over the course of the week, she'd discovered from the few times he'd spoken of the appointment or his vision, he'd become instantly irritable.

Ben glanced at his pocket watch and snapped it shut again. "By the way, Katie, you've made quite an impression on Aaron and Ellie. She can't say enough good things about you." On a wink, he turned and jogged away from them.

Katie felt a warm blush color her cheeks as they walked in silence for several moments.

"He's right, you know…"

"Right about what?"

"Ellie has really taken to you." His voice was as low and soothing as a cool breeze on a hot day. "Last night when the two of them stopped by, she couldn't stop talking about you. Said you were beautiful, inside and out."

Embarrassment flamed hot now. Her knees went weak and her mouth grew dry. She couldn't seem to be around him without noticing every little thing about him and being affected in ways she'd never experienced.

But she was Joseph's teacher. Nothing else. She had to keep telling herself that.

"Sorry if I embarrassed you." His deep, mellow voice had countless other effects on her besides soothing her. His voice incited a warm quiver in her stomach and a slow, steady tremble up her spine. "When Ellie said that, it blew the very first image I had of you when Ben called you up from the street."

She slowed to a stop. "There's a step here. Gauge its height with your foot, then move ahead." When he continued without incident, she went on to ask, "What image did you have?"

He puffed out his cheeks on a big sigh. "Oh, just that you were a prune-faced old woman with a sharp nose and even sharper tongue. Good thing I didn't ride away into the sunset with that impression all week."

She smiled at his description, recalling how sour and gruff he'd been when she'd first met him. "Likewise, it's a good thing I didn't hold you to my first impression, either."

Wincing, he pulled at his collar as though it was suddenly too tight for comfort.

"For a while there, I thought my uncle's high opinion of you was overrated." She came to a stop and stared up at him. "But now, I think that it might just be underrated."

Chapter Five

"If there's one thing I cannot abide, it is an overbearing woman!" Julia proclaimed with a flourish. "Mrs. Duncan...why, the way that woman prattles on, you'd think she owned half the town. The woman is overbearing, I tell you. Overbearing!"

Joseph slid a hand across his mouth, masking his grin. He figured it took an overbearing person to know one, and Julia was close to an expert in the ways of overbearing women.

"Mrs. Duncan does—"

"She was nothing if not imperious," she interrupted with a terse huff. "Out of the goodness of my heart, I offered my valuable expertise in helping to organize the box social and barn dance for the Glory Days celebration. And she refused! Flat-out refused, I tell you."

"Maybe she already has things arranged," he offered in a lame attempt to console her.

He couldn't imagine why she'd come looking for consolation from him. Between the meal catastrophe when she'd stormed off mad and the indifference he'd shown her at church yesterday, he sure didn't expect her to try and cozy up to him again. But from the minute she'd barged into his solitude some fifteen minutes ago, she'd been as much as crawling into him, mining for sympathy.

He'd been sitting on his porch awaiting Katie's arrival to start a second week of training when Julia's taut, brisk steps brought her up the walk. Funny, the second he realized the footsteps weren't Katie's, disappointment crept over him like a dark cloud blocking out the sun's warmth.

Training his ear to the street, he listened for Katie's approach, feeling a strange sense of regret knowing he wouldn't really need her after his appointment next week. When his vision returned, Katie wouldn't have to. He had to admit, having her around every day had been nice. She'd gotten under his skin with her sweet but confident disposition, her sunny encouragement and the way she made him feel so at ease. So much like himself again.

"I just do not understand that woman!" Julia wailed, jerking him out of his thoughts. "Apparently she just doesn't want the celebration to be a success. Here I was only trying to help, and I—" A loud sob broke her lamentation.

The sound of her sniffling gave the indifference in Joseph's heart pause. Honestly, he felt sorry for Julia. She was an oddity out here in the west, away from her eastern friends and high-class ways. She was cultured. A large brilliant diamond in the midst of an earthy environment, and the startling radiance, which had caught his eye once, seemed almost offensive to him now. Like a shocking blast of light piercing a protective cocoon.

Unable to ignore her loud cries, he took a couple steps forward, reaching out to her. If there was one thing he couldn't bear, it was a woman upset and crying. His compassion always got the best of him.

"Aww, come here." He found her shoulder and gently pulled her to his side, her stiff skirt bristling like crisp rice paper against his britches. "I'm sure Mrs. Duncan doesn't really mean anything by it. She's just been the one in charge of organizing this shindig every year. Don't take it personally."

Julia sniffed daintily, and he could almost feel her big, emerald-eyed gaze upon him. "Do you think? I mean, I only wanted to help and then she—" Her voice broke on another sob.

For several moments he held her, feeling as awkward and stiff as a gruff old hermit embracing the Queen of England. But the way her sobs were subsiding, he was glad that at least his pathetic try at sympathy was helping.

"Good morning," came Katie's voice from his walkway.

Joseph turned, slipping his arm off Julia's shoulders.

"I—I'm sorry if I interrupted something." Her voice seemed to lack the warmth he'd grown accustomed to. "I thought we were beginning at eight-thirty this morning."

"It's fine. No need to apologize," he quickly responded, shoving his hands inside his pockets. "I was sitting out here waiting for you when Julia stopped by. We were just talking."

Sensing Julia's wilting spine stiffen, he silently

groaned. He shifted his feet on the hard-packed earth, noting that the sizzling sparks she emitted could've started a wildfire.

"Come on up," he offered, in an attempt to ease the awkwardness Katie must have felt.

"Miss Cranston, good morning." Even though she'd stopped mere feet from him, Katie sounded strangely distant.

He wished he could see her face, to gauge what kind of reaction registered there. Was she given to hiding her emotions? It dawned on him how little he knew of her, of what made her tick, what made her shudder in fear and of what made her heart leap.

And he determined to rectify that as soon as possible. If they were going to work side by side, even if it was for just another week, he wanted to know more about Katie Ellickson. Something about her drew him, compelling him to ignore common sense and step beyond a professional relationship to friendship.

"Miss Ellington." Julia's icy response could have frozen a flower on the spot.

"Ellickson," Joseph corrected with a shake of his head. Sliding a hand down his shirt, he checked for misaligned buttons. "I'm ready to start if you are, Katie."

Katie lightly cleared her throat.

Then Julia's parasol snapped open next to Joseph's head, and he sidestepped, startled and irritated.

"I certainly thought you would be done after an entire week of working with him, Miss *Ellickson*." Although Julia's voice was as smooth as honey, it lacked any sweetness. He could almost see her red lips clipping off each word with sharp precision. "All day long even?

Why, goodness, surely there can't be *that* much information to cover. You must be new to this."

He raked his fingers through his hair. "Actually, she's not new to this at all."

Ben had ticked off her qualifications on that first morning, and at the time Joseph hadn't given a horse's behind about any of it. But he cared now. "Far as I can tell, the glowing recommendations accompanying her are too conservative."

"Whatever could you possibly learn from her? I mean, you're a grown man, fully capable—except for those silly bandages obstructing your vision. You're used to life on your own. I cannot see what more you could need to learn."

Joseph gave a frustrated sigh. "You'd be surprised."

"All right, so perhaps you needed help eating at first. How well I remember *that* disaster. My dress..." she began with a whine. "Well, never mind that. But if you were to ask me, she's just confusing things, complicating simple matters with all of her five o'clock, three o'clock, six o'clock, ten o'clock gibberish. In my humble opinion—"

"I don't remember asking for your humble opinion," Joseph ground out. If he hadn't heard the brazenness of her sentiments for himself, he might not have believed she could be so thoughtless.

"I was just trying to help." Syrupy innocence dripped like putrid tonic from her words. She sidled up next to him and perched a hand on his bicep, trailing her fingers down his forearm. "Of course you know that I just want the best for you. Our relationship means a great deal to me."

Struggling to keep his composure, he picked up her hand from his arm as though it were a dead fish, dropping it back down to her side. "Julia, *I* need to get to work. And you—*you* need to leave."

"Very well." She took a couple steps away from him when he heard her pivot firmly. "Oh my, how could I be so remiss," she breathed, coming to stand in front of him again. "I came to give you a message from Daddy. That large furniture order he entrusted you with…well he hopes you understand how *very* important it is that it be completed—on time."

Joseph clenched his fists, trying to remain calm. When her father had placed the order over four weeks ago, Joseph had agreed on the completion date, exactly three months from the time of the order. He'd agreed to front all expenses with the understanding that he'd find hearty compensation in the end. Normally he wouldn't have put so much on the line, but the money he'd make from this one job would more than cover wages; it would pay for an extensive addition onto his shop, as well as some new tools.

Three months gave ample time to finish each piece to the standard he was known for. After all, he didn't want to jeopardize his reputation, not to mention this job. Aaron had been at it alone now for four weeks and even though he hadn't alluded to any problems, Joseph had a horrible feeling that they were losing precious time.

Thinking about everything that hinged on the return of his sight, a thick knot balled his stomach.

"It'll be done," he finally said. If it didn't get completed, he wouldn't have a livelihood left to resume.

"Wonderful! I'll let Daddy know." Without another word, Julia clattered back toward the heart of town.

When the sound of her brisk footsteps faded into the distance, he sighed and rested the pads of his fingers over his bandaged eyes. Frustration and irritation weighed heavy on him. But mostly he felt sick that Julia had been so unkind to Katie.

"Listen, Katie, I'm sorry about that." He shook his head, shoving his hands on his hips. "I don't know what came over her. I mean, I haven't ever seen this side of her and I—"

"You don't have to explain." The understanding in her voice pierced his heart all the more.

"No, she shouldn't have—"

"It's fine. I don't need an explanation."

He stepped toward Katie, wanting to reach out to her, to encourage her the way she'd encouraged him so many times with words or with a simple touch. For a week she'd poured herself out for him, a stranger really. Enduring, encouraging and lending faith when his was flagging.

"I just want you to know—"

"Please. Not another word." He could hear the light brush of her hand against her dress. "Now, then, if you're ready, why don't we begin for the day?" The suggestion she made was bolstered by levity that seemed forced. And he'd spent enough time with her to hear the difference.

"No," he stated simply.

"No?" Her voice was almost a whisper.

"That's right. No." He offered her a sidewise grin. "I have another idea. A surprise."

She gave an audible sigh. "What might your surprise be?"

"Well, it'll still require your assistance—that is if that's all right with you?"

"Of course. What can I do?"

Tucking his hands in his pockets, he felt a wave of sudden shyness. "I thought a picnic might be just the right thing today. What do you think?"

"A picnic? That would be lovely." The smile in her voice gave Joseph all the encouragement he needed.

After he and Katie packed a picnic lunch of cold meat, cheese and bread, they set out with Boone at their side for a day by the stream, a place Joseph had loved for years.

"Boone knows his way better than any hound dog, but just in case he's having an off day, let me know when you spot a big cottonwood edging the stream." Joseph gently grasped Katie's arm as they walked. "If my guess is right, we should be about there."

"I think it's right in front of us, about an acre ahead."

He caught the faint gurgling sound of the mountain stream. "Is it the biggest tree out here?"

After a short pause, she answered, "Yes. There's an old rope hanging from one of the branches. Is that the tree you're looking for?"

Childhood memories with his brothers came rushing back. They'd scale the rope, hand over fist to sit on the thick branches that spread like sturdy arms from the tree's broad trunk. "That's the one." Breathing a sigh of relief, he quickened his pace. "It's been a while since I've been here. I didn't know how much I missed this place."

"I can see why. It's beautiful."

"It is, isn't it?" Tilting his head back, he breathed deep, invigorated by the clear mountain air. Although he wished he could see it for himself, he could conjure up a clear mental picture of the landscape. Tall pines infusing the area with rich, dark green patches of color. Slate gray rocks positioned here and there in an order all their own. The quaint little valley nestled in between the mountains.

"It must be a beautiful day," he said. "The sun's already bearing down and it can't be past ten o'clock. How 'bout if we find some shade so you don't get too hot?"

"I don't mind the sunshine if you don't."

Slowing his pace, he came to a stop, turning her toward him. Tenderly slipping his fingers down her slender arm, lightly covered in soft cotton fabric, he grasped her hand—so petite in his, so smooth, so perfect. When he held her hand, his nerve endings hummed to an altogether different awareness. He could hear her breath catch in her throat, could almost feel her pulse pounding a rapid beat at her wrist. Threading his fingers through hers, he gave her hand a gentle squeeze, thankful for her presence today.

"No... I don't mind sunshine at all." Joseph's throat had gone thick and suddenly raw. "Sunshine."

Every moment spent together made him desire her brightness in his life all the more. As much as he wanted to rein in his heart, he felt helpless to hold it back. He may as well have been trying to lasso the wind. Like warm embers glowing to life by a gentle breath, his feelings for Katie sparked brighter.

Was he playing with fire? What if he'd never see anything more than dim shadows for the rest of his life? He wouldn't strap a woman with that—especially not Katie. Even though she was used to being around blind people, he wouldn't think to saddle her with that until death do them part. She deserved a whole man, not half a man. No matter how seemingly normal she said his life could be without sight, he'd never be a whole man, able to see trouble before it came, able to protect the ones he loved, able to provide an adequate living.

No. He'd have to bat down his heart until he knew what his future held. If his vision was restored, there'd be nothing stopping him from pursuing Katie. But if his vision didn't change, he'd have to settle for simple friendship with her.

Shrugging off the pain searing his heart at the thought, he released her hand and reached down to ruffle the fur on Boone's boxy head. "Come on, boy. I intend to enjoy the sunshine while I can."

Katie's hand still tingled from his touch. It felt as though his long, work-worn fingers lingered there, entwined in hers still, even though she and Joseph had been settled beneath the majestic tree for nearly an hour already. She brushed her fingertips across her lips. However gentle and tentative his grasp, the contact had affected her far more than she could've imagined.

And far more than she could allow to happen again.

She had to remain professional. She couldn't allow her emotions to wander about, unchecked. It just wasn't safe. Not when everything within her felt a strange pull to this man.

She stared down at the colorful scrap quilt where Joseph had stretched out on his back, hands stacked beneath his head. Her gaze roamed to his lips. The smile she'd glimpsed there the past few days had warmed her from the inside out. Her gaze lingered on his defined chest muscles stretching taut his cotton shirt. What would it be like to rest in the strong protection of his embrace? He was beautiful and honorable. So masculine and so...so taken!

She slammed her gaze down to where she'd clasped her hands in her lap. He obviously had an attachment to Miss Cranston that Katie would never be able to figure out. Why a humble man like Joseph would be attracted to a woman like Julia Cranston—so full of herself and thoughtless—was beyond Katie. She'd dismissed the possibility in the past couple of days, thinking perhaps the relationship was just one-sided, but after seeing the way he'd embraced Julia this morning, Katie's certainty crumbled like a day-old biscuit.

She was so confused. Had she read more into Joseph's touch and his sentiments than he'd intended? She must have.

But she hadn't missed the way he'd caressed her hand not more than an hour ago. Something had happened in that moment that had made them both struggle to breathe evenly. For some reason, his touch hadn't evoked the fear she'd battled since the attack a year ago, but instead filled her with comfort. And for the first time, she felt as if there might be hope for freedom.

Did she innately trust Joseph? She was beginning to think so. But as much as she felt a compelling draw toward him, she had to maintain her professionalism. Even if he did echo her feelings, he'd dismiss them if he discovered what had happened to her. There were just certain stains that could never be removed—no matter how hard you tried.

Katie drew her knees up to her chest, shutting out the shame that pricked her once again.

"So, Sunshine…" Joseph's soothing voice lifted her attention as though he'd gently crooked a finger beneath her chin. He rose on an elbow, facing her. "When you're not teaching, what do you enjoy doing?"

She peered at him. "We're not here about me, Joseph."

"That's where you're wrong," he responded with a shake of his finger. "What sort of things do you enjoy? Reading? Needlework? Big dogs that resemble bears?" A smile spread across his face as he reached to where Boone had dropped his hulking, dripping-wet form just off the blanket.

Katie laughed at the memory. "That was definitely not one of my better moments." She reached to stroke Boone's massive paws, noticing the fur that grew between his toes. "I'm sorry, boy. I hope you've forgiven me."

Joseph pushed himself up to sit and leaned back on his hands. "I'm sure he has. He doesn't hold grudges."

"Good. I'd hate to be on his bad side."

"Boone doesn't have a bad side."

"That's good to know. But you have to admit, it'd be unnerving to have a run-in with a dog like him. I thought I was a goner that first day on your porch."

She peered over at Boone, whose big brown eyes eased shut as though he was pretending not to eavesdrop on their conversation. In one deliberate, weighted movement, he rolled onto his back, his paws poking up in the air.

Katie laughed. "Not that you'd think he meant harm the way he looks now. You should see him, Joseph."

"Oh yeah?" he asked, smiling. "What's he doing?"

She leaned over to run her hand up and down the dog's long form. "He either wants his tummy scratched or he's sunning himself. He rolled over and has his feet stuck up in the air like wild flowers."

"He's done that since he was a young pup. He was one of Ben's strays, you know. Just a bag of bones with the most forlorn look in his eyes when we first found him. But Ben gave him lots of love and good care. I couldn't help myself from pitching in."

"The poor thing. That must've been horrible to see him like that."

"It was. But he's well-cared for now. Aren't you, boy?" Joseph ruffled the dog's fur. "Go on, Boone, play to your heart's content. It may be a while before we get back here."

When the dog lumbered off toward the stream, breaking out into an awkward lope, Katie turned back to Joseph. "Do you think he'd sense danger?"

Joseph nodded. "Boone's smart. He may look dead to the world the way he lazes about all day, but believe me, he has a keen awareness of people and what goes on around him. Far as I know, he's never bared his teeth at anyone, but I'm sure he'd sense it if someone meant harm. And I wouldn't be surprised if he did something about it, too."

Katie watched as Joseph leaned his head back for several moments. The sun splayed over his face in a golden glow, and a look of utter contentment spread across his features, his mouth curving slightly in a look of pure pleasure. The radiance diffused through the tree's silvery leaves enhanced his chestnut waves, turning them into strands of rich burnished bronze.

She couldn't deny the way she felt so safe and protected out here with Joseph. Ever since the attack, she'd avoided remote areas like this, determined to keep herself far from harm. But this place, this haven tucked away from the world, was so peaceful. Katie could easily see why Joseph had so many good memories here. She already felt refreshed.

"This was a good suggestion, coming out here today."

He snapped his attention toward her, his brows raised over the white bandage. "You didn't answer my question. What do you enjoy doing?"

Nervously, she picked at imaginary pieces of lint on her robin's-egg-blue print dress, then smoothed her hands down her skirt to her brown laced boots. She didn't like being the center of attention—especially after the attack. For the past year her job had been a good hiding place for her. She'd poured herself and every waking moment into her students. It was a small consolation that they weren't able to see her—that way she'd not have to worry about unwanted attention.

"Katie," he urged. "My question?"

The sideways grin Joseph sent her way did something uncommonly wonderful to her insides. Her stomach fluttered with the inexperience of a butterfly with new wings. Warmth crept through her like liquid sunshine.

"What makes Katie smile? What do you enjoy doing?"

"Hmm…what makes me smile?" she echoed, unable to keep her gaze from taking him in once again. "I'm glad to see you so relaxed."

"That I am, thanks to you. But we're not talking about me." He shifted to face her. "What about your family? Do you enjoy spending time with them? You must miss them."

Sliding her hands over her boots, she fingered each hook with great deliberation. "Oh, believe me, I do. But Uncle Sven and Aunt Marta are wonderful."

Joseph drew a knee up and draped his arm over it. "If things go well next week at my appointment like I think they will, do you think you'll go back home right away? I'd hate to see you take off so soon."

Katie sent up yet another silent prayer that he'd see again. But already she dreaded the emptiness she'd feel not being with him every day.

"I won't go home if I can help it." Unbidden, images of Frank Fowler, his eyes full of all manner of evil, played through her mind. "I have no desire to go back—" She cut her words off, her cheeks flushing hot beneath her hands.

"Can I ask why?"

"Why what?" Pulling her legs securely against her chest, she tried to block out the shadowy images that had instantly and without mercy assaulted her thoughts.

"Why are you avoiding going home? Is there a problem?"

"Oh, it's nothing," Katie dismissed, brushing at her skirt, wishing she could just as easily brush away the memories. "I'm just enjoying my time in Boulder. That's all."

"Enjoying your time, huh? I've been a real pleasure to be around, haven't I?" He smirked. "Is there more to it?"

"Nothing more." She winced at the quaver in her voice.

"Katie, I may not be able to see you, but I can hear a difference in your voice. And I've never heard you sound like this before. Want to talk about it?"

When a loud crack sounded from the tree line, she jumped, unable to stop a small scream from piercing the air.

"What? What's wrong?"

Her heart lurched to her throat as she scrambled over to Joseph and clung to his arm. "Did you hear that?"

"Hear what?" He set a hand on hers.

She craned her neck, searching the dense grove of trees, sure she would find Frank there. "That—that loud crack?"

Squeezing her eyes tight, she fought in vain to ignore the memories that came now in crashing waves. Frank Fowler's leering gaze. His long, tapered fingers clamping down around her arms, her neck, her breasts. His cigar-tainted breath hovering over her like a poisonous cloud.

She bit back a cry and swallowed against the sickening lump in her throat. Tightened her grip around Joseph's arm as though her very life depended upon it.

When she opened her eyes, she saw Joseph's forehead creased in concern. "It's all right, Katie," he soothed, wrapping his arm around her shoulders. "I think what you heard was Boone. He probably stepped on a branch and snapped it in two."

She shot her gaze back toward the stream to see

Boone emerge from the trees, his four sturdy legs braced and head hung low. As though building up momentum, he finally broke out into a full-body shake, sending tiny, sun-glinted droplets of water spraying from his glistening black fur.

"I—I'm sorry," she breathed, retreating to the other side of the blanket again.

"Please, don't apologize. Whatever has you so shaken, I want to help. I'm a good listener."

Katie fought for control over her emotions. She bent her head to her shoulder and swiped at the perspiration beading her brow. Rocking back and forth, she silently reminded herself that she was safe now, hundreds of miles away from Frank Fowler.

"I appreciate your concern," she finally squeezed out. "But it's something I'd rather not talk about."

"Sometimes it helps to talk." He slid his fingers slowly across the blanket toward her, as if searching for her hand. "Can you give me your hand, Katie?"

Katie stared at his outstretched hand, already missing the safe protection of his arm around her. Her heartbeat sped up inside her chest. She wanted to trust him, wanted to believe he could help her. Seeing the way his hands bore all the marks of hard work and sacrifice, she nearly groaned with the need to feel his strength, his support, his care.

"Listen. I realize you haven't known me long, but I mean it when I say I want to help." His words were offered like some lifeline.

Although she'd vowed that no one would ever know what had happened over the past year, a desperate part of her yearned to tell someone her secret. Someone she could trust. Someone she could lean on. Someone she could run to when the haunting memories nipped at her heels.

Like now.

She gulped back the all-too-familiar bile burning in her throat, slid trembling hands to her face and covered her mouth. Blinking hard, she fought to focus on Joseph's strong, capable hand. But the images, the haunting memories clouded her vision, turning the bright day upside down.

Frank Fowler's sharp, aristocratic features, his tall, foreboding frame, loomed like a sinister demon. A highly respected citizen, part-owner of the railroad and a deacon in the church—some thought he was fit to be a genteel lady's winning catch.

But Katie knew better. He was an awful, hurtful man, who'd done the unthinkable, not once, but twice. He'd stolen her—all of her—the first time in a dark copse of trees. Leaving her dress torn and dirty, her simple trust in others wounded and her purity sullied forever. He'd said that she'd always be his. Left her with a pointed threat that if she ever told a soul, someone she loved would die. He'd said that no one would believe her anyway, not when her father had lost a long and bitter court battle with him over a land dispute. Frank had promised that she'd be the shame of the community, a pawn in her father's hands, lying in a bid to discredit Fowler.

Katie had been desperate to tell someone, but what if Frank was right? She'd never forgive herself if something happened to a loved one because she couldn't keep her mouth shut. She'd lived with the secret for twelve months now. And she'd have to take it with her to her grave. No one could know.

She couldn't—wouldn't break her silence, now or ever.

"Katie? Are you all right?" Joseph's voice, his calming, rich voice, broke through her pain.

With quavering hands, she rubbed her eyes, wiped her perspiration-beaded brow and willed her body to stop quaking so. "Yes. I'm fine."

"Are you sure? Because you don't act like you're fine."

"Boone just startled me, that's all," she responded, her voice sounding almost normal again.

On a long pause, Joseph slowly braced his hand behind him again. "If you say so. But if ever you do feel like talking, I'm here."

She tried to shake off remnants of the haunting memories, but they were like tiny, stinging shards of glass. How she wished she could feel Joseph's hand around hers right now, assuring her everything would turn out fine. But she couldn't risk losing her job, and she definitely couldn't risk losing her heart. And she would, because no man—no matter how kind, how considerate, how upstanding—would want her once he knew she was soiled.

Inhaling slowly, she struggled to gather her composure as she rose to her feet. "We really should head back and get something accomplished today."

He gave his head a shake. "Far as I'm concerned, we're accomplishing plenty. I'm getting to know you a little better."

"That's what I mean," she countered, adjusting the

pleats draping her skirt. "We shouldn't be wasting our time talking about me."

Joseph stood in one slow movement, every bit of his tall, muscled form exuding strength and fluidity. He took one step her way and set his hands on her shoulders. "Katie… I want you to listen to me. You're not a waste of time. You're *far* from a waste of time."

Chapter Six

Joseph knew he should be relieved to have his brothers here, but for some reason he sensed this was more than just a shoot-the-breeze kind of visit.

He shifted uncomfortably in the wingback chair, feeling like a worm caught in the baking sun. Unable to stand the tension permeating the room, he finally broke the silence. "So, what's going on? I don't need eyes to see that you came here for a reason. I can't imagine what I've done this time. I've been on my best behavior with Katie." Which hadn't taken any effort since she was so easy to like. "We even spent the morning with a picnic down by the stream."

He couldn't miss the creaking of the sofa or the boots scuffing on the floor.

"So...who's going to talk?" he queried.

Ben cleared his throat from the winged-back chair opposite Joseph. "I guess what we're wanting to know is...how important is it that the furniture order be done on time?"

Foreboding crawled down his spine. "What do you mean, how important is it? It's important."

"*How* important?" Ben's reply was unnervingly measured.

"If the job doesn't get done, what'll that mean?" Zach's no-nonsense tone of voice grated on Joseph's nerves.

Joseph braced his elbows on his legs, steepling his fingers beneath his chin. "Aaron, I thought you said things were coming along. I believe those were the words you used. So are they?"

Aaron sucked in a deep breath. "Well, when we first st—"

"Just answer my question," Joseph ground out.

Zach huffed. "He will if you'll snap your jaw shut and let him."

"Quiet, Zach!" Joseph fired off, then shoved himself out of the chair and stood firm. "Is the job coming along or not?"

"Well, no," Aaron answered hesitantly.

He balled his fists, an unbelievably helpless feeling taunting him. "I thought you had everything under control."

"Take it easy," Ben urged. "He's been at it from early morning to late at night for almost five weeks straight."

Guilt for his quick temper pricked. He struggled to tamp down his irritation. "I know you've been working day and night, Aaron, but we've got to get this done."

"Remember, it's a very large order." Ben cleared his throat. "An entire restaurant worth of furniture."

Jamming his fists on his hips, Joseph felt every

muscle in his body jerk taut. "So, what's the problem? Tell me."

"Ease up, Joe," Zach spoke from the sofa. "Aaron's been doing the best he can."

"The best he can?" he repeated. Raking his fingers through his hair, he grasped at what little calm he had left. If it wasn't for his injury, he wouldn't be in this mess. "Aaron, tell me, what is the status with Mr. Cranston's order? Because so far every time I've asked you how things are going, you've said that things were fine. Have you been giving me the straight story or not?"

"Both." Drumming his fingers on the arm of the sofa, Aaron made a loud hissing exhale, then continued. "I don't see how the job's going to get done at the rate things are going. There's no way, Joseph, even with Ben and Zach helping out."

"What about when I'm able to work again after I get home from Denver?" He crossed his arms at his chest.

"You're forgetting one small thing," came Ben's voice, low and sobering. "What if you don't get your sight back?"

"That's *not* an option, Ben," Joseph shot over his shoulder.

The wingback chair scraped against the wood floor as Ben shifted. "We all want you to see again. But the fact remains that you might not distinguish more than the dark gray shadows you saw the first time I took off the patches. And the doctor in Denver may not have any alternatives for treatment."

His skin prickled. "I hate this!"

Balling his fists in front of his face, he wished he could just pound his eyes and bring back his vision.

Frustrated, he hastily stalked toward the entryway, coming to a sudden, humiliating stop when he collided with the wall. Gritting his teeth, he braced trembling hands up along the wall. Leaned his forehead against the cool plaster.

"Right now I can't make it down the street without help and I may not have a business left, all because of this." Pressing hard against the wall, he added, "I *have* to see again."

"I hope you do, Joe-boy. Believe me, I do," came Aaron's voice just behind him. "I'm sorry. I should've said something sooner, but I didn't want to make things worse for you than they already are. Even if you do get your vision back, though, I'm afraid we still might be too far behind."

"Too far behind?" He pushed his fists against the wall, wanting to just shove them all the way through.

"I'll talk to Mr. Cranston." Aaron's voice was swathed with forced optimism. "I'm sure he'll understand if I have a chance to explain everything."

Joseph spun around and pulled his shoulders back. He wanted to lash out, take his anger and deep-seated desperation out on something or someone. Instead, he slowly headed back to the chair, inwardly gauging his steps as Katie had taught him.

"You're not going to go making excuses for me. Even if you did, I already know the answer." Turning, he sank down into the tall, padded chair. "Mr. Cranston is a shrewd businessman. We made a deal. Signed a contract. His hands are probably tied just like mine."

Joseph braced his elbow on the arm of the chair and leaned into his hand, attempting to massage away the pain in his head that suddenly bore down upon him without mercy. "You know as well as I do that I fronted all the money for materials and labor. I stand to lose the shop if we don't deliver on time."

"So, what do we do?" Aaron moved to stand next to Joseph.

"Right now I can't do much," he said, trying for a more contrite tone. "I know I've heaped a lot on you, Aaron—especially with Ellie not feeling well. And I know that you, Ben and Zach have been over there helping when you can. If you can just hang on a little longer till these bandages come off, I'll make it up to you. I promise."

"What about the finish work?" Aaron asked, dropping down to squat beside the chair.

Joseph pressed his fingers to his bandaged eyes. "When I return from Denver next week, I'll work night and day if I have to, to catch us up so we won't be late."

"But what if—" Aaron began.

"My vision doesn't return? It will. God *will* give me back my sight. He has to."

Joseph bit back a curse. He slapped the knife down on the counter, resisting the urge to shake off the throbbing pain assailing his finger. He'd been cutting vegetables—Katie's latest lesson—and had cut more than just the carrot.

"What's wrong?" Katie approached his side, her arm lightly brushing against his.

He covered one hand with the other, trying to snuff out the anger that had sparked so quickly. "Nothing."

He was learning the hard way that he couldn't afford

to let his focus drift or he was vulnerable to mishaps. Every task he did seemed to require double the effort, double the energy, double the focus. And double the patience.

He'd been agitated *all* day. Couldn't seem to keep his mind on any task—not after his brothers had paid him a visit last evening. He'd lain awake through the night wracking his brain, searching for a way to complete the job on time.

Katie lifted his hand, her touch light, sure and warm. "It's not *nothing*. You're bleeding, Joseph." Cradling his hand in hers, she drew him over to the washbasin and began pumping the squeaky handle. "We'll get this cleaned up."

"I can do it." He pulled his hand from her grasp.

"If you insist," she stated, stepping away from him and leaving him instantly wishing for her closeness again. "Can you tell me where to find something to put on that?"

"On my cut?"

"No, your wounded pride," she shot back.

He winced. "So I'm irritated. You would be too if you cut yourself like a youngster."

He directed her to where he kept medicinal supplies while he ran his forefinger under the stream of water, feeling it trickle into the wound. If he could see, he'd be able to handle the situation easily. Knowing he couldn't see past the bandages covering his eyes firmly established his irritation like a stubborn weed with tentacle-like roots that crept into his dignity.

After she'd returned, she gently wrapped his hand in a cloth and led him over to the table. "You seem to forget that other people cut themselves, too. It doesn't matter whether you can see or not, it's bound to happen."

"Other people can see whether they're bleeding all over the floor," he retorted, feeling justified in his response.

She pulled out two chairs. "Here, sit down while I bandage your finger."

He sat down directly in front of her and fought the urge to ask her to leave. Fought even harder the sensations provoked by the way she cradled his hand in hers.

"The cut's pretty deep," she breathed, gently turning his hand as though to get a better look. "Maybe we should have Ben take a peek at it. You might need a few stitches."

"No." Every muscle in his body pulled taut. "I don't need Ben to take a look at it."

"Are you sure?" She gently dabbed at his finger with a cloth. "I could go and find—"

"No! I said I'm fine. I don't need him."

"Joseph Drake, you are as grumpy as a wounded bear."

He couldn't argue with that. Why was it so hard to submit to the soothing ministrations of this one who cared, who didn't see his weakness as something to exploit? For several moments he sat there, torn between wanting to distance himself from her and wanting to trust her in his vulnerability.

Refusing to center on the upheaval he felt, he decided to focus on her hands, so smooth and tender on his skin. With the faintest of strokes from the pads of her thumbs, she began to calm the tension that commanded his body.

"Here," she said, handing him a cloth. "Apply pressure to stop the bleeding while I get a wrap prepared."

He did as she'd directed, acutely aware of the slightest brush of her legs against his.

"What's wrong, Joseph?" Her words were guarded.

"It's just a cut. Like I said, I'm fine."

"That's not what I mean." She cradled his hand in hers again and carefully lifted the cloth from his finger. "Good. It looks like the bleeding's stopped. We'll get this fixed in no time." She began applying an ointment to his cut, her touch so gentle. "You seem on edge. You have been since I showed up this morning. Did something happen?"

On a long exhale, he felt his tight neck muscles relax a little. "I'm sorry. I just have a lot on my mind."

"Anything I can help you with?"

"No." With a wry grin he added, "Not unless you're as good at building furniture as you are teaching."

When she stopped her ministrations, he could feel her gaze on him. "Is there a problem out at the shop?"

"Yes. You could say that," he admitted, then related the circumstances he faced.

"What are you going to do? I mean is there any way Mr. Cranston could postpone the date a few weeks?"

As she began to wind a bandage around his finger, he was sure she was unaware of the way her warm, comforting touch sent sensations through him.

Straight to his heart.

It seemed there was no way to keep from being affected by Katie. He'd have to send her away to accomplish that, and he wasn't sure he was willing to go to that extent. In just two short weeks she'd become a part of his life. A bright, promising part of his present and hopefully his future.

"There's no way he'll postpone," he answered, distracted by the tightening in the pit of his stomach. "Either we deliver on the date, or lose it all."

"Could Zach or Ben help Aaron out?"

"They're already pitching in where they can. But there's only so much they can do. Ben's a great doctor and Zach's a natural with horses, but of their own admission, they're not cut of the same cloth as Aaron and me."

"Oh, I see." She secured the bandage with a knot.

When she finished, he set his elbow on the table, holding his hand up to ward off the throbbing. Her touch had been so comforting that he wished she hadn't been so efficient.

"What about you, Joseph?" Katie rose and crossed to the sink where she pumped water. "I'm sure you could do things in the shop."

Shifting uncomfortably in his chair, Joseph figured she might as well have kicked him in the shin. "I never thought I'd say this but you're starting to sound like Julia."

"I'm sorry." She set a hand on his shoulder. "I didn't mean for the suggestion to sound unfeeling." Katie grasped his good hand. "Here's some water."

He felt the cold stoneware and gripped the cup as she sat down in front of him again. "Thanks."

"What I'm trying to say is…why *couldn't* you try some of the work out there? From what I hear and the proof I've seen, you're a master at the craft. Couldn't you—"

"Don't be ridiculous." Gulping down the water, he

swiped the moisture from his lips with his shirtsleeve
and set the cup on the table. "If you've forgotten already,
I sliced my finger cutting vegetables." He held the bandaged finger in front of him. "With a saw or chisel in
my hand, I'd be a bloody mess."

"No, you wouldn't," she shot back.

Joseph shook his head. "You're not being realistic."

"No, Joseph. I'm being completely realistic. You're
just being stubborn. I told you on our first day together
that I wouldn't coddle you, but help you to find independence." She rose and pushed in her chair. "And that's
what I'm here to do."

He drew his lips into a grim line, not sure whether
to be angry or relieved. She could be so compassionate
and then turn right around and goad him without shame.

"Why couldn't Aaron spend his time putting the furniture together, while you focus on the finish work and
sanding? Don't you depend a lot on touch to do that
kind of thing?"

With a grunt, he slouched in the chair, sliding his
long legs out in front of him. "Nice thought," he said,
draping one boot over the other. "But it'd never work."

"Why wouldn't it work?" He could hear her gathering the medical supplies on the table. "I see you often,
smoothing your hands over things as though searching for imperfections. It's in you, Joseph. You can't get
away from it."

"Well, I'll be a dad-burned donkey if it ain't Sam
Garnett!" Mr. Heath, the mercantile owner proclaimed.
"How have you been?"

The shopkeeper's jubilant greeting perked Katie's

curiosity. She cocked an ear toward the door without turning away from the elegant hair combs she'd been inspecting. She was trying to decide which one to buy with some of the pay she'd received yesterday, at the end of her second week of work.

Honestly, she hadn't wanted to take one dime from Joseph, feeling more than ever that her time with him was not a job at all, rather a privilege, a pleasure. He'd gotten visibly irritated when she'd balked at taking the envelope. Said he wasn't interested in charity. Insisted she take the money.

"Mr. Heath, you're a sight for sore eyes. It's good to see you," the stranger called, his deep voice echoing in the room.

"You, too, Sam. You, too. It's not often we get a city-slick lawyer in these parts."

From the corner of her eye, she saw the two men shaking hands across the long glass-front counter. Even from her vantage point she noticed that the man wore a crisp three-piece suit, professionally tailored.

"What brings you to these parts?" Mr. Heath inquired.

"I need to tie up some loose ends on my folks' land since they passed away."

"We sure are sorry about their passing. They were good people." Mr. Heath's voice went unusually quiet.

"Thank you." After a short pause, Sam added, "That wave of influenza hit hard last winter, didn't it?"

"Yes, sirree. But thank goodness it didn't last long. Since Ben Drake came back from his schoolin' and started practicin' his medicine here it seems like we've been fairin' better through things like this."

"Ben's a good doctor. I've no doubt about that." Sam took his rounded top hat from his head, tapping it into perfect form.

"So, will you be headin' back to the big city right away? Or can you stay a spell?"

Katie held up a comb as though examining it, but her attention kept getting pulled to the man named Sam. She didn't feel the same unnerving wariness she normally had around strange men, and that surprised her. Maybe it was because he was a native to the area. Or maybe it was the way he'd been received by Mr. Heath like a richly decorated hero come home from war.

"I thought it'd do me good to take in some fresh mountain air to clear my head." His voice swelled with satisfaction. "I decided to take a month's leave from the law firm and mix a little business with pleasure."

"If that ain't a fine how-do-you-do!" Mr. Heath slapped Sam on the shoulder. "Me and the missus— why we'll be lookin' forward to havin' you over to our place for supper. Bet you don' get cookin' like the wife's back in the big city."

"Probably not. I'm looking forward to that already. Thank you for the invitation." Sam reached into his pocket and pulled out a slip of paper. "Here I came in to say hello and get these few things, and I end up with a dinner invitation. I believe I'm getting the better end of the deal."

"Ya say ya need a few things, do you? Well, what can I do you for?"

Katie briefly glanced toward the exchange and listened to the conversation, all the while peering at the same comb she'd held for the past several moments.

She didn't mean to eavesdrop but couldn't help it. The wood floors and high ceilings only aided in carrying the sound of their voices.

The tall stranger, whose dark hair accentuated his almost Romanesque features, handed the list to Mr. Heath. "I'll be staying at Mrs. Royer's boarding house, so I won't need much."

"Don't think there's a selfish bone in that woman's body. She'll take good care of you. Mother you till you wish you were eight again." Mr. Heath quickly perused the list. "I'll get these things. You just make yourself at home." He turned to start filling the order and called over his shoulder, "You might notice some changes we've made since you were last here."

When Sam turned and leaned against the counter, his arms folded across his chest, Katie snapped her attention back to the combs. She stared down at them, wondering why she was so curious about this man.

"It's good being back in your store," Sam called out. "I can't count how many times Joseph and I would stop by and try to finagle you out of a licorice whip or a peppermint stick in return for a good hour's labor."

Katie's pulse skittered. Was he talking about Joseph Drake? Were the two of them friends?

"You were good help, too," came Mr. Heath's response from the far side of the room. "That is, when you weren't tryin' to impress some lil' lady. Couldn't get an honest *minute* of labor outta ya then."

She bit back a smile at the thought of Joseph and this man, vying for some girl's attention. And as she easily recalled the feelings she'd had when she'd held Joseph's hand while doctoring his cut, she couldn't imagine him ever having to work too hard for any girl's affection.

After several more moments Sam said, "You *have* made some additions to the mercantile. Business must be good."

"Had to add those two new rows of shelving to house the extra goods. Our customers expect an ample selection, you know." Mr. Heath poked his head out from the back room. "And speaking of Joseph, take a look at that new counter he made. She's a beauty. Ain't another one like it."

Katie glanced at the beautiful counter in front of her. Another tribute to Joseph's expert craftsmanship. Another reason why she had to help him get his life back again.

When she spotted Sam approaching from out of the corner of her eye, she tried her best to appear fully transfixed on the items before her.

"Good afternoon, ma'am. I don't believe I've had the pleasure of making your acquaintance." He stopped next to her and held out his hand. "My name is Samuel Garnett. And yours?"

She stared stupidly up at him, and with minimal grace shoved her hand toward him. "I'm Katie Ellickson."

When he gently grasped her hand in his, her cheeks grew warm. Much to her chagrin, her embarrassment had never been easily hidden, not when her fair skin told an undisguised story.

She abruptly pulled her hand from his. "It's nice to meet you, Mr. Garnett."

"You must be new to town. I don't believe I remember seeing you here the past few times I've made it back. I would *never* forget a face like yours." He studied her face, his liquid brown gaze intent.

"New?" She gulped. "Yes, I moved here from Iowa a little over two weeks ago."

"What brought you here?" When he glanced down at her finger as though looking for a ring, her hands trembled.

"I—I came to start a new life." She immediately cringed at her ridiculous choice of words, no matter how true they were.

"The old life not so good, eh?" His eyebrows arched over his dark, penetrating eyes.

"Oh, no—I mean—it was fine. Well…more than fine." She shook her head and laughed nervously. "I'm terribly sorry. I don't know what has come over me."

"Forgive me," he said, offering an apologetic grin. "I didn't mean to make you uncomfortable nor did I mean to pry. I guess it's just the lawyer coming out in me. You know, always wanting to know every little fact. Let me try again."

Backing up a few paces, he started toward her. "Good afternoon. I don't believe I've ever met you. My name is Samuel Garnett. And yours?" His eyes twinkled with delight.

She hesitated for a moment, unsure whether she should run from this very bold man, or stay put. That he was a longtime friend of Joseph made her relax a little. When she peered up at him, noticing the kindness in his strong features, she held her hand out to him and smiled. "I'm Katie Ellickson."

"Well, Miss Ellickson, I hope we'll be seeing each

other again. Perhaps at church tomorrow?" Brows raised, he tilted his head toward her, as if waiting for a response.

"Yes, Mr. Garnett. I'll see you at church."

"I have your order together, Sam," Mr. Heath called out.

Mr. Garnett slid his gaze to the counter and pointed to one of the combs. "My vote is this one," he whispered, giving her a warm smile. "A sure compliment to your beauty."

Katie felt her cheeks flush. Again. He was a charmer—that was for sure. But she didn't know why in the world she was responding like some smitten schoolgirl.

"What do you keep yourself busy with besides lawyering?" Mr. Heath's booming voice filled the room. "Is there a missus yet? Young 'uns?"

He started back over to Mr. Heath. "I've been so busy at the law office with all the movement west, I haven't had time for much else."

Katie felt his gaze directed her way and angled a glance to see him leaning casually against the counter on one elbow. Staring at her as though there was nothing else in the room.

"I actually might start thinking about settling down," he continued with the hint of a smile. "Especially if I happen to find the right lady."

Chapter Seven

"Why is it so unbelievable to think that Joseph has feelings for you?" Ellie prodded. She graced Katie with one of those cat-that-ate-the-canary kind of smiles, and rubbed a hand lightly across her protruding belly.

Exasperated, Katie gave her friend a wide-eyed look. "I'm his teacher. I seriously doubt he's thinking beyond that."

"Just because you're his teacher doesn't mean he couldn't develop feelings for you."

Raising the dainty flowered teacup to her mouth, Katie breathed in the warm cinnamon scent, then took a sip. She remembered how agitated Joseph had been yesterday after he'd cut himself. And then when she'd suggested he could work in the shop without sight, he'd gotten downright belligerent.

No. She doubted very much that he felt anything but irritated by her.

"I'm sure he feels nothing of the sort," Katie dismissed. "I'm more like a thorn in his flesh than a rose in his garden."

But then she replayed, as she had countless times, the softness with which Joseph had touched her, the gentleness and respect with which he'd treated her on their picnic. His words had been like warm caresses and his momentary touch had set her off-kilter. Even the memory incited the same skittering feeling all the way down her spine to her toes.

Surely she must be reading into all of that. How could he possibly have feelings for her when he had so much to deal with as it was? His lack of sight. His work. A general upheaval in his life. And there was always Julia, with her thoughtless, manipulative, even abrupt, ways. Julia, with her striking dark tresses, porcelain-white complexion and piercing emerald gaze. She was a beauty, probably pure as the wind-driven snow. Probably flawless in every way.

Except in the way she treated Joseph.

Vindictiveness rose within Katie like a sword unsheathed. She'd never felt so hostile toward another person, so hungry to dish back the same thoughtless handling.

She tried to rein in the errant emotion, chiding herself for being so hard on Julia. Maybe there was an understanding side of Miss Cranston that had drawn Joseph in the first place.

If so, Katie just couldn't seem to look past the obvious manipulation she saw happening. The woman had conveniently been walking in the direction of Joseph's home on more than one occasion this week and had stopped once, keeping his attention for a good hour with some drivel about getting nominated to cochair the Boulder Ladies' Committee. Katie had gladly made herself scarce at the time, although she couldn't help stealing glances of the two out on the porch, noticing how clingy Julia was with Joseph, like a barnacle hugging tight to a ship's hull.

Shaking off the disturbing image, she folded her hands in her lap. "Joseph has so much to think about right now. I'm sure he has no thoughts of me other than as a teacher."

"Whatever you say." Ellie shrugged, tucking strands of strawberry blond hair into her loose braid. "But Aaron and I—even Ben—agree that he's a different man since you've come. You've been good for him, Katie." The mischievous smile she sent Katie faded fast when she stood from the table. She winced and set hands to the small of her back.

"Is something wrong?" Katie asked.

"No, no. I'm fine." Ellie fixed a smile on her face. "You definitely have a way with Joseph. We *all* think so."

"I'm sure you're just noticing that Joseph is feeling more comfortable with himself and his surroundings. He's been getting to know his world through touch," she said, unable to ignore the ready memory of just that. The way his fingertips irrevocably branded her flesh with absolute tenderness.

Bowing her head, she blinked hard and glanced down at the handkerchief she twisted in her hands. "I do think he's beginning to trust me, though. I'm glad of that."

"Well, that's something." Setting a fist to her waistline, Ellie dabbed at the perspiration beading her upper lip with her white apron. "You've gotten a lot farther with him than the rest of us would've been able to."

A sudden flush worked its way up Ellie's cheeks, inciting another swell of concern in Katie. "Do you need to sit down?"

Ellie trailed her hands down her dress, plucking at the wide stretched pleats. "It seems like these days, with less than a month to go, and the baby being so low, I'm more comfortable on my feet."

Standing, she moved over to grasp Ellie's hand, unable to shake the concern she felt. "Can I do something for you?"

"Really, don't worry." Ellie smiled and squeezed Katie's hand. "I hope you don't mind me saying so, but I'd be elated if Joseph did have feelings for you. You'd be the perfect sister-in-law."

"Ellie! How can you say that?"

"Because you'd be wonderful. Besides, I'm tired of being the only woman among the Drake brothers," she added, swiping her brow and taking a deep breath as though she'd just run a mile. "Those brothers need to each find themselves a bride. And I've decided that you'd be the perfect start."

Crossing her arms at her chest, Katie shook her head. "You're picking the wrong flower in the field here."

"You can't stop me from hoping."

Ellie was right. Katie couldn't stop her from hoping. At times she could barely stop herself from hoping. Too often for her own comfort, she'd catch herself daydreaming about Joseph, fancying herself as his bride. Sharing a full, beautiful life with him.

But it seemed as if the more she dreamed of that, the more her shame overshadowed her like a threatening storm cloud.

Swallowing past the lump in her throat, she tried to remain levelheaded. "You're right. I can't stop you from hoping. But let me assure you that nothing like that could ever happen."

"You two are perfect for one another. Besides…" Ellie added, resting her arms on her belly. The scrupulous perusal she gave had Katie squirming. "I've seen that *look* in your eyes when you speak of him—or when you spotted him at church."

Katie pinned her gaze to the rag rug. "What *look* is that?"

Out of the corner of her eye, she saw Ellie slowly twirl around like a belle at a ball. "That starry-eyed, soft look that happens when a woman…feels something for a man."

Katie unsuccessfully bit back a smile. At times like this, she wished she was better at schooling her expressions. "I won't dispute your observation," she said simply.

"Ah ha! I knew it!" Ellie clasped her hands beneath her chin. "Just last night I was telling Aaron that—"

"But—" she interrupted, holding out her hand, "—that's the extent of it."

Katie crossed to the window. For several moments she stared out through clear glass at the protected valley, bathed in a late-afternoon August glow. Would there ever be beauty like that, all warm and promising in her life? Maybe she was selling Joseph short. Maybe he wouldn't allow her past to define their future. Maybe he could look beyond her shame.

What was she thinking? She knew how upright men wanted their brides unstained. Fowler had told her as much. He'd hissed the reality in her ear, his words striking her like buckshot, piercing her in so many ways that she didn't know how to begin putting herself back together.

Turning away from the window, she passed a wary glance to her friend. "There are things from my past that—" Katie stopped midsentence when Ellie grabbed her abdomen and bent over, drawing in a sharp breath.

"Ellie, what's wrong?" She scurried over and set a hand of support at Ellie's back. "What's going on?"

A muffled cry came through clenched teeth. After several moments Ellie straightened, her hands clamped to her abdomen.

"Have you had pain like this before?"

"Not sh-sharp cramping like this." She gasped for air. "But I'm sure it's nothing."

"That wasn't nothing," Katie argued. She helped Ellie to a chair, noticing how her friend's whole body trembled. "I'm going to go get Ben and Aaron."

Ellie snapped out her arm and grabbed for Katie. "No, I'll be fine. Please don't bother them."

"Sorry," Katie responded, patting her friend's hand. "But I'm certain they'll want to know."

"Katie, really, Aaron can't afford to be gone from the shop right now," Ellie pleaded, her brow beaded with perspiration, her cheeks flushed. "There's too much to do. I don't want him worrying about me."

Dipping a washcloth in cool water from the basin, she laid it on Ellie's forehead. "I understand how urgent things are in the shop. But I know he'll agree that you take precedence over anything there. Now, I'm going to help you to bed and then, if you'll be all right for a short while—"

"I'll be fine—I'm fine now. You don't need to go." Her hands drifted to her protruding stomach where she carefully caressed the life inside. "Please, I'm feeling better already."

"I'm not taking any chances. This baby could be on the way and I'll feel much better knowing that you're well-cared for."

After she got Ellie situated in bed, she ran the one-and-a-half-mile distance to Boulder, all the while praying that God would help Ellie and the little baby yet unborn.

Bounding up the boarded walk to Ben's office, she flung the door open. "Ben, are you here?" she called between panting breaths. She peeked into the back room, then ran out of the office and to the mercantile. "Mr. Heath, do you have any idea where Ben Drake is?"

"Well, yes, as a matter of fact, he was just here. Said he was gonna be stoppin' by to pay Joseph a visit."

She called her thanks on the way out the door and hurried over to Joseph's home. Picking up her skirts, she leaped up the three steps to his porch and rapped on the door.

"Ben, are you here?" Katie called out.

The door swung open. "Katie, what's wrong?" Ben's face was etched with obvious concern.

"It's Ellie. She needs you. Something's wrong."

"What happened?" He stepped out onto the porch.

"I—I'm not really sure. I just know she didn't look good. She's in pain. Cramping. I'm very worried about her."

"Joseph, is Aaron still in the shop?" Ben called.

"Yes, he should be." Joseph emerged from the front room. "You go ahead and get what you need at the office, Ben. We'll have Aaron meet you down there."

Ben called his agreement as he ran down the walk. After Katie rushed behind Joseph's house to the shop and alerted Aaron, she jogged back to find Joseph waiting for her.

"I do hope Ellie will be all right," Katie choked out, winded. Her strength bolstered just being in Joseph's presence.

"She's in good hands," he assured her. "Ben will take good care of her—Aaron, too."

Pulling in a deep breath, she walked alongside him to the front porch, grateful for his company. In a very unladylike fashion, she collapsed next to Joseph on the steps, resting her head in her hands in an effort to calm herself.

When she felt his gentle touch at the small of her back, her heart skipped a beat. A tingling sensation, thick as honey, spread through her entire body and her heart threatened to beat right out of her chest at the reassuring warmth of his touch.

When she hauled herself to sit up straight, his hand remained settled, a warm claim at her back. A shiver worked down her spine, and she was certain he could feel her heart beating right through her rib cage. Her head swam with emotions, sensations that made her light-headed.

"It's good you were there, Katie." His caring tone made her all the more weak-kneed. "Ellie needed you."

"Yes, but I should've been more attentive to her." A

wave of guilt assaulted her. "At first when I asked, she said she was fine. And then I was so busy telling her why it wasn't possible that you and I—"

She clapped a hand over her mouth, downright mortified at her careless choice of words. Shoving herself up to standing, she established some much-needed space between herself and Joseph. His touch was way too disarming and threatened to break down her protective walls.

He stood, edging slightly closer. "Why it wasn't possible that you and I what?" His voice was low and smooth.

Her knees began to tremble beneath her soft yellow day dress. The air grew stiflingly thick as she peered up at him, her stomach pulling taut at his all-consuming focus. Sliding her gaze over his form, her focus riveted on his shoulders. They were firm, thick with muscle and broad enough to support the biggest burden. In the short time she'd known him she'd seen him bear trials a lesser man would've buckled under.

Oh, that she could trust him with her troubles.

Moving her gaze down to his muscle-roped arms, she quivered. Katie could almost feel his sinewy arms, placed protectively around her shoulders, shutting out her fears. She closed her eyes, indulging herself in the notion.

Emotions that rocked her deep inside, intensified.

She squeezed her eyes tight, willing the feelings not to surface. Not now. If she couldn't control her emotions, she'd have to quit working with him. And he'd made so much progress. He'd been giving a grand effort in his training, and if his vision didn't return, there was still so much more she could show him, so much more she could open up for him.

Besides, she was only making it harder on herself. There was sure to come a time when the sparks that arced between them would fade from brilliance, snuffed out by her past.

"Katie, are you there? You're awfully quiet," he breathed, easing her back to reality.

Her entire body trembled now, an uncontrollable shaking that stemmed from deep within. For months she'd run ragged, fighting to keep the walls she'd erected firmly in place. If someone breached that barrier, the secret she'd diligently hidden would be exposed.

But right here…right now, she ached to have a shoulder to lean on. An arm to support her.

She startled as Joseph settled his hands on her shoulders, then lightly slid them down her arms.

"You're trembling," he said, his voice husky.

She swallowed hard, staring up at him. Hugging her arms tight to her chest, she fought against her unruly emotions.

Every nerve ending sprang to life as he trailed his fingers, whisper-soft, to the nape of her neck. Cradling her head in his hand, he inched closer and drew her to his chest.

Katie stiffened, feeling his hard upper body beneath her cheek. Curling her arms snuggly at her chest, she warred against the innate need to feel protected, cared for. She teetered on the edge. But as he lightly stroked her hair, trailing his fingers to her back, calm settled over her like a thick blanket.

His warm breath filtered through her thick tresses

and she melted against his chest. Drawing in a quivering breath, she took in the woodsy male scent that was Joseph. She uncurled one fist, placing her fingertips reverently against the rigid muscular wall in front of her, feeling his untapped power beneath her touch.

He rested his chin on top of her head, and a rush of warmth poured over her as though she'd just stepped into glorious, welcoming sunshine.

"I know that you probably regret coming out here to work with me." His voice grew rough with emotion. "Even on my good days, I've taken out a lot of frustration on you."

She wanted to stop him, realizing that he'd misunderstood her, but she couldn't find her voice. She was completely overcome by the sensations he stirred inside her.

"Don't let my gruff exterior scare you, Katie. I'd never—never hurt you." Like a hearth fire's soothing glow, his husky voice penetrated the swirl of emotion. "I care too much about you."

Joseph could kick himself for how he'd responded to Katie yesterday—embracing her like he did and saying what he had. But she'd been so upset about Ellie—and rightly so. Ellie was not doing well and Ben had put her on strict bed rest until the baby arrived.

Joseph's heart had squeezed at the compassion and care he'd seen in Katie, and he'd relished the few moments when he'd held her close. It had felt so right. *She* had felt so right in his arms. It had taken every bit of strength he had to finally release her.

Now, as he stood outside the church waiting for Ben, he still didn't feel as though he had control over his traitorous heart. He'd done his best to rein in his run-away emotions around Katie, but his heart beat sure and strong, the ancient rhythm pervading every breath, thought and moment. Even knowing she was most likely there in church this morning set his pulse to pounding.

Everything about her tugged at Joseph's heart, making him want to comfort her, encourage her, protect her. And for some reason, he couldn't help but wonder if maybe breaking through the barriers she'd set up around herself might be the biggest challenge he'd ever faced.

But considering his uncertain future, he couldn't allow himself to get too close. He'd spent far too much time thinking of Katie. The way her gentleness soothed his deep-seated fear and the way her patience had given him needed confidence. She'd made him feel like a man again.

Turning his face to the cool breeze, he marveled at how he'd become captivated so quickly. But from what he'd heard, she'd had the same effect on others, too, winning hearts like some long-lost heroine.

"Hey, there, Joseph!" a voice called out, startling him from his musings. "I've been looking all over for you."

Joseph turned toward the familiar voice. "Sam?"

"It's me, all right!" Dry grass crunched beneath Sam's feet as he approached Joseph. "Am I ever glad to see you."

Joseph stretched out his hand to give Sam a firm handshake and wasn't surprised to find himself pulled into a manly embrace. When Sam released his hold, Joseph noted how his friend seemed more filled out than the last time he'd seen him. His shoulders felt broader and his chest fuller.

"Good to have you back in town, Sam," he said, resisting the awkwardness that suddenly assailed him.

But if anyone could put him at ease, it was Sam. His friend had a way of making others feel comfortable, no matter what the circumstance. Joseph would never forget that day, years ago, when thirteen-year-old Jacob returned to school after sustaining burns in a barn fire. Humiliation had been written all over the boy's face as he clearly avoided interaction with other kids. But at the first recess, Sam made a point to draw him into a game of kickball. From then on, it was as though everyone else seemed to know how to respond.

"It's good to be back," Sam replied, his voice sounding deeper than Joseph remembered.

"I heard that you arrived yesterday."

"I can believe that. Boulder's gossip mill seems to be in perfect working order."

He threw his head back and laughed, knowing full well that he'd been the brunt of informational tidbits lately. "Ha! That's an understatement. And to think we used to make sport out of feeding it, then watching it fly into high gear."

"We were shameless, you and me. I'm not sure how we both ended up riding the right side of the fence."

He grinned at the strand of memories that inched through his mind. "Glad I got it out of my system when I was young."

"I'm sorry about your accident. I heard about it when I got into town." Sam's voice sounded solemn but not pitying, and for that Joseph was thankful. "How are you getting along?"

Joseph pulled his shoulders back, not surprised at

the way Sam cut a sure path right through formalities. "Ah… I'm great, just have to put up with this ridiculous costume for another day or two." He gestured to the bandage circling his head. "Should be good as new in a couple of days."

"I understand you're going to go see a doctor in Denver?"

"I leave tomorrow." Joseph nodded, shoving his hands into his pockets. "Are you planning on being in town for a while?"

"That's the plan." Sam gave a long exhale. "What do you say we get in some fishing while I'm here?"

"I wouldn't miss an opportunity to show you up with a pole again. You and I both know who always caught the biggest—"

"Well, well, well," Sam breathed, his voice thick with adoration. "There she is."

"Who?" Amused, Joseph couldn't help but grin.

"Only the most beautiful woman in Boulder. Wait— make that *this* side of the Rockies." In the long moment of silence that followed, Joseph could almost imagine his friend's adoring gaze fixed on the little lady as though she were a rare jewel. "I was smitten by her at first sight, Joseph. Smitten."

"That captivating, eh?" Curiosity nipped at him like a pack of unruly pups.

"Yep. That captivating," Sam agreed in a case-closed kind of tone.

"You never were one to miss a pretty lady. You've had a soft spot for them as long as I've known you."

"What about you?" Sam shot back with a nudge to Joseph's arm. "If my memory serves me right, I think we had our fair share of fights over girls throughout the years. We scrapped over the best of them, didn't we, Joseph?"

He winced. "Maybe we did."

"No maybes about it. That's probably why neither of us got married. In the end, we always deferred to one another."

On a low chuckle, he nodded his agreement. "So, who is she? I probably know her."

"I wouldn't be so sure. She said she's new to Boulder. I met her yesterday—right after I arrived on the afternoon stage. What a way to start off my stay here."

Was Sam referring to Julia? He always did seem drawn to brunettes. And if he kept himself as tailored as he did the last time Joseph had seen him, then Julia was sure to notice.

It had started irritating Joseph how Julia couldn't seem to help dropping hints about his attire. Apparently she preferred a fancy three-piece suit, and frankly, he'd wear nothing rather than be confined to a suffocating suit day in, day out.

"Come with me. I want you to meet her." Sam grasped Joseph's arm and started walking.

"Nah. Really, I don't need to meet her." He slowed to a stop. If it was Julia, there'd be awkwardness that he had every hope of avoiding.

"Are you sure?" Sam spoke low, leaning toward him. "I want to know what you think. You're a good judge of character."

Wanting to be good-natured about this, Joseph shoved down his unease—after all, it wasn't every day he got to do a favor for his friend. He conceded with a sigh.

"That's the spirit!" Sam maneuvered Joseph forward once again. "I just want to know what you think of her."

"Just don't say I never did anything for you."

"Good morning, ma'am." Sam's gallantry had the corner of Joseph's mouth quirking.

He sniffed the air around him, searching for Julia's strong perfume on the breeze. It'd be a dead giveaway this close, but surprisingly the air was free of the choking scent.

When Joseph felt Sam ease to a stop, he sidestepped out of his friend's grasp.

"I'd like to introduce you to a friend of mine." The timbre of Sam's voice was as smooth as a finely sanded heirloom. "This is Joseph Drake, we go way back. Joseph, this is—"

"Good morning, Joseph."

He snapped his focus down, furrowing his brow. "Katie?"

"You know each other?" Sam chuckled.

Gritting his teeth, Joseph tried not to show his shock, but confusion swirled around him. A stranger, he'd bargained on, seeing as how new people were moving into the area almost daily. And Julia, he wouldn't have been shocked by because she seemed to have a knack for spreading her presence around town.

But Katie? Sam had set his sights on Katie?

Joseph swallowed hard, the hair prickling at the back of his neck as the realization sank in. A herd of emotions raced through his mind, the front-runner being irritation. That Sam was referring to Katie had him thoroughly unsettled. Even though Joseph had laid no claim to her other than as his teacher, why did he feel sick knowing that Sam had taken notice?

Shrugging his shoulders, he jammed his hands into his pockets. "Katie's my instructor. She's been working with me."

"You didn't tell me that you knew her." Sam chuckled.

"You didn't ask," Joseph responded wryly. "And I couldn't exactly see her, remember? I figured you'd stumbled across someone new in town that I hadn't met since I've been laid up."

"Well, what do you know?"

"Yeah," he agreed under his breath. His jaw muscles clenched tight. "What do you know?"

"How are you today, Joseph?" Katie asked, breaking his ire.

"Just fine." He tried to shove off his shock. "Yourself?"

"I'm well, thank you." She paused for a moment, then said, "You're probably really looking forward to your appointment?"

"That I am."

"You better believe I'll be thinking of you as you go, my friend," Sam said, giving Joseph's shoulder a firm squeeze. "I hate to cut out so soon here, but I'm being flagged down over by the wagons. I'll catch up with you later, all right?"

Joseph nodded. "Sounds good. You know where to find me."

"Miss Ellickson, it has been a pleasure seeing you once again." Sam's voice was low with sincerity, and

Joseph could easily imagine him sweeping his hat off on a dramatic bow.

"Nice to see you, too," Katie responded with equal sincerity that had Joseph inwardly cringing.

When Sam strode away, Joseph couldn't help speculating what kind of eye contact had transpired between the two of them just then. He set his back teeth at the grim possibilities that were floating through his mind, but when Katie moved a step closer, that pleasing lily scent of hers distracted him.

"I hate to say it, but it looks like you've been left high and dry again," she said next to him.

"Yeah. It appears that way." He chuckled, sweeping his focus around as if confirming that fact. "Guess there's no sympathy for the wounded guy, huh? That's just fine by me, as long as I'm not left here all night, there's no harm done."

"Well, rest assured, Joseph, I won't let that happen."

"Thank you kindly, ma'am." He tipped his head toward her and smiled.

"So, how are you really feeling about your appointment Tuesday?"

Joseph raked a hand through his hair. "I'm anxious, nervous, excited.... How's that for emotions?"

Katie sliced the air through her teeth on an inhale. "That pretty much covers most of them."

"One minute I'm chomping at the bit to go and get it over with," he said, balling his fists tight. "So I can move on with my life—whatever it looks like. The next minute, I'm climbing the walls with excitement that I'll actually see again."

"Oh, I hope so, Joseph," she breathed, touching his

arm for a brief second. "I really do. We'll definitely have to celebrate when you get home."

"We will. You'll still be here, won't you?" he asked, selfishly hoping that she wouldn't head back to Iowa—ever.

"I'll be here."

"When I can see again," he focused down at her, "I'll enjoy every sunrise, every sunset, every cloudy sky—" he cut himself off, shaking his head as doubts suddenly assailed him. "But then when I think about the possibility of being permanently blind..." he continued, jamming his hands into his pockets and grimacing. He swallowed hard. "If I can't see anything more than the gray shadows when Ben removed the bandages two weeks ago, I don't know what I'll do, Katie. I really don't."

"I'm sorry, Joseph, that must be very difficult." Her voice...her sweet understanding ways, gave him such comfort.

"I mean, I try not to even think about being blind because if I do, I get scared—and angry. Really angry. At myself for being careless, at the world for being sighted," he said, his mouth drawing into a tight line. "And at God if He doesn't answer my prayer for healing."

After a long, not uncomfortable moment of silence, Katie finally spoke. "I'm sorry you're going through this. I can't imagine how hard it must be to consider the possibility and what all of that would mean for you."

Angling his head down, he dug the toe of his boot into the hard ground. As good as it was to admit how he really felt to someone, he was determined to keep things light. "Yeah! I mean, what do you do with someone like me who's used to being self-sufficient?" He held his arms out as if offering himself. "If I can't see, I'd have to find some kind of employment, because I'm sure as anything not cut out for the ladies' quilting circle."

Katie gave a wistful sigh. "Yes, I don't imagine you'd be welcome there. After all, they do call it the *ladies'* quilting circle."

Jamming his hands on his hips, he cocked his head to the side. "Who knows, maybe they'll make an exception."

"Probably not," she retorted, her quiet laughter putting him so at ease.

"Well, I guess I'll have to ford that creek if I get to it. For now, however, I'm going to ask you for a lead home seeing as how Ben must've gotten caught up again."

"Absolutely. I'd be glad to."

"All of the worrying, excitement and outings are tiring." On a hearty exhale, he puffed out his cheeks as he reached for her arm. "Between this snappy little teacher that's been running me ragged and the—"

"Ha! That's not a very nice thing to say, Mr. Drake," she retorted, her voice filled with mock exasperation. "I might not be so willing if you keep that up."

"Nah…you'll walk with me because you feel sorry for me with these bandages on and all," he teased.

Her light laughter was the most wonderful music to his ears. "Not hardly, sir. I do, however, enjoy your company."

Chapter Eight

Joseph had been to Denver dozens of times. But none of his experiences had ever been like this. Every sound within earshot seemed amplified tenfold. The nickering horses—their hooves clomping on the barren ground, the carriages creaking across the rutted roads and the boardwalk echoing with the click of boots.

Standing at the entrance to the stagecoach house, his nerves buzzed with all the sensations. His ears rang from countless unfamiliar voices coming from every direction.

He pulled back his shoulders and steadied himself against the rough-hewn clapboard at his back. His journey to Denver hadn't exactly started the way he'd planned. After Ben had shown up early this morning, announcing that he was unable to go along, frustration had hit hard and fast. Joseph had anticipated this day like his next breath. This appointment was his doorway to freedom from the suffocating confines of blindness. But when Ben went on to explain that he couldn't leave because Ellie's condition was shaky at best, Joseph didn't give the appointment a second thought.

That Ben had asked Katie and her Uncle Sven to accompany him instead set Joseph's thoughts on a completely different course, driving him into a dense thicket of emotions. He didn't know whether to be glad for another opportunity to be with her, to hear her sweet mellow voice, feel her warm gentle touch. Or be irritated at having to wrestle his rebellious emotions into submission again.

He definitely couldn't deny the feelings he had for Katie now. Especially since he'd run into Sam yesterday. He'd tossed and turned all night trying to reason it all out. Sam was his friend, a good friend. Joseph wouldn't let anything come between their long-standing friendship. But when he thought about Katie, he didn't know if he could just let her slip away.

His prayers for restored sight took on a whole new focus. Being able to see again wasn't just about having his life back—it was about being free to follow his heart to Katie. And if Sam was inclined to do the same, then at least the playing field would be fair.

Katie. She was a ray of sunshine on a cloudy day, a gentle rain soaking the thirsty ground. Side by side, they'd enjoyed the eight-hour journey with Sven, sometimes in comfortable conversation and other times in amicable silence. But upon arriving less than twenty minutes ago, the ease of the trip was quickly swallowed by the hectic pace of the booming city.

The tinny sound of the piano coming from the saloon just doors away, and the raucous laughter knifing through the warm evening air set the hair at the back of his neck on end. With the hour nearing dinner time, Denver's night life was probably just beginning. Joseph would be a heck of a lot more at ease when he had Katie checked safely into the nice hotel he'd stayed at not far from here. The restlessness he felt waiting for her to return from the washroom made him wish that he'd taken Sven up on his offer to see them to the hotel. But Joseph knew that Sven had a hearty list of things he needed to do while they were here. Running a busy lumber mill back home, supply ordering trips like these were meant for business only.

He pushed away from the building, tilting his head from side to side to remove the kinks in his neck from the long ride. As he slid his fingers over his buttons, he felt, more than heard, someone cross slowly in front of him, stopping as if to give him a thorough perusal.

For a fleeting moment he wondered if Katie had returned, but he knew she wouldn't sneak up on him unannounced. It could be that he was the object of rude scrutiny from some stranger, his bandage standing out like a white flag of surrender flying high in enemy territory.

He loathed feeling as if he was on display like some sideshow and would be so glad to be rid of the ridiculous getup.

Joseph drew himself to his full height, jamming his hands into his pockets. Catching the remnant of stale liquor hanging in front of him, he sniffed the air, scowling as he steadied himself against the prickly sensation working up his spine and neck, setting his hair on end.

Then he heard Katie's voice from around the corner. "Excuse me, sir. Please let me pass by."

He jerked his focus to the right, furrowing his brow and listening intently. The slight tremor he'd sensed in her voice set his pulse pounding.

"Katie, I'm over here." He turned to the right and stepped cautiously, trailing his hand along the building as he tried to gauge the length of the wooden platform.

Fierce protectiveness rose within him like some dormant warrior—as did the reality that he couldn't see a thing. That she might be in trouble made every nerve snap to attention.

"Where you goin' in such a hurry, sweetheart?" a man's voice cut through the city noise, taunting flecked in careless chunks through the words. "I just wanna talk is all."

"Katie?" he called again, hearing a small scuffle.

"Well, whata we have here?" the man tossed in Joseph's direction, his sloppy drawl summoning an image in Joseph's mind that had him moving faster. He heard the man spit, the juicy wad plinking against something metal. "With all them bandages he's wearin', I'd say you must be his nurse, lil' lady. Ain't that somethin'?"

A throaty chuckle rumbled from the man. With a low whistle, he added, "Yep. Wouldn't mind havin' a perty nurse like you tend to my—"

"That'll be enough!" Joseph slapped the side of the building and stalked toward the direction of the man's voice. "You can step away from her now," he ground out, his jaw muscles tensing, a heated flush working up his neck and face. When his foot found the edge of the platform, he stopped.

He stretched out his hand. "Katie, come on, darlin',"

he spoke, the endearment coming as easily as his next breath. "Let's get to the hotel."

"Well, now…what're ya gonna do iffin' I don' let 'er pass?" the man slurred on a contemptuous snicker. "Chase me?"

When laughter, thick and dark, erupted from the rogue, anger shot through Joseph like a cannon blast, ripping through his calm reserve. He'd knock the scoundrel to kingdom come if only he could see him. But the lack of control he had over the situation and insufficiency he felt stared him in the face.

His neck tensed as tight as a pulled cord. He sucked air through his teeth and kept a hand on the side of the building as he lowered his foot, hoping to locate a step.

"Get away from her," Joseph warned, a foot connecting with the second step and then another with the hard ground.

He wanted to tear off the bandages, but what if he obliterated the wraps and found nothing had changed? No light to illumine his path, no clear image, no sight by which to make his way in life.

"It's all right, Joseph," Katie urged, her words far from convincing. He could hear her struggling to free herself.

When he pushed away from the building, aiming toward the sound of Katie's voice with his hands outstretched, all he could think about was getting her out of harm's way. And of how he could never watch over her if he couldn't see.

What kind of protector would he be? How could he ever ensure her safety?

The questions ricocheted through his mind mercilessly, but he shoved them down. He couldn't afford to think about those things now. Katie needed him.

"What's going on out here?" A man's voice pierced his silent nightmare as he came to stand beside him. "Is there a problem?"

"Nope. No problem as I can see," the drunk who'd stood near Katie answered, the sound of his heavy, unsteady footsteps quickly carrying him away from the stagecoach house.

"Everything is fine now, thank you," Katie answered, her voice still trembling.

"All righty, then," the man responded as he trudged up the steps and walked back inside the building.

Humiliation, cold and harsh, crumbled over Joseph like a wall of ice. He tried not to think about what would've happened had the man not appeared from inside the building.

"Katie?" he breathed.

When he felt her touch at his arm, relief nearly bowled him over. As did the sickening realization that without his sight, he was as useless as a bug on his back. She deserved more than having to look to others for her protection.

When she drew in a shuddering breath, he turned and wrapped his arms possessively around her, pulling her close to his chest. The quaking he felt coming from her shook him. Shook him to the very core, stirring up the insecurities he'd faced these past five weeks.

He just had to get his sight back.

When Joseph's appointment finally arrived, flagrant insecurities haunted him from the previous day. He was desperate to finally see again, and was beyond grateful that the day had finally arrived because he didn't ever want Katie to have to go through that again.

She'd tried dismissing the event as nothing, but Joseph knew it had affected her far more than she was letting on. He'd kept his arms around her for some time, and it was long moments before her shaking subsided and her breathing evened out.

After they'd checked into the hotel and met up with Sven for supper, they'd all parted ways until morning. Sleep eluded him once again because he'd lain awake thinking of Katie. The horrible reality of his limitations if he didn't regain his sight was at the forefront of his mind.

In the early morning hours he'd finally pushed through the morbid thoughts and slept. He was going to see again. Surely God loved him enough to answer his desperate pleas. Surely the providence of Katie coming into his life wouldn't be dangled like some carrot just out of reach.

With a gentle grasp on Katie's arm, he steadied himself, anxious to finally get this day behind him and get on with his life. But as he crossed the threshold to the office he couldn't seem to shake the feeling that a thousand guns were aimed directly at him—their sights firmly set upon his vulnerability.

Shortly after arriving, they were ushered into an exam room where a lingering scent of antiseptic pervaded. While they sat waiting for the doctor, his mind and body buzzed with anxious energy. He dragged his fingers through his hair and shifted uncomfortably, unable to recall a time when he'd been so nervous. The anticipation of seeing again had his stomach bound in a tight knot.

Worse, the fear of not seeing again had his heart grinding to an agonizing halt.

"It'll work out, Joseph." Katie touched his shoulder, her fingers lightly, briefly stroking his tense muscles.

"Thanks." He turned to her, knowing that his attempt at a smile fell painfully short. "I'm sure it will, too."

He caught her fingers, pulling them down to cradle her hand. He rubbed his thumbs the length of each soft, slender finger and up to her dainty wrist, where he felt the wisp of lace edging her sleeve.

"Do you know what I want my first sight to be?" His voice grew tight with emotion as the door creaked open. "I want to see you," he whispered, releasing her hand and standing from his chair.

"Good afternoon. I'm Dr. Becker." The man's voice boomed confidence as his feet swept steadily across the wood floor like fine-grained sandpaper. "You must be Mr. Drake."

Joseph faced the doctor. "Good afternoon, Doctor." When he returned the man's handshake, he noticed how the doctor's hand felt considerably smaller in his own.

"And you must be Mrs. Drake?"

Joseph sat down next to Katie again. "Miss Ellickson is a teacher who's been working with me."

"Oh, I see. Well, it's nice to meet the two of you," the doctor said simply, exuding nothing but pure professionalism. "I hope we can help you today, Mr. Drake. Your doctor—and brother, I understand—informed me of your situation."

Joseph heard him shifting some papers and assumed

he was probably skimming over Ben's notes that they'd left with the nurse. The muscles in his jaws worked overtime, and his forearms ached from the tight fists his hands formed.

"Uh-huh." A long silence followed. "Now, let's see. It's been over five weeks since the accident?"

After the doctor gathered firsthand details of the accident from Joseph, he gave a harsh cough. "I know you probably want to get this over with, so why don't we do just that."

Joseph's pulse picked up. His stomach churned.

"Let me tell you that I'm hopeful. Knowing that you were able to see some dim shadows when the patches were originally removed is a very good sign. Very good, indeed. Hopefully we'll see even more improvement today."

"That's what I'm hoping for," Joseph said with a nod.

"Your brother did the right thing in ordering bed rest," the doctor confirmed. "Now, I'm going to remove these wrappings around your head first."

His nerve endings thrummed. His ears rang and his pulse pounded heavily as a heated flush worked up his chest, neck, head. Every noise suddenly annoyed him, especially the short-winded whistling sound as Dr. Becker breathed.

The doctor snipped at the bandage with cold metal scissors, then began unwinding. "I'll have you open your eyes slowly, so it won't be too bright. It can be overwhelming at first."

"I suppose," he responded with a forced chuckle. His heart slammed against his chest wall. "I'll take overwhelming."

A suspense-filled silence hung in the air, making it stifling. Joseph wanted to reach to Katie, but resisted the urge. The confidence he'd felt only a week ago, an hour ago, a moment ago, seemed like a mirage in a hot, dry desert.

Once the bandages were finally off, he sighed with relief. The air was cool, liberating against his skin.

"Now, I'm going to lift off these patches." Dr. Becker's voice was girded with caution. "Are you ready?"

Nodding, he gripped the arms of the chair and steadied himself, as if waiting for a stunning fireworks demonstration, full of light, color and form.

Or was he waiting for the knockout blow in a fight?

"Now, Joseph, be patient and let your eyes adjust to the light. I want you to slowly open your eyes."

He tightened his grip on the arms of the chair, every muscle tensed with anticipation as he leaned forward. He felt confident again, and hopeful as he determined to look Katie's way just as soon as the glorious light seeped into the offending darkness. Slowly easing his eyelids open, he blinked.

Was there something in his eyes?

He clutched the arms of the chair and blinked again. But he couldn't seem to find anything more than the dim shadows he'd seen before.

"I—I don't know. I can't tell," he said hesitantly.

Desperately wanting to believe that remnants of the bandages still remained on his eyes, he reached up, his hands trembling as he felt where the patches had been.

Nothing.

"It's all right," Dr. Becker offered. "We'll go over

here by the window. The sun is bright this afternoon. Let's see if your eyes can register more light here."

Joseph struggled to his feet when he felt the doctor's hand beneath his arm. Once standing, his knees threatened to buckle. He closed his eyes as he was led across the room. When they stopped, the doctor placed Joseph's hand upon a wide wooden sill, smooth and polished under his fingertips.

"Do you see anything now?" The measure of hope in the doctor's voice gave encouragement.

Opening his eyes wide, he again searched for light-bathed images. He opened and shut his eyes several times. Sweat beaded his brow. His breath came in short pants. Desperate, he searched wildly.

Nothing.

Dr. Becker stood directly in front of him, appearing like a vague, undefined image in a thick, unrelenting fog. Try as he might, Joseph couldn't make out color or even the most obvious detail.

He turned his head toward where Katie was sitting, straining to see her through the dense gray filling his vision. He saw nothing, but heard her whisper, "Joseph?"

The weight of the doctor's hand upon his shoulder was a faint contact point as he felt himself drifting farther away. The stark reality of his fate threatened to drive him to the darkest depths.

Turning back to the window, the warm, inviting sun bore down upon his face as if mocking him, but again he couldn't make out anything more than a murky shadow of light.

How could this be?

Slamming his eyes shut, he opened them with the

fading hope of finding something more than formless shadows. Trembling, he plowed his fingers through his hair, then pulled a hand down over his face, his fingertips briefly resting upon eyes that couldn't see. Slowly he raised his chin, fighting not to fall prey to complete and total despair.

I'm blind. Oh, God, I'm blind.

The realization hit like a sudden blast, annihilating hope.

Never had he felt more alone or forsaken.

Where are You, God? Don't You know I need my sight?

His silent plea, one he'd prayed hundreds of times, seemed to hang suspended in the dark unknown.

"There's no change," he finally admitted, his jaw tense, his stomach churning. "It's no better than before."

"I'm sorry, son. This must come as a surprise." Dr. Becker's tone was tight, forced. "Let's go back over here and sit down."

Every single step felt short and clumsy once again, as if all the progress he'd made with Katie had been a figment of his imagination.

After the doctor performed a couple of tests, he rested his hands upon Joseph's shoulders. "I'd hoped to have more encouraging news for you. I know this must be difficult."

He wanted to run far away. But he probably couldn't make it out of the room without attendance, let alone the building.

"You'll get through this, Joseph. I know you will." An undercurrent of shared discouragement and sadness was evident in Katie's voice as he felt her familiar, comforting touch upon his arm. "Give yourself time."

"This isn't an easy lot in life," the doctor added. "But in time you will grow accustomed to life without sight and your other senses will compensate for the lack in vision. There have been some significant advances made for the blind." The words were meant to lend hope, but nothing could mask the pity in the doctor's voice. "And it sounds like, with Miss Ellickson here, you're already on the right road."

Although he was thankful for what Katie had taught him over the last two weeks, he realized now that he'd been going through the motions, counting on things taking a favorable turn for him.

"Is there any chance that restoration could still take place?" He forced the tremble from his voice as he mined for some vein of hope. "I mean, could it be that maybe my eyes just need more time? Maybe you should wrap them again."

The doctor gave a measured sigh. "I don't make a habit of leaving my patients with false hope. I find that that can be counterproductive, so I'll be very honest with you."

The nervous cough coming from Dr. Becker had Joseph bracing himself for words he somehow knew would set his fate in stone. He wanted to cover his ears. Storm out of the room.

He'd never run from a challenge, though. Could he find it within himself to face this one head-on? The way he saw it, he didn't have much of a choice. God had ignored his pleas and left him high and dry.

"With this kind of head trauma and the amount of

time that has gone by since the injury, I regret to say that we've likely seen as much restoration as we're going to get."

Joseph stared into the darkness while listening to the bleak prognosis. He set his face like the calm of a glassy sea. Inside, however, huge waves battered his soul.

"It's apparent the damage done was very serious and irreversible," the doctor continued. "If there was going to be a return of sight, we would've seen it by now."

Chapter Nine

The trip home was strained at best. For most of the journey Katie had sat squeezed between Uncle Sven and Joseph, and crammed to capacity into the stage along with the other six travelers. Joseph had leaned his head back, shutting his eyes tight beneath furrowed brows. The way he held his body so rigid and fists so tight, she would've thought they were careening down a mountainside. He surely felt that his life had just hit a steep, rocky slope.

The times she'd tried to make conversation, she'd feel him tense as though he couldn't bear her presence. Finally, she'd given up. She understood how devastated he must be.

What she couldn't understand was why he'd wall himself off from her. Hadn't she developed a trust with him? Hadn't he found comfort with her as much as she'd found with him?

Even Uncle Sven couldn't break Joseph's dark silence. When the stagecoach arrived back in Boulder after supper, Katie had quietly insisted on walking Joseph home, hoping that if he felt less crowded by others, she could get him to open up.

Peering over at him now as she led the way home, compassion again welled inside her. He'd banked on regaining his sight and had gotten no return. The anger creasing his brow and frustration clenching his jaw spoke volumes of his distress.

On a measured sigh, she turned her attention back to the path and gasped. Tripped down a step, her arm jerking free from his tentative grasp. "Whoa!" Katie cried. "Be careful—"

He followed a split second later. He reached in vain for something to steady himself as he dropped face-first to the packed dirt like felled timber.

"Oh no! I'm so sorry." She scrambled to kneel beside him.

"What in the—"

"It was my fault, Joseph." She placed a trembling hand on his back, inwardly scolding herself for being so distracted. "I wasn't paying attention."

"Apparently," he snarled over his shoulder. He lay sprawled out in the middle of the road for a moment, then shoving her hand away, quickly levered himself up. With his face set in a scowl, he slapped his hands together, sending a plume of dust into the evening air. "I don't need you to walk me home. I'll do it myself."

"I'm sorry, Joseph. Really I am." She stared up at him, confused. Up to now he'd been quiet, not explosive. "I should have been more attentive to where I was going."

"My house can't be far from here. What…another block?" He turned his head opposite his desired direction. Kneeling, he patted his hand along the ground, feeling for his bag that had flown from his hand, scattering the few things within.

"A little over two blocks, actually." Katie shook her head at his stubbornness. "Here, let me get that for you."

"No! I can do it myself," he ground out.

He stretched out his arms and swept them across the ground in broad movements. Scooting forward, he repeated the action, finally locating his bag and all but one item. When he'd stuffed them back inside, he stood, his chest rising and falling in rapid rhythm.

With trembling knees, she crossed to retrieve the shirt he'd missed. "You forgot something," she uttered, unable to resist the urge to breathe in Joseph's scent woven within the threads.

When she handed it to him, her heart squeezed as she watched the embarrassment tainting his features. Maybe his vision hadn't changed, but the Joseph she knew was not who stood before her now. He'd erected a wall the size of a mountain around himself, and he was intent on keeping her out.

She couldn't make herself look away as he focused directly on her, his sightless gaze bearing into hers.

"Please let me walk the rest of the way with you."

"I told you I'd do it myself," he retorted, stuffing the shirt in his bag.

She sighed. "Fine. Go right ahead."

Hugging her arms to her chest, she witnessed his brow crease and his fists clench as though he'd expected her to put up a fight. From her experience, she knew that it was best to just let him find out the hard way—as long as doing so didn't pose any danger. Had the streets been busy, she would've put up a fight and dragged him home regardless of his protests.

"Fine," he echoed. He shoved a hand in his pocket, but not before she noticed the tremble undermining his composure.

After a moment's pause, she slowly walked away, her heart constricting inside her chest, her gaze fixed on him. He stood at the side of the road, a study in stoicism with his shoulders drawn back, head held high and his chin set. At a quick glance, he didn't look as if he needed help. Maybe in a couple of weeks after more training, maybe in a month. But right now, at the very least, he'd need the aid of a cane.

After nearly a minute, he made a tentative move forward to cross the street, then another and another. Dragging his fingers through his hair, he came to an abrupt halt.

She stopped in her tracks. A soft moan escaped her lips as raw fear played across his features in the evening light. Bracing herself, she walked back to him, her heels lightly ticking across the boardwalk.

He turned his head in her direction, a look of irritation sweeping over his face.

Standing in front of him, she struggled with many different emotions. She was angry with him, frustrated by him, but mostly she felt so very sad for him.

He gave a loud, long exhale. "If you could just point me in the right direction, I can do the rest."

How did he think he was going to get home without help?

"I'm sure I can figure it out," Joseph added firmly, as if he'd read her thoughts.

"Why don't you stop being so *stubborn,*" she urged, unable to keep her irritation at bay. "It's all right to let someone help, you know."

"Easy for you to say," he ground out, his frustrated gaze set down the road.

Hugging her arms to her chest, she sighed. "You're right. It's a lot easier for me to say those things when I don't have to face this." She took a step closer, then gently grasped his hand, inwardly cringing when he jerked at her touch. "Please," she whispered. "Let me help you."

When he didn't pull away, she placed his hand at her elbow and led him home, acutely aware of the stiffness in his touch.

At the familiar sound of the front gate opening, he relaxed ever so slightly. And when they reached his porch, she turned to find his unseeing gaze fixed on her, his eyes—the most beautiful golden brown she'd ever seen. The first time she'd really caught a glimpse of his eyes this morning, she'd nearly lost her breath. Prominent cheekbones and perfectly shaped brows served as a masculine frame, enhancing his stunning eyes.

Surely they'd once sparked with life like his brother's. But right now, exhaustion, fear and anger weighed heavily on him as he lifted his chin a notch.

Hearing a rustling at the side of the house, she glanced over to see Boone lumbering into the evening shadows, his tail wagging lazily from side to side in greeting.

"Hello, Boone." She knelt to pet the dog.

"Hey, boy." Joseph hunkered down and reached out, his hand connecting with hers on Boone's back.

For a moment neither one of them moved. Comforting warmth spread through her when he swept the pad of his thumb over her hand in a light caress. Much as she'd tried to remain professional concerning Joseph, something had changed over the past two weeks. Her heartbeat quickened at his comforting presence. Stirred at his soothing voice. She found herself longing for his touch. Longing for his nearness to lend her hope and confidence. And to calm her deep fears.

Katie deserved a whole man. And whole, he was not.

Joseph swallowed hard, burrowing his fingers next to Katie's into Boone's fur as he thought about what he had to do. For her sake, he had to sever all feelings other than those of friendship. His blindness was a thorn in his flesh, and he sure wasn't going to inflict its sting upon a wife. Especially someone as sweet, as special, as Katie.

Had things turned out differently for him, he might've proposed marriage by now. There was really nothing keeping him from still doing that except that if she said "I do," he'd forever wonder if it was out of pity or some warped sense of obligation. Over the past two weeks they'd shared tender moments laden with unspoken promises that maybe she felt some misplaced duty to fulfill.

He couldn't live with himself if that was the case.

But he didn't know if he could live without her, either. Each day he looked forward to being with her, having her near, hearing her voice. And whenever he'd held her or when she'd given him encouragement by a simple, innocent touch, the connection had bolstered him with strength he needed to face this challenge.

Since his appointment this morning, he'd been as

rigid and unyielding as the mountains surrounding this valley. And right now he was starving for comfort.

So maybe he could indulge himself just once more before he let her go. He wanted to walk away with the memory of her warm and soft and caring touch.

After a long moment of silence, he slowly came to standing, pulling her along with him. Joseph focused down at where he cradled her hands in his. He traced a path with the pads of his thumbs. Heard and felt her quiet sigh.

He threaded his fingers with hers. And for a moment in time, he closed his eyes, imagining that he could see again. He'd hold her close. Look deep into her eyes. He'd protect her the way she deserved. Drive away her fears with his love.

Joseph dragged in a deep breath and with it the delicate scent of lilies. So simple, so natural and so Katie.

If he didn't go inside now, he might never let her go. And that set off warning bells that clanged loudly, slicing through his longing.

He couldn't allow himself to do that and then dismiss her like some discarded waste. She didn't deserve that.

He slowly slid his hands from hers, committing to memory this moment as he opened his eyes to the harsh darkness. "I'm sorry for my impatience, Katie. I'm just not very good company right now."

"No. Don't apologize," she whispered.

He stepped away from her and shook his head, slamming his eyes shut. He was sending her mixed signals, being so harsh just moments ago out on the street and then showing tenderness.

"Joseph, I—"

"I really should just get inside," he blurted.

"It's been a hard day, I know."

When he grasped the cool door handle, he shuttered away the warmth and affection he'd felt just a moment ago, steeling himself to do what needed to be done. It was for her sake.

"Katie, I think it's best that you not come over tomorrow." His voice sounded flat as he stared downward.

"Oh? So—so you want me here Thursday, then?"

He swallowed hard. "No. Not Thursday, either. I don't know when—or *if* I want you to come back."

Something felt innately right when she was by his side.

The moments when their hands touched or his leg brushed against hers in the stagecoach, or every single time she spoke his name or a word of encouragement, he felt something that was undeniable—a connection that seemed as though it'd been established even before their paths had crossed just two weeks ago.

But he could barely stand himself right now. He didn't need to subject her to his anger or his rampant emotions. His response when he'd fallen flat on his face had surely tested her patience with him. It was an accident—accidents happened. He was in for his fair share of them in the future.

Joseph shook his head, recognizing that until he could resign himself to his blindness, he wouldn't be good company for anyone. Especially not Katie. Even then, if he did decide to ask her to work with him again, there could never be anything more than friendship between them.

He would *not* strap Katie with the burden of living with a blind man for the rest of her life.

Stepping through the doorway after Boone, Joseph stumbled slightly, then steadied himself by grabbing the doorjamb. His balance wasn't too keen after being on the road for so long. In fact, his whole life seemed off balance now and he didn't know when he'd get his bearings again.

He dropped his bag at the door and shuffled forward, each uncertain step a reverberating reminder of his affliction. All day long he'd wanted to revolt against the imposing darkness. He'd wanted to scream, throw something, run, but instead he'd shut himself up tight like a tender young tree in a mature forest, crowded, dark and confined.

Alone now in the privacy of his own home, he could give in to the compulsion to release his anger, but he just didn't have the strength. What good would it do now, anyway?

He massaged the tight knots at the back of his neck, realizing just how weary he was. Every muscle in his body ached from the rigid stance he'd assumed all day.

With outstretched hands, he carefully counted his steps until he reached the bedroom at the back of the house. As usual, Boone found his place at the foot of the bed while Joseph crawled into bed, not even bothering to remove his clothes or boots.

He lowered his head to his pillow and closed his eyes, wishing that this horrible nightmare would finally come to an end. But opening them, the nightmare loomed as real as ever.

Boone laid his chin on Joseph's knee and Joseph

smoothed his hand over the dog's soft fur. He could almost feel Katie's fingers there, beneath his again. It had almost been his undoing. He'd wanted to hold her.

And be held.

But he steeled himself against the deep need for reassurance. Like it or not, his well-ordered world had been overrun with an all-consuming darkness.

Why had God sentenced him to this sightless, black prison?

He'd silently railed against God on the long trip home, demanding an answer. He'd received none, and questioned if he was fighting a war more for his soul than for his livelihood.

When Boone nuzzled his soft wet nose into Joseph's palm, Joseph gathered in a shaky breath.

"How could you allow this, God? What did I do to deserve this?" he whispered. It was an honest question void of the accusation that had filled his unspoken barrage earlier.

Opening his eyes to nothing once again, he clenched his fists and trembled.

That still, small voice Joseph had learned to recognize as God's came once again, beckoning for his trust.

Hungry for any response, he let it sink in. It wasn't the answer he was looking for, but it was a reply. And he wanted desperately to know that God hadn't forgotten him.

"I want to trust You, God. But I don't know how. I'm so used to taking care of things on my own. Who am I now?" The shop and deadline that loomed in the not-too-distant future swirled through his thoughts. "Everything I've worked so hard for in the past—it's just slipping away."

Even though he couldn't see God, he knew that He was here with him. An unexplainable peace he needed now more than ever seemed to blanket him.

Joseph was desperate to understand, desperate to hold on to that comfort. "Help me, God. Please," he whispered.

Lying with his eyes wide open, he stared into bold, unrelenting darkness. The peace he'd felt just moments ago was already slipping away as he searched in vain for a fragment of brightness in his dark world.

If there were a moon to light the sky or stars to illuminate the heavens, he'd never know.

"Oh, God! No!" Joseph woke with a jolt.

He sat up, panting. Grasped the edge of the mattress and held it as though it were a lifeline keeping him from falling into a deep chasm. Sweat drenched his body as he tried to force the nightmare from his mind, but the images lingered.

"Lord, please. I *need* to know You're here." His breathing was ragged.

Even in his dreams he was living out his present nightmare all over again. The scene replayed once more in his mind.

A woman stood off in the distance at the edge of the woods. She was calling to him. Begging him to come. He started toward her. Turning momentarily away from her, he saw an endless black hole. Its expanse stretched as far as the eye could see. It pulled at him. Dragged him backward. Into a place so bleak that he clawed at the ground to remain in the light. Hearing her faint cries, he strained to free himself. But it was wholly engulfing and he kept slipping farther...farther away into darkness.

He forced his mind away from the hopelessness. Wiping his brow, he struggled to still his turbulent emotions. Joseph slowly lowered himself to his pillow with a long, shuddered breath.

Darkness was his enemy now. Forever mocking him. Forever taunting him.

"Ellie lost the baby?" Katie whispered, echoing Ben's words.

She didn't think things could get much worse since Joseph had received such devastating news about his vision, then proceeded to close the door on his training, sending her away last night. But when she knocked on Ben's door just moments ago to inform him that she and Joseph had arrived home with Sven a day earlier than planned, she stood stunned, her eyes wide with disbelief.

"Late last night." Ben slid a hand over his unshaven face. Dark circles shadowed his eyes as he stared down at his hands. "I tried everything I knew to do, but it wasn't enough. The little guy just wouldn't come around."

Katie swallowed hard. A torrent of emotions and images swamped her as she slid trembling fingers up the tiny pearl buttons to her neckline, clasping the small brooch.

She remembered how Ellie would lovingly caress the baby she carried inside her. How Aaron would, without embarrassment, ease his large, work-worn hands around his wife's belly. They'd been so excited about the birth of their first child.

Katie couldn't imagine the overwhelming grief they must feel. She dabbed at tears pooling in her eyes, knowing that if she allowed herself to fall apart now, she might not be able to get herself back together.

"How is she doing?" she forced out, clearing her throat as she followed him to his buggy. "How is Aaron? I mean…is there anything I can do?"

His shoulders hanging low, Ben sighed with a nod. "Yes, there is. Right before I left there this morning, Ellie asked for you and Joseph. She wants to see you." He hauled his doctor's bag up to the black leather seat. "I think it would do both of them good to have the two of you there."

"Well, of course. Of course I'll go." She grabbed his offered hand and climbed into the seat. Glancing to the west where Aaron and Ellie lived in a cabin outside of town, an ominous shiver passed through her as she spotted the dark gray bank of clouds crawling over the horizon.

"It was a good thing you caught me when you did," Ben said, grabbing the reins. "I was coming after supplies, then going straight back out there. Aaron's trying to get a coffin made and tending Ellie, too. She's still not out of the woods."

"Will she be all right?" she braved.

His mouth formed a grim line. "I don't know. It wasn't an easy delivery. She lost a lot of blood."

"I'll do whatever needs to be done. Just let me know."

As the buggy lurched forward, rolling over the rutted ground, he glanced at her. "I saw Sven on the way here and he told me about the appointment. It must've been a difficult trip for all of you. I'm sure Joseph is very upset."

On the way to pick up Joseph, Katie proceeded to tell Ben about the day, from the way Joseph had courageously handled the discouraging news, to his silence and the unfortunate incident on the walk home. She was careful not to dishonor Joseph in any way, but she felt that Ben should know the extent of things.

He pulled in a deep breath, blowing it out in one big gust of air. "I really hoped things would turn out better than that. But I can't say I'm surprised." Furrowing his brow, he jammed his hat down on his head. "Did you get much out of him after the appointment?"

"I'm afraid not. I tried, but he wasn't in any mood to talk, and I don't blame him."

Thunder rolled in the distance, penetrating the silence. "This is one of the toughest things he's had to face." Slicing a glance her way, he added, "It's a good thing he has you."

Katie blinked back hot tears as she stared down the street toward Joseph's house. "I'm not sure he sees it that way. And I doubt that he'll be too keen on my coming along today, either. He didn't want me coming back to work with him."

Ben gave her hand a brief, comforting squeeze. "He may be stubborn. But knowing Joseph, he'll put aside his trials if it means being there for Ellie and Aaron." With a jerk of the wrist, he slapped the reins, urging the horses to move a little faster. "When it comes to doing for others, he always looks past his own needs."

Chapter Ten

Joseph's heart clenched at the unmistakable sound of Aaron working a saw in the barn. Each pass of the sharp-toothed blade through the wood echoed like some mournful cry as Joseph approached the barn with Ben.

When Joseph had learned of the baby's death, he'd felt deep sorrow. It had multiplied as they'd arrived a few minutes ago and he'd sat by Ellie's bedside. Her voice sounded so small, so sad, so weak. And in spite of the warm August day, her hand had felt like ice in his. When she'd tried to comfort him about his own discouraging news, Joseph had fought hard to bat down the raw emotions that flapped like gaping wounds in his soul. It was just like her to encourage others in the midst of her own pain and loss. He'd tried to offer the same in return, but what could he say that would possibly bring any consolation?

That God was with them? That God had a plan in it all? That God would turn it all for good?

Having heard enough of that from well-meaning folk over the past few weeks, he was weary of assuaging an-

swers like those. True as they may be, sometimes sentiments like those seemed trite. Sometimes just the quiet
strength of another's presence was worth more than a
whole book of words. Besides, wasn't God more than
capable of showing Himself to be true, sovereign, loving? Did he really need folks to defend His honor or
what He allowed in our lives?

Thunder rumbled through the valley and the saw
blade groaned to a halt. A lump rose in Joseph's throat
as he took a tentative step out of Ben's lead and into
the barn.

"I'm sorry, Aaron," he expressed, as Ben headed back
toward the house. "So very sorry for your loss."

Aaron's feet scuffed over the dirt floor and stopped in
front of Joseph. After several seconds, Joseph reached
out and found his brother's arm, pulling him into a
strong embrace.

"I'm sorry, too, Joe-boy," Aaron rasped, his tall frame
quaking in Joseph's arms. "Both about my baby…and
your vision." Stepping out of the embrace, he added, "I
can tell…it's not any better, is it? Your vision?"

Joseph slid his hands into his pockets. "No. But don't
worry about me. And don't worry about things at the
shop. Take all the time you need," he urged, knowing
full well that time was ticking away and the deadline
loomed closer. Right now, though, it didn't matter. Not
when Aaron and Ellie had just lost their baby, and she
was struggling for her own life. "Just get Ellie better.
That's all you need to think about now."

Aaron drew in a fractured breath.

Joseph tried to focus his unseeing eyes on his brother.
He'd always believed that eye contact, man-to-man, was

important. But with the dim lighting inside the barn, murky shadows were barely visible through the gray haze. Outside in the daylight, he could at least make out the barn's faint, rough outline or a person's foggy silhouette.

"I'll be here for you, Aaron," he finally said. "Whatever you need. Just ask. I'll do my best."

Aaron grasped his arm and pulled him over to the small workbench in the barn. "I could use your help trying to get this built." He paused, clearing his throat. "So we can bury him...our little Jeremiah."

The lump in his throat grew larger just hearing his nephew's name. He wanted to help, but how could he build something when he couldn't see?

Moreover, how could he tell his brother no?

Then Katie's words came back to him. Her encouragement that he could be a carpenter even without sight. That his skill had as much to do with touch as anything else. Although she had no carpentry experience, she'd had students in the past who'd succeeded in the trade. She'd assured him that there were many things he could do if his vision wasn't what it had been.

Awkwardly, he raised his hands and felt the wood that Aaron had already cut. The pieces were so small. Just like little Jeremiah, whose lifeless body Ben had wrapped and placed in a handmade crib that should've cradled life, not death.

While he slid his hands over the individual sections of the crude box, he heard quickened footsteps approach the barn and turned his attention to the doorway.

"Aaron," Katie breathed. "Ellie's asking for you."

Without a word, Aaron squeezed Joseph's shoulder and ran back toward the house.

A wave of compassion rose within Joseph. Had he ever married, he would've counted himself a blessed man to know love like Aaron and Ellie's. Aaron had found someone he cherished, and who treasured him.

Swallowing hard, he turned back to the wood pieces and began estimating the width and length. When Katie approached his side, he stilled his hands on the wood. "He wants me to help build a coffin."

Rain, steady and serene, made a pitter-patter sound on the barn roof as Katie stood silently beside him. The faintest aroma of fresh rain mixed with the lily scent she wore wafted to his senses, making him already miss her sweet presence.

"I don't think he's trying to push you too fast, Joseph. I just think he wants to know you're here for him."

"I know. I told him I'd help out and I intend to make good on my promise," he said with a nod. Turning, he leaned back against the workbench. "I'm probably not a good judge since I couldn't see her, but the way Ellie sounded in there…he needs to be with her. Doesn't he?"

Katie sniffed in front of him. Several moments passed in quiet and with each one he fought the urge to reach out and comfort her. But holding her was sure to weaken his resolve. Once she was in his arms he'd be overcome with the sense that she somehow belonged there.

But she was upset. Even though Katie had known Ellie for only a brief time, they'd become close friends. Just moments ago Ellie had urged him not to let Katie get away—an urging that Joseph had silently pushed aside. Now that he couldn't offer himself as a whole man, he had to let Katie go.

Sooner or later, he'd have to get used to having her around and not wanting her for his own. She'd told him once already that she had no intention of going back to Iowa. If she stayed, Sam would probably pursue her with more allure than a snake charmer. When Sam wanted something, he usually went after it with lightning speed and solid assurance.

Hearing her quietly sniff again, he shrugged off his silent deliberation and shoved away from the workbench. "Come here, Katie," he whispered, reaching out and pulling her to himself.

He drew his arms around her, spanning a hand at her small waist, and one at her back.

On a quiet sob, she curled her arms in front of her and relaxed against him. Like sunshine on snow, she seeped into him, melting his defenses. Closing his eyes, he took in her scent, her form, her sweet presence in his arms. For a full, magnificent moment, he held her as if they belonged together.

Pressing his lips to the top of her head, he knew that he could bring her comfort.

But when he opened his eyes to find the darkness again, he realized that that'd be about it. He couldn't protect her. He couldn't drive his own team of horses without her by his side. And he probably couldn't provide enough for a family to live on. What could he do if he couldn't be a carpenter?

The image of himself, begging on some street, a tin cup held out to those with pity, crawled through his mind.

Joseph cringed at the picture. No matter what happened, he'd never, *ever* be reduced to that. He had too much pride and resourcefulness. He might not make a nice, comfortable living again, but he'd never beg.

Katie deserved far more than he could give her. She deserved the world—and more. He could only give her a small bit of comfort. But comfort couldn't put food on the table or see danger and circumvent it.

On a shudder, she finally spoke. "Ellie doesn't look good. Not at all." Her voice was so solemn that it made his heart hurt. "She's so pale and very weak. I'm really worried, Joseph."

He trailed his hands to her arms, cherishing this touch as he stepped back away from her. "Me, too. And I know that Ben is—I can hear it in his voice. He'll do all he can medically, and we can pray and do what we can here to help them."

Brushing against the wood pieces behind him, he slowly turned around to try to make sense of the pile. "I don't even know where to begin. I mean, I've made one of these before.... I just haven't ever done it without sight."

Katie sidled up next to him. "It looks like Aaron put the pieces in piles according to size."

That struck him as odd—Aaron was never so organized before. Joseph furrowed his brow and carefully slid his hands over the neat piles, remembering how Aaron's haphazard ways had always driven him mad.

Katie grasped his hand and set it on a pile. "These are the longer, narrow boards." Then she slid his hand to another pile. "And these, the wider, short boards."

"They must be the outside end pieces," he added,

making mental notes as she continued showing him each pile.

After she'd placed a hammer, nails and the pieces he needed within his reach, he was about to give it his best try when Aaron came back inside the barn. He said that Ellie had finally fallen asleep, and Katie excused herself to return to the house and do some quiet chores while Ben kept tabs on Ellie.

"So, do you think you could help me with this?" Aaron's voice was ragged with emotion. "It's not a task a fella wants to do alone. You know?"

"Of course I'll help."

The pain and grief Aaron had to be feeling and the way he kept going regardless inched through Joseph's mind. When had Aaron gotten so mature? When had he grown up to become the man who worked beside him with patience, steadiness and precision?

Joseph pondered those things while they completed a job no father would ever wish to do. While they made the finishing touches on the small, modest coffin, Joseph didn't feel as if he'd offered much in the way of expertise. But he was sure that being there for his brother, walking through that heartbreaking task together, meant more than if he'd built the most splendid, elaborate coffin fit for a king...or a baby prince.

Dawn's first light barely cracked through the pouring rain, gray skies and cool temperatures. Katie quickly donned a pale green dress made of thin wool challis and over that, her cloak. With a covered basket heavy with food prepared by Aunt Marta, and a roofed buggy made ready by Uncle Sven, she picked up Joseph and they drove out to Aaron and Ellie's early.

With the baby's death and funeral all in the same day, and Ellie's unstable condition, Ben had dropped them off just before midnight. But at least there'd been a positive turn of events before they'd left the cabin, as it seemed that Ellie's bleeding was lessening some. Katie had lain awake and prayed all night for her friend, but something ate away at her, undermining any peace she had.

Morning hadn't come soon enough.

When they neared the cabin, she narrowed her gaze to see through the wind-whipped rain. Staring ahead at the large old pine tree that stood as a silent, settled guardian at the foot of the baby's grave, she caught sight of a dark form hunched over at the fresh mound of dirt.

"Is that—Aaron?" Alarm slithered through her.

"Where? Where is he?" Joseph leaned forward, clutching the seat.

Urgency overwhelmed her and she pushed the horses faster. "I can't tell. The rain…it's—" The breath whooshed from her lungs as the image came more clearly. Cupping a hand to her mouth, she held back her moan.

"What is it, Katie? What's wrong?" Joseph grasped her arm, his touch the only thing that kept her from crying out.

Disbelief knifed through her. Her heart twisted in pain. "It—It's Ellie. She's lying on the grave."

"What about Aaron? Is he there?"

She nodded, swiping at the tears pooling in her eyes. "Yes, he's there. He's holding her." Struggling to hold back the deep sob that threatened to release, she fo-

cused on driving the horses into the rain-soaked yard.
"Oh, dear God, no," she whispered, a lump lodging in
her throat at the unmistakable stain of red she saw covering Ellie's muslin nightgown.

Joseph catapulted down from the bench, reached up
and found her hand. "Take me there. Please, Katie," he
urged.

"Oh, Joseph, it's awful," she whispered. Thunder
clapped, shaking the ground. "Something terrible must've
happened."

When she and Joseph approached the grave, Aaron
lifted his head, his boyish features contorted in anguish
and his tear-stained face streaked with dirt. "I've lost
her, Joseph." He nuzzled his face into Ellie's strawberry
blond hair, dripping wet and plastered to her ashen face
by the rain.

Katie's insides balled tight at the wounded cry. She
breathed a desperate prayer for Aaron as thunder rumbled over the valley floor.

Dropping to his knees in the mud, Joseph felt his way
to where his brother clutched Ellie's limp body. "What
is it, Aaron? What do you mean you've lost her?"

Katie's stomach churned. She was unable to move or
think beyond the horrific fact that Ellie was dead. How
could she be? Hadn't she taken a turn for the better?
Her bleeding had lessened. That's what Ben had said....

Quaking from head to toe, Katie peered through her
watery gaze at the bloodred stain, already being diluted
by rain. The sight of Aaron's broad shoulders shaking
with silent sobs twisted her heart. She slipped out of her
cloak, spreading the light wool over him and adjusting
it so it draped over Ellie, too. Stooping to kneel beside

Joseph, her breath caught and heart dropped at the sight of the small booties Ellie had knit for the baby, clutched in her lifeless, dusky hand.

"She didn't want to—to leave the baby," Aaron cried as a blast of thunder shook the ground. His voice was so forlorn that Katie thought her heart might break in two. "After you left last night she begged to see Jeremiah's grave. But she wasn't strong enough, Joseph. She wasn't strong enough."

"I know, Aaron," Joseph soothed.

Katie bit back a sob when he grasped Aaron's shoulders, as though trying to lend him strength. "I know how much she wanted to be here to lay the baby to rest." Joseph's voice was thick with emotion. "But she was so weak from the blood she'd lost."

Closing her eyes to the sight of her friend's lifeless body, Katie recalled how frantic, how inconsolable Ellie had been when Katie had sat with her yesterday, during Jeremiah's funeral. She'd held Ellie until the grieving mother had cried herself to sleep.

Unwilling to believe that Ellie was really dead, Katie stretched her hand toward her friend. She touched Ellie's arm, which dangled stiffly from her husband's embrace. Her stomach churned at the hard, cold feel of Ellie's fair skin. The touch left no question as to whether death had left its distinctive, chilling mark.

Pulling her hand back, she blinked away hot tears stinging her eyes. For a moment, her vision narrowed to a black, cavernous tunnel and she thought she might pass out. Inhaling deeply, she glanced up to see Aaron's face crumple in agony.

He stared at Joseph, his desperate gaze begging for

relief from his torment. "I told her I'd take her as soon as she got strong enough. I promised her I'd bring her out here to see where we laid our son to rest—under our favorite tree."

Smoothing back rain-soaked hair from her eyes, Katie slid her gaze up to the tree. She swallowed hard and took in the initials surrounded by a heart that had been carved into the thick trunk. Remembering when Ellie had told her about Aaron's first true and hopelessly romantic declaration of love.

"Ellie begged me to bring her out here, Joseph." Aaron settled a desperate kiss on his wife's forehead as though hoping that his love for her would be enough to bring her back to life. "I wanted to. But I didn't th—I didn't think she'd be strong enough. And the rain…"

"I know, Aaron. It's all right." With a compassion that gripped Katie's heart, Joseph tentatively reached up and wiped at the tears streaming down his brother's face. "You did the right thing. You're a good, loving husband."

His brother shook his head sharply. "No. No, I'm not," he moaned, rocking Ellie's limp body back and forth over the fresh grave. "I should've stayed awake all night watching over her. She was so upset. I couldn't have nodded off for long when—" His words broke on a loud sob.

Tears trickled down Joseph's face and mingled with the droplets of rain beading his face. Katie allowed her own tears to fall as he slid his hand down to find Ellie's face and then to her arm, as though feeling for himself, whether the cold, hard touch of death was really there.

Aaron pulled in a broken breath. He lifted Ellie's

hand that held the little booties to his mouth, pressing his lips to each finger. "Somehow she made it out here by herself. I found her here at daybreak. Laying dead on Jeremiah's grave."

A quiet groan escaped Katie's lips. She squeezed her eyes against the tears, knowing that Aaron's pain must be almost more than he could bear. To see this man, so strong and capable, and so full of despair, made her weep for him.

"I'm so sorry." Joseph's low voice was barely audible over the pounding thunder and unyielding downpour.

Aaron rained kisses over his wife's serene, pale face, his whole body shuddering with quiet sobs. He stared into his Ellie's face for a long, agonizing moment as though memorizing her beautiful, delicate features. Then he pulled her even tighter to himself, rocking her back and forth again in some silent rhythm that perhaps only heaven knew.

Joseph grasped Katie's arm and leaned close. "We need to get him inside. Can you help me?"

She lightly squeezed his hand, blinking off the rain-drops beading her lashes. "Yes. Just tell me what to do."

For the next few minutes Katie wavered between strength and weakness as Joseph coaxed Aaron step by heartbreaking step back to the cabin. Although Aaron was exhausted physically and emotionally, he refused to relinquish his wife's body to Joseph's strong arms. Witnessing the way Joseph took charge of the situation with the utmost compassion as he helped his brother back to the house made Katie's heart nearly break.

When they reached the door, she turned and peered through the heavy drizzle to stare at the fresh mound under the tree. Tears came hard as she saw where Ellie had lain, her lifeless body heaped on the grave, her blood soaking into the earth where Aaron had buried their firstborn son.

Chapter Eleven

The three days since Ellie's funeral had felt like a month. And the six days since Joseph's appointment in Denver, like a year. The hours had dragged by and his agitation had grown tenfold knowing that Aaron had resumed work on the furniture order at the crack of dawn this morning. Over the past couple of days Joseph had urged Aaron to take plenty of time off, insisting that a weekend full of family and friends visiting and offering condolences, food and help wasn't a sufficient amount of time.

And now here it was Monday morning and Aaron was back at work, pouring himself into things.

Joseph hadn't stepped foot in the shop since his accident. He'd banked on digging into things upon the return of his sight, and that hadn't happened. Since his return from Denver, there'd been one tragedy after another. But knowing that his brother was in the shop this very moment, working so hard to escape the pain of his loss, drove Joseph to try and find his way to the building at the back of his property, to help if he could.

In spite of the long list of trials, the order deadline hadn't been lengthened even a day. And even though the chance of completing it on time was slim to none, he had to at least try.

Standing on his back porch, he gave a sharp whistle and immediately heard the sound of Boone's large, heavy paws padding across the ground. The dog gently burrowed his head between Joseph's knees, a trait he'd recently adopted.

"Hey, boy. How are you doing?" Joseph bent to scratch him behind the ears. "Do you want to go to the shop with me?"

Boone lightly pressed his full body against Joseph's legs and Joseph slid his hands down the dog's back. He could feel the way Boone lobbed his tail from side to side, his back end moving almost independently of the rest of his body.

"I take it that's a yes." He chuckled.

Boone didn't get to go to the shop often because his hair wreaked havoc with the work. Like homing pigeons, the fine hairs inevitably landed on whatever had been freshly varnished.

"Do you think I could tag along? Unless Aaron's been snitching, I bet we could find some jerky for you in my stash." He stepped down from the porch and trailed the dog.

"Good job, Boone," Joseph encouraged as he opened the shop door and poked his head inside.

"Aaron? Are you here?" he called, his voice echoing in the large wood-filled room.

He was surprised when there was no reply, so he stepped inside with Boone scurrying in beside him, no doubt determined to cash in on the tasty incentive. Closing the door, Joseph reached down and ruffled the unruly hair on Boone's head, then stood upright. He found the can of jerky he kept by the door and gave a couple of pieces to Boone.

"Aaron, you here?" he called again, wondering if maybe he'd caught his brother at a bad time, when words were hard to find. No matter how strong Aaron had seemed over the weekend, Joseph knew very well that his brother was devastated.

Aaron's pain was far worse than the sting of going blind. That awareness had struck Joseph deep over the past few days, bringing some needed clarity and perspective to his situation. Life without sight was difficult, but maneuverable. But Aaron's heartache seemed cruel.

Swallowing hard, he inhaled the distinctive scents surrounding him. The fresh-cut wood, the varnish, the stain. Even the old leather chair by his desk. He closed his eyes and drank everything in, strangely invigorated by the experience.

When Boone dropped to his place at the door, Joseph stepped forward, the familiar, muffled crunch of sawdust bits beneath his feet, like some kindhearted grandfather drawing him out of hiding.

He reached out, his fingertips connecting with the large workbench that sat like a massive centerpiece in the room. Grasping the bench's thick edge, he ran his hands across the surface, noticing how scarred, how well used it was. After a long moment, he turned and moved over to the wall, feeling for where the small hand tools were usually hung. He carefully worked his fingers over the wall, surprised to find each tool suspended neatly in its place, as though he'd never been gone.

A little farther and he reached his desk. Afraid he might find the surface littered with papers and tools, he tentatively set his hands on the desk. He patted the expanse of oak and furrowed his brows. There were no tools, no papers. Just one neat pile at the left-hand corner where he'd always set aside any paperwork related to ongoing jobs.

Aaron had not only kept the shop from complete disarray in Joseph's absence, but he'd managed to maintain a condition that was tidy. The shop was essentially just as he'd left it.

"You make me proud, Aaron," he whispered, determined to tell his brother that face-to-face.

He skimmed his hand over the old and slightly torn leather chair pushed into his desk, then moved on to find a row of unfinished furniture. A good number of the pieces were lined up in the back of the shop, their broad surfaces rough and awaiting the fine finish for which he'd gained a reputation.

A small tremor of satisfaction shook him from deep within. And a sense of belonging settled over him like a warm, life-giving breeze after a cold, harsh winter. This was a part of him. This shop and the work done here was not only a solid part of his past, but a promising part of his future.

Moving over to the workbench again, he used it as a guide as he slowly worked his way around the room, savoring the revelation. An overwhelming sense of contentment stole over him and he found himself eager to work with his hands again.

But when his fingertips came into contact with the large steel clamp bolted to the workbench, icy aversion sliced through him. He pulled back as though bitten.

Images of that day when he'd fallen from the ladder came hard and fast. Reaching to grab a board. Losing his balance. Falling backward. He'd tried to right himself. He'd groped for something to hang on to.

Trembling, he raised his hands to the cold, hard steel. Held his breath and slid his fingers over the unyielding shape. Bleak and dank to the touch, it seemed as though it mocked Joseph and his blindness. With a strong grip and an even stronger determination, he held the vise and outlined the shape, with its combination of sharp edges and rounded curves.

Standing here now, he knew that he couldn't go back and change things. Instead, he removed his hands from the vise, breaking free from all the what-ifs and lingering regret. For the first time since his accident, he didn't feel overwhelmed, or depressed, or even bitter... but resolved.

Although he could begin to embrace the idea that he could be a carpenter again, he would never let himself grow used to the idea of taking a wife.

Standing in the mercantile, his hands positioned nervously on the glass counter, Joseph jerked to attention at a familiar odor.

Julia. He'd know her cloying scent a mile away.

The sound of her footsteps lightly tapped across the scarred plank floor, her overwhelming perfume blocking out the various dry goods scents that wafted to his senses.

He clenched his hands into fists, steadying himself as he stood there waiting for Aaron to return from the storeroom with Mr. Heath. Almost a week had passed since Aaron had buried Ellie beside their baby boy. Aaron had spent every waking hour at the shop, working his hands raw, then sleeping on a cot near the stove in the shop. He'd submerged himself in his job, rather than seeking out others for comfort. Joseph had worked alongside him and considered it a small victory that today his brother had agreed to accompany him to the mercantile.

"Well, Joseph Drake! I didn't dream I'd run into you today," Julia announced, slipping up next to him.

He turned toward her, sure that by now she must know the outcome of his appointment. With Ellie's funeral, there'd been enough friends and townsfolk around that she'd have heard.

"Didn't plan on running into you either." He shifted uncertainly, pulling his shoulders back.

When she perched her hand on his arm, her touch stirred up unease. "I see you have those awful wraps off. Quite frankly, I can't imagine how you could stand them for so long. I'm absolutely certain I would've ripped them off, had it been me."

He forced a congenial look her way. "Can't say I miss them much."

Julia trailed her fingers up his arm to his shoulder. "So…is it true?" she uttered conspiratorially. She leaned toward him, her powdery perfume nearly gagging him. "You're…blind?"

He cringed when she whispered the last word as though it was socially impolite, offensive. He still had a hard time admitting the truth—that he was blind. In the presence of others, except his brothers, Sam and especially Katie, he sensed awkwardness. As though people didn't quite know what to say or do. Well-meaning though they may be, sometimes people would treat him as though he was deaf, mute *and* blind.

If Katie was around, she'd almost always come to his rescue, though never by making it look as though she had to—a small detail for which he was thankful. She had a very tactful way of diverting attention.

He hadn't asked for her to return to work with him again, though he surely felt the lack. Joseph was grateful for the two weeks he'd had with her, knowing that without them, he'd be fumbling around like a babe in nappies. He'd been trying to get by without help from his brothers, but some things he just couldn't manage on his own.

Maybe when he was certain he could be around Katie without feeling the intense draw he still experienced, he'd ask her to come back. And if Sam would just get the ball rolling and propose marriage, then she really would be off-limits. Sam had commented that they'd had several in-depth conversations on her aunt and uncle's front porch, and that he was just waiting for the "right" time to tell her of his intentions.

For now, Joseph had to fight his own desire for her.

Through the deaths of Ellie and the baby, Joseph had gotten a closer glimpse into Katie's character. Her compassion, her strength and her gentle caring ways. She was everything and more of what he wanted in a wife. He cared deeply for her. But she could never know. And Sam could never find out.

When he felt Julia's breath fan across his face, he jerked his attention back to her lingering question. "Yes. It's true. I'm blind," he answered, loud enough to make her uncomfortable.

Her tsk-tsk-tsk set the hairs of his neck on end. "That's what I'd heard, though not from numerous sources. Just one *very* reliable source." On a dramatic sigh, she patted his arm. "Of course, you can imagine my surprise. I scarcely believed it, since you were absolutely certain things would be fine. But now that I'm here, seeing with my very own eyes, I must concede that it is true."

"Yep. It's true," he echoed, waving a hand in front of his face for effect. "Can't see a thing. If you'll excuse me…"

Slipping away from her, he tried to picture the layout of the mercantile, wanting to move as far away from her as possible. But uncertainty assaulted him and instead he scooted down to the end of the counter. A heated flush worked up his neck and his pulse pounded in his ears. Drumming his fingers against the glass, he willed his brother back. Now!

Although he tried to look nonchalant and unaffected by her presence, doubts as to whether he'd buttoned his shirt correctly suddenly assailed him, undermining what little composure he had. He resisted the urge to check, knowing for certain that she was still standing there. He could smell her, for goodness's sake. And he was sure she was staring at him. He could easily imagine her curious gaze, taking his full measure as if he were a piece of meat that had spoiled.

He hated this!

Jamming his hands into his pockets, he pulled his shoulders back. He could loathe this kind of incident and let it get the best of him or get used to it, knowing that people would be curious whether he liked it or not.

And Julia was curious to a fault.

"So, did you want to ask anything else?" he began, drawing his mouth into a tight line as he raised his brows. "There must be some kind of burning question on your mind, like maybe if I've made a mess of a meal lately?"

After a stunned silence and imperious sniff, she muttered, "Uh...no."

A self-satisfied grin stole across Joseph's face. And even though Julia still stood there, no doubt glaring at him, he didn't even try to wipe it off. It felt too good.

The sun had begun a leisurely descent in the western sky, sinking low and dragging with it the minute bit of light Joseph treasured. He sat on the porch steps and stared into the sky, letting the waning light of day wash over him before night crept in and the dim shadows turned dark again.

He'd worked in the shop with Aaron from sunup until now, and was exhausted from the level of concentration he'd maintained all day—every day. He wondered if, given time, things would grow easier. Every task seemed twice as hard and took twice as long. Even though they'd made surprising headway on the order, finishing it on time was still a long shot.

But he wasn't about to go down without a fight and lose his shop because of some intimidating deadline. He'd do whatever it took to make sure the job was finished on time. And though Aaron probably didn't care one bit whether he received anything extra, Joseph was eager to reward his brother heftily for the hard, laborious work he'd given to complete the job.

The distant cadence of footsteps over the boardwalk generated a long, wistful sigh from Joseph. What he wouldn't give to walk to and from without relying on someone else. Since he'd joined Aaron in the shop over a week ago, his brother had picked him up in the morning or Joseph had coaxed Boone to let him tag along, bribing him with a handful of treats. If he kept that up, Boone would be so round that Katie's initial impression that the dog was a black bear wouldn't be so far off the mark.

The memory brought a low chuckle from Joseph. He didn't think he'd ever forget that day, when she'd squeezed behind him, afraid she was going to be bear lunch.

For an instant he'd felt useful, normal. But the bandages he'd had on his head had been a stark reminder that things had changed for him, he just hadn't known how much at that time.

In most every aspect of life he had made adaptations, from the way he prepared a meal, to something as small as making sure he'd pushed in a chair. Sooner rather than later, he'd have to start using the cane. That's why he sat holding it now, determined that today would be the day. Hadn't Katie said that it would make things easier for him? Affording him independence he was desperate to taste again? It had been almost two weeks since he'd returned from Denver, and though he'd come to some sort of resolution regarding his blindness, he still avoided the thing. It was as if using the cane as his guide would somehow solidify his fate.

He held the finely sanded object in his hands, feeling its length and narrow circumference. He tried to imagine himself with it, walking to the mercantile or to church or to the hotel restaurant. Humiliation rose hot and ready to sting.

Joseph ignored the caustic burn, forcing his focus to the cane. He set it on end at his feet and tapped the small tip on the hard ground again and again, determined to come to terms with this. He'd never imagined that a stick of wood, so insubstantial and harmless, could loom like some evil enemy.

"Good evening, Joseph." Katie's warm voice startled him.

He shot off the step, the cane dropping to the ground with a quiet thunk. "Hello."

"Sorry if I startled you," she called from the gate, the mellow lilt of her voice soothing something deep inside him.

He passed a hand through his hair, wondering if he looked as ruffled as he felt. "Don't worry. No harm done."

The gate opened and closed with a restful creak. "I just wanted to stop by and say hello. I hope you don't mind."

"No. Not at all. Come on up and have a seat." He gestured to the steps with a smile, then sat down beside her, recalling how he'd wanted to check in on her a couple hundred times.

She'd been so strong through Ellie's death. Joseph had been grateful to have Katie with him that morning. He'd worried plenty about her, but he couldn't very well check in on her when he couldn't make it to Sven and Marta's on his own. Besides, he didn't think he was ready to be in her quiet yet compelling presence without feeling so out of control of his own emotions. Even now his heart raced inside his chest.

Sam had told him just yesterday that he was encouraged by the interactions he'd had with Katie and hoped to make his intentions for her known by the time he left for the city in a week or two. If Sam didn't make a move soon, Joseph might just have to prod his friend some, even though doing so would be like ripping his own flesh.

"I hope you've been well," he finally said, turning to face Katie. "What's it been? A week since I saw you last?" he asked, the irony of his own words hanging before him.

She gave his arm a brief squeeze and sighed. "I've been busy. Things have been so hectic for Uncle Sven at the lumber mill that I've been helping him with his ledgers."

Joseph furrowed his brows in surprise. "Do you like to do that sort of thing?"

"I don't mind it, really. I'm willing to try anything."

Regret prickled Joseph. He knew very well that she enjoyed her job as a trainer and teacher. She was good at it, too. If he could get over his feelings for her, he'd ask her back in a heartbeat. But with the order he and Aaron were trying to finish in the shop, he wasn't sure when he'd even have time to work with her. In the evenings he was usually so tired.

But being with her right now, it suddenly dawned on him how energized he felt.

"So, you looked like you were deep in thought," she probed.

He felt for the cane on the ground, then drew it up on end in front of him. "It's this thing."

"That *thing* again, huh?"

He sighed. "I know I need to get used to using it, but for the life of me, I can't seem to bring myself to do that."

"I understand. Just know that once you've gotten the hang of it, you'll wonder why you didn't take it up sooner."

He nodded. "Probably."

After a settling silence she cleared her throat. "Ben said that you've been working with Aaron. How's that been going?"

"Surprisingly well." Joseph turned toward Katie. "He has the patience of Job, and believe me…he's needed it working with me. I get so frustrated not being able to see what I'm doing," he ground out, tightening his grip on the cane. "But Aaron's been a great help, and between the two of us we've devised some pretty good systems."

"I'm so glad," she breathed, resting her hand on his arm.

Warmed by her touch, he chose to ignore the fact that he was nearing dangerous territory. "You were, too, you know."

"I was what?"

"A great help. I thought about what you'd said, that I could do carpentry work again, and that gave me hope."

"I'm glad, but really, your talent didn't diminish an

ounce when you had your accident, Joseph. You just needed to discover that for yourself."

"I suppose," he finally admitted as he rolled the cane between his palms. "Listen, I'm new at this cane and I was wondering if maybe you'd give me some pointers."

"I'd be—"

"I know you're not officially working with me," he interrupted, half expecting she might turn him down. After all, he'd sent her packing when they'd returned from Denver. "I just wondered, as long as you're here...."

"Of course, I'll show you. I'd be glad to."

"I'll pay your wages for whatever time I use," he added.

"Don't be ridiculous!" She gave his arm a playful shove.

Standing, Joseph cocked his head down at her and smiled. "So, the lady has a feisty side...."

Katie stood, sighing. "I get that way when I have to."

He held the cane in front of him and readied himself as though facing a firing squad. "All right, then. Have at it."

Katie chuckled as she came to stand next to him. "Hold the cane this way." She lightly grasped his hand and adjusted his grip as he struggled to focus on her instruction, instead of on her touch. "Now move the cane back and forth like this."

As she demonstrated, standing behind him and threading her arm around his, he felt his resolve crumbling fast. "If there's something in your way or a step ahead of you, you'll know."

Doing what she'd instructed, he took a turn to his

gate and back, counting steps and moving the cane the way she'd advised.

"Perfect," she commented as he stopped beside her.

He smiled. "Good instruction I guess, Sunshine." Tilting his head toward where she stood beside him, he pulled in a long breath, dragging a hand over the stubble on his chin. "I could use some practice, though. You wouldn't want to go on a walk with me, would you?"

"A walk sounds very nice." Katie's voice was light as the late-summer breeze filtering through his cotton shirt.

They took off down the street, and Joseph tried to remain fully concentrated on his technique.

"That's it," she encouraged as he slowed to a stop some distance from his home. "Just make sure you're keeping it far enough in front of you that if you come across an obstacle, you'll be able to stop in time."

He pulled his head around, searching for light. Finding none, he figured they must be beneath a tree. "If I'm correct, I'm standing outside the boarding house, right?"

Joseph wondered if Sam was there. He could hear the faint sound of voices floating through open windows, but he didn't pick up Sam's low timbre among them, which was probably for the best. If his friend walked out here now, Joseph didn't know how he'd react to Sam's tangible attraction for Katie.

He often wondered if Katie felt the same attraction to Sam. Why wouldn't she? Sam was a successful, good-hearted man.

A whole man.

"Yes, we're a little over four blocks from your home."

She came to stand in front of him and grew quiet. "Can you see anything, Joseph?"

The tenderness in her voice melted his heart. It had from the moment she'd said one word to him. She was so caring. So considerate. So full of kindness.

Yes, he could see clearly that she was perfect for him—that's what he could see. But he wasn't perfect for her. And never would be.

Determined not to dwell on what could never be, he shoved the disappointment aside with a shake of his head. "With the sun going down and being under the tree here, I can't see much of anything. In daylight, though, I can see gray silhouettes. It's a far cry from vivid sight, but at least it's something."

While they stood in companionable silence, a wagon rolled by. Its wheels clacked and the horses' hooves clomped over the hard-packed ground. He pictured the wide street, the gracious boarding house, the wagon and horses. The expanse of skyline, sparse grass and the majestic mountains hemming in the valley.

But as Joseph focused down toward Katie, he wondered once again what she looked like. He'd heard enough from Sam and his brothers to know that she was beautiful. He'd love to see her for himself. Just once.

On a deep breath, he drew his sightless gaze from her. "Well, this was easier than I thought," he confessed.

"It'll certainly make things easier," she agreed, the sweep of her hand rustling down her skirt. Katie paused and after several moments cleared her throat, her voice gone dreamy, as if she'd just awoke from a long, restful nap. "You're looking good, Joseph. I'm so glad to see you smiling."

Right now he wished that he hadn't become so astute to the emotions layered in a person's voice. Even though he'd like to pretend it wasn't there, he couldn't miss the deep affection, even longing in her sweet lilting voice.

Chapter Twelve

"Hello there, Miss Ellickson." The voice, low and pleasant, halted Katie on her perch. "Aren't you a fetching sight?"

Grasping the ladder for support, Katie twisted around from where she'd been hanging decorations for the Glory Days celebration to find Sam smiling up at her. Without a doubt, the man was dashingly handsome with his dark hair, stunning smile and trim build.

But seeing Sam didn't do to her insides what seeing Joseph did. Being with Joseph made her heart beat fast and hard, made her stomach quiver and made a smile form on her face that was hard to wipe off.

"Hello, yourself." She returned his smile.

Knowing she probably looked a sight, she brushed at the strands of hair that had fallen out of her loose chignon. When she began descending the ladder, she gasped as his hands circled her waist and gently hauled her to the ground.

"Thank you," she breathed.

"At your service, lovely lady." His playful bow made

her chuckle. "What are you doing climbing ladders anyway? Surely others can do that job." He glanced around the square.

"I'm fine. With two brothers, I spent many an afternoon climbing trees and haylofts." Katie laid her hammer and nails in the basket at her feet, then brushed her hands together.

"Oh?" He raised his perfectly shaped brows. "Climbing trees, huh? I know the best climbing tree around if you ever get the inclination. Joseph and I spent hours up in that tree."

A trickle of longing worked through her at the mention of Joseph's name. Wiping at the beads of sweat on her brow, she caught Sam grinning at her. "Sounds like you two had fun."

"That we did. Sometimes a little too much fun," he confessed, his mouth still set in a smile. He rested a hand at the small of her back, leading her into the shade of a tall oak, its branches draped outward like open arms of welcome. Folding his arms at his chest and leaning against the rough bark, he settled an intense gaze upon her.

"What?" she asked, furrowing her brows. She wiped her face with her sleeve and did a quick scan of her dress for signs of dirt. "Do I have a smudge of dirt somewhere?"

"You look perfect."

Embarrassment swept through her and she busily focused on smoothing out her robin's-egg-blue skirt, splashed liberally by a print of small white flowers.

"In fact, I don't believe I've ever seen a woman look so beautiful." His voice was thick with adoration. "I tell you, Katie, I'd be hard-pressed to find such elegance anywhere."

She raised her hands to her cheeks where a heated blush embarrassed her further. Fighting to collect herself, she peeked up at him.

He dipped his head. Tenderly held her gaze.

Around Sam she felt as if she was the only other person walking the earth. He was a very kind man, generous with his compliments, though sincere. From all she'd heard, he was well-respected and loved in his hometown.

But there was Joseph.

She found herself thinking of him often. All the time, really. The way he'd held her, making her feel so protected and cared for, not evoking any of the fears she'd initially had with him. It hadn't taken long for her to realize he meant her no harm. Joseph Drake was a man she could trust with her life.

But could she trust him with her heart?

Clasping her hands in front of her, she scanned the city square where several people busily worked to complete the decorations in time for the celebration that started tomorrow.

"So what brings you out here?" She turned toward him. "Did you volunteer to help with the preparations, too?"

"I regret to say that I did not." He drew his mouth into a mock grimace, then settled a very direct, but warm gaze upon her. "I was hoping that perhaps I could whisk you off to dine with me on this beautiful afternoon. Does a picnic pique your interest?"

"A picnic?" Katie echoed in surprise.

She was sure he'd be a wonderful companion for a picnic. He'd been nothing but a gentleman each time she saw him, and he'd shown so much compassion in the aftermath of Ellie and the baby's death almost two weeks ago.

Katie's heart squeezed at the memory of her dear friend. She sorely missed Ellie, their honest conversations and friendship. At times like these she wished for her friend's honest guidance.

"I'm sorry, Sam. I—I appreciate your offer, but there's still so much to do here," she faltered, wishing it was Joseph standing here asking her to go on a picnic.

There was something far more than just a passing fancy for Joseph resonating in her heart. His muscle-roped arms had made her knees weak, and the strength she'd found in his embrace gave her a security she'd never known. His hand at her back set her nerve endings humming, arousing sensations so innate she'd be hard-pressed to subdue them.

She'd relished the opportunity to help him out the other day when she'd given pointers on using his cane, but she had fading hopes that he'd ask for more than that. He was very busy and had made no effort to contact her about returning to work with him.

She hugged her arms to herself. Joseph had been pleasant enough the past two weeks. But since he'd found out his vision wasn't returning, he seemed set on suppressing the warmth and interest he'd shown her before, shutting himself off like a snowed-in mountain pass.

Turning, Katie sighed as she viewed all of the undec-orated venues that stood like roughly clad women awaiting their transformation into finely dressed ladies. "I'm afraid I won't be able to slip away, even for a short time."

Sam stepped back, setting his hand to his heart. "You wound me, Katie. Here I was hoping to take you away to the perfect place."

"The perfect place?" She angled her head.

"Yes." He stepped forward, inches from her. "You see, Katie, I'm not a man to make rash decisions. Nor am I a man to stand idly by while something so perfect is within my reach." He raised a long finger to touch the tip of her nose. "I have every intention of asking you to be my wife."

"But I—" She topped midstream.

Be his wife? Had she heard him correctly?

Surely he was just teasing her. He often did. He was always calling her "m'lady" or "lovely lady" or whatever else suited his fancy at the time.

She raised a hand to capture the laughter that erupted at his playfulness. Bringing her watery gaze to rest on his, her laugh piddled out to a weak chuckle when she witnessed the sincerity in Sam's expression.

Her cheeks flushed instantly hot.

"Can I look forward to seeing you tomorrow?" He captured her hand, lightly brushing her knuckles with his lips.

Mutely she nodded, staring blankly at him as she drew her hands together, fingering where his lips had just been. For a moment she wondered what it would be like to be married to Sam. Surely he'd cherish her. The depth of honesty in his eyes spoke volumes. His kindness and genuine concern would make any woman happy, she was sure.

Katie just knew she couldn't be that woman. Especially since she was soiled. If Joseph never opened his heart to her again, she didn't think Sam, or anyone for that matter, would want her the way she was.

With a finger crooked beneath her chin, he lifted her head. "I'm going to be looking for your decorated box at the box lunch auction. Then you will be mine for the afternoon."

Katie clutched the box lunch in her hands, half tempted to fling it under the wheels of a passing wagon and head back to her aunt and uncle's house. Instead, she trudged onward, the lovely little handbag Ellie had made for her swinging from her wrist as she made her way to the town's celebration.

Her heart was heavy, weighed down by loss. After talking briefly with Aaron last night and seeing his drawn features full of grief and pain, she'd settled on avoiding today's festive atmosphere altogether. But Aunt Marta and Uncle Sven had strongly suggested she attend, assuring her that nothing would be gained by staying home, alone in her sadness.

They were probably right. Isolation wouldn't help. Besides, Katie needed to knit herself into this community and make it home. She couldn't go back to Iowa— not as long as Frank Fowler was there. Attending today was as good a way as any to get to know her neighbors and fellow townspeople.

Seeing how charming the town square looked with wooden booths and townspeople alike dressed in their finest made her smile. Ellie had been so enthusiastic about this day, with its box lunch auction, lively barn dance and fireworks display.

Katie forced a smile on her face and returned a wave to a young woman across the way. Scanning the square, she noticed how the adorned booths flanking each side of the open area drew attention, like beautiful paintings hung in a prestigious gallery. A swell of pride rose within her knowing that she'd played a small part in the visual splendor.

Lifting her chin a bit, she stepped across the grass sparsely peeking through the reddish soil, and tugged on the hem of her new silk taffeta bodice. She smoothed down her matching skirt, appreciative of the indulgence her aunt and uncle had insisted on purchasing for her. With no children of their own, they'd often sent gifts to Katie and her siblings.

Although Katie had several nice dresses, she'd never owned one that made her feel as elegant as this one did. The periwinkle-blue color was like that of the late-summer blooms dotting the countryside. The stylish scoop neckline her aunt had urged her toward was edged with a graceful white lace collar, and clasped by a delicate silver brooch. Her other dresses touted more traditional, full skirts with room for several petticoats. But this one was cut in a slimmer fashion—a design the dressmaker said was all the rage out east.

When Katie reached the long threshing table located on the flag-draped auction platform, she stared in amazement. Dozens of boxes lined the table, like twittering schoolgirls dressed for their first dance. Some were tied up with twine—plain as the dirt beneath her feet—and others were bedecked in such elaborate detail they teetered on the edge of being garish.

She'd been forewarned that being a young, single female in this community, some considered it her womanly responsibility to proffer a box for eligible bachelors to bid on. Wishing that she'd avoided this event, she tucked her decorated box lunch in among the others, glad that there was nothing spectacular to call attention to hers. That was just as she'd wanted it. Not too plain and not too overstated, the pale blue ribbon was tied neatly, without fuss or flourish around the box. Three small daisy blooms and a touch of greenery she'd picked from her aunt's garden garnished the top of the light maple box. Eyeing her offering one last time and hoping for a swift lunch with an agreeable companion, she gave a small sigh.

Her attention was suddenly grabbed by one box in particular, displayed prominently at the front of the table. Picking it up, she turned it over in her hands and studied it. The package was fixed with a sparkling green ribbon and festooned with overly large flowers, and had Katie wondering if the creation was Julia's handiwork. A distinctive aroma even lingered about the parcel… perhaps a remnant of the owner?

Setting the box down, Katie was unable to hide her slight grin. Julia was like a spoiled child insisting on being the center of attention.

If Joseph was present today, Julia might focus her overbearing, inconsiderate ways on him again. The very thought needled Katie. She could only hope that Julia would find some small amount of tact in her reservoir of social etiquette.

Coaxing her white gloves from her hands, Katie glanced around the square again when her gaze collided headlong with Sam's. He stood with Joseph just inside the grassy square.

Warmth stole up her cheeks remembering what he'd said yesterday about becoming his wife. Surely he didn't mean it—she'd done her best to convince herself of that all night long. Chided herself for thinking he could actually be interested in her. After all, why would he set his sights on her when he had a whole city of fine women to choose from?

Had he been sincere, she faced a hard decision. One she'd rather not think about. It seemed advantageous, if not cowardly, for her to steer clear of him altogether.

But Sam was so nice. So much fun to be around. She didn't have the heart to shun him or avoid him just because her heart still beat a steady rhythm for Joseph.

When she skimmed her attention their way again, he promptly removed his hat and bowed, his dark hair gleaming in the sunlight. Straightening, he gave her a ready smile and a long, slow look that had her heart swelling ever so slightly.

Twisting her gloves over in her hands, Katie smiled back, feeling like a cat in a room full of rockers. She could be perfectly congenial to him—he'd make that easy. If she could just act as if he'd not made his intentions so blatantly known yesterday, then things would be fine.

She glanced their way again. Both men looked exceedingly handsome today. Sam in his dark gray suit and matching bowler hat. And Joseph... Joseph in his bronze-colored vest, ecru shirt and brown breeches that hinted at his powerful legs.

Her cheeks flushed warm as she raised her gaze to the rebellious locks of wavy chestnut hair that fell across Joseph's forehead and then to the length that skimmed his neckline. Her gaze lingered on him and a shiver of longing passed through her. She sorely missed his companionship and the safe refuge he offered. The mere sight of him and the vivid memory of his strong, protective embrace called from within her a chorus of emotions and sensations that were irrevocably unsettling.

"Ah, Joe…" Sam breathed, his voice gone thick with adoration. "I don't remember the scenery being quite so beautiful around here."

"You really have been away too long," Joseph teased.

He clutched his cane as he walked beside Sam across the town square, struggling to keep his head above a wave of self-consciousness. Other than going to and from the shop he hadn't ventured out in the public with his cane, and right about now he felt like the Glory Days celebration sideshow.

With a great deal of lost time yet to be made up on the order, Joseph had been set to work with Aaron in the shop today. But his brother had all but pushed him out the door to attend the town's festivities with Sam.

Pulling his shoulders back, he tried to ignore the self-consciousness he felt now. He didn't want his insecurities to affect his time with Sam. "Has the valley changed that much since you left?" he asked.

He caught a fiddle's faint song lilting over the jumble of voices in the vicinity. Took in the different aromas that bombarded his senses—the home-cooked foods, late-summer blossoms, even the grass beneath his feet. In past years he'd really enjoyed himself at this annual celebration, but this year he doubted he'd have much to write home about.

"I don't mean *that* kind of scenery, my friend. I mean the any-way-you-look-at-her, gorgeous woman due north," Sam quipped, making Joseph squirm. "Katie is elegance and purity all wrapped into one beautiful package, just like that box lunch I just saw her set on the table."

"So you know which one is hers, huh?" Joseph asked, trying his best to sound interested. "Guess that's a good thing."

"Yep. It'll be easy enough to spot with that huge green ribbon and big flowers she tied around it." Sam gave a subdued whoop. "Yep. It's a beautiful day, indeed. But this mountain valley—luscious as it is on a day like today—doesn't hold a candle to m'lady, Katie."

Joseph swallowed hard, determined not to let Sam's words get to him. He might well spend each day with his heart aching and each night imagining her in Sam's arms, but he'd do it for Katie's sake. It'd be torture, plain and simple, but what choice did he have? His friend deserved a woman like Katie. A sweet woman with strength of character and kindness of heart—and as Sam had said—a woman with unequalled beauty.

Katie deserved a man who wasn't encumbered by blindness.

"Katie, it's good to see you," Sam greeted as he slowed to a stop. "Wonderful day for the celebration, isn't it?"

"Yes, it is," she responded, a hint of hesitance in her voice. "How are you gentlemen today?"

"Even better now that I've seen you." Sam took a step forward and a chill wriggled down Joseph's spine. "You look lovely today, Katie."

"Thank you." Her voice was quiet. "How are you, Joseph?"

He shoved a hand into his pocket. "Fine. And yourself?"

"I'm doing well." Melancholy burdened her sweet voice.

Joseph grew immediately concerned because he could almost always count on her sunny demeanor. "You sound a little down."

"Just missing Ellie today. She was so excited for this event."

He nodded, a reminiscent smile tipping his mouth. "She was like a little girl when it came to things like this. I'm sure Aaron won't be here at all today."

"Probably not," Katie agreed.

"He's going to need time and a lot of prayer," Sam added, followed by a long moment of silence. "I believe I saw you put a box lunch on the table, Katie."

She sighed. "I hear it's mandatory if you're single."

"According to Mrs. Duncan and her followers, yes," Sam agreed with a chuckle. "Every year, for as long as I've been around, that woman has hit the streets campaigning for the event. The way she goes at it, visiting every household in the valley, you'd think she was Herod himself, seeking out all firstborn males—or single females as the case may be."

The sound of Katie's quiet laughter seeped into Joseph, making him wish he was a little closer to her.

"I'll say this for her, she's very persuasive." Katie gave a big sigh. "If I didn't know better I'd think my entrance to heaven hinged on this alone."

"You can bet that she'll make sure everyone is involved, even if she has to hold a gun to their heads," Sam quipped.

Joseph reminded himself once again that he had no claim on her. She wasn't his. But she wasn't really Sam's either.

"I wonder, Katie, who will be the highest bidder on your box lunch?" Sam shifted his feet lightly over the ground.

"I'm sure that whomever I dine with will be just fine."

Joseph balled his fists, clenching his jaws tight as he envisioned Sam sweeping Katie off for a private lunch. Were he able to see, he'd pay whatever it took to secure a picnic with Katie, making sure he was the first and last to bid on her box.

"Joseph Drake! Well, I never in my wildest imagination thought that I'd see you here today." Julia's voice and overpowering powdery scent cut a brassy path through the pleasant atmosphere. "Miss Appleton," she clipped off, the greeting colder than an icehouse in January.

"Ellickson, Julia," Joseph corrected, shaking his head.

"And who is this man with you, Joseph? Is he yet *another* teacher?" Julia's voice was so loud that Joseph had to resist the urge to plug his ears.

"This is Sam Garnett, a friend of mine."

"Really," she oozed, making Joseph marvel at how she could make her voice rise and fall an entire octave in one word.

"And I'm blind, Julia." He tightened his grip on his cane, unable to miss how Katie cleared her throat. "Not deaf."

"A pity it is, too, Joseph." She perched her fingers on his forearm and sidled up next to him. "A pity."

He stepped out of her touch and closer to Katie.

"Knowing Joseph, he won't let his lack of sight get the best of him," Sam said, gently slapping Joseph on the back. "He's not one to shrink from difficulty."

Joseph didn't doubt that Sam was coming to his rescue, but for some reason he didn't feel as if he needed rescuing.

"Mr. *Garnett,* you say?" Julia's skirt swished and Joseph wondered if the gown she wore was the one he'd spilled grape juice on. "Would that be from the Boston Garnetts?"

"No. The Boulder Garnetts, Julia. Sam grew up here. His folks passed on a year ago."

"How dreadful," she simpered. Barely missing a beat, she continued. "Why have I not had the privilege of making your acquaintance, Mr. Garnett?"

"I'm not sure why." Sam sounded amused.

"I'm not sure, either," Joseph echoed, seeing as how Julia made Boulder's business her business. "He's been in town three weeks." He nudged Sam's arm. "This is Julia Cranston."

"It's a pleasure to meet you, Miss Cranston."

Joseph wanted to laugh at Sam's gallantry, but didn't

dare. Sam was probably playing with Julia and no doubt enjoying her drama and outlandish personality. He'd always had patience for things like that, where Joseph had decided that he preferred things straightforward.

"Mr. Garnett," Julia said as though greeting a king.

Joseph could only imagine the coy look she was sure to give Sam. The slight tilt of her chin. The way she'd peer at him sideways with her big emerald eyes.

"Are you in town for a visit or have you plans to stay?"

"Just a visit. Though who knows, I may decide to stay if the fancy strikes me," Sam responded.

"Well, now, that is good to hear, Mr. Garnett," she gushed. "I presume you'll be participating in the box lunch auction? Though primitive compared to eastern entertainment, it promises to be quite a marvelous event."

Sam chuckled. "I wouldn't miss it."

"Joseph, do you plan on having someone do your bidding for you?" Julia asked, her tone almost motherly. "Since you are unable to see, that is?"

He pulled a forced smile. "No, Julia. I don't."

She tsk-tsked. "Oh...what a pity, I tell you. The auction will positively be the talk of the town."

Joseph held his cane between both hands and drew it against his chest when Julia gasped.

"Are you lame, Joseph?" she nearly shouted, stepping in front of him. "Did you hurt your leg?"

"*Why* would you ask that?"

Julia huffed, her stale breath fanning across his face. "Well, you're carrying a cane. What else is one to think?"

"You tell me," he shot back, enjoying her confusion.

He could hear her hands brush against her skirt, the material slipping under her touch. "Naturally I assumed that perhaps you'd fallen and hurt yourself. Given your condition, it would certainly be a strong possibility, you know."

He smiled, feeling a tangible sense of satisfaction. "No, Julia. My leg is fine."

"Oh, well, the cane is fetching with your outfit, Joseph," she dismissed with a verbal flourish. "I didn't take you as one to make a fashion statement, but then, wonders never cease."

"Thank you."

"Miss Appleby," she continued.

"Ellickson," Joseph and Sam spoke in unison.

"Have you a box lunch to offer today?" she asked, almost accusing in her tone.

"I do," Katie responded simply.

"Splendid. Don't you worry one bit. I'm quite certain that some young bachelor is bound to place a bid on it. The men around here, though they lack the class of those back east, seem polite enough."

Katie chuckled, apparently unruffled by Julia's barbs. And that made Joseph proud. "I'm not worried."

"Though, being new to town, mind you," Julia continued as though she was some authority on the matter. "I wouldn't expect for your box to draw an overwhelming amount of money. You do understand, don't you, dear?"

"Thank you for the warning, Miss Cranston. I'll be sure to prepare myself."

Chapter Thirteen

Joseph jammed a booted foot up on the lowest fence railing, amused as he listened to Mr. Heath—mercantile owner turned auctioneer for the day—ramble off the bidding. He tipped his head back to the afternoon sun's full brightness, enjoying the faint bit of light he could see. With his cane secured against the fence, he bent over and braced an arm on his knee.

Every single year he was caught off guard by Mr. Heath's surprising cadence as it filled the town square. Oohs, aahs and cheers erupted from the crowd when a box went for a whopping six dollars and fifty cents— no small change in these parts.

"Who bought that one?" Joseph leaned toward Sam. He could easily envision his friend, the relaxed way he'd hold his arms at his chest and the way he'd drape one foot lazily in front of the other, as he leaned back against the railing.

"I think it went to Jacob Watson. That banker has a payroll that could outfit three large ranches." A deep chuckle resonated from Sam. "Or maybe Julia's wardrobe."

Joseph grinned at his friend's assessment. "It might take more than a banker to keep her happy."

"She's something else, isn't she?"

"That's an understatement." Threading his fingers through his hair, Joseph dragged in a breath. "She means well. But sometimes…"

"You handled her well-meaning words with finesse, my friend. I was proud of you."

"Thanks."

"No, really, I mean it. You're acting more and more like yourself again, and I'm glad to see it." Sam clapped him on the arm. "You know, Julia really isn't all that bad. She's oblivious to how her words come off, but socialites can be like that. Until you tame them, that is."

"It's hard to hate her," Joseph agreed, sliding his hand across the fence to make sure his cane was still there. He'd had to use Sam's arm as a guide a few times so far today. But mostly he'd put into action what he'd learned from Katie.

"I took Julia on a few outings before my accident. Nothing serious, though. Not as far as I was concerned, anyway. My blindness has made her noticeably uncomfortable around me now."

Sam puffed out a sigh. "That has to be hard to take."

"Yeah…at times."

"I just met her, but from what I can tell, Julia's similar to women from more affluent circles," Sam explained. "Most likely she doesn't know what to do with you because she's never really had to deal with sickness or injury."

Joseph nodded. "You're probably right. But whether it's her or someone else, I'm going to have to get used to that sort of thing," he added with a conciliatory sigh. "I just know that I'll never get married, that's all."

He sensed Sam turning toward him. "What do you mean, that's all? You've been planning on marrying for as long as—well, for as long as you and I've been noticing girls."

Joseph raised his brows, hoping he came close to making eye contact. "You're one to talk, Mr. I'm-not-married-yet-either," he shot back with satisfaction. "And, for the record, I did have a lady who had captured my attention."

"Well, then? Where is she?" Sam pressed, his voice low.

"I gave her up."

"What did you do that for?"

"I had my reasons. Besides, without my sight I'm not exactly *prime* husband material."

Sam huffed, shifting his feet on the hard ground. "You're not getting sympathy from me with *that* attitude."

"I wasn't looking for sympathy," Joseph countered.

Sam might live in a world of honesty and directness, but he just didn't understand what it was like to feel so useless and unable to do what a man should. Joseph couldn't exactly fault him for that. "Listen, I have a lot to focus on with relearning things. I really don't need a woman in my life to distract me."

"*That,* Joseph Drake, is the most ridiculous thing I've heard in my life!" Sam jabbed a finger into Joseph's chest. "And believe me...being a lawyer, I've heard plenty of lame excuses."

Joseph pushed his friend's hand away. "Call it what you like. It doesn't change a thing."

After a long silence, Sam finally spoke. "Hey, they're holding up the box with the big green ribbon for auction. That's Katie's box."

Joseph sucked in a long, steadying breath, praying he could stay indifferent. "Well, then, you better pay close attention."

The bidding began at fifty cents, working up to two dollars, then three, three-fifty...

Joseph could almost feel the intensity coming from Sam. He knew the man was focused on one thing only. Securing Katie's box lunch for himself.

Five dollars, five-fifty, six dollars...

"I'm bidding against money bags over there," Sam whispered in a conspiratorial tone. "From the looks of him, he must be some wealthy rancher. Ah well, he doesn't know how competitive I can be, Joe."

He wanted to cheer his friend on, but felt as if he'd betray his own heart if he were to root for Sam. While sleep eluded him again last night, Joseph had decided that he'd do his best to congratulate Sam and Katie if they were to marry. But each step they took to the altar would twist the noose around his heart a little tighter.

Seven dollars, eight dollars, nine dollars.

For a split second, Joseph thought about raising his hand and getting in on the bid—all he had to do was make sure he was the last one called upon. But he couldn't do that to Sam. And he couldn't do that to Katie.

This is for Katie's sake.

Ten dollars, eleven dollars...thirteen dollars.

A hush came over the crowd as the auctioneer spoke. "Seems we have a high-priced lunch here, folks. The young lady who dolled up this box with all this frippery and what-not must be quite a catch. Do I hear fourteen dollars?"

"Fourteen dollars," Sam called out triumphantly, as though he'd just obtained the state of Colorado in some land auction.

"Do I hear fourteen-fifty?" the auctioneer queried, then paused. "Fourteen going once...going twice.... Sold! To Mr. Garnett for fourteen dollars!"

Sam let out a long, wistful sigh. "That, my friend, was money well spent," he said, his victorious grin glaringly apparent in his voice.

Joseph's heart tightened inside his chest. It didn't matter a coyote's hide what he wanted or that the mutual attraction to Katie was undeniable. What mattered was what was best for Katie.

He held out his right hand to Sam and forced a smile to his face. "Congratulations. You won," he said, feeling the full, painful brunt of those words. "I'm sure you didn't waste one cent of your money."

After an awkward silence, Sam moved his hand up to grasp Joseph's arm. "You feeling okay? You look a little pale."

"I'm fine," Joseph shot back as he jerked his foot down from the fence railing. He willed the irritation out of his voice. "Just not used to all this activity, I guess. I think maybe I'll go back home when the auction is over."

"You're welcome to join Katie and me for lunch."

"Now who's being ridiculous?" He reached toward the fence, carefully feeling for his cane. "You may be a great lawyer, Sam, but you're a lousy liar."

"All right, so you got me there," Sam retorted, placing the cane in Joseph's hand. "Are you sure you don't want to stick around? Ben and Zach are here. I could find them for you."

"I'd rather not." Hearing another round of bidding begin, Joseph grasped his cane between both hands, wondering if he could trust his sense of direction enough to make the seven blocks home, alone. "I think they had plans of their own."

"Apparently," Sam remarked with a low chuckle. "Zach's in on this round. Whew! That rancher he works for must be paying him good money."

"I don't think so. He probably just has a stash saved from his poker days."

Joseph pulled his head around and stared at the murky silhouettes of the buildings behind him, trying to decipher where, exactly, he was on the square. But everything appeared roughly the same height. Not one detail, large or small, could he make out through the dense haze.

"He must. The bid is already up to nine dollars."

Curious now, Joseph turned his attention back to the auction. "I wonder what young woman he's set his sights on."

Sam clucked his tongue quietly. "I don't know, but it looks like he's got some pretty stiff competition going with Ethan Hofmann."

Ten dollars, eleven, twelve...

"Neither one of them look like they're ready to drop

out," Sam informed. "Ethan has those big meaty arms of his folded over his chest. I think he's trying to intimidate your little brother. If you ask me, he does look modestly imposing."

"Zach can take care of himself." Joseph chuckled, knowing that given Zach's respectable size and surprising agility, Ethan Hofmann didn't stand a chance. "Zach hasn't said a thing about being smitten by some lady. Do you know whose box it is?"

"No idea. I just paid attention to the one Katie set on the table. Sparkling green—"

"Ribbon. Big flowers. I know," Joseph cut in, irritated.

Thirteen, fifteen, eighteen…

"What is Zach thinking spending money like that?" Joseph ground out under his breath. He nudged his friend's arm. "Does he look drunk? He vowed he hasn't been drinking, but if that boy's drunk, when I get done with him he'll wish he'd stayed out on the ranch mucking stalls."

There was a long pause as the bidding continued to escalate. "He doesn't appear unsteady on his feet. And he sure doesn't look like he just dragged himself out of a saloon. He looks sound to me, Joseph."

Twenty dollars, twenty-one.

"Folks, we must have ourselves some kind of royalty livin' here in Boulder, with the price this box is bringin'," the auctioneer bantered even as laughter rolled through the crowd. "Just look for the bright pink blush, fellas. You'll know who fixed up this perty little number with the blue frippery and—what are them—little daisies?"

Joseph braced a hand on the fence, genuinely amused at the expectancy swirling around the square. "Can you tell who's got the telltale blush?"

"Hard to tell who the box belongs to. Seems like all of the ladies have been pinching their cheeks today."

Twenty-two, twenty-three, twenty-three-fifty.

"What in the world is he thinking bidding more than half a month's wage?"

"I don't know. But he's looking over this way and has a smile a mile wide. Ethan, on the other hand," Sam added, in a sympathetic tone, "appears to be noticeably uncomfortable right about now. He's all red-faced. I can see the perspiration on his brow from clear over here. Either his collar suddenly got tight or he's bidding out of his league."

Joseph threw his head back and laughed, and for a blessed moment in time, he felt normal again.

Twenty-five, twenty-seven, twenty-eight.

"Twenty-eight-fifty going once…going twice…sold!" Mr. Heath proclaimed as the crowd broke out into loud whoops and hollers. "Folks, that there is the *highest* price we've ever had a box go for. Zach, I ain't heard of you playin' the tables lately. What with money like that, it must be burnin' a hole in them britches you're wearin'."

A fresh round of laughter burst across the square, Joseph's and Sam's included. Joseph shook his head, trying hard to wipe the smile off his face. "Here we all thought he was starting to make good decisions. Be responsible. Guess he had a relapse."

Sam jabbed his arm. "Young love. Gets a man every time."

"Foolish love, maybe," he retorted. But Joseph couldn't deny that had he been bidding and that had been Katie's box, he would've done the same thing. He would've spent more if needed.

"He's coming this way," Sam whispered. "Try to go easy on him. I'd hate to see that look of pleasure he's flaunting like a prized mare turn sour."

Joseph slid a hand over his freshly shaven jaw. Shoving a hand on his hip, he pulled his shoulders back and tried for his best concerned, older brother look.

Zach came up beside him and grasped his arm. "You owe me twenty-eight-fifty, Joe-boy!"

"Twenty-eight-fifty?" he echoed, unable to wipe the smile from his face. "You're a funny man, Zach. You know darn well I'm not paying your bill for some la-dy's—"

"You sure will, Joe-boy. And you'll do it gladly, too."

Joseph just laughed. Leave it to Zach to go to some wild extreme just for a laugh.

"Why, I would'a bid twice as high for Katie's box to put a smile back on your face."

It'd been four hours since the auction and Katie still felt the heat of embarrassment as she walked with Joseph to the barn where the dance was about to begin. She supposed she should be flattered, but the idea that someone would pay such an outrageous amount for anyone's box lunch, let alone hers, was awkward, to say the least. And that Zach would bid as if he owned the town and then gleefully dump the bill in Joseph's lap was downright mortifying.

At the time, she hadn't been sure whether to protest

or just let things fall where they may. When she'd realized what Zach had intended all along, it had been painfully obvious that Joseph wasn't pleased. He was stiff with tension and looked as though he might snap his cane in two—his hands were fisted so tight. If he'd been a lesser man he probably would've flat-out refused to oblige Zach and his innocent, good-natured gesture.

Instead, Joseph had forced a half smile on his face and picked up the expensive box, then escorted Katie out to the mountain stream. It'd been awkward at first, but after they'd settled at the stream's bank, where the melodic trickle of water gurgled around bends and over rocks, and the sun's warmth peeked through the luscious pines and hearty aspens, Joseph seemed to relax. They'd slipped into the kind of easy conversation she treasured with him.

Katie cherished every single moment of the afternoon. She'd just spent four blessed hours with Joseph and she hoped she could be content with that.

"There you two are," Sam called jogging across the street toward them. "You were gone so long I almost rallied the Rangers and sent them out after you."

Katie peered up at Joseph to see his mouth suddenly pull into a taut line. The awkwardness she'd sensed from him earlier this afternoon multiplied tenfold.

"Guess I lost track of time." Joseph released his gentle hold on her arm. "That's easy to do out by the stream."

Sam glanced her way. "He showed you our old haunt, eh?"

A wistful feeling came from deep within as she stared up into Joseph's face. "Actually this is the second time. It's such a peaceful, serene place. So picturesque."

"How about you, Sam? How was your lunch?" Joseph asked.

"I'm glad to say that I had a nice time." There was a mischievous gleam in Sam's eyes as he narrowed his gaze on her. "But I could've sworn I was bidding on your box, Miss Katie Ellickson. I just know I saw you set a box with a big green ribbon and flowers on the table. I figured it had to be yours."

"Oh, I'm sorry for the confusion, Sam. Mine was the one with the pale blue ribbon... Well, you know that now, I guess. For some reason, that other box had caught my eye and I wanted to get a better look at it." With a certain amount of irony, she silently recalled holding the box. "Perhaps it was the flowers. They were just so... so large." She remembered Julia's potent, recognizable scent that had lingered like some caustic odor around the gaudy package. "You must've been glancing my way when I set it back on the table."

"Hmm." With a furrowed brow, Sam tapped his forefinger against his lips. "Apparently."

Joseph angled his head toward Sam. "So, what lucky lady was fortunate enough to go on a picnic with you?"

Sam paused. "None other than Miss Julia Cranston."

"Really?" Joseph's mouth twitched with a barely bridled grin. "I hope you had a nice lunch with her."

Feeling a giggle working its way up her throat, Katie set her hand to her mouth and coughed to ward it off. Honestly, she felt genuinely sorry for poor, unsuspecting Sam.

"I'll admit, I was disappointed that it wasn't you, Katie," he said, slicing his warm gaze to her. "Nevertheless, I did enjoy myself," Sam assured, giving her arm a tender squeeze before he clapped Joseph on the shoulder. "I must say, Joseph, I was taken aback when Zach handed over his...prize."

Joseph dragged in a breath. "So was I."

Sam passed a slow, studying gaze from Katie then back to Joseph. "Is there any reason in particular why he'd do that?"

"You'll have to talk with him about that."

Hugging her arms to her chest, Katie peered up at Joseph. "I hope that Zach won't really make you pay all that money."

"Don't worry about the money." He focused down at her, his eyes...those beautiful, dark amber-colored eyes radiant with instant warmth that seeped all the way to her toes. "Spending time with you would've been a bargain at ten times the price."

Katie silently drank in the moment, reveling in the unexpected show of affection from him.

"Well, kids, the fiddles are tuning up." Sam pulled her out of her small indulgence and nodded toward the large barn. "That means the barn dance is about to start. Do you enjoy dancing, Katie?"

"I love to dance," she breathed, then leaned toward Joseph and quietly spoke. "Do you want a guide into the barn?"

He lightly grasped her arm. "Sure. Thanks."

"And you, Sam, do you enjoy dancing, as well?" she asked.

"Love it!" He clapped his hands once, then rubbed them together as though warming himself over a fire.

"How about you, Joseph?" she asked, steering him around a large dip in the ground. "Do you dance?"

"*Does* Joseph dance? I'm surprised your reputation hasn't preceded you, my friend." Sam reached around Katie, needling Joseph with a friendly pat. "Joseph Drake may as well have been born-and-bred nobility, the way he dances. Come to think of it, all the Drake brothers can twirl a lady around the dance floor like they stepped out of some castle ballroom."

Sam leaned toward her and whispered conspiratorially. "The menfolk hate them for it, too. Makes us all look bad."

"This year they'll have two less Drakes to hate. Aaron's not here and you won't catch me out there doing any dancing."

"What harm could a waltz or two do?" Sam prodded.

When they stepped into the barn doorway, Joseph stopped beside Katie and pulled his head back as if adjusting to the change in lighting. "Without my sight, I'd be like a bull in a barn full of newborn chicks out on a dance floor."

"You never know, it might just make you feel more like yourself again," Sam urged.

"I'm feeling like myself without dancing, thank you." He dropped his hand from Katie's arm and held his head high. "If one of you'll point me in the right direction, I'll just find my way to where all the men with two left feet line up. You two go on ahead." With nonchalance, he gestured them away with small sweeping strokes of his hand. But his jaw muscles clenched, and his casual manner didn't quite reach his voice. "Enjoy yourselves. Dance all night."

Confusion tugged at Katie's heart, threatening to tear it in two. She just couldn't understand how Joseph could look visibly irritated when Sam showed her attention, yet seemed bent on shoving her straight into his friend's arms.

As good and as nice as Sam was, it wasn't his arms she dreamed of holding her. She yearned for Joseph's strong, muscled arms encircling her, making her feel tenderly cared for…and loved.

She swallowed hard. Joseph seemed set on shutting down his feelings for her. Even if he did want her, he very well might not feel the same way knowing the truth of her past.

But she could dream. No one could steal that from her.

Several moments of silence ensued. Sam continued to stare at Joseph as though seeing his friend for the first time, and then turned a hesitant, lingering gaze on Katie.

"Katie, if you wouldn't mind, I'd be honored if you'd grace me with a dance before the night's out," he uttered calmly, suddenly lacking the excitement he'd shown only moments ago.

She glanced at Joseph, then to Sam. "Well, I—"

"Yoo-hoo, Samuel!" Julia's shrill voice demanded attention.

The hair on the back of Katie's neck stood on end as she witnessed the woman whisk across the wide-planked floor with graceful elegance. Her dark silky hair was pulled back in a fashionable twist and her cobalt-blue dress glimmered in the barn's soft yellow glow. Julia's striking emerald eyes glinted hard as steel as she shot a look of warning at Katie, then slithered up next to Sam like a snake to sun.

"My dear Samuel, the music is about to begin," she

cooed, trailing a finger down his arm. "You promised me the first dance. Remember?" she whispered, soft enough not to wake a baby. Loud enough for Katie to hear.

Sam peered at Joseph again, then with what seemed a deliberate, painstaking length of time, passed his gaze back to Katie. When her eyes met his, she found something strangely different there. Something that almost made her sad for Sam.

While he gave Katie a single measured nod, he responded to Julia. "I did promise you the first dance, Julia."

He peered down at where Julia possessively looped her arm through his and gave the woman a genuine but dim smile as he patted her hand. "If you'll excuse me, Joseph, Katie, I have a dance to enjoy."

Katie swallowed hard, watching Sam lead Julia out on the dance floor with gentlemanly grace and undivided attention. He was such a good man, so warmly attentive. She said a silent prayer for him, yet wondered if it was Julia she really needed to pray for. Sam, perceptive and astute as he was, seemed to be able to see past all of the flash and flourish Julia acted out like some grand performance. She might not be prepared for the candid and guileless way with which Sam operated.

Chapter Fourteen

The night had just begun and Joseph already wished that it was over. Slowly inhaling the rich summer air, he listened as Sam ushered Julia toward the dance area, reminding himself that he'd vowed to go the distance tonight. If he was going to get on with as normal a life as possible, he wanted to start living it like he had in the past. Living like he had a future.

When he sensed Katie shifting beside him, he leaned toward her and asked, "Would you like something to drink? I'm pretty sure I caught a whiff of apple cider. If it's anything like in past years, I'm sure it's good."

"That sounds delicious. Thank you," she answered, her sweet voice raised a notch, compensating for the loud music and the dancer's stamping feet as the announcer called for the Virginia reel.

"Do you mind leading the way?" He reached up and grasped her arm. "I'm a little uncertain with all the people. Can't rely on shadows when it's so dark in here."

She briefly touched his hand at her elbow. "Not at all. It's just over here, to the left."

As she weaved through the crowd, Joseph returned several greetings sent his way, trying to appear as casual as possible. *Other than the fact that he was holding on to Katie's arm with one hand and the long cane in the other, no one would guess a thing was different about him,* he mused sarcastically.

He took in all the sounds around him...the voices, the music, the apple press grinding in the background. When the edge of his cane came into contact with a barrier, he reached out and touched the waist-high board that doubled as a beverage counter for these gatherings. He felt the nudging of people beside him and behind him, and was threatened with a moment of panic, but knowing Katie was there gave him confidence.

"I'm right behind you," she spoke low, edging closer.

"What'll it be, Joseph?" Mr. Heath's easy timbre was a welcome sound.

He smiled. "Two glasses of cider, please."

"Coming right up!"

"Joseph Drake, it does my heart good seeing you here today." Mrs. Duncan scooted next to him and barked out an order for cider.

"I'm glad I could make it," he answered, picturing the older woman's round, rosy-cheeked face.

"This event just wouldn't be the same without you." When she patted his arm as though she was burping a baby, a sliver of irritation wriggled down Joseph's spine. "I suppose you're bored stiff and just chomping at the bit for things to do now that you're blind."

Not wanting to appear rude, he endured her thick-handed touch and ungainly words. "Well, actually—"

"It's a shame about your eyesight and all, young man.

The whole town thinks so." Her stale breath fanned across his face and he could easily picture Mrs. Duncan's pinched features framed in wisps of carrot-orange hair. "A pure waste of a promising young man, that's what it is."

He set his back teeth. "I wouldn't consider—"

"You needn't feel ashamed of yourself," she half yelled as she pushed closer, bumping into him with her doughy-soft figure. "It's a cryin' shame you never married, seeing as how you'd probably be grateful for someone to take care of you now. But as handsome as you are, I'm sure you could find some young woman who'd be agreeable to marrying you in your condition."

Joseph threaded his fingers through his hair, striving to maintain his patience. After all, this was Mrs. Duncan, and it was no secret that she spoke her mind, the words flying from her mouth without a thought.

"Oh, really? Is that so?" he finally said, as though responding to news about the local logging industry.

"I don't usually do this sort of thing, but my niece, well, she may not be beautiful by some men's standards, but she's a good girl. Practical, nurturing and strong as an ox," she said, each quality emphasized by a sharp poke in his chest.

Joseph balled his fists around his cane and when Katie's hand came to rest at his back, he felt a sense of relief.

"She's from Longmont," Mrs. Duncan announced, her voice carrying through the barn as the music came to a snappy halt. "She'll be arriving before winter sets in. I'd be more than happy to introduce—"

"I appreciate the thoughtfulness," he interrupted,

holding up his hand in hopes that she'd just drop the subject.

"I'm sure you'd find her pleasant-enough company. Why, she can read, cooks real good and is charitable just like me," she added as the music began again. "Mind you, it's not as if I've given this a lick of thought, but if the two of you married, you could just move in with Horace and me. We have plenty of room."

"Does she have all of her teeth?" came Katie's voice from behind him, the sharp but humorous bite in her words cracking a smile on Joseph's face.

Mrs. Duncan huffed and pressed in closer, making Joseph's level of irritation shoot upward. "As I was saying…the two of you could live with Horace and me."

He suddenly felt more compassion for Horace Duncan than he'd ever felt for another soul. "Mrs. Duncan, I—"

"That way Horace could tend to the *manly* things around the house." When she sidled even closer, it was almost his undoing. "Since you're not able-bodied, why, it'd be the perfect arrangement."

"Mrs. Duncan! Really, I'm *not* interested," he ground out, his voice raised a notch. Closing his eyes, he steadied his nerves, thankful again that Katie was behind him.

"Well!" The woman gasped. "I was *just* trying to help."

"I'll let you know if I need your help."

After Mr. Heath handed him the mugs of apple cider, he turned and gave Katie hers, then followed her lead back through the crowd.

"That was outrageous," Katie whispered.

"That's Mrs. Duncan for you," he clipped off, swallowing a mouthful of cider along with his pride.

When they reached the benches that were lined up around the barn's perimeter, Joseph secured his cane against the wall and sat down. He rested against the thick, sturdy walls as he tried to compose himself. His sour mood was in direct contrast to the light, playful music.

"I'm sorry that happened," Katie spoke next to him.

Hearing the quiver in Katie's voice, he knew he'd have to ignore his frustration or her evening would be lost on him. He didn't want that. She loved to dance and deserved to enjoy herself tonight, but if she stuck around feeling sorry for him, she might bow out of the frivolity, and Sam had yet to dance with her.

"Are you all right?" Her voice was tentative enough to broach a hibernating bear.

"I'm fine. Don't worry about me."

"But Mrs. Duncan…she was so thoughtless," she added.

"She's not known for her tact." He hoped his casual dismissal was convincing. "Go have fun now. I'm sure there are plenty of men waiting in line to dance with you."

When Ben chose to stop by at that very moment and pull Katie out on the floor for a lively number, Joseph tried to be grateful. He sat back on the bench, determined to enjoy the pleasant music, rhythmic stamping of feet and the satisfying sounds of laughter woven like a cheerful cord through the night. While the evening wore on, one dance after another, he remained resolute on staying to the end.

"Having fun over here?" Sam sounded winded as he sat down with an unceremonious plop next to Joseph.

"Sure. The music's good, as always. And I have a great view from here," Joseph retorted, smirking.

"So…the man has a sense of humor?"

Joseph gave his friend a disingenuous grin and stretched his legs out in front of him, hooking one ankle over the other.

"Where's Katie?" Sam asked on a deep exhale.

"I'm not sure. Last I knew she was out there with Zach."

After a pause, Sam said, "There she is, dancing with Mr. Heath—that sly, old dog."

A smile tipped the corner of Joseph's mouth. "Does she look like she's having fun?"

"She's glowing," Sam responded with a certain reverence. "Has been all night."

Hearing Sam say that, Joseph was very glad that he'd jerked himself out of his irritation earlier. Had he not, she might still been sitting beside him missing out on the evening.

"Katie sure is something, Joseph." Sam cleared his throat. "Listen, I came over here to let you know that Julia's come down with a headache and asked if I could see her home. You know, since I bought her box lunch…"

"Of course. Go ahead."

"I'll be back later to walk you home," Sam added.

"I'm sure I can get Ben or Zach to see to it. I might even be able to make it myself."

"You might as well get a lead. I know I would if I were you." Sam's voice suddenly grew serious. "There's something else…. I was wondering, since I haven't danced with Katie yet and there are probably a few waltzes left, I thought that maybe you could do the honor for me."

Joseph gave his head an adamant shake. "Sam, you're a good friend, but—"

"It's just a waltz. You could do it in your sleep."

"I'm flattered by your confidence in me," he shot back sarcastically. "But I'm *not* getting out on that dance floor."

"What will it hurt?" Sam prodded.

"If I talk with her again, I'll let her know that you had to leave and were sorry you couldn't dance with her. I'm sure she'll understand."

Even as Joseph uttered the words, he wished he could take them back. Just one dance. Why couldn't he find it in himself to at least try one dance? One more chance to hold her, to touch her, to burn into his memory her scent, her soft skin, the sound of her sweet voice so near him.

"You know that I'd never leave without extending her my deepest regrets. I already did that." Sam paused a moment, the uncomfortable silence drowning out the fiddle music in the background. "There's no good reason why you can't dance *one* waltz with her."

Joseph stared straight ahead, wide-eyed. "Being blind isn't good enough reason for you?"

"Just try. Dance with Katie," Sam urged, his words sounding as though they'd passed through gritted teeth.

Joseph pushed himself up from the bench and drew his mouth into a tight, grim line. "Stop badgering me about this. Please."

"Let me put it this way," Sam ground out, coming to stand right in front of him. "I could continue to set my sights on Katie, falling over myself to win her affection, but it wouldn't do me a bit of good." When Sam moved closer, Joseph bridled to meet him, nose to nose. "I want you to listen, and listen good. There's a fall-off-your-horse gorgeous woman out there who takes my breath away. But believe me, it's been painfully obvious all night that she has eyes for only *one* person in this room," he said, jabbing a finger in Joseph's chest. "And it *ain't* me."

The words permeated every inch of Joseph, weighing down the protest that struggled to break free. He stared into darkness, confusion hanging over him as Sam walked away. A swirl of emotions rocked his mind and heart. Frustration at the helplessness that still snaked through him, challenging his sense of value. Dread that dare he follow his heart he'd find that he really did lack what it took to be a worthy husband.

And hope. Hope that *if* he dared to follow his heart, he'd find things to be far different than what he feared. He'd discover that Katie cared for him, not out of pity or loyalty, but because of who he was, blind or not.

Sensing his stubborn resolve slipping away like water through a sieve, he reminded himself again why he shouldn't be the one to pursue Katie. He wasn't a whole man—like Sam. He couldn't take care of her like a husband should. He couldn't love her like—

But he could love her. Maybe he already did love her.

All at once, the insecurities that had permeated his mind these past weeks now smelled more like pride than truth. And the gallant motivation that had held his focus captive seemed as unclear as the indistinct shadows in his world.

Turning to grab his cane, a tremble worked through him as he realized that Sam had just relinquished the object of his desire... Katie. He'd as much as pushed Joseph toward her, the last few words he'd said ricocheting through Joseph's mind like a bold flash of light jerking him from some strange, dark dream.

He was still reeling from the sentiment when he felt a light touch on his arm, and instinctively knew it was Katie.

"Joseph?"

He squeezed his eyes shut, trying to remind himself of why she deserved more. But he couldn't seem to grasp even the smallest bit of prior reasoning.

"Are you feeling under the weather?" she asked, her touch working like a mesmerizing fire to calm his uncertainty, her light lily scent like an intoxicating draw. "Would you like to step out back for some air?"

"Sure," he heard himself saying.

He swallowed hard, fighting to sink his teeth into his resolve again. Each time he started to protest with some excuse as to why he couldn't go with her, he felt his tongue get thick, his mouth go dry with the unspoken words. When he grasped her arm and walked with her around the dance area, each step felt like a thousand mile's distance from his former rationale.

"Are you sure you're not feeling ill?" Katie asked as they walked into the cool night air. "You look a little flushed."

He shook his head, working his cane in front of him. "No, nothing like that."

His footsteps fell in perfect rhythm with Katie's across the hard ground as they neared the spot where a new fence line had been erected to flank the lot. Slowing to a stop next to her, he felt helpless to drag up even one argument.

As another melody ended from inside the barn, Joseph concentrated on the noises surrounding him. The crickets chirping their own playful song, pigeons cooing from their roost in the barn, the light wind whispering through the nearby pines.

When he thought he heard movement from the area of the trees, he turned, training an ear that way. Had someone run into the trees when they'd come out here? Perhaps some of the children who seemed to delight in spying on private moments? Listening closely, he knew for a fact that he didn't want an audience right now.

After he was satisfied that they were alone he pulled his attention back to the moment and heard her sniffing the air.

"Do you smell that?" she asked, sniffing again.

"Smell what?" he responded, wondering if maybe she'd caught the scent of fire in the distance. He dragged in a long breath, but the only distinct scent he caught was a faint whiff of some kind of tobacco smoke.

"Oh, I'm sure it's nothing," she dismissed on a shaky sigh.

"Are you sure?"

"Yes—I mean, I just thought I smelled cigar smoke out here. But I'm sure it's fine."

"I smell it, too. In these parts you could throw a rock and probably hit someone who smokes those things."

"I'm sure you're right." She sighed.

He tried to ease the tension cording his neck muscles, letting the music wash over him like some gentle waterfall. "It's a beautiful night," he uttered, awkwardly searching for something to say.

"Gorgeous." Katie gave a wistful sigh, making Joseph yearn to see the expression on her face. "Oh, Joseph. The sky is *so* beautiful tonight."

He swallowed hard. "What does it look like?"

"Hmm… Like a deep, dark blanket soaked with brilliant stars," she breathed, her carefully selected words painting a vivid, poignant picture. "And the moon—it's full. Like some perfect, priceless pearl hung over the barn just for this occasion."

Joseph's heart squeezed tight. Closing his eyes, he felt an irrepressible smile curl his lips. Although he'd never told her, she intuitively knew how important words were to him now, and had made such a touching, magnificent effort just for him.

Never once had he felt pity from her or been treated with kid gloves. Never once had she responded to him as though he was incapable of handling a situation. She'd been a friend and a driving force in helping him find his way to normalcy.

She'd warmed to his show of concern, melted to his touch and given a part of herself he knew hadn't come easy for her. She'd given him her trust.

"Katie," he said, his voice low as he turned toward her. He clutched his cane between his hands, his knuckles tight. His heart thudded against his chest. "Would you dance with me?"

Throwing his cane to the side, he held his hand out to her.

When she slipped her hand in his, a connection traveled far beyond his fingers, flowing all the way to his heart.

The musicians began a familiar waltz and he closed his eyes, picturing the surroundings. The hard-packed ground, flat and free of obstacles. The barn with its doors swung wide, spilling a soft yellow glow of lantern light out into the dark night. The long, thick row of hearty pines, their boughs draped heavily with snug cones this time of year. The setting wasn't some grand ballroom or even a crude barn, but as far as Joseph was concerned it was the most perfect setting for a waltz.

With a slow intake of breath he set his hand at her back, pulling her a little closer, relishing the way she trembled ever so slightly at his touch. Before he lost his courage, he took the lead, stepping back, side, together, forward, side, together. Back, side, together...

He danced with Katie, drawing her nearer as he glided her across nature's ballroom with just the moon and the stars as his witness. He held this beautiful treasure, feeling something tug at his heart, then settle deep inside his soul.

After the song ended and another began, Joseph slowed to a stop, the space between them charged with some invisible, tangible force. He twined his fingers with hers, splayed his other hand at her waist. His heart drummed a steady, fast beat, and his breathing grew shallow.

Wanting to drink in this moment, he grasped both of her hands and drew them to his chest. He stared down at where he grazed her fingers with the pads of his thumbs. Felt her soft skin that belied her perseverance and hard work.

"Sam asked me to dance with you in his stead." He raised his sightless gaze. "But that dance—that was for me."

A small whimper came from her lips. "Oh, Joseph, you are so sweet."

He stared down at her, straining to see through the darkness. "I wish I could see you, Katie," he ground out, swallowing hard. "From the moment I first met you, I've wanted to see your face."

She drew his hands to her cheeks, holding them there for a long moment. "You can."

Awkward shyness crept over him at the idea of taking in her features with his fingertips. When he hesitated, she gave his hands a tender squeeze.

"It's all right," she whispered.

He swallowed hard, and then with a feather-light touch, moved his hands little by little over her smooth skin. Her warm, shallow breath fanned his palms, seeping into him like the welcoming spring sun thawing the frozen ground.

When she released her hold, he gently, hesitantly slid his fingertips to her forehead where a line of silken hair framed soft skin. Then to her brows, perfectly arched over closed eyes, her lids, satiny as rose petals. Her lashes, dense and long, fluttered like a butterfly's wings beneath his fingertips.

He smiled.

Then skimmed his fingertips down a little farther to high cheekbones that rimmed eyes he knew must sparkle with life and wonder. To her small nose, just the right size for her perfect oval-shaped face. He trailed his fingertips down to her mouth, where full, soft lips met his trembling touch. He moved the pads of his fingers slowly, reverently over her supple mouth, admiring the most perfect, flawless Cupid's bow. From these perfect lips came a constant flow of encouragement that had changed his life forever.

Cupping his hands around her face, he lowered his head, his lips settling on hers. He adored her with a soft, gentle kiss, the slight brush of his mouth against hers, awakening every emotion he'd tried so hard to bury.

Joseph pulled back and slid his fingertips down the line of her jaw to her silky smooth neck where her pulse, beating hard and fast, met his touch.

"You're so beautiful, Katie." His voice came as a harsh whisper. "So beautiful."

He wrapped his arms around her and held her tight, loving the way she snuggled into his chest as though hiding herself in him. She molded so flawlessly to him, her body the perfect mix of soft, rounded curves and long, steady lines.

Boldly, he smoothed trembling hands up to the nape of her neck, where petal-soft skin seared his sensitive fingertips. He breathed deep, resting his cheek against her head.

His heart skipped a beat and his pulse pounded faster, louder in his ears. In spite of the cool August night, he was suddenly warm. He released her, shuddering as an unexpected revelation hit him soundly. He'd never felt like this before, so moved, so taken by beauty he couldn't even see.

Chapter Fifteen

$\mathbf{K}$atie could hardly believe the sensations and emotions that still rocked her as she made her way behind the barn again. Regretting every step away from Joseph's consuming presence and exhilarating touch, she'd left him waiting in front of the barn for Zach, remembering that she'd forgotten the treasured purse Ellie had given her out by the trees. She'd said she'd be right back because he'd insisted on walking her home, and she was now inching along the tree line peering into the deepening darkness to find the purse.

As she neared the place where they'd danced, she set a hand to her lips, recalling how she'd been hard-pressed to find her voice after Joseph had kissed her. She reveled in the way he'd held her, demonstrating to her what it means to be cherished.

The thick grove of pines whispered softly to her in the slight breeze. She stood, hugging her arms to her chest, relishing the memory of his embrace. Peering up at the stars, she swayed back and forth, made a slow lazy turn, compelled by the age-old love song Joseph had awakened in her heart.

He was the best thing, the most wonderful thing that had ever happened to her. God bless her Uncle Sven and Ben for asking her to come out here and work with Joseph.

A fading dread tried snatching her attention as she remembered how, after suffering through that first awful attack a year ago, her soul had been shattered. Then to have the same horrible man stalk and accost her again, leaving her with the lethal threat of a loved one's death and the wicked assurance of her ill repute, she'd given up hope of ever entrusting another man's touch to promise something other than pain.

But tonight she'd allowed herself to fully melt to Joseph's wonderful touch. His strong hands meant her no harm, only tender care, and his powerfully muscled body was like a shield of protection.

She swallowed hard, lifting her chin a notch.

Frank Fowler may have taken her innocence, but for the first time since he'd devastated her, she felt as if maybe, just maybe she could be free. Free from the clutches of his control. Free from the threat that promised she'd always belong to him. That no man would want her.

Doubt nipped like jealous demons at her newfound joy. Katie fluttered her eyes closed, knowing that she had to tell Joseph about her past, but not knowing how. She could only hope that he'd still find her desirable.

The uncertainty that perhaps he would reject her made her wonder if she'd ever be free from Frank's grip.

A chill worked up her spine, setting her hair on end.

That scent, that bitter, musky cigar scent had been here by the pine trees when they'd stepped outside. For a brief second, her breath had caught in her throat and her blood had gone ice-cold. She'd remember that scent till her dying day. The way Frank Fowler's tainted cigar breath had fanned over her face, making her struggle for fresh air. For weeks after both attacks, the taste lingered on her tongue and she'd wondered if it was like some evil, sick mark. A lasting stain of contamination.

She caught a whiff of it again, and an icy chill blasted through her. She hugged her arms closer to her chest. Tried to ignore the familiar fear that had plagued her for so long.

She was being silly—plain and simple.

Like Joseph had said, many people smoked cigars. It was probably the pungent residue of someone else's crude vice. Besides, she was clear out here in Colorado, hundreds of miles from Frank Fowler. But even as she reminded herself of those things, fear coursed through her. She wanted to run and hide, but instead she slowly turned, determined to resist the urge to dart back inside—

A hand grabbed her hard and firm. Another wrapped around her waist, pulled her back against a solid wall of flesh.

She screamed. Struggled to break free from the hard, unrelenting grip. Kicked hard against the man's shins, her hair prickling on end.

"Help! Someone, help!" she got out before the man clamped a hand over her mouth.

She snapped her jaws shut, catching skin between her teeth.

"You little wench!" the man snarled, grinding his hand against her face.

That voice. Never in her life would she forget that voice.

Frank Fowler.

She fought to wrench her head around to see him, but he had a powerful grip on her. When he removed the hand from around her waist and reached for something, she broke free.

But he yanked her back, dragging her, kicking and fighting, away from the barn and farther into the trees. She thrashed about. Shrieked for help. But her screams died fast when he jammed an acrid-smelling wad of cloth into her mouth, and tightened his grip around her middle.

"Didn't think you'd see me here, did you?" he growled.

Her pulse pounded in her ears and her stomach churned with nausea as she strained to see in the darkness. The deeper into the trees he hauled her, the farther from help she was. And the lights from the barn were being doused one by one.

She tried again to scream, but it just came out as a muffled groan.

"Thought I'd pay you a little visit. But I'm disappointed, Katherine. I didn't expect to find you throwing yourself at some man." He dragged the backside of his hand down her cheek, his icy, rough touch sending a shiver of horror through her body.

She yanked her head away from his touch, sickened by the foulness of his words.

He gripped her chin and jerked her around to face

him. "Here you are, off in some remote mountain town acting like a brazen woman." He heaved her hard against himself, his tight grip sending pain stabbing like hot irons through her. "How soon you forget that you belong to me."

She didn't move a muscle. Didn't make a sound. She wouldn't give him the satisfaction.

"I suppose with him being blind, you're as good as he's going to get." He spun her around to face him and slowly pulled her up next to his unyielding body. "He'll have to find some other soiled dove because you won't be around to show him your kind of charity."

Her heart clenched tight. She forced his ruthless, cutting words away from her heart. If she didn't, she'd be right back where she started before she came out here to Boulder a few weeks ago. Before she started finding healing.

He dipped his head. Dug his fingers deeper into her flesh.

Refusing even a glance his way, she averted her gaze, trying to devise a way to get to safety. She could barely see in the darkness, but if she could just make her way back through the trees and run toward where she could still hear the faint sound of people's voices....

"Don't think you're going to escape from me now."

She swallowed the bile burning in her throat. Tears sprang to her eyes. She blinked them away, knowing that he'd love it all the more if she showed weakness, finding some sick satisfaction in seeing her vulnerability.

Joseph. She just wanted Joseph. To feel his arms wrapped around her, a refuge of warm protection.

"You're mine, Katherine," he taunted, his cigar-tainted breath fanning her face as he grabbed her bodice. "And I'm going to take what rightly belongs to me—again."

Her eyes grew wide as she stared at his black form, barely visible. When she saw his white teeth gleaming in a smile, she wrenched her arms, fighting to break free. Kicked at his legs. Bucked against his tightening grip.

He gave her a brutal shove, hurling her to the hard ground, where he pinned her firmly beneath him.

Her shoulder jammed into a protruding rock and she whimpered. Ignoring the searing pain in her shoulder, she scrambled to get out from underneath him, grunting with her effort. She couldn't bear this again. Not again.

For a brief moment, she felt herself drifting away, far away from the humiliation and agony of what seemed inevitable. But she had to fight back. She couldn't let it happen again.

Katie slid her hands over the ground, frantically searching for something she could use as a weapon. A rock, a branch, anything. When he snatched her wrists and slammed them above her head, she knew the possibility for escape was dwindling.

"Now, let's see if you can please me," he growled.

She felt the barrel of a gun, its cold, hard steel jammed into her ribs. As he thrust the gun deeper, she knew there was no way she'd escape now.

Katie squeezed her eyes tight and stifled a whimper as she held very still.

He laughed, an evil laugh that made her stomach

churn. When Frank released her hands for a brief moment, she heard his belt give way.

Now. She had to make her move now!

Balling her fists, she jabbed them hard into his groin. Kicked and bucked to get him off her.

He yowled and drew back, leaning off balance. "You'll pay for that," he ground out.

Katie pushed hard against him.

He teetered.

She scrambled to get up. Felt a surge of hope as her feet gained ground.

He grabbed her leg. Held on with crushing force.

She kicked with all her might and as she grabbed for the cloth in her mouth, he gained his feet and caught her hand.

"You want it that way? Fine," he spat out, spittle spraying her face.

He jammed the cloth into her mouth again. Gripped her arms tight and slammed her into a tree.

Her whole body convulsed with sharp, stabbing sensations.

With an eerie calm, he held the gun at her heart, his breathing heavy and ragged. "You'll either stop your fighting and come with me," he growled, "or you'll die right here. Right now." He drove the barrel of the pistol deeper into her ribs. "What'll it be?"

She clenched her eyes shut. Forced her thoughts to rest on the sweet memory of Joseph, his protective strength, tender caressing touch and his warm, promise-filled kiss. She'd have to take that beautiful memory with her to her grave, because there was no way she'd go with Frank Fowler without a fight.

* * *

Joseph's blood ran cold as ice at the sound of a gun cocking not fifteen feet in front of him. His heart pounded loud as thunder.

He crouched low, advancing forward step by silent step, honing in on the repulsive noise of the man's ragged breath. And the heart-wrenching sound of Katie's whimper. He could only hope that the element of surprise would be enough to save her.

While he'd waited for Zach outside the front barn doors minutes ago, he'd heard a scream. Then another. The voice had sounded too much like Katie's. He'd charged toward the cry in spite of the taunting that crept through his mind, reminding him of his blindness. He'd called for Zach on the run, but there was no time to waste. He had to get to Katie.

His pulse pounded hard and fast now. Untapped power pumped through his veins at breakneck speed. He tightened his grip on the thick branch he'd found on the ground, hoping, praying it would be a solid weapon and not decayed on the inside.

He heard the man shift, his feet crunching against the dried bed of pine needles.

When Katie made another whimper, the hairs on the back of his neck prickled to ready attention. He'd kill the man—whoever he was—before he'd let him harm his sweet Katie. When he'd gotten within earshot and heard the man threaten Katie, Joseph had felt something snap inside him. It took every amount of self-control he possessed to move with stealthy silence in the cover of darkness, using his sharpened sense of hearing to his greatest advantage.

He clenched his jaw taut, drawing on the raw anger coursing through his veins. Narrowed his focus on the sound of her attacker's heavy breathing. He took a careful, measured step forward. Tried to determine the man's height and where he stood in proximity to Katie, each second praying she'd be all right.

Joseph's heart slammed against his chest. His pulse pounded in his ears. He inhaled quietly, steadying himself. Bolted forward, zeroing in on the man's heavy panting. Hauled the bulky branch over his shoulder. Aimed his focus and brought it down with full, concentrated force.

A gust of air whooshed from Joseph's lungs as the power-packed branch thudded heavily against the man.

With a grunt, the man's gun dropped to the ground with a solid clink of steel.

Katie whimpered.

The man gave an eerie howl, his breath forced through clenched teeth.

"Run, Katie! Run!" Joseph commanded.

Her skirts swished with sudden movement. Her feet shuffling slowly, laboriously over the bed of pine needles.

"Joseph! Where are you?" Zach's call came from near the barn, as Katie's assailant spat a vile string of curses.

"Over here. In the pines," Joseph yelled.

Joseph could hear the man struggling over the ground. He honed in on the sound. Brought the branch back. Focused every bit of power he had into his taut muscles. He let the swing loose. As the branch sliced through the air toward its point of focus, a gunshot sounded. The awful, unmistakable noise ricocheted through the dense grove of trees.

The branch slammed against the man, dropping him to the ground with a dull thud.

Joseph's stomach convulsed with horror as Katie whimpered not more than fifteen feet away. Fell hard to the ground.

"Noooo!" Joseph raged, aiming his raised branch at where the man lay, moaning.

"What are you going to do now, blind man?" the man jeered, his words forced between clenched teeth. "I'm going to kill you, too."

Joseph's emotions stormed between fierce wrath and enormous sorrow. All he wanted to do was get to Katie. Hold her in his arms. But when he heard the man's low, evil chuckle, he felt something untamed, something wholly violent, rise within him and he launched himself in the man's direction, landing hard on top of the attacker.

The man cocked the gun again.

Joseph zeroed in on the sound and grappled for the weapon. When his fingers connected with metal, he grasped hard, crushed the man's hand and flung the gun well out of the way.

Every muscle in his body bunched rock-solid. He balled his fists and pummeled Katie's attacker.

The man's fingers bit into Joseph's wrists, but Joseph jerked free. Then swung harder, faster, deeper. Slamming his fists into the man's face, one blow after another after another. Time stood still as he punished the man with every bit of force he could muster. So relentless that the form beneath him no longer tried to fight back, but was out stone-cold.

"Joseph, stop! He's not worth it." Zach grabbed Joseph's arms, pulling him back.

He wrenched from Zach's hold and sprang to his feet. "She fell somewhere over this way," he breathed, panting hard as he moved in the direction he'd last heard her. "Can you see her?"

"Who?" Zach asked.

"Zach, he shot her. He shot Katie."

"It doesn't look good." Ben's voice was low and grave, renewing the ominous sense of dread that darkened the night. "The bullet lodged just above Katie's heart and she's lost a lot of blood."

"What can you do? Is there anything?" Joseph pulled a painfully bruised and battered hand over his face as Zach grasped his shoulder.

Katie's Aunt Marta sniffed quietly. "Oh dear. My poor, poor Katie-did."

"Vhat else is der to do?" Sven echoed, his quivering voice belying his hulking size. "Der must be someting."

Ben's feet shifted heavily on the wood floor. "If she has any hope at all, I need to operate and remove the bullet—repair what I can. But as weak as she is right now, I'm afraid I'd lose her on the table."

Joseph trained an ear to the other room where Katie lay. "What are her chances otherwise?"

"Dis should not be," Marta whispered harshly. "Vhat kind of evil man vould do dis? Shoot our Katie like dis?"

"I don't know. I've tried asking her a few questions,"

Ben added in a hushed tone. "But I don't want to upset her."

"If'n Miss Ellickson 'members anything," Sheriff Goodwin offered, his gravely voice contrasting sharply with the hushed atmosphere, "it'd be a might helpful, seein' as how that varmint somehow slipped through our hands."

Joseph jammed his hands into his pockets, his jaw muscle tensing. He recalled how Zach had pried him off the man. Since Katie's attacker posed no threat being unconscious, they'd immediately tended to Katie. By the time the sheriff came along, the man had come to and had almost reached his gun. No doubt he would've used it.

But the sheriff put a bullet into him first.

Had the shot been as accurate as the one that took down Katie, the man would either be dead or in custody. Instead, the man had howled, but doggedly plowed on, managing to escape by stealing a tethered horse not far from the site.

"Seein's how she ain't in any condition to talk, I gotta git back to the jail. The deputy's gatherin' a party to track 'im down." The sheriff hacked loudly, then scuffed across the wood floor toward the front door. "Don' you worry none, folks. We'll git 'im."

When the door closed solidly behind the sheriff, Joseph felt the old familiar taunts snaking through his head…. He wasn't whole. Couldn't see danger if it stared him in the face. That he'd never be a protector. What if the man came back and tried to finish the job? Would Katie ever be safe?

"All I can say is…pray." Ben's admonition broke

through the terrifying questions playing through Joseph's mind. "Pray like you've never prayed before."

While Sven began talking to God, his low Swedish timbre hanging in the room like some comforting blanket, Joseph felt his way back to the adjoining room. He stood next to Katie's bed and lowered his head, settling a kiss on her clammy brow.

"I'm going to die, aren't I?" she whispered, her weak, sweet voice barely audible.

"You can pull through this, Katie." Hunkering down, he trailed his fingers lightly down her right arm and found her delicate hand, grasping it in his. "You've got to."

"Did they catch—him?" Her voice caught with pain.

Joseph shook his head, wishing he'd finished off the guy when he'd had a chance. "Not yet. But they will."

Katie suddenly squeezed his hand tight and tensed in pain, making his heart ache for her. After a few moments she relaxed her grip, but his concern wouldn't be relieved.

"The whiskey should start working soon," came Ben's whisper next to Joseph's ear. "It'll help make her more comfortable."

Joseph nodded once in acknowledgment, then focused his sightless gaze on Katie. He smoothed a hand over hers, desperate to ease her suffering. "Just hang on, Katie. You're strong. You're going to make it."

"You're so good, Joseph." She slid her hand from his and set quivering fingers to his early morning shadow of a beard. "Such a good man."

He folded her hand in his and swallowed hard. "Not half the person you are."

"I hoped… I hoped that you and I—"

"That you and I what, Katie?" Joseph pulled her slender fingers to his lips and kissed them.

When he caught a whiff of the unmistakable metallic smell of blood, icy dread blew through him like a silent omen. He could almost feel the warmth of life slowly ebbing from her.

Sitting here feeling so helpless to change the course of things, he couldn't imagine how hard it had been for Aaron seeing Ellie struggle as she had. Finding her lifeless body, the warmth and cheer that Ellie emanated, gone.

Joseph may not have known Katie for long, but already he felt sick at the thought of not having her in his life.

Swallowing hard, he blinked back tears, determined to stay strong for her. He'd do anything to ease her pain. Anything to make her smile. Anything to make her last moments here on earth as meaningful as possible.

"Whatever you want, darlin', I'll do it for you," Joseph murmured softly, the endearment easy on his lips.

"I hoped that we'd—" She coughed suddenly, tensing again.

He eased her hand open and threaded his fingers through hers. Gave her hand a gentle squeeze, wishing he could somehow give her his strength. "Katie?"

Fear gripped hard. Trembling, he set his hand to her chest and felt the faint rise and fall there.

Joseph exhaled slowly, unspeakably grateful that she was still alive. And seething mad at the man who'd done this.

"The pain…it's not so bad now," she finally said.

"It's that medicine." Her weak voice was almost child-like, and with the way he felt her relax, he figured the laudanum and whiskey was finally working. "What a good doctor. I like Ben."

"I like Ben, too," he agreed, his throat tight. "He's doing what he can to make you comfortable, darlin'." Closing his eyes, he hoped, prayed that she'd live through this. "What is it you hope for? Just ask me. Please."

She pulled in a shallow breath. "Mmm…it's nice having you here, Joseph. So handsome. So beautiful. I was smitten with you…from the moment I saw you." Her voice was wistful, dreamy. Her words slow on the tongue.

They stirred Joseph to the depths of his soul. She was smitten with him? Surely the whiskey and lauda-num were having an effect on her…

"I dreamed of marrying you…." Her words trailed off like some long-forgotten love letter floating on the breeze.

Joseph's heart clenched tight inside his chest at the sentiment. His pulse thrummed loud in his ears. He lowered his forehead to her hand. Brushed it lightly over her fingers.

His throat constricted at the thought that Katie might not make it through the night. She had so much life yet to live, so much to give. She'd selflessly lavished her knowledge and patience on him these past few weeks— and he hadn't even begun to thank her. Until tonight when they'd danced, he'd fought off the growing feel-ings for her, but now he was certain he'd crossed over from deep fondness to love. So if marriage to him was her wish—very possibly her last wish—he'd do anything in his power to grant her that.

"Zach," he called over his shoulder.

Joseph pressed a gentle kiss into her palm, praying that she could hold on to his deep love. He leaned over and whispered next to her ear. "Katie, will you be my bride?" He swallowed hard. "Will you marry me?"

She gave a small gasp. "That's so sweet, Joseph." Her words were thick on the tongue. "Just what I wanted."

"What do you need?" Zach spoke low next to him.

"Go get Reverend Nichols." He smoothed a hand over hers. "If Katie wants a wedding, she's going to have one."

Chapter Sixteen

"I do," Katie whispered, blinking against the tears burning her eyes. She gazed up at Joseph, trying to focus on him, but she had a hard time fixing on anything for longer than a moment. "I do," she repeated.

This certainly wasn't what she'd dreamed of for her wedding day—lying in a doctor's office, her vision and mind fogged by remedies to help ease her pain, and a gunshot that had stopped her cold.

Katie didn't want to knock at death's door, even though she felt herself moving closer and closer toward that timeless passage. Even though she had an assurance that God was with her every step of the way, she wanted to live, but with each second that passed, she felt life slowly draining from her body.

It was peaceful, really. And Joseph was here. Her sweet Joseph. He'd been so kind to give her this last wish.

He was such a contrast to Frank Fowler. The thought of the evil man sent an icy chill through her and made her throat constrict with suffocating force. She couldn't think of him—she wouldn't think of him. This was her wedding day.

Joseph gently squeezed her hand, staring down at her with those beautiful, deep amber-colored eyes.

Willing her focus there, she tried to gather strength from him. She wanted to curl completely into the warm security of his embrace, lose herself in his tender strength. But weakness had swallowed her body and she couldn't lift her arm on her own.

Instead she eased her tongue across her dry lips, trying to remain fixed on Joseph. On staying alive.

"Reverend Nichols, please make this quick," came Ben's admonition from down by her feet. "I need to do surgery as soon as possible."

"Of course, of course," the reverend agreed. "So then, Joseph Drake, do you take Katherine Ellickson to be your lawfully wedded wife? To have and to hold—"

"I do. I do to all of those things." Joseph's voice was laced with urgency as he set a trembling hand to her forehead.

"Oh my, let's see now...where were we? For richer, poorer, sickness, health, 'til death—"

"I said, I do," Joseph spoke again, more forcefully.

"Oh my, my, my." Reverend Nichols leafed through his Bible. "Well, then, I—I pronounce you man and wife."

Joseph leaned over her and pressed his mouth, feather-light, on hers. He lingered there for several moments before he drew back slightly. "Hello, there, Mrs. Drake," he whispered.

His sweet words and warm breath whiffed softly over her face, sending a slow, invigorating tremor through her. She was heady with the aftermath of his kiss and the medicine that was fast taking over her ability to stay awake.

"All right, folks. The wedding's over." Ben sounded unusually short-tempered. "I need to see to her now. You're going to have to leave."

Katie blinked several times, trying to focus on each person as they briefly stopped at her side. Her Aunt Marta's pinched features and Uncle Sven's red-rimmed eyes made her heart hurt.

"Love you," Katie murmured, struggling to form the two words as they each bent to place a kiss on her brow.

Sleepy. She was so sleepy. Her eyelids drooped. Weighed down by a force she could no longer deny, she shut her eyes, listening as Ben ushered the small gathering from the room.

"I'm not going anywhere, Katie," Joseph spoke close to her ear, his low, mellow voice lulling her further.

She tried to lift her hand to touch him, but her arm... it was so heavy.

"I don't usually allow others in here with me when I perform surgery, Joseph," came Ben's voice. "You know that."

"Yes, I know. But you're going to have to bend the rules this time, because I'm not leaving her side."

"Joseph, you should at least go in the back room and lay down for a while." Ben's voice sounded rough and weary from the grueling night. "Get some sleep if you can."

"No, thanks." He rolled his head from one side to another. Sitting up a little straighter in the wood chair, he smoothed his hand over Katie's. "I'll stay right here beside Katie."

Ben exhaled. "It's six-thirty in the morning and you've been here since midnight. I'm watching her closely. I promise I'll call for you if it looks like she—"

"I said I'm not going anywhere." He pulled his swollen, stiff hands over his face, the scruff of new growth meeting his touch. He tried to ignore the way his knuckles throbbed, painfully aware of how heavily he relied on touch now.

For a brief moment he thought about the shop and the unfinished order that was screaming for time and attention. But it'd have to wait. He wasn't about to leave Katie's side now.

"If you say so." Ben came around the bed to stand next to him. "At least let me take a look at your hands now that we have a quiet moment. They're a mess, Joseph."

He shook his head. "I'll be fine."

"Maybe. But it won't do you or Katie a bit of good if you're fighting an infection." He lightly grasped Joseph's right hand and turned it over, palm side then knuckle side up.

"Listen, I don't want you wasting time on me when Katie needs you. This can wait," he said, drawing his hand back.

"It won't take me but a few minutes to get those cuts cleaned, medicated and bandaged." Ben crossed over to the cupboard in the corner of the room and quietly rustled around, lifting metal lids that clanked softly against glass jars. "Someday, maybe, I'll hire an assistant to help out here—goodness knows I needed one last night. You could've done with a few stitches when you first came in, but it's too late now. Your hands should heal fine, it just might take a little longer and it won't look as pretty."

"That's fine by me. I won't be able to see them, anyway."

A deep sense of gratitude welled inside Joseph as his brother began smooth and efficient ministrations. This, after he'd performed a three-hour, tedious operation to remove the bullet and patch up Katie as best he could. Then a quiet vigil spent by her bedside, taking her pulse regularly and monitoring every little nuance.

"I'm glad Katie's in your care." Joseph swallowed hard.

"I hope I can help her," Ben said, his hands stilled against Joseph's. "I couldn't seem to help Ellie or the baby. That does something to a man who's supposed to bring healing."

"You're a good doctor, Ben," Joseph responded, knowing that often his brother carried a heavy weight of responsibility when a patient died. "Sometimes, it's just the way of things—and you're fighting against God as much as you are death."

"Yeah, well, I promise I'll do everything I can for Katie."

"Do you think she's going to pull through?" Joseph trained an ear and listened once again to the shallow, thin breathing coming from Katie—his wife.

His wife. The thought tumbled through his mind like a tender acorn looking for fertile soil to settle in and grow. He was a married man now. In spite of the vow he'd made after finding out he was blind, he'd jumped headlong into matrimony. And whether he was blessed to be Katie's husband for a few hours or days, he was going to do the best he could to love her.

"I wish I had an answer for you, but it's too early to tell." Ben began wrapping bandages around Joseph's knuckles. "Having almost lost her twice in the last two hours isn't a good sign. But both times she came around—which shows that she's still fighting for her life."

"Katie's strong," Joseph whispered, silently pleading with God to let her live.

He closed his eyes as different moments from the past hours swirled through his mind like a cluster of dust devils in the summer. He didn't know if he'd ever forget her panicked scream that had stopped him cold or the heart-wrenching sound of her whimper when she was downed by the bullet. And he knew for certain he'd never forget the way she'd lovingly touched his cheek or the way she'd so innocently expressed her secret desire to be his bride. Each memory made him yearn to hold her tight and never let her go.

"It's a noble thing you did, marrying her." Ben spoke low, his voice sounding thick with emotion.

There was nothing heroic in what he'd done. He'd done what was right, and given Katie his life in hopes that she'd have joy for however long she might live—minutes, hours, maybe longer. She'd selflessly given hers these last weeks to offer him comfort and confidence for the rest of his life.

Joseph swallowed hard. "Nothing noble about it. I'm sure you'd do the same."

On a sigh, Ben wrapped the last of Joseph's battered knuckles. "Well, you didn't have to do that for her as a kind of last wish. But you did and it meant the world to her."

Joseph blinked back the tears burning his eyes. He raised a bandaged hand and sought out hers. "She deserves a lot more than that."

Ben's hand came to rest on Joseph's shoulder. "I may have been eager to move the ceremony along so I could tend to her gunshot, but honestly, I didn't want it to end. I believe I witnessed a beautiful act of love here last night."

Joseph wrapped his warm hand around hers, praying. Praying that it'd be enough to pull Katie through.

"Cain't say as we have any leads yet." Sheriff Goodwin's boots clomped loudly over the floor toward Joseph.

"How can that be?" Joseph furrowed his brow, unable to mask his aggravation.

"Wish I could tell ya."

Steadying his temper, Joseph slid his hand to Katie's shoulder. Deep concern for her weighed down every heartbeat and thought. She'd not regained consciousness, but seemed to be growing restless. Given her weakened condition, if infection had come calling, her slim chance for survival could diminish to nothing. Even though he'd been married to her for barely a day, he couldn't imagine life without her.

"What are your plans to catch him?" he finally asked.

"We been workin' on this since one o'clock this mornin'." The sheriff puffed a mouthful of stale coffee breath in Joseph's direction. "Got half'a Boulder scouring the countryside."

"And you don't have a single lead?"

"Well, this mornin', 'round nine, we thought we had ourselves a trail headin' west'a here, but the thing went cold on us." Goodwin hacked, sending an abrasive sound echoing through the room.

Clenching his jaw in irritation, Joseph moved down to the foot of her bed, hoping the sheriff would follow suit.

"Most'a the boys don' know what he looks like, but I told 'em he shouldn't be hard to spot with the way you laid into 'im. Not many men walkin' 'ound with their faces rearranged. We're lookin' everywhere. He cain't git too far head'a us. I'd say by noon tomorrow we'll have 'im."

"I hope you're right."

He curled his fists tight around the footboard, ignoring the pain in his knuckles as he wrestled with the sense of helplessness assaulting him. If he could see, he'd ride out with the rest of the party. Push day and night. Because each minute that man remained out there untouched by the law, the more Joseph's apprehension grew regarding Katie's safety.

"I think that it'd be a good idea to have someone guarding this building round the clock—until you apprehend him."

"That ain't necessary," the sheriff said.

"It sure is necessary!" Joseph retorted in a harsh whisper. "The man could come back to finish the job."

"Hey, there, now. Simmer down." Sheriff Goodwin braced his hand against Joseph's chest. "All I was sayin' is... Aaron's out there doin' the job. That boy's been standin' guard since the search party formed. Ain't no one gonna git by him."

Joseph whipped his head around at Ben's familiar footsteps entering the room. "Aaron's out there?"

"I just found out myself." When Ben moved to Katie's bedside, Joseph felt a measure of relief that his brother was back tending to her once again. "We've been so busy watching Katie all night long that I hadn't stepped outside until just a few minutes ago."

Joseph raked his fingers through his hair, his knuckles bound with bandages. "I need to talk with him."

"Take your time," Ben responded.

"I won't be long." He felt as though he had to sever life and limb to leave the room. Stopping next to Ben, he said, "Her skin seems hot to the touch and she's been restless."

Ben groaned. "I'll check her over."

Emotion constricted Joseph's throat as he slid his hand over the bed to Katie's head. He smoothed wisps of silky hair from her hot, damp forehead and placed a kiss there. "Don't give up, darlin'," he whispered. "You can make it."

Weariness creaked through his bones as he walked out of the room, feeling his way along the hallway toward the front door. He opened it and stepped out onto the porch, pulling in a slow breath of fresh air.

"How's Katie?" came Aaron's voice in front of him.

Joseph shook his head and took two more steps until he was standing beside his brother. "I don't know what to tell you. It's not good. She's not good."

Aaron cleared his throat. "Sorry I haven't been inside to see her, or you. I've thought about you both plenty and prayed a lot, but I just don't think I can see her like this yet." He coughed. "With Ellie and the baby passin' away, I just—"

"You don't have to explain." Joseph placed a hand on his brother's shoulder and felt a slight shudder. "I understand."

When a wagon rolled at a leisurely pace past the office, he could hear the faint sound of a conversation. People were probably well aware of what had transpired last night—the shooting, the operation, the wedding. Information like that just didn't stay concealed long in a town like Boulder.

"It's all too fresh in my mind, you know?" Aaron said. "But when I heard about Katie, I wanted to help."

"It means a lot that you're here. I know she'll be safe."

"I hope she pulls through, Joseph. I'm prayin' for her—for you. A person doesn't have to look long to see that you two are meant for each other. Ellie said so from the get-go."

Joseph gave a reminiscent smile. "She told me."

"And don't worry about the order in the shop. When I'm not here keepin' watch, I'll be workin' at it. Sven and some of the other men are helpin' out, too."

"I'll be back when I can, but right now—"

"Right now you need to be with Katie...your wife."

"My wife," he repeated. "That has a nice ring to it."

The door opened suddenly behind him. "Joseph, she's taking a turn for the worse. I don't think she has much time left."

Joseph held a cool, damp cloth to Katie's forehead, hoping for some kind of improvement, but nothing seemed to work. It had to be nearly midnight by now, and Ben had just left the room to see Sven and Marta out. The four of them had maintained a constant vigil at Katie's bedside for hours, praying for the violent fever to release its burning grip. Sam had stopped by, too, and joined in prayer with them for Katie.

Her skin blazed hot beneath Joseph's fingertips as she lay eerily still. The restlessness she'd shown earlier had passed.

"God, please don't let her die." He stared into the darkness, blinking against the moisture pooling in his eyes.

There'd been moments when God's abiding peace and comforting presence had rested like a warm glow in the room, and Joseph had been sure God had come to take her home. He didn't pretend to know God's plan for Katie, but if he had any say in the matter, she'd remain earthbound. Live to journey through a long life with him. Be his wife and lover, bear their children.

Apart from pausing for a brief moment to eat the plate of food Marta had threatened to shovel down his throat, he hadn't left Katie's side. Having been awake for almost two days straight, he was beyond tired. His head pounded and his hands throbbed with a dull ache, but he barely paid these things an ounce of attention.

Lifting the cloth from Katie's brow, he dipped it in a basin of cool water, squeezed it out, then set it on her brow once again. "It's all right. I'm here," he soothed.

He tenderly wiped the cool moisture over her brow, down both cheeks and to her mouth. Alarm shot through him at how quickly the heat radiating from her body permeated the cloth.

He drew a trembling thumb over her full lips, cringing at how they were already dry and cracked from fever. Dabbing the cloth to her mouth, he moistened her lips, trying everything Ben had shown him to do to keep her as comfortable as possible. After dipping the cloth in the basin yet again, he placed it on her brow.

Bone-weary, he sank to the chair, gathering her hand in his. "Please…please don't take her, God."

His heart twisted with the deep yearning to see her live.

Twisted even tighter at the thought of seeing her suffer.

Tears welled up in his eyes. Spilled over onto his cheeks as he realized that he had to be willing to let her go, though he'd really only held her as his for a day.

She was his. His teacher. His friend. His beloved bride. He loved Katie. Loved her with his life, his breath, his heart.

Leaning over the bed, he rested his arms against the feather mattress, and his head against the back of her hand. Joseph breathed deep, trying to catch her light, lily scent. But all he could smell was the metallic odor of blood, mixed with the perspiration beading her body.

He prayed for some movement from her, but all he felt was the saltiness of the tears sliding down his cheeks. He brushed his mouth gently against the back of her hand, feeling the searing heat from her skin against his tear-dampened lips.

There were so many things he wished he'd said and now it might be too late. But if there was even a small part of her that could hear him, he had to tell her what was in his heart. If she died never knowing how much he really cared and how sorry he was, he wasn't sure he'd be able to live with himself.

Joseph drew in a steadying breath. "Katie, if you can hear me, darlin', I need you to listen carefully."

Burrowing his face into his shoulder, Joseph wiped his tears against the once-sturdy cotton fabric that now hung limp and wrinkled. Then he pressed his lips against her fingers, kissing each one, gently, slowly.

"If there was ever a time I wished I could go back and relive, it would be the last few weeks."

He held her hand, wishing for even the slightest response from her. But her hand hung limp in his.

"I've been a fool. A prideful fool who couldn't see the forest for the trees. I've been working so hard, tackling every task you set in front of me and diving into things back at the shop. I've been trying to make my life have meaning again." A steady trail of tears slid down his face as he lowered her hand to the mattress and laid his head next to her.

"When I found out that my vision wasn't going to get any better, I shut you out. I pushed away the one person who'd brought my life more meaning than anything else could've."

He grasped her fingers and drew them beneath his cheek, wanting to breathe her in for as long as he could. "I don't have a good explanation for the way I've behaved." His throat ached with a pain he'd never known. Closing his eyes, he wished he could hear her voice, see her face. "You've been so strong. You've honored my wishes when they were nothing but pride. I'm so sorry I pushed you away when all I really wanted was to pull you close and never let you go."

Joseph pressed a kiss into her palm. "I love you, Katie. I thank God that He brought you into my life. And if the only way I could've come to know you was through my blindness—" his voice broke as the weighty, sobering realization hit him full force "—then it was worth it. I'd willingly go through it all again if it meant coming to know you and love you like I have."

A wave of profound emotion crumpled his face. He bit back a sob. "You see…that's why you have to get better."

Chapter Seventeen

Joseph peered off into the distance, the growing fog hampering his view. He caught sight of a woman, her golden hair tumbling down her shoulders in soft waves, the blue of her eyes piercing through the mist and gathering darkness.

Katie?

She beckoned him from the edge of the woods. Calling to him. Begging for him to come.

He started toward her, knowing that he had to help her.

But something from behind grabbed at him. Demanding his attention. Turning momentarily away from her, he saw an endless black hole. Its expanse stretched as far as the eye could see. It pulled at him. Daring him to focus on it, dragging him into a place he knew was so bleak that he clawed at the ground to remain in the light.

Hearing her faint cries, he strained to free himself from its engulfing grip, but kept slipping farther...farther away into utter darkness.

Until finally he forced his attention ahead of him, to-

*ward where Katie had stood. Wrenching away from the
murky curse that lay behind him. He bolted toward the
woman whose cries had gone silent, a memory carried
on the night breeze.*

*Cut through the fast-growing shadows to the timber-
line, scanning the area, searching for her. Darting forward into the darkness, his heart clenched tight with the
horrific thought that he might've lost her.*

*He called to Katie. Then again, more frantic, once,
twice.*

Katie blinked once, twice.

Her name…someone had called her name.

She eased her eyes open to see light, brilliant and
warm, shining around her in golden streams of glory.
She fluttered her lids against the brightness, wondering
if she'd died and gone to heaven. Comforting peace en-
veloped her in downy softness. A bird's lilting melody
drifted to her ears. Opening her eyes again, she tried to
get her bearings about her.

Where she was? Why did she feel so completely exhausted?

And what in the world was tickling her hand?

Gathering her strength, she lifted her head slightly
and angled her gaze downward.

Joseph.

Katie's heart squeezed. Her beloved Joseph, asleep
and as handsome as ever, had laid his head near her
hand, the loose waves of his hair spilling over, dangling
feather-light against her skin. A smile worked itself from
deep down and spread across her face, warming her

with more contentment than she'd ever felt. This wasn't heaven, but it was close.

Laying her head against the pillow, patchy memories floated through her mind of the past hours—days maybe? The attack and the terrible dread it provoked in her. The gunshot…

Her pulse pounded inside her head as a huge wave of fear threatened to overtake her. She slowed her rapid breaths and resisted the taunting evil, determined to commit her thoughts to hopeful things.

Like her wedding…

Her throat swelled thick with emotion, her stomach quivered with excitement. Staring up through tears at the ceiling, she tried to make sense of it all. She recalled saying, "I do." She just didn't imagine she'd be facing her fanciful dream-come-true today. Instead, she thought she'd be strolling with her Creator through an endless field of radiant flowers or maybe basking in the consuming resonance of an angelic choir. As she'd spoken her vows, Katie was certain she'd been set on an eternal quest to know God's unfathomable riches and love. She would've gladly gone, too.

But something had called her back. Someone.

Joseph. Her beautiful Joseph.

His words—his passionate declaration of love and heart-wrenching plea for her to live—had called to her. They'd broken through her pain, her fever and fear, blanketing her in a love she never imagined feeling on this side of heaven.

When he'd poured out his heart to her, she'd tried to tear away from the fever's fiery grip enough to respond. Squeeze his hand…anything. But it was all she could do to focus on living through each minute, drawing another breath into her weakening body. And although, at times, she felt alone in her pain, she knew she wasn't. God had been there comforting her and carrying her through the night.

And Joseph was there, too. Wiping her brow, praying for her, trying to soothe her pain.

Joseph.

Remembering how she'd shared her secret thoughts with him, she felt a heated blush warm her cheeks. What had gotten into her? Facing death must've stripped away any amount of comportment and good judgment she embraced. Or maybe it just put things into the right perspective. Maybe God wanted to show her a glimpse of His goodness and love right here on earth.

Katie raised her hand from the mattress and worked her fingertips into Joseph's hair, loving the way the thick waves wrapped around her fingers. She slid her tongue over her dry, cracked lips.

"Joseph," she whispered in a raspy, weak voice. Swallowing, she tried again. "Joseph…"

Joseph slowly blinked his eyes open to the dull gray that met his gaze every morning. The nightmare he'd had last night came pouring back through his thoughts. The call for help. The woman standing at the edge of the timberline. The evil darkness. He'd dreamed the same thing several times since his accident. Had always dismissed it as just another reminder of his blindness and the sense of helplessness that plagued him.

Only this time, he saw it differently. The dream wasn't as much about his blindness but about Katie.

And instead of being dragged by the darkness, he'd broken from its grip and gone toward the woman—toward Katie. Calling to her.

"Joseph," came the faintest of voices lifting him from the swirling of thoughts.

He raised his head from the mattress, felt the light brush of delicate fingers against his face.

His heart lurched to a sudden halt. "Katie?" His breath caught in his throat. Trembling, he reached to touch her. "Is it really you?"

"Hello, there, sleepyhead." She spoke weakly, the sweet sound of her voice making his eyes burn with ready tears.

When she settled her hand in his, disbelief swept through him. Was she really alive? Or was this just a dream?

Joseph couldn't control the quivering of his hand as he slid it up her slender arm to her face, where her eyelashes fluttered feather-light beneath his fingertips. Her perfectly shaped lips curved into a sweet, warm smile.

Closing his eyes, he released a pent-up sigh. "I thought I'd lost you," he choked out.

His horror, grief and sorrow faded fast. And fear—fear that he'd never have more than just a memory of Katie.

Joy flooded through him with exhilarating force. He'd never experienced anything so intense. So profound.

Leaning closer to Katie, he closed a hand around hers, relishing the way her skin no longer radiated with fiery heat. He swallowed hard against the emotion constricting his throat.

Katie nuzzled into his palm, and a warm, moist tear slid down her satiny cheek onto his hand. "I couldn't go. Not when you were calling me back."

He wiped her tear away. "Oh, God, thank You," he breathed, pressing a lingering kiss to her brow. "Thank You, God."

Trailing his fingertips lightly over each of her beautiful features, he felt the soft kiss she brushed against his hand and knew he could never get enough of her.

"Oh, Katie, I'm so glad you're back. I don't think I'll ever be able to let you out of my sight again." He gave a slow shake of his head and grinned. "What I mean is... I'm not sure I'll ever want to be away from you."

He settled the pads of his thumbs at her mouth, grinning at the way she melted to his touch.

She gave a contented sigh, the corners of her mouth tipping to a smile. "You won't get any argument from me."

"Good." He kissed each of her fingertips.

"You're hurt. What happened to your hands?"

"It's nothing. Just a few bruises."

"Are you all right?" she asked, concern cloaking her voice.

"I'm fine. The question is, are you in pain?"

When she shifted slightly, he felt her stiffen and grew immediately concerned. "Don't try to move. Just lay still and let me help."

"I guess I'm a little worse off than I thought." She pulled a breath through clenched teeth. "And tired. So tired."

"I'm sure you are." While he adjusted the pillow behind her and pulled the quilt up to her chin, a lingering fear prickled the hair on his neck. The horror of her scream and pitiful sound of her muffled moans filtered through his thoughts. Lowering himself to the chair, he pulled his hands down his face, wishing he had some kind of assurance about the future.

The familiar taunting voices ricocheted through his mind, vomiting the same vile curses he'd entertained for too long.

But he had been here from the beginning, providing comfort and prayer and love. He'd protected. And he'd circumvented danger in spite of his blindness. He hadn't given his abilities more than a moment of thought when he'd followed the cries. Had used his honed sense of hearing to his advantage, while working the cover of darkness to the assailant's disadvantage.

He held her hand, brushing his lips against her fingers. "I'm so sorry about what happened to you. I came as fast as I could, darlin'."

"And you got there just in the knick of time." She squeezed his hand.

"When I was close enough to hear the things he was saying to you—the things he wanted to do to you—I got so enraged I almost lost my advantage, Katie. I could've gotten you killed."

"Don't think about that," she pleaded. "You saved me, Joseph. You saved me."

He lowered his head, pulling in her scent and the sound of her strong, even breaths. "I don't know who he is or why he attacked you…but I'm so glad he didn't take your innocence."

* * *

Katie blinked back the tears crowding her eyes as Joseph left in search of Ben. His measured, quiet steps, and the way he held his shoulders back and head high, belied the fatigue that must weigh on him.

Alone now, she gazed up at the embossed-tin ceiling, trying to ignore the sick rush of nausea that coursed through her. Not from her injury, or medicine, or the fever.

But from the words that her beloved husband had spoken....

I'm so glad he didn't take your innocence.

She pulled in a shuddering breath, trying not to crumple beneath the overwhelming misery that stalked her like some rabid dog, threatening to poison her happiness.

Katie swiped at a single tear that trickled down her face, feeling afresh the deep cutting edge of those words. The pain they evoked, far worse than the gunshot or raging fever. It had taken everything she possessed to shut down the instant reaction she'd had—the small gasp and groan. She'd been quick to blame it on a sudden stabbing pain which thankfully propelled Joseph out of the room to find Ben. Giving her a few blessed moments to gather herself before her emotions wholeheartedly betrayed her.

Had Joseph been able to see, he would've known that something was amiss. She could try to hide the truth from him awhile longer. Except for the small fact that they were now married. Husband and wife. Destined to consecrate the union.

When Joseph discovered that she was used—irrevocably dirty—would he even want her? He'd said himself that he was glad her innocence hadn't been taken. And Frank had promised that no man would ever want her. She and Joseph had said their vows, but maybe, given the fact that he'd committed to the marriage thinking he was giving her a last, dying wish, it wouldn't really count. After all, she did remember the reverend being rushed through the ceremony.

The rapid clap of footsteps approaching from down the hall set her heart racing. She faced the warm sunlight pouring through the lace-curtained window and closed her eyes, forcing herself to relax as she tried to feign sleep. Even though her secret was still safe for now, she just couldn't face anyone. Not Ben. And definitely not Joseph.

"Katie," Ben spoke, his voice low as he neared her bed. "Katie, are you awake?"

When she felt his hand against her forehead, and Joseph's tantalizingly familiar grasp around her fingers, she stayed as still as a mouse in a field full of hungry cats. She focused on taking long, even breaths, on trying to keep her eyes from moving beneath her closed lids.

"Is she all right?" The level of worry laced through Joseph's whispered words seized her heart.

And the painful realization that he deserved more than he thought he was getting was almost her undoing. She braced herself against the emotions that blasted away at her shallow wall of strength.

"She must've worn herself out from talking," Ben murmured as he placed his thumb and two fingers around her wrist to take her pulse. "Her fever's nearly gone and she's fast asleep again. But her pulse...it's a little rapid. We'll have to continue to keep a close eye on her."

* * *

Guilt weighed so heavy over Katie. Each time Joseph offered a kindness or did some sweet deed, the knife twisted deeper into her heart.

."Are you comfortable, darlin'?" Joseph asked again, hunkering down next to where she sat in the rocking chair.

His words heaped burning coals on Katie's conscience and had her wishing she could just tell him the truth of her past.

Glancing around the bedroom—their shared bedroom—she felt her head swirl with sudden dizziness.

It had been four days since she'd been shot, and though she was feeling so much better physically, emotionally she felt as if she'd been riddled with bullets. It was the least of her concerns that Frank hadn't been found—dead or alive. But that her secret might somehow be exposed before she had the chance to tell her husband, worked overtime to unravel her peace and security. Her stomach lurched every time she thought of how she'd allowed Joseph to think he'd married a spotless bride.

She'd looked for opportunities to tell him, but something always snatched away her courage at the last moment.

Joseph had been very open about his feelings for her. How glad he was that she was his wife. How he looked forward to the day when they would have children.

Katie slammed her eyes shut, her head pounding with a sudden onslaught of painful thoughts. "I'm fine," she finally responded when concern creased Joseph's brow.

The lie was a bitter draught on her tongue as she

glanced out the window to see the noonday sun shining with full force.

When she heard a tap at the door, she glanced over to see Uncle Sven poke his head into the room. His blue eyes shone through the crinkle of a wink, bolstering her heart a little. "I bring da trunks in und set dem by da door, Joseph. Mind dat you don't trip on dem, jah?"

She forced a smile at her uncle as Joseph moved toward the doorway.

"Thanks, Sven. I'll bring them in here when I get the chance." He turned back to her for a moment, the glint of joy in his deep amber eyes making her heart skip a beat. "I'll go get you a glass of water."

Katie slid her fingers along the wood buttons trailing down the bodice of her golden wheat-colored dress as she eased herself out of the chair.

"Jah, vell… I should go den, too, Katie-did. Da day is not half over und I haf plenty of vork to do yet." He moved toward her, sweeping off his wood-shaving dusted hat. Staring at her for a long moment, his gaze filled with worry.

The gentleness and fatherly wisdom shimmering in his eyes made her heart lurch.

"I love you like you are my own child," he said, smoothing wisps of hair back from her face. "Und I know dat you haf many tings to tink about over dis past days. But der is someting dat is heavy on your heart, jah?"

"Yes, I do have something on my mind," she admitted, threading her arms at her waist.

He gave her arm a gentle squeeze. "Can I help?"

Easing her hand over Uncle Sven's, she felt the weathered touch of age and hard work. "Just pray."

He peered at her for a moment longer when Joseph walked back in the room. "I vill pray," he whispered as he leaned over and planted a quick kiss on her cheek. "Marta...she brings by dinner tonight."

"Please tell her that we appreciate that." Joseph nodded and shook her uncle's hand. "By the way, thank you for everything you've done in the shop. Aaron says we're almost on schedule now with all the help we've had. I'm not sure how I'll ever be able to repay you."

Uncle Sven's mouth pulled tight, his chin quivering ever so slightly, forcing Katie to look away for fear that she'd cry. "Just take goot care of my Katie-did."

Joseph cleared his throat. "That I can do, sir."

After Uncle Sven left, Joseph stood in front of her and threaded his fingers around hers. "Welcome home, darlin'."

"Thank you, Joseph." Her heart pulled tight inside her chest as she stared down at where he held her hand. "Thank you for everything."

He leaned in closer to her, moving his fingers up to touch her face...her mouth. Then placed a kiss, warm and gentle, against her lips. Her cheeks. Her chin.

Katie closed her eyes, her breath caught. Stomach clenched. Her pulse thrummed at the base of her throat as he slid trembling fingertips almost reverently down her face.

His name was on her lips when he pressed another kiss to her mouth.

His touch...his tender, loving ways, left her feeling protected, treasured and loved.

When she finally opened her eyes, she found him inches away, staring at her with a steadfast gaze that belied his blindness. It was as if he was looking somewhere deep inside of her.

"Katie?" He dipped to place a chaste kiss on her lips.

She swallowed hard and drew a wad of her skirt in her grip. What would happen when he found out that she was coming to the marriage bed tainted by another man?

"Katie?" he said a second time.

"What?" she squeaked.

"I know that maybe you're worried about, well, us sleeping in the same bed now that we're married. I want you to know that until you're well, we won't do anything but sleep. All right?"

She shook her head, speechless.

"I would never do anything you weren't ready for. Do you understand?"

"I understand," she agreed, a yawn coming over her and insisting on her full attention.

He smoothed her freshly washed hair—a luxury she owed to her aunt—from her face. "You're tired, darlin'."

She was exhausted. "Well, maybe a little."

His mouth lifted in one of those sideways grins that sent a quiver all the way down to her toes. "Why don't you rest, then?"

Once she'd settled on the bed, she breathed deep, drawing comfort from Joseph's lingering scent on the pillow as he stared down at her.

Would he look at her like this after she told him? The fear of seeing his visible disappointment had Katie's insides knotted tight. Scraping together whatever courage she could find within herself, she knew that no matter what the outcome, she must tell him...tonight.

When he pulled a quilt over her from the foot of the bed, she felt herself drifting away, the agony of things left unsaid ushering her into fretful slumber.

Chapter Eighteen

"We ain't got no leads, but we're still lookin'."

It wasn't what Joseph had wanted to hear. He'd hoped that the sheriff had come over to tell him that they'd found the rogue dead. Unable to bring Katie any more harm.

The sheriff scuffed loudly across the front porch, making Joseph thankful the bedroom was located at the back of the house where Katie wouldn't be awakened.

"I know I got 'im. Sure as shootin'." He stomped a foot, sending Boone scurrying off the porch. "If'n he's laid up somewhere without some kind'a medical attention, he'll be festerin' so bad the wolves'll turn their noses up at 'im."

Joseph's jaw ticked. "Suppose he stopped at someone's home? Got help along the way?"

"He could'a, but we been checkin' with every livin' soul within thirty miles a this place."

Pulling his hands over his face, Joseph leaned back against the clapboard siding. "Ben said that someone found the Donaldsons' horse grazing near their home just last night."

"Yep." Sheriff Goodwin hacked, then spat, the wad plunking against the ground. "Don' look none worse for the wear neither. That means the scoundrel's either dead somewhere or he's on foot. Either way, we're bound to run across 'im, and with everyone on the alert 'round here, he'd be a fool to try and come back. Got wanted posters all over and sent a rider to the neighborin' towns to alert the law there."

"Sounds like you're doing everything you can."

"Miss Katie ain't been here long, but the whole town wanted to pitch in one way or t'other. She must be some special lady." The sheriff clucked his tongue, probably sporting that self-satisfied look he'd get.

"She's very special," Joseph agreed.

"If'n I was to guess..." When the sheriff sucked in a long breath, Joseph imagined Goodwin hooking his thumb inside his holster the way he always did when he was about to make some kind of proclamation. "I'd say the man's gone and died in some old shack somewhere. And Lady Luck just ain't been on our side enough to find his sorry be-hind yet."

Joseph tamped down his ire. "Let me know when you do."

"You'll be the first to know."

"I appreciate it."

"Well, time's a'wastin'," the sheriff announced, slapping his hat against his leg. "I got myself a town meetin' this evenin', but I'll be over to guard the place late tonight, if'n that's all right by you?"

Without sight, Joseph might not do the best job standing guard, but he could be prepared. He'd loaded his guns and made sure the locks on the two doors were secure. He'd even added a lock from inside the root cellar, in case Katie needed to hide. And he could care for his wife, tend to her needs, love her the best way he knew how.

Joseph shoved his hands in his pockets. "That'll be good."

After the sheriff rode off toward the heart of town, Joseph strode back inside, Boone at his heals. "You and me, Boone, we're pretty lucky, aren't we?" he asked, bending to stroke the dog's long thick back as he locked the door behind him.

The aroma from the food Marta had brought over not long ago drifted through the kitchen to his senses, and his stomach growled with hunger.

"You liked Katie from the beginning, didn't you, buddy? You warmed right up to her, and she took a liking to you, too," he said, easily moving to the front room where he opened the mantel clock and felt the position of the hands to find that it was past six o'clock.

He walked back to the kitchen with Boone meandering along beside him, his furry feet buffing the floor and his toenails ticking quietly. Kneeling, he wrapped his arms around Boone's furry neck. "Just between you and me, I'd say I'm the luckiest man alive to have married such a beautiful lady. And you're lucky she likes dogs—not that you're like other dogs—but she obviously doesn't mind sharing a house with you. In fact, I think she really likes having you around."

When Joseph stood up again, he turned his focus to the bedroom down the hall. "Now we've got to get her to feel the same about me, because ever since she came to after the fever, she doesn't seem to want me around."

After a painfully quiet dinner where conversation came hard and moments passed with a guardedness that blared brightly, Joseph walked Katie into the front room to sit on the sofa for a while. He wished that she'd allow him to help carry whatever it was that seemed to be burdening her.

Resting his elbows on his knees, he was unable to deny the way her voice had lacked the sparkle of life that was Katie.

She gave a shaky sigh, then inhaled as though she were about to say something. When she stopped short, Joseph could feel the heavy, tension-charged air. But what could his sweet, innocent Katie possibly have to tell him that would be so bad?

He set his hand on her arm, wishing that he could see her faint shadow, but the dim mist of day had dispelled and a black curtain had lowered once again.

Could it be that she was nervous about sharing a bed starting tonight? He'd tried to allay any fears she'd had earlier. If there was one thing he didn't want, it was a bride who came to his bed out of some kind of obligation.

He wanted her heart, first and foremost.

"It's a little chilly tonight," he commented, turning toward her on the sofa.

"A little."

He reached for the blanket he kept on the back of the sofa, then wrapped it around her shoulders, taking care not to bump the wound that was heavily bandaged beneath her dress.

Joseph eased a little closer to her. "Katie, I know that this is all sudden—the marriage and all, but I want you to know that I'm so glad you came into my life."

She sniffled again, something he'd heard her do a dozen times over the last half hour. "That's sweet. So sweet."

"I just wish I could've given you a real wedding. In a church. With flowers and a ring and…and that kind of stuff."

"It was perfect. Really."

"It worked under the circumstances, but I want to make it up to you somehow. Maybe we can have a reception of some kind. Do you think your family could travel out here for that?"

She paused. "Perhaps."

"We'll plan that if that's what you want, darlin'. Just as soon as you feel up to it."

"You're very good to me, Joseph."

"Not good enough."

She made a small groaning sound in the back of her throat and his attention was pulled up short. "Darlin', what's wrong?"

She pulled her hand away from his. Took a slow, measured breath. "Everything. Everything's wrong."

Joseph dragged a hand over his face as he wondered if she was in the throes of regret. Maybe she felt trapped by her whimsical, passing fancy that she'd been so free to share, thinking she was dying.

But what could they do about it now? They were married. Joseph wasn't about to give her up. He loved her—so much that it hurt. He'd spend the rest of his life showing her, too.

"Katie, if you're having second thoughts, I understand. But we can work through them."

"No. It's not that at all." Her voice was strained with emotion.

"I want you to feel at home here. I know that it'll take a while with everything you've been through and the adjustments I'm still making. But I'll do whatever I can to make this as easy as possible for you. This is your home now."

"And it's a beautiful home," she offered, her voice breaking. She sniffed. "I love it."

"When you're feeling up to it, I want you to make any changes you want." He gave a broad gesture around the room. "I've been a bachelor for too long and I'm sure you'll probably want to add some nice feminine touches."

Her muffled cries broke his heart. "I wouldn't change a thing, Joseph. Not one thing."

He found her hand and grasped it in his. "Well, what's wrong, darlin'?"

Silence filled the air, and so did the faintest sound of something falling behind the house followed by a low curse. He shot his focus toward the noise, every single nerve ending springing to the alert. A warning knell, sure and strong, rang through him with deafening clarity.

"Joseph, I—I have to t-tell you something," Katie ground out. "Something awful."

He instinctively knew that each word came with a high cost.

"You don't know what you got yourself into marrying me." Katie pulled in a fractured breath at the same moment he heard another rustle.

"Katie, I need you to do something for me," he interrupted, wishing for all the world that he could've taken the time to bring her comfort. But there was no time for that now.

He levered himself off the sofa and grabbed a loaded gun from above the door. Angled his head toward another sound as he helped her stand, pulling her toward the kitchen.

"What is it? What's wrong?" she asked, sniffling.

"I need you to take this gun down into the root cellar and lock the door behind you," he said as he held out an oil lamp for her. "Can you do that?"

"Why?" she whispered, her voice quivering. "What is it?"

"Just promise me you won't open the door for anyone else but me. Do you understand?"

He felt her tremble beneath his touch as he held the trap door open for her. "Everything's going to be all right."

"But Joseph, I—"

He lowered his head and settled a kiss to her brow, breathing in Katie. He loved her beyond words and hoped he'd get to show her for years to come.

"Go now, darlin'."

When he lowered the door and heard her lock it, he strode through the house to the back entrance. Prayed that God would help him. Pleaded that Katie would be safe as he grabbed another gun he'd loaded.

God, where's the sheriff? He prayed silently, suddenly remembering that the sheriff wasn't going to be here to guard until late. *I need help here.*

There was always Boone. Except that Boone usually took his nightly stroll through town about now, picking up a furry friend or two along the way. The dogs had taken to using their large brown, expressive eyes to win a scrap of meat here or a slice of bread there.

Quietly unlatching the back door, he passed through and stepped with stealthy precision around his house.

Listened. Honed in on the small grunt coming from near the side of the porch. And the heavy breaths that sliced through clenched teeth. The dry grass crunched and scratched as if the person was limping.

Joseph crept forward. Caught the fading scent of a cigar. The same aroma that had lingered in the area where Katie had been attacked.

His pulse pounded harder, ricocheting through his head, arms, legs.

Thoughts of Katie lying soaked in fevered sweat, fighting for her life, splashed into his mind and his blood instantly boiled hot with rage. His muscles bunched, pulling taught, ready for use.

Riveting his focus on the man's ragged breaths, uneven steps and the direction they were aimed, Joseph breathed a prayer of thanks that he still had the advantage. Apparently too engrossed in his sick quest or the pain that was hampering his movements, the man seemed unaware that Joseph was close at his heels.

Joseph was less than ten feet away now and could hear Katie's name hissed through clenched teeth. Could smell the rank scent of infection coming from the man.

He tightened his grip on the gun and narrowed in on his target.

If the man had scared up a weapon somewhere, Joseph had to be ready. He listened for the sound of clanking steel. Heard nothing and prayed to God the man wasn't armed.

Raising the gun, he took another step forward. Another. Then another. Zeroed in on the sounds of the man's labored breathing. The raking of his foot across the ground. The putrid scent of raw, infected flesh.

Joseph aimed the gun and fired.

He heard a *thwap* followed by an animal-like yowl.

Joseph dived forward and grabbed the man.

A vicious string of curses filled the air as the attacker tried to wrench free from Joseph's grip.

He could feel the sharp bite of a knife pierce his thigh. Ignored the searing pain and squeezed harder.

"Drop the knife, now!" he ground out. With one quick movement, he hooked an arm underneath the man's right bicep and jerked it up behind the man's neck.

The villain drove the blade deeper into Joseph's thigh.

He clenched his teeth, trying to disregard the pain as he locked an unyielding grip on the attacker's neck.

When he heard the front door unlatch, his heart sank. "Katie, get back inside!" he yelled, jamming a fist deep into the man's gut. "Go back in there and lock the doors!"

"Joseph, no. No!" she cried, her feet sweeping over the porch and down the steps.

"Ah, just who I wanted to see," the man hissed on a cough.

Followed by a low, steady growl.

Boone!

Joseph could hear the dog advancing from the side, his growl deepening. When the man jerked back and let out another howl, Joseph tried to maintain his hold.

"Call your dog off!" the man spat, trying to wrench his arm free from the dog's strong jaws.

But Boone must've sunk his teeth deeper, because the man suddenly released the knife and roared in pain.

When Katie moved closer, Joseph's sense of alarm heightened. "Get inside and lock the doors!"

"No, I won't." She was close enough that he could hear her breath now. "I got the knife, Joseph. I got the knife."

"Good, honey, good." Joseph grunted as he hooked a leg in front of the man's shins. "Now, get back, Katie! Go back inside!"

Tripping the man's legs out from underneath him, Joseph maintained his hold as they both fell forward to the ground. He could feel warm sticky blood seeping from the attacker's side as he wrenched the man's other arm up behind his neck and pulled up harder and tighter, until the man cried out in pain.

Boone didn't miss a beat but regained his hold behind Joseph, this time sinking his teeth into the man's calf. The scream that followed boomed like the hordes of hell.

"Hold him, Boone!" Joseph encouraged through gritted teeth.

"What in the world?" came the sheriff's voice into the yard. "Joseph, is that you?"

"Over here, sheriff." Katie's voice quavered close by.

The sheriff's booted feet clumped over the ground hard and fast. "You got 'im, Joseph. You got 'im."

Before he released him over to the sheriff, he wrenched the man's arms up even tighter and dipped his head down to the villain's ear. "You will never—" he warned through a clenched jaw, grinding the attacker's face down into the dirt, "—come near my wife again."

Katie's attacker struggled to jerk his head back. "You must like your women soiled, blind man," he hissed into the dirt, his voice low and barely audible. "'Cause that's all she is."

Joseph wanted to jam his fist down the rogue's mouth and rip his tongue out for saying such a vile thing about Katie. He ground the attacker's face into the dirt and held him there for a long moment. He gave one last power-packed push and propelled himself to standing, thankful the filthy words weren't loud enough for Katie to hear.

When the sheriff approached from the side and Joseph backed away, he heard a small scuffle, a single gunshot and an evil curse as the man collapsed to the ground.

"Stupid move." Goodwin spoke as if he was inspecting a piece of meat. "This time we stopped 'im fer good."

A shudder of relief reverberated through Joseph while the man lay silent on the ground. And Boone sniffed around the body, as if ensuring that the job was done.

"Wish my bullet had'a done the job the first time," the sheriff apologized, grunting as though he was hoisting the body. "Your husband, he done the right thing, Miss Kate. This dirt-poor excuse for a man won't be hurtin' you no more."

"Thank you." Her whispered words tore at Joseph's heart.

He stepped toward Katie as Goodwin dragged the body away.

"I'll just get his sorry be-hind out'a the way for ya."

Joseph nodded, letting loose a pent-up sigh. "Thanks. By the way, could you maybe send Ben over with his bag?"

Although he wished he could just ignore the wound and escape into the security of his house with his wife, the warm, moist feel of blood dripping down his leg made him think twice.

"Sure 'nough."

Joseph moved toward Katie, Boone at his side. He held out his hand to find her. "Darlin', are you all right?"

She stepped into his arms and melted into his embrace. "I'm fine. But Joseph—your leg—you're bleeding."

"Nothing that a stitch or two won't fix." Joseph nestled his face into her hair and dragged in her light lily scent. "You had me so worried. He could've hurt you. You should've stayed inside."

"I knew you wouldn't let him hurt me. And I couldn't let him hurt you."

He cupped her face. "Thanks for your help, darlin'."

Clenching his jaw, he closed his eyes as her words cycled through his mind. Not long ago the idea that he'd needed help would've pricked his dignity, infecting him with stubborn pride. But tonight, for the first time, he saw that the measure of his strength and ability to protect didn't necessarily lie in his hands alone.

But in God's.

And in those around him who loved enough to sacrifice.

Feeling Boone's weight leaning heavily against his leg, Joseph knelt down next to the dog. Drove his fingers through Boone's long, thick fur. "Thank you, my friend."

Chapter Nineteen

"You're all patched up, Joseph. Good as new." Ben snapped his bag shut and walked into the kitchen. "And you, Katie, are looking very well considering the night you've had."

Walking beside his brother, Joseph felt the tight pull of the dozen or so stitches Ben had sewn in the privacy of the bedroom while he'd cleaned up and changed. "Thanks, Ben. I appreciate you coming out so late."

"What are brothers for?" He braced a hand on Joseph's shoulder. "But the next time I dismiss the idea of getting an assistant, remind me of this moment, would you? It has been a whirlwind day—a whirlwind week—and I'm tuckered out."

With a chuckle, Joseph nudged his brother. "Get out of here, then. Go home and get some rest."

"Can I send some of Marta's cooking along with you?" Katie asked, stepping up beside them.

Ben blew out a full breath of air. "Much as I love her food, I'm so tired I don't think I could eat. I just want a bed," he said, opening the front door. "And a pillow. And a blanket."

"Go." Joseph laughed and gave his brother a playful push out the door.

"I'll check in on you two tomorrow. But not too early."

Joseph hooked one arm over the top of the door. "Fine by me. Thanks."

"Good night, Ben," Katie called, dipping her head beneath Joseph's arm and nestling into his side.

After Joseph closed the door, he turned and wrapped his arm around Katie, ushering her to the front room where he'd built a fire. He sat next to her on the sofa, breathing deep, taking in the room's comforting atmosphere. The crackling of the fire and radiating warmth. The popping sounds as flames licked up the dry wood, and mellow, earthy scent as it burned in the hearth.

And the wonderful feel of his wife here beside him, safe.

"Joseph, I have to tell you something," Katie whispered.

He reached for her hand. "I'm sorry, darlin'. You'd started to say something earlier and I—"

"I know. You heard the sounds. I understand you were protecting me." Katie threaded her fingers through his. "But really, this time I have to just say it."

Joseph hooked his other arm around the back of the sofa, setting his focus completely on her. "I'm listening."

"I—I knew him, Joseph. I know who he is."

When he heard the faintest, muffled whimper come from his bride, his stomach knotted. Blood slammed through his veins. He remembered the vile words the

man had spoken—that he must like his women soiled—
and his heartbeat ground to a staggering halt.

Had her attacker really violated her like that?

She dragged in a long breath. "Remember after I
woke from the fever and you said that you were—that
you were glad that man didn't take my innocence?"

God, no.... No. It couldn't be.

He couldn't have....

"Well, he did. He took my innocence." She jerked her
hand away from him. "He was a deacon in my church
back home. I thought I could trust him. I had no idea.
No idea," Katie muttered the words over and over as if
she'd unlocked an ancient door, the foul secret finally
spilling out into the light.

He wrestled to control the rage that instantly rose
within him as he reached out and pulled her into his
arms. She shuddered uncontrollably against him, and
thoughts of his beautiful, sweet wife being used like
that coursed through his mind, feeding the fierce anger
boiling within him. How could someone do that to her?

"You're safe now," he whispered. He smoothed a
hand down her hair, his throat gone raw with emotion.
His eyes burning with unshed tears. "Shh.... It's all
right."

Katie stiffened and pushed away from his embrace,
sniffling. "No, it's not all right." Bravery and courage
as he'd never seen girded her voice, making his eyes
pool with tears.

She scooted away from him, the distance feeling like
some wide chasm. "You thought you were marrying a
spotless bride. But I'm not. I never will be." Katie sniffed

again. "Nothing can ever, ever, *ever* give me back what I lost to him."

Joseph reached across the sofa, to find her hand. "Everything's going to be all right, Katie."

"Don't you understand?" she pleaded, her voice rising in volume as she backed farther away from him. "He attacked me more than once. I fought him, but it didn't do me any good. I was desperate to tell someone, but he said he'd kill me or my family. I didn't know where to turn, what to do. And he was always there in church, staring—"

The sofa shook with her violent trembling, and his heart weighted with sorrow. To think that she'd carried this devastating secret alone sent stabbing pain straight through him.

And righteous anger coursing through his veins.

That her attacker lay dead was of little value or comfort.

"I shouldn't have let him do that to me," she whimpered, her voice so small, so innocent that he wanted to hold her and never let her go. "I could've somehow stopped it."

Joseph slowly edged next to her, then scooped her up and settled her onto his lap, being careful to avoid his freshly stitched wound. He wrapped trembling arms around her. Gently pulled her head to rest against his shoulder. "Katie, sweetie, it's not your fault. None of it is your fault."

"But it is," she whispered, as though it was her duty to convince him. She was all tense and quaking like a harmless rabbit cornered by a hungry wolf. "He said that it was—all my fault. He said that I was the one who brought it on myself." She drew her arms into a tight ball at her chest and wrestled in a shaky breath. "That I had flau-flaunted myself in front of him. But I don't see how. I—I didn't think I did that."

Joseph cupped her chin and raised her gaze to his. "He was wrong, Katie. He was a sick man and he was wrong."

"But, Joseph!" Katie grasped his hand at her chin and held tight. "He took away the one thing I could've given to you and you alone."

Closing his eyes, Joseph shook his head at the lies— the filthy, sick lies that man had planted into her sweet, innocent head. "No, he didn't."

Her grip grew tighter. "How can you say that?" she cried in a voice so full of agony that it broke his heart.

A tear slid down his cheek. "Because, darlin', he didn't take your heart."

Katie had never felt more invigorated or alive as she stood before Joseph in their bedroom.

After she'd poured out her heart to him two days ago, disclosing her well-guarded secret about the attacks, she was emotionally spent. She knew he'd be compassionate, but had fully expected to see some kind of underlying regret evident in his eyes, or his voice, or his touch. And wouldn't have blamed him for it.

She was sure she'd never forget the way she'd felt when he'd held her so tenderly, responding in the gentle, caring way he had. He'd shown compassion, support and love. Pure, unconditional love that gave her hope.

And for the first time in a year she took the smallest glimpse at freedom from the haunting darkness of her past.

Glancing at the welcoming glow of shadows that danced and flickered across the wall from the fire Joseph had banked in the small bedroom hearth, she knew she was home. Right where she belonged.

Her body quaked. No longer with the painful uncovering of her secret, but with the anticipation of Joseph's touch.

"You're beautiful, Katie," he breathed, his voice husky as he reached up and stroked her hair. "So beautiful."

Apprehension rose within her at what was sure to happen tonight. They'd spent the past two days and nights recuperating, but she knew that tonight... Could she let her guard down so completely as to find joy in something that for a year had meant sorrow? She wanted to, for Joseph, but he'd told her that if she wasn't ready, he'd wait. As long as she needed.

And although a part of her felt horribly self-conscious and utterly unworthy, another part of her yearned for the nearness with Joseph.

She peered up at him, captivated by the warmth and sensitivity she found in his gaze and the serenity she found in his expression. Compelled by the absolute gentleness with which he treated her, as though she was a priceless, treasured jewel.

She swallowed hard, fighting to ignore the residue of lies that had made a deep rut in her heart. The thick groove was there and she had no earthly idea how it could ever be removed.

The kiss he settled against her lips made her tremble

all the way down to her toes. "I couldn't have asked for a more perfect bride."

Tears stung her eyes as his words washed over her like a gentle, cleansing rain. Her head swirled with intoxicating emotion and her breath caught.

"So lovely," he whispered, contentment tipping his lips.

Her inhibitions began to crumble.

"So sweet." Joseph pressed a kiss to her neck, his warm breath fanning over her in a wash of liquid heat.

He made slow work of the next kiss he placed on her lips.

"So very innocent." He deliberately measured out the words as if he was marking her with a new name, etching it on her heart. Her soul. Her mind.

He skimmed his hands whisper-soft over her shoulders, then moved his hands to her waist, and Katie shivered at his magnificently tender touch.

He pulled her close to his warmth and strength. Every caring touch of his hands bringing her another measure of healing.

Joseph's eyes were closed as he trailed his fingertips, feather-light, down her neck, shoulders and arms.

He cupped her face in his hands then and stared down at her, the depth in his gaze drawing her, beckoning her. "Katie, I love you," he ground out. "Do you hear me? I love you."

Her shame fell away then, shattering into a million pieces.

She stared through joyous tears up at Joseph, her heart soaring to heights she'd never known.

When he settled his arms gently around her and pulled her close, she felt completely encompassed by a love that gave her wings to fly. To explore the beautiful, wondrous, God-given design of intimacy.

"Joseph, I feel so safe when I'm in your arms," she whispered, wrapping her arms around his chest and splaying quivering fingers against his back.

Joseph wasn't sure if he'd ever be able to express to her how much those words meant. With them she restored a foundation that had crumbled eight weeks ago when he'd lost his vision.

When she rested her cheek at his heart, his throat tightened with instant emotion. He nuzzled his face into her hair, loving the way she felt in his arms.

Her heart belonged to him and him alone.

He gloried in the revelation, unable to keep the smile from washing over his face. He'd seen beauty around him all his life. The mountains. The streams. The innocence of a child.

But to be entrusted with a heart so giving, and pure, and beautiful brought more joy than he'd ever known.

"You are so beautiful, Joseph. So perfect for me. I love you." Katie's sweet voice was laced with a strong sense of relief—as though she'd finally found what she was looking for.

He dipped his head to settle his mouth on hers, his lips brushing hers with a promise. The way she melted to his touch made his heart squeeze and allowed him another glimpse of God's abiding love and power to restore.

* * * * *

SPECIAL EXCERPT FROM

LOVE INSPIRED
INSPIRATIONAL ROMANCE

Temporarily in her Amish community to help with her sick brother's business, nurse Rachel Blank can't wait to get back to the Englisch *world...and far away from Arden Esh. Her brother's headstrong carpentry partner challenges her at every turn. But when a family crisis redefines their relationship, will Rachel realize the life she really wants is right here...with Arden?*

Read on for a sneak preview of
The Amish Nurse's Suitor *by Carrie Lighte,*
available April 2020 from Love Inspired.

The soup scalded Arden's tongue and gave him something to distract himself from the topsy-turvy way he was feeling. As he chugged down half a glass of milk, Rachel remarked how tired Ivan still seemed.

"*Jah*, he practically dozed off midsentence in his room."

"I'll have to wake him soon for his medication. And to check for a fever. They said to watch for that. A relapse of pneumonia can be even worse than the initial bout."

"You're going to need endurance, too."

"What?"

"You prayed I'd have endurance. You're going to need it, too," Arden explained. "There were a lot of nurses in the hospital, but here you're on your own."

"Don't you think I'm qualified to take care of him by myself?"

That wasn't what he'd meant at all. Arden was surprised by the plea for reassurance in Rachel's question. Usually, she seemed so confident. "I can't think of anyone better qualified to take care of him. But he's got a long road to recovery ahead, and you're going to need help so you don't wear yourself out."

"I told Hadassah I'd *wilkom* her help, but I don't think I can count on her. Joyce and Albert won't return from Canada for a couple more weeks, according to Ivan."

"In addition to Grace, there are others in the community who will be *hallich* to help."

"I don't know about that. I'm worried they'll stay away because of my presence. Maybe Ivan would have been better off without me here. Maybe my coming here was a mistake."

"*Neh*. It wasn't a mistake." Upon seeing the fragile vulnerability in Rachel's eyes, Arden's heart ballooned with compassion. "Trust me, the community will *kumme* to help."

"In that case, I'd better keep dessert and tea on hand," Rachel said, smiling once again.

"Does that mean we can't have a slice of that pie over there?"

"Of course it doesn't. And since Ivan has no appetite, you and I might as well have large pieces."

Supping with Rachel after a hard day's work, encouraging her and discussing Ivan's care as if he were…not a child, but *like* a child, felt… Well, it felt like how Arden always imagined it would feel if he had a family of his own. Which was probably why, half an hour later as he directed his horse toward home, Arden's stomach was full, but he couldn't shake the aching emptiness he felt inside.

She is going back, so I'd better not get too accustomed to her company, as pleasant as it's turning out to be.

Don't miss
The Amish Nurse's Suitor *by Carrie Lighte,*
available April 2020 wherever
Love Inspired books and ebooks are sold.

LoveInspired.com